F PAL
PALME

D0977005
12

Silver Bells

✢✢✢✢✢

Also available from Diana Palmer

DIANA PALMER

Silver Bells

HARLEQUIN®

entertain, enrich, inspire™

Recycling programs
for this product may
not exist in your area.

ISBN-13: 978-0-373-77718-1

SILVER BELLS

CONTENTS

Man of Ice

Prologue

DAWSON Rutherford hesitated on the front steps of the Mercer home. As the butler held the carved wooden door open for him to enter, he was only absently aware of music and voices and the clink of ice in glasses. He couldn't remember ever feeling so unsure of himself. Would she welcome him? He smiled with cold mockery. When had Barrie Bell, his stepsister, ever welcomed his presence in recent years? She'd loved him once. But he'd killed her feelings for him, as he'd fought to kill all the violent emotions she inspired in him since her mother had married his father.

He pushed a big, lean hand through his short, wavy gold hair, only barely disrupting its neatness. His pale green eyes were thoughtful as he stood there, elegant and dramatically handsome, drawing the gaze of women. But he had eyes for none of them. They called him the "ice man." And it wasn't because he came from a cold country.

Through the open door he could see her on the steps, her long, wavy black hair curling down her bare shoulders, sparkling in a silver dress. He was all she had left since both their parents had died, but she avoided him. He couldn't blame her, now that he knew at last about the other casualty of his turbulent relationship with Barrie; one that he'd only just found out about recently.

He hesitated to go in there, to see her again, to talk to her. They'd argued at their last meeting over the same issue he was going to bring up now. But this time he needed it as an excuse to get her back to Sheridan, Wyoming. He had to undo five years of pain and heartache, to make up to her for what she'd endured. In order to do that he was going to have to face some private demons of his own, as well as the fear he'd taught her to feel. He didn't look forward to it, but it was time to erase the past and start over. If they could…

One

THERE was a cardinal rule that people who gave parties never invited both Barrie Bell and her stepbrother, Dawson Rutherford, to the same social event. Since the two of them didn't have a lot of mutual friends, and they lived in different states, it wasn't often broken. But every rule had an exception, and tonight, Barrie discovered, was it.

She hadn't really wanted to go out, but Martha and John Mercer, old friends of the Rutherfords who'd taken a interest in Barrie since their move to Tucson, insisted that she needed a diversion. She wasn't teaching this summer, after all, and the part-time job that kept her bank account healthy had just ended abruptly. Barrie needed cheering up and Martha was giving a party that was guaranteed to accomplish it.

Actually it had. Barrie felt brighter than she had in some months. She was sequestered on the steps of the staircase in the hall with two admirers, one who was a bank executive and the other who played guitar with a jazz band. She was wearing a dress guaranteed to raise blood pressures, silver and clinging from its diamanté straps at her lightly tanned shoulders to her ankles, with a long, seductive slit up one side of the skirt. The color of her high heels matched the dress. She wore her long, wavy black hair loose, so that it reached almost to her waist. In her creamy-complexioned, oval face, bright green eyes shone with a happy glitter.

That was, they *had* been shining until she saw Dawson Rutherford come in the front door. Her sophisticated chatter had died abruptly and she withdrew into a shell, looking vulnerable and hunted.

Her two companions didn't connect her stepbrother's entrance with Barrie's sudden change. Not, at least, until a few minutes later when he spotted her in the hall and, excusing himself to his hostess, came to find her with a drink in his hand.

Dawson was more than a match for any man present, physically. Some of them were spectacularly handsome, but Dawson was more so. He had wavy blond hair, cut conventionally short, a deep tan, chiseled, perfect facial features and deep-set pale green eyes at least two shades lighter than Barrie's. He was tall and slender, but there were powerful muscles in that lithe body, which was kept fit from hours in the saddle. Dawson was a multimillionaire, yet being the boss didn't keep him from helping out on the many ranches he owned. It was nothing unusual to find him cutting out calves for branding on the Wyoming ranches, or helping to drive cattle across the spinifex plains of the several-thousand-square-mile station in Australia's Channel Country. He spent his leisure hours, which were very few, working with his Thoroughbred horses on the headquarters ranch in Sheridan, Wyoming, when he wasn't buying and selling cattle all over the country.

He was an elegant man, from his hand-tooled leather boots to the expensive slacks and white silk turtleneck shirt he wore with a designer jacket. Everything about him, from his Rolex to the diamond horseshoe ring on his right hand, screamed wealth. And with the elegant good looks, there was a cold, calculating intelligence. Dawson spoke French and Spanish fluently, and he had a degree in business.

Barrie's two companions seemed to shrink when he

appeared beside them, a drink cradled in one big, lean hand. He didn't drink often, and never to excess. He was the sort of man who never liked to lose control in any way. She'd seen him lose it just once. Perhaps that was why he hated her so, because she was the only one who ever had.

"Well, well, what was Martha thinking, I wonder, that rules were made to be broken?" Dawson asked her, his deep voice like velvet even though it carried above the noise.

"Martha invited me. She didn't invite you," Barrie said coldly. "I'm sure it was John. He's laughing," she added, her gaze going to Martha's husband across the room.

Dawson followed her glance to his host and raised his glass. The shorter man raised his in acknowledgment and, catching Barrie's furious glare, turned quickly away.

"Aren't you going to introduce me?" Dawson continued, unabashed, his eyes going now to the two men beside her.

"Oh, this is Ted and that's…what was your name?" she somewhat abruptly asked the second man.

"Bill," he replied.

"This is my...stepbrother, Dawson Rutherford," she continued.

Bill grinned and extended his hand. It was ignored, although Dawson nodded curtly in acknowledgment. The younger man cleared his throat and smiled sheepishly at Barrie, brandishing his glass. "Uh, I need a refill," he said quickly, because Dawson's eyes were narrowing and there was a distinct glitter in them.

"Me, too," Ted added and, grinning apologetically at Barrie, took off.

Barrie glared after them. "Craven cowards," she muttered.

"Does it take two men at once to keep you happy these days?" Dawson asked contemptuously. His cold gaze ran down her dress to the low neckline that displayed her pretty breasts to their best advantage.

She felt naked. She wouldn't have dreamed of wearing clothing this revealing around Dawson normally. Only the fact that he'd come to the party unbeknownst to her gave him the opportunity to see her in this camouflage she adopted. But she wasn't going to spoil her sophisticated image by letting him know that his intent regard disturbed her. "There's safety in numbers," she replied with a cool smile. "How are you, Dawson?"

"How do I look?" he countered.

"Prosperous," she replied. She didn't say anything else. Dawson had come to her apartment only a few months ago, trying to get her back to Sheridan to play chaperone to Leslie Holton, a widow and former actress who had a piece of land Dawson wanted. She'd refused and an argument had resulted, which led to them not speaking at all. She'd thought Dawson would never seek her out again after it. But here he was. And she could imagine that the widow was still in hot pursuit of him—or so her best friend Antonia Hayes Long had told her recently.

He took a sip of his drink, but his eyes never left her face. "Corlie changes your bed every other day, hoping."

Corlie was the housekeeper at Dawson's Sheridan home. She and her husband, Rodge, had been in residence since long before Barrie's mother had married Dawson's father. They were two of her favorite people and she missed them. But not enough to go back, even for a visit. "I don't belong in Sheridan," she said firmly. "Tucson is home, now."

"You don't have a home any more than I do," he shot back, his voice cold. "Our parents are dead. All we have left is each other."

"Then I have nothing," she said harshly, letting her eyes speak for her.

"You'd like to think so, wouldn't you?" he demanded with a cold smile. And because the flat statement wounded him, he added deliberately, "Well, I hope you're not still eating your heart out for me, baby."

The accusation made her feel even more vulnerable. Her hands clenched in her lap. In the old days, Dawson had known too well how she felt about him. It was a weapon he'd used against her. She glared at him. "I wouldn't waste my heart on you. And don't call me baby!"

His eyes narrowed on her face and dropped to her mouth, lingering there. "I don't use endearments, Barrie," he reminded her. "Not in normal conversation. And we both remember the last time I used that one, don't we?"

She wanted to crawl under the stairs and die. Her eyes closed. Memories assailed her. Dawson's deep voice, husky with feeling and need and desire, whispering her name with each movement of his powerful body against hers, whispering, "Baby! Oh, God, baby, baby…!"

She made a hoarse sound and tried to get away,

but he was too close. He sat down on the step below hers and settled back on his elbow, so that his arm imprisoned her between himself and the banister.

"Don't run," he chided. "You're a big girl now. It's all right to have sex with a man, Barrie. You won't go to hell for it. Surely you know that by now, with your record."

She looked at him with fear and humiliation. "My record?" she whispered.

"How many men have you had? Can't you remember?"

Her eyes stared straight into his. She didn't flinch, although she felt like it. "I can remember, Dawson," she said with a forced smile. "I've had one. Only one." She actually shivered.

Her reaction took some of the antagonism out of him. He just stared at her, his pale eyes unusually watchful.

She clasped her arms tightly over her breasts and her entire body went rigid from his proximity.

He moved back, just a couple of inches. She relaxed, but only a little. Her posture was still unnatural. He wanted to think she was acting this way deliberately, in an attempt to resurrect the old guilt. But it wasn't an act. She looked at him with eyes that were vulnerable, but even if she cared as much as ever, she was afraid of him. And it showed.

The knowledge made him uncomfortable. More uncomfortable than he usually was. He'd taunted her with her feelings for him for years, until it was a habit he couldn't break. He'd even done it the night he lost his head and destroyed her innocence. He'd behaved viciously to push away the guilt and the shame he felt at his loss of control.

He hadn't meant to attack her tonight, of all times. Not after the argument he'd had with her months ago. He'd come to make peace. But the attempt had backfired. It was the way she was dressed, and the two eager young men sitting like worshipers at her feet, that had enraged him with jealousy. He hadn't meant a word he said, but she wouldn't know that. She was used to having him bait her. It didn't make him feel like a man to punish her for his own sins; it made him sick. Especially now, with what he'd only just found out about the past, and what had happened to her because of him…

He averted his eyes to her folded arms. She looked like a whipped child. She'd adopted that posture after he'd seduced her. The image was burned indelibly into his brain. It still hurt, too.

"I only want to talk," he said curtly. "You can relax."

"What could we possibly have to say to each other?" she asked icily. "I wish I never had to see you again, Dawson!"

His eyes bit into hers. "Like hell you do."

She couldn't win an argument with him. It was better not to start one. "What do you want to talk about?"

His gaze went past her, to the living room, where people were laughing and drinking and talking. Happy, comfortable people. Not like the two on the staircase.

He shrugged and took another swallow from the glass before he faced her again. "What else? I want you to come home for a week or two."

Her heart raced. She averted her gaze. "No!"

He'd expected that reaction. He was ready to debate it. "You'll have plenty of chaperones," he informed her. "Rodge and Corlie." He paused deliberately. "And the widow Holton."

She looked up. "Still?" she muttered sarcastically. "Why don't you just marry her and be done with it?"

He deliberately ignored the sarcasm. "You know that she's got a tract of land in Bighorn that I have to own. The only way she'll discuss selling it to me is if I invite her to Sheridan for a few days."

"I hear that she's hanging around the ranch constantly," she remarked.

"She visits regularly, but not overnight," he said. "The only way I can clinch the land deal and get her to go away is to let her spend a few days at the ranch. I can't do that without you."

He didn't look pleased about it. Odd. She'd heard from her best friend, Antonia Long, that the widow was lovely and eligible. She couldn't understand why Dawson was avoiding her. It was common knowledge that she'd chased Powell Long, Antonia's husband, and that she was casting acquisitive eyes at Dawson as well. Barrie had no right to be jealous, but she was. She didn't look at him, because she didn't want him to know for sure just how vulnerable she still was.

"You must like her if you're willing to have her stay at the ranch," she said. "Why do you keep plaguing me to come and play chaperone?"

His pale green eyes met hers. "I don't want her in my bed. Is that blunt enough?"

She flushed. It wasn't the sort of remark he was in the habit of making to her. They never discussed intimate things at all.

"You still blush like a virgin," he said quietly.

Her eyes flashed. "And you're the one man in the world who has reason to know that I'm not!" she said in a harsh, bitter undertone.

His expression wasn't very readable. He averted his eyes to the carpet. After a minute he finished his drink. He reached through the banister to put the glass on the hall table beyond it.

She pulled her skirt aside as he reached past her. For an instant, his deeply tanned face was on an unnerving level with hers. She could see the tiny mole at the corner of his mouth, the faint dimple in his firm chin. His upper lip was thinner than the lower one, and she remembered with sorrow how those hard lips felt on her mouth. She'd grieved for him for so long. She'd never been able to stop loving him, despite the pain he'd caused her, despite his suspicions, his antagonism. She wondered sometimes if it would ever stop.

He turned sideways on the step, leaning back against the banister to cross his long legs in front of him. His boots were immaculate, as was the white silk shirt under his open dinner jacket. But, then, he made the most casual clothes look elegant. He was elegant.

"Why don't you get married?" he asked suddenly.

Her eyebrows went up. "Why should I?"

His quiet gaze went over her body, down her full, firm breasts to her narrow hips and long legs. The side slit had fallen open in the position she was sitting, and all too much of her silk-clad leg was visible.

He watched her face very carefully as he spoke. "Because you're twenty-six. In a few more years, it will be more difficult for you to have a child."

A child… A child. The color drained out of her face, out of her eyes. She swallowed a surge of nausea as she remembered the wrenching pain, the fear as she phoned for an ambulance and was carried to the hospital. He didn't know. He'd never know, because she wouldn't tell him.

"I don't want to marry anyone. Excuse me, I have to—"

She tried to get up, but his lean hand shot out and caught her forearm, anchoring her to the steps. He was too close. She could smell the exotic cologne he always wore, feel his breath, whiskey-scented, on her face.

"Stop running from me!" he growled.

His eyes met hers. They were relentless, intent.

"Let me go!" she raged.

His fingers only tightened. He made her feel like a hysterical idiot with that long, hard stare, but she couldn't stop struggling.

He ended the unequal struggle by tugging slightly and she landed back on the steps with a faint thump. "Stop it," he said firmly.

Her eyes flashed at him, her cheeks flushed.

He let go of her arm all at once. "At least you look alive again," he remarked curtly. "And back to normal pretending to hate me."

"I'm not pretending. I do hate you, Dawson," she said, as if she was programmed to fight him, to deny any hint of caring in her voice.

"Then it shouldn't affect you all that much to come home with me."

"I won't run interference for you with the widow. If you want that land so badly…"

"I can't buy it if she won't sell it," he reminded her. "And she won't sell it unless I entertain her."

"It's a low thing to do, to get a few acres of land."

"Land with the only water on the Bighorn property," he reminded her. "I had free access when her husband was alive. Now I buy the land or Powell Long will buy it and fence it off from my cattle. He hates me."

"I know how he feels," she said pointedly.

"Do you know what she'll do if you're not there?" he continued. "She'll try to seduce me, sure as hell.

She thinks no man can resist her. When I refuse her, she'll take her land straight to Powell Long and make him a deal he can't refuse. Your friendship with Antonia won't stop him from fencing off that river, Barrie. Without water, we'll lose the property and all the cattle on it. I'll have to sell at a loss. Part of that particular ranch is your inheritance. You stand to lose even more than I do."

"She wouldn't," she began.

"Don't kid yourself," he drawled. "She's attracted to me. Or don't you remember how that feels?" he added with deliberate sarcasm.

She flushed, but she glared at him. "I'm on vacation."

"So what?"

"I don't like Sheridan, I don't like you, and I don't want to spend my vacation with you!"

"Then don't."

She hit the banister helplessly. "Why should I care if I lose my inheritance? I've got a good job!"

"Why, indeed?"

But she was weakening. Her part-time job had fallen through. She was looking at having to do some uncomfortable budgeting, despite the good salary she made. It only stretched so far. Besides, she could imagine what a woman like Mrs. Holton would do to get her claws into Dawson. The widow could compromise him, if she didn't do anything else. She could make up some lurid tale about him if he didn't give out...and there was plenty of gossip already, about Dawson's lack of interest in women. It didn't bear thinking about, what that sort of gossip would do to Dawson's pride. He'd suffered enough through the gossip about his poor father and Antonia Long, when there wasn't one shred of truth to it. And in his younger days, his success with women was painfully obvious to a worshiping Barrie.

"For a few days, you said," she began.

His eyebrows lifted. "You aren't changing your mind!" he exclaimed with mock surprise.

"I'll think about it," she continued firmly.

He shrugged. "We should be able to live under the same roof for that long without it coming to bloodshed."

"I don't know about that." She leaned against the banister. "And if I decide to go—which I haven't yet— when she leaves, I leave, whether or not you've got your tract of land."

He smiled faintly. There was something oddly calculating in his eyes. "Afraid to stay with me, alone?"

She didn't have to answer him. Her eyes spoke for her.

"You don't know how flattering that reluctance is these days," he said, searching her eyes. "All the same, it's misplaced. I don't want you, Barrie," he added with a mocking smile.

"You did, once," she reminded him angrily.

He nodded. His hands went into his pockets and his broad shoulders shifted. "It was a long time ago," he said stiffly. "I have other interests now. So do you. All I want is for you to run interference for me until I can get my hands on that property. Which is to your benefit, as well," he added pointedly. "You inherited half the Bighorn property when George died. If we lose the water rights, the land is worthless. That means you inherit nothing. You'll have to depend on your job until you retire."

She knew that. The dividend she received from her share of cattle on the Bighorn ranch helped pay the bills.

"Oh, *there* you are, Dawson, dear!" a honied voice drawled behind him. "I've been looking just everywhere for you!" A slinky brunette, a good few years younger than Barrie, with a smile the size of a dinner plate latched onto Dawson's big arm and pressed her ample, pretty chest against it. "I'd just love to dance with you!" she gushed, her eyes flirting outrageously with his.

Dawson went rigid. If Barrie hadn't seen it for herself, she wouldn't have believed it. With a face that might have been carved from stone, he released himself from the woman's grasp and moved pointedly back from her.

"Excuse me. I'm talking to my stepsister," he said curtly.

The woman was shocked at being snubbed. She was beautiful and quite obviously used to trapping men with that coquettish manner, and the handsomest man here looked at her as if she smelled bad.

She laughed a little nervously. "Of course. I'm sorry. I didn't mean to interrupt. Later, perhaps, then?"

She turned and went quickly back into the living room.

Barrie was standing where she'd been throughout the terse exchange, leaning against the banister. Now she moved away from it and down the steps to stand just in front of Dawson. Her green eyes searched his quietly.

His jaw clenched. "I told you. I'm not in the market for a woman—not you or anyone else."

Her teeth settled into her lower lip, an old habit that he'd once chided her about.

He apparently hadn't forgotten. His forefinger tapped sharply at her upper lip. "Stop that. You'll draw blood," he accused.

She released the stinging flesh. "I didn't realize," she murmured. She sighed as she searched his hard face. "You loved women, in the old days," she said with more bitterness than she knew. "They followed you around like bees on a honey trail."

His face was hard. "I lost my taste for them."

"But, why?"

"You don't have the right to invade my privacy," he said curtly.

She smiled sadly. "I never did. You were always so mysterious, so private. You never shared anything with me when I was younger. You were always impatient to get away from me."

"Except once," he replied shortly. "And see where that got us."

She took a step toward the living room. "Yes."

There was a silence, filled by merry voices and the clink of ice in glasses.

"If I ask you something, point-blank, will you answer me?" he asked abruptly.

She turned, her eyes wide, questioning. "That depends on what it is. If you won't answer personal questions, I don't see why I should."

His eyes narrowed. "Perhaps not."

She grimaced. "All right. What do you want to know?"

"I want to know," he said quietly, "how many men you've really had since me."

She almost gasped at the audacity of the question.

His eyes slid down her body and back up again, and they were still calculating, the way they'd been all evening. "You dress like a femme fatale. I can't remember the last time I saw you so uncovered. You flirt and tease, but it's all show, it's all on the surface." He scowled. "Barrie..."

She flushed. "Stop looking into my mind! I hated it when I was in my teens and I hate it now!"

He nodded slowly. "It was always like that. I even knew what you were thinking. It was a rare kind of rapport. Somewhere along the way, we lost it."

"You smothered it," she said correcting.

He smiled coolly. "I didn't like having you inside my head."

"Which works both ways," she agreed.

He reached out and touched her cheek lightly, his

fingers lingering against the silky soft skin. She didn't move away. That was a first.

"Come here, Barrie," he invited, and this time he didn't smile. His eyes held hers, hypnotized her, beckoned her.

She felt her legs moving when she hadn't meant to let them. She looked up at him with an expression that wasn't even recognizable.

"Now," he said softly, touching her mouth. "Tell me the truth."

She started to clamp down on her lower lip, and his thumb prevented her. It smoothed over her soft lower lip, exploring under the surface, inside where the flesh was moist and vulnerable. She jerked back from him.

"Tell me." His eyes were relentless. She couldn't escape. He was too close.

"I...couldn't, with anyone else," she whispered huskily. "I was afraid."

The years of bitterness, of blaming her for what he thought he'd made of her were based on a lie. All the guilt and shame when he heard about her followers, when he saw her with other men—he knew the truth now. He'd destroyed her as a woman. He'd crippled her sexually. And just because, like his father, he'd lost control of himself. He hadn't known what she'd suffered until a week ago.

He couldn't tell her that he'd wrangled this invitation from John because he needed an excuse to see her. He hadn't realized in all the long years how badly he'd damaged her. Her camouflage had been so good. Now that he did know, it was unbelievably painful.

"Dear God," he said under his breath.

His hand fell away from her cheek. He looked older, suddenly, and there was no mockery in his face now.

"Surprised?" she taunted unsteadily. "Shocked? You've always wanted to think the worst of me. Even that afternoon at the beach, before it...before it happened, you thought I just wanted to show off my body."

He didn't blink. His eyes searched hers. "The only eyes you wanted on your body were mine," he said in a dead voice. "I knew it. I wouldn't admit it, that's all."

She laughed coldly. "You said plenty," she reminded him. "That I was a tramp, that I was so hot I couldn't—"

His thumb stopped the words and his eyes closed briefly. "You might not realize it, but you aren't the only one who paid dearly for what happened that night," he said after a minute.

"Don't tell me you were sorry, or that you felt guilty," she chided. "You don't have a heart, Dawson. I don't think you're even human!"

He laughed faintly. "I have doubts about that myself these days," he said evenly.

She was shaking with fury, the past impinging on the present as she struggled with wounding memories. "I loved you!" she said brokenly.

"Dear God, don't you think I know?!" he demanded, and his eyes, for that instant, were terrible to look into.

She went white, paper white. Beside her skirt, her hands clenched. She wanted to throw herself at him and hit him and kick him, to hurt him as he'd hurt her.

But slowly, as she remembered where they were, she forced herself to calm down. "This isn't the time or the place." She bit off the words. Her voice shook with emotion.

He stuck his hands into his pockets and looked down at her. "Come to Wyoming with me. It's time you got it all out of your system. You've been hurt enough for something that was never your fault to begin with."

The words were surprising. He was different, somehow, and she didn't understand why. Even the antagonism when he saw her had been halfhearted, as if he was only sniping at her out of habit. Now, he wasn't especially dangerous at all. But she didn't, couldn't, trust him. There had to be more to his determination to get her to Wyoming than as a chaperone.

"I'll think about it," she said shortly. "But I won't decide tonight. I'm not sure I want to go back to Sheridan, even to save my inheritance."

He started to argue, but the strain of the past few minutes had started to show in her face. He hated seeing the brightness gone from it. He shrugged. "All right. Think it over."

She drew in a steadying breath and walked past him into the living room. And for the rest of the evening, she was the life and soul of the party. Not that Dawson noticed. A couple of minutes after she left him in the hall, he went out the door and drove back to his hotel. Alone.

Two

IT WAS a boring Saturday. Barrie had already done the laundry and gone to the grocery store. She had a date, but she'd canceled it. Somehow, one more outing with a man she didn't care about was more than she could bear. No one was ever going to measure up to Dawson, anyway, as much as she'd like to pretend it would happen. He owned her, as surely as he owned half a dozen ranches and a veritable fleet of cars, even if he didn't want her.

She'd given up hoping for miracles, and after last night, it was obvious that the dislike he'd had for her since her fifteenth birthday wasn't going to diminish. Even her one memory of him as a lover was nothing she wanted to remember. He'd hurt her, and afterward, he'd accused her of being a wanton who'd teased him into seducing her. He could be kind to the people he liked, but he'd never liked Barrie or her mother. They'd been the outsiders, the interlopers, in the Rutherford family. Barrie's mother had married his father, and Dawson had hated them both from the moment he laid eyes on them.

Eleven years later, after the deaths of both their parents, nothing had changed except that Barrie had learned self-preservation. She'd avoided Dawson like the plague, until last night, when she'd betrayed everything to him in that burst of anger. She was embarrassed and ashamed this morning to have given herself away so completely. Her one hope was that he was already on his way back to Sheridan, and that she wouldn't have to see him again until the incident was forgotten, until these newest wounds he'd inflicted were healed.

She'd just finished mopping the kitchen floor in her bare feet and had put the mop out on the small balcony of her apartment to dry when the doorbell rang.

It was almost lunchtime and she was hungry, having spent her morning working. She hoped it wasn't the man she'd turned down for a date that evening, trying to convince her to change her mind.

Her wavy black hair lay in disheveled glory down her back. It was her one good feature, along with her green eyes. Her mouth was shaped like a bow and her nose was straight, but she wasn't conventionally pretty, although she had a magnificent figure. She was dressed in a T-shirt and a pair of worn jeans. Both garments had shrunk, emphasizing her perfect body. She didn't have makeup on, but her eyes were bright and her cheeks were rosy from all her exertions.

Without thinking, she opened the door and started to speak, when she realized who was standing there. It definitely wasn't Phil, the salesman with whom she'd turned down a date.

It was always the same when she came upon Dawson unawares. Her heart began to race, her breath stilled in her throat, her body burned as if she stood in a fire.

Eyes two shades lighter green than her own looked back at her. Whatever he wore, he looked elegant. He was in designer jeans and a white shirt, with a patterned gray jacket worn loose over them. His feet were encased in hand-tooled gray leather boots and a creamy Stetson dangled from one hand.

He looked her up and down without smiling, without expression. Nothing he felt ever was allowed to show, while Barrie's face was as open as a child's book to him.

"What do you want?" she asked belligerently.

An eyebrow jerked over amused green eyes. "A kind word. But I've given up asking for the impossible. Can I come in? Or," he added, the smile fading, "isn't it convenient?"

She moved away from the door. "Check the bedroom if you like," she said sarcastically.

He searched her eyes. Once, he might have taken her up on it, just to irritate her. Not since last night, though. He hadn't the heart to hurt her any more than he already had. He tossed his hat onto the counter and leaned against it to watch her close the door.

"Have you decided whether or not you'll come back to Sheridan?" he asked bluntly. "It's only for a week. You're on summer vacation, and John told me that you'd been laid off at your part-time job." He looked at the counter and said with calculation, "Surely you can survive without your flock of admirers for that long."

She didn't contradict him or fly off the handle. That was what he wanted. She made points with Dawson by remaining calm.

"I don't want to play chaperone for you, Dawson," she said simply. "Get someone else."

"There isn't anyone else, and you know it. I want that land. What I don't want is to give Mrs. Holten any opportunities for blackmail. She's a lady who's used to getting what she wants."

"You're evenly matched, then, aren't you?" she replied.

"I don't have everything I want," he countered. His eyes narrowed. "Corlie and Rodge will be in the house, too. They miss you."

She didn't answer. She just looked at him, hating him and loving him while all the bad memories surfaced.

"Your eyes are very expressive," he said, searching them. There was so much pain behind the pretense, he thought sadly, and he'd caused it. "Such sad eyes, Barrie."

He sounded mysterious, broody. She sensed a change in him, some ripple of feeling that he concealed, covered up. His lean fingers toyed with the brim of his Stetson and he studied it while he spoke. "I bought you a horse."

She stared at him. "Why?"

"I thought you might respond to a bribe," he said

carelessly. "He's a quarter horse. A gelding." He smiled with faint self-contempt. "Can you still ride?"

"Yes." She didn't want to admit that it touched her to have Dawson buy her a present. Even a plastic necklace would have given her pleasure if he'd given it to her.

His eyes lifted back to hers. "Well?"

"You have Rodge and Corlie to play chaperone. You don't need me."

His pale eyes held hers. "Yes, I do. More than you know."

She swallowed. "Look, Dawson, you know I don't want to come back, and you know why. Let's just leave it at that."

His eyes began to glitter. "It's been five years," he said coldly. "You can't live in the past forever!"

"The devil I can't!" she snapped. Her eyes hated him. "I won't forgive you," she whispered, almost choking on the words. "I won't ever, ever forgive you!"

His gaze fell, and his jaw clenched. "I suppose I should have expected that. But hope springs eternal, don't they say?" He picked up his hat and turned back to her.

She hadn't gotten herself under control at all. Her

slender hands were clenched at her sides and her eyes blazed.

He paused just in front of her. At close range, he was much taller than she was. And despite their past, his nearness disturbed her. She took a step backward.

"Do you think I don't have scars of my own?" he asked quietly.

"Men made of ice don't get scars," she managed to say hoarsely.

He didn't say another word. He turned and went toward the door. This wasn't like Dawson. He was giving up without a fight; he didn't even seem bent on insulting her. The very lack of retaliation was new and it disturbed her enough to call to him.

"What's wrong?" she asked abruptly, even as he reached for the doorknob.

The question, intimating concern, stopped him in his tracks. He turned as if he didn't really believe she'd asked that. "What?"

"I asked what was wrong," she repeated. "You aren't yourself."

His hand tightened on the doorknob. "How the hell would you know whether I am or not?" he returned.

"You're holding something back."

He stood there breathing roughly, glaring at her. He

shifted, restless, as highly strung as she remembered him. He was a little thinner these days, fine-drawn. His eyes narrowed on her face.

"Are you going to tell me?" she asked him.

"No," he said after a minute. "It wouldn't change anything. I don't blame you for wanting to stay away."

He was hiding something. She knew instinctively that he didn't want to tell her. He seemed vulnerable. It shocked her into moving toward him. The action was so unexpected, so foreign, that it stilled his hand on the doorknob. Barrie hadn't come toward him in five years.

She stopped an arm's length away and looked up at him. "Come on, tell me," she said gently. "You're just like your father, everything has to be dragged out of you. Tell me, Dawson."

He took a deep breath, hesitated, and then just told her.

She didn't understand at first.

"You're what?" she asked.

"I'm impotent!"

She just looked at him. So the gossips weren't talking about a cold nature when they called him the "ice man." They were talking about a loss of virility.

She hadn't really believed the rumors she'd heard about him.

"But…how…why?" she asked huskily.

"Who knows?" he asked irritably. "What difference does it make?" He took off his hat and ran a lean hand through his hair. "Mrs. Holton is a determined woman, and she thinks she's God's gift to manhood." His face clenched and he averted it, as if it tormented him to tell her all of it. "I need that damn tract of land, but I have to let her come to Sheridan to talk to me about selling it. She wants me, and she'll find out, if she pushes hard enough, that I'm…incapable. Right now it's just gossip. But she'd make me the news item of the century. Who knows? Maybe that's her real reason for wanting to come in the first place, to check out the gossip."

Barrie was horrified. She moved back to the sofa and sat down, hard. Her face was drawn and pale, like his. It shocked her that he'd tell her such a thing, when she was his worst enemy. It was like offering an armed, angry man a bullet for his gun.

He saw her expression and grew angry. "Say something."

"What could I possibly say?" she whispered.

"So you do have some idea of how devastating it is," he murmured from a rigid face.

She folded her hands in her lap. "Then I'm to run interference for you? Will the threat of a sister stop her?"

"That isn't how you'd come back to Sheridan."

She lifted both eyebrows. "How, then?"

He fished a small velvet box out of his pocket and tossed it to her.

She frowned as she opened it. There were two rings inside, a perfect emerald in a Tiffany setting and a matching wedding band set with diamonds and emeralds.

She actually gasped, and dropped the box as if it were red-hot.

He didn't react, although a shadow seemed to pass over his eyes. "Well, that's a novel way of expressing your feelings," he said sardonically.

"You can't be serious!"

"Why can't I?"

"We're related," she blurted out, flushing.

"Like hell we are. There isn't one mutual relative between us."

"People would talk."

"People sure as hell would," he agreed, "but not about my...condition."

She understood now, as she hadn't before, exactly what he wanted her to do. He wanted her to come back to Sheridan and pretend to be engaged to him, to stop all the gossip. Most especially, he wanted her there to run interference while Mrs. Holton was visiting, so that she wouldn't find out the truth about him in a physical way while he tried to coax her into selling him that vital piece of land. He could kill two birds with one stone.

To think of Dawson as impotent was staggering. She couldn't imagine what had caused it. Perhaps he'd fallen in love. There had been some talk of him mooning over a woman a few years ago, but no name was ever mentioned.

"How long ago did it happen?" she asked without thinking.

He turned and his green eyes were scorching. "That's none of your business."

Her eyebrows arched. "Well, excuse me! Exactly who's doing whom the favor here?"

"It doesn't give you the right to ask me intimate questions. And it isn't as if you won't benefit from getting her to sell me the land."

She flushed and averted her face.

He rammed his hands into his pockets with an angry murmur. "Barrie, it hurts to talk about it," he snapped.

She should have realized that. A man's ego was a surprisingly fragile thing, and if what she'd read and heard was correct, a large part of that ego had to do with his prowess in bed.

"But you could…you did…with me," she blurted out.

He made a rough sound, almost a laugh. "Oh, yes." He sounded bitter. "I did, didn't I? I wish I could forget."

That was surprising. He'd enjoyed what he did to her, or she certainly thought he had. In fact, he'd sounded as if the pleasure was… She shut out the forbidden thoughts firmly.

He bent and retrieved the jewelry box from the floor, balancing it on his palm.

"It's a very pretty set," she remarked tautly. "Did you just buy it?"

"I've had it for…a while." He stared at the box and then shoved it back into his pocket before he looked at her. He didn't ask. He just looked.

She didn't want to go back to Sheridan. She'd

learned last night and this morning that she was still vulnerable with him. But the thought of Dawson being made a laughingstock disturbed her. He had tremendous pride and she didn't want that hurt. What if Mrs. Holton did find out about him and went back to Bighorn and spread it around? Dawson might have recourse at law, but what good would that do once the rumors started flying?

She remembered so well the agony her stepfather and Antonia Hayes had suffered over malicious gossip. Dawson must be remembering as well. There was really no way to answer suspicious looks and whispers. He seemed to have had a bad enough time from just the gossip. How would it be for him if everyone knew for certain that he wasn't capable of having sex?

"Barrie?" he prompted curtly.

She sighed. "Only for a week, you said?" she asked, lifting her eyes to surprise a curious stillness in the expression on his lean, handsome face. "And nobody would know about the 'engagement' except Mrs. Holton?"

He studied his boots. "It might have to be in the local papers, to make it sound real." He didn't look at her. "I doubt it would reach as far as Tucson. Even if it did, we could always break the engagement. Later."

This was all very strange and unexpected. She hadn't really had time to think it through. She should hate him. She'd tried to, over the years. But it all came down to basics, and love didn't die or wear out, no matter how viciously a heart was treated. She'd probably go to her grave with Dawson's name on her lips, despite the lost baby he didn't even know about, and the secret grief she'd endured.

"I need my mind examined," she said absently.

"You'll do it?"

She shrugged. "I'll do it."

He didn't say anything for a minute. Then the box came out of his pocket. "You'll have to wear this."

He knelt just in front of her, where she sat on the sofa, and took out the engagement ring.

"But it might not fit…"

She stopped in midstatement as he slid the emerald gently onto her ring finger. It was a perfect fit, as if it had been measured exactly for it.

He didn't say a word. He had her hand in his and, as she watched, he lifted it to his mouth and kissed the ring so tenderly that she stiffened.

He laughed coldly before he lifted his eyes to hers, and if there had been any expression in them, it was gone now. "We might as well do the thing properly, hadn't we?" he asked mockingly, and got gracefully to his feet.

She didn't reply. She still felt his warm mouth on her fingers, as if it were a brand. She looked down at the ring, thinking how perfect the emerald was. Such a flawless stone was easily worth the price of a diamond of equal size.

"Is it synthetic?" she asked absently.

"No. It's not."

She traced around it. "I love emeralds."

"Do you?" he asked carefully.

She lifted her eyes back to his. "I'll take good care of it. The woman you originally bought it for, didn't she want it?" she asked.

His face closed up. "She didn't want me," he replied. "And it's a good thing, considering the circumstances, isn't it?"

He sounded angry. Bitter. Barrie couldn't imagine any sane woman not wanting him. She did, emotionally if not physically. But her responses had been damaged, and he hadn't been particularly kind to her in the aftermath of their one intimacy.

Her eyes on the emerald she asked, "Could you, with her?"

There was a cold pause. "Yes. But she's no longer part of my life, or ever likely to be again."

She recognized the brief flare of anger in his deep voice. "Sorry," she said lightly. "I won't ask any more questions."

He turned away, his hands back in his pockets again. "I thought I might fly you up to Wyoming today, if you don't have anything pressing. A date, perhaps."

She stared at his back. It was strangely straight, almost rigid. "I had the offer of a date," she admitted, "but I refused it. That's who I thought you were. He said he wouldn't take 'no' for an answer...."

Just as she said that, an insistent buzz came from the doorbell. It was repeated three times in quick succession.

Dawson went toward it.

"Dawson, don't you dare!" she called after him.

It didn't even slow him down. He jerked open the door, to reveal a fairly good-looking young blond man with blue eyes and a pert grin.

"Hi!" he said pleasantly. "Barrie home?"

"She's on her way out of state."

The young man, Phil by name, noticed the glare he was getting and the smile began to waver. "Uh, is she a relative of yours?"

"My fiancée," Dawson said, and his lips curled up in a threatening way.

"Fi…what?" Phil's breath exploded.

Barrie eased around Dawson. "Hi, Phil!" she said gaily. "Sorry, but it only just happened. See?" She held out her ring finger. Dawson hadn't budged. He was still standing there, glaring at Phil.

Phil backed up a step. "Uh, well, congratulations, I'm sure. I'll, uh, see you around, then?"

"No," Dawson replied for her.

Barrie moved in front of him. "Sure, Phil. Have a nice weekend. I'm sorry, okay?"

"Okay. Congratulations again," he added, trying to make the best of an embarrassing situation. He shot one last glance at Dawson and returned down the hall the way he'd come, very quickly.

Dawson muttered something under his breath.

Barrie turned and glowered up at him. "That was unkind," she said irritably. "He was a nice man. You scared him half to death!"

"You belong to me for the duration of our 'engagement,'" he said tautly, searching her eyes. "I won't take kindly to other men hanging around until I settle something about that tract of land."

She drew in a sharp breath. "I promised to pretend

to be engaged to you, Dawson," she said uneasily. "That's all. I don't belong to you."

His eyes narrowed even more, and there was an expression in them that she remembered from years past.

He looked as if he wanted to say more, but he hesitated. After a minute, he turned away.

"Are you coming with me now?" he asked shortly.

"I have to close up the apartment and pack…"

"Half an hour's work. Well?"

She hesitated. It was like being snared in a net. She wasn't sure that it was a good idea. If she'd had a day to think about it, she was certain that she wouldn't do it.

"Maybe if we wait until Monday," she ventured.

"No. If you have time to think, you won't come. I'm not letting you off the hook. You promised," he added.

She let out an angry breath. "I must be crazy."

"Maybe I am, too," he replied. His hands balled into fists in his pockets. "It was all I could think of on the spur of the moment. I didn't plan to invite her. She invited herself, bag and baggage, in front of half a dozen people and in such a way that I couldn't extricate myself without creating a lot more gossip."

"There must be other women who would agree to pose as your fiancée," she said.

He shook his head. "Not a one. Or didn't the gossip filter down this far south, Barrie?" he added with bitter sarcasm. "Haven't you heard? It would take a blowtorch, isn't that what they say? Only they don't know the truth of it. They think I'm suffering from a broken heart, doomed to desire the one woman I can't have."

"Are they right?" she asked, glancing at the ring on her finger.

"Sure," he drawled sarcastically. "I'm dying for love of a woman I lost and I can't make it with any other woman. Doesn't it show?"

If it did, it was invisible. She laughed self-consciously. She'd known there were women in Dawson's life for years, but she and Dawson had been enemies for a long time. She was the last person who'd know about a woman he'd given his heart to. Probably it had happened in the years since they'd returned from that holiday in France. God knew, she'd stayed out of his life ever since.

"Did she die?" she asked gently.

His chin lifted. "Maybe she did," he replied. "What difference does it make?"

"None, I guess." She studied his lean face, seeing new lines in it. His blond hair had a trace of silver, just barely visible, at his ears. "Dawson, you're going gray," she said softly.

"I'm thirty-five," he reminded her.

"Thirty-six in September," she added without thinking.

His eyes flashed. He was remembering, as she was, the birthdays when he'd gone out on the town with a succession of beautiful women each year. Once Barrie had tried to give him a present. It was nothing much, just a small silver mouse that she'd saved to buy for him. He'd looked at the present with disdain, and then he'd tossed it to the woman he was taking out that night, to let her enthuse over it. Barrie had never seen it again. She thought he'd probably given it to his date, because it was obvious that it meant nothing to him. His reaction had hurt her more than anything in her life ever did.

"The little cruelties are the worst, aren't they?" he asked, as if he could see the memory, and the pain, in her mind. "They add up over the years."

She turned away. "Everyone goes through them," she said indifferently.

"You had more than most," he said bitterly. "I gave you hell every day of your young life."

"How are we going to Sheridan?" she asked, trying to divert him.

He let out a long breath. "I brought the Learjet down with me."

"It's overcast."

"I'm instrument rated. You know that. Are you afraid to fly with me?"

She turned. "No."

His eyes, for an instant, were haunted. "At least there's something about me that doesn't frighten you," he said heavily. "Go and pack, then. I'll be back for you in two hours."

He went out the door this time, leaving her to ponder on that last statement. But she couldn't make any sense of it, although she spent her packing time trying to.

Three

IT WAS stormy and rain peppered the windscreen of the small jet as Dawson piloted it into his private airstrip at Sheridan. He never flinched nor seemed the least bit agitated at the violent storm they'd flown through just before he set the plane down. He was as controlled in the cockpit as he was behind the wheel of a car and everywhere else. When he'd been fighting the storm, Barrie had seen him smile.

"No butterflies in your stomach?" he taunted when he'd taken off his seat belt.

She shook her head. "You never put a foot wrong when the chips are down," she remarked, without realizing that it might sound like praise.

His pale green eyes searched her face. She looked

tired and worried. He wanted to touch her cheek, to bring the color back into her face, the light back into her eyes. But it might frighten her if he reached toward her now. He might have waited too late to build bridges. It was a sobering thought. So much had changed in his life in just the past two weeks, and all because of a chance meeting with an old buddy at a reunion and a leisurely discussion about Tucson, where the friend, a practicing physician, had worked five years earlier in a hospital emergency room.

Barrie noticed his scrutiny and frowned. "Is something wrong?"

"Just about everything, if you want to know," he remarked absently, searching her eyes. "Life teaches hard lessons, little one."

He hadn't called her that, ever. She'd never heard him use such endearments to anyone in normal conversation. There was a new tenderness in the way he treated her, a poignant difference in his whole manner.

She didn't understand it, and she didn't trust it.

A movement caught his eye. "Here comes Rodge," he murmured, nodding toward the ranch road, where a station wagon was hurtling toward the airstrip. "Ten to one he's got Corlie with him."

She smiled. "It's been a long time since I've seen them."

"Not since my father's funeral," he agreed curtly. He left the cockpit and lowered the steps. He went down them first and waited to see if she needed help. But she'd worn sneakers and jeans, not high heels. She went down as if she were a mountain goat. She'd barely gotten onto the tarmac when the station wagon stopped and both doors opened. Corlie, small and wiry and gray-haired, held her arms out. Barrie ran into them, hungry for the older woman's warm affection.

Beside her, Rodge shook Dawson's hand and then waited his turn to give Barrie a hug. He was at least ten years older than Corlie, and still dark-headed with a few silver streaks. He was dark-eyed and lean. When he wasn't managing the ranch in Dawson's absence, he kept busy as Dawson's secretary, making appointments and handling minor business problems.

The two of them had been with the Rutherfords for so long that they were more like family than paid help. Barrie clung to Corlie. She hadn't realized how much she'd missed the woman.

"Child, you've lost weight," Corlie accused. "Too many missed meals and too much fast food."

"You can feed me while I'm here," she said.

"How long are you staying?" Corlie wanted to know.

Before Barrie could answer her and spill the beans, Dawson caught her left hand and held it under Corlie's nose. "This is the main reason she came back," he said. "We're engaged."

"Oh, my goodness," Corlie exclaimed before a shocked Barrie could utter a single word. The older woman's eyes filled with tears. "It's what Mr. Rutherford always prayed would happen, and me and Rodge, too," she added, hugging Barrie all over again. "I can't tell you how happy I am. Now maybe he'll stop brooding so much and smile once in a while," she added with a grimace at Dawson.

Barrie didn't know what to say. She got lost in the enthusiasm of Rodge's congratulations and Dawson's intimidating presence. He must have had a reason for telling them about the false engagement, perhaps to set the stage for Mrs. Holton's arrival. She could ask him later.

Meanwhile, it was exciting to look around and enjoy being back in Sheridan. The ranch wasn't in town, of course, it was several miles outside the city limits. But it had been Dawson's home when she came here, and she loved it because he did. So many memories had hurt her here. She wondered why it was so dear to her in spite of them.

She found herself installed in the backseat of the station wagon with Corlie while Dawson got in under the wheel and talked business with Rodge all the way up to the house.

The Rutherford home was Victorian. This house had been built at the turn of the century, and it replaced a much earlier structure that Dawson's great-grandfather had built. There had been Rutherfords in Sheridan for three generations.

Barrie often wished that she knew as much about her own background as she knew about Dawson's. Her father had died when she was ten, too young to be very curious about heritage. Then when her mother married George Rutherford, who had been widowed since Dawson was very young, she was so much in love with him that she had no time for her daughter. Dawson had been in the same boat. She'd learned a bit at a time that he and his father had a respectful but very strained relationship. George had expected a lot from his son, and affection was something he never gave to Dawson; at least, not visibly. It was as if there was a barrier between them. Her mother had caused the final rift, just by marrying George. Barrie had been caught in the middle and she became Dawson's scapegoat for the new chaos of his life. George's remarriage had shut Dawson out of his father's life for good.

Barrie had tried to talk to Dawson about his mother once, but he'd verbally slapped her down, hard. After that, she'd made sure personal questions were kept out of their conversation. Even today, he didn't like them. He was private, secretive, mysterious.

Rodge took her bags up to her old room on the second floor, and she looked around the hall, past the sliding doors that led to the living room on one side and the study on the other, down to the winding, carpeted staircase. Suspended above the hall was a huge crystal chandelier, its light reflected from a neat black-and-white tile floor. The interior of the house was elegant and faintly unexpected on a ranch.

"I'd forgotten how big it is," Barrie mused.

"We used to do a lot of entertaining," Corlie reminded her. She glared at Dawson. "Not anymore."

"I'll remember you said that," he replied. "Perhaps we'll throw a party for Mrs. Holton when she gets here."

"That would make a nice change," Corlie said. She winked at Barrie. "But I expect she's going to be something of a nuisance to a newly engaged couple. I'll help run interference."

She smiled and went off to make coffee.

"Oh, dear," Barrie murmured, seeing more complications down the road.

Dawson shoved his hands into his pockets and searched her face. "Don't worry," he said. "It will all work out."

"Will it?" She grimaced. "What if Mrs. Holton sees right through us?"

He moved a little closer, near enough that she could feel the warmth of his body. "Neither of us is used to touching or being touched," he remarked when she stiffened. "That may be awkward."

She remembered how he'd pushed away the woman at the party in Tucson. Barrie was afraid to come that close, but they were supposed to be engaged and it would look unnatural if they never touched each other.

"What are we going to do?" she asked miserably.

He sighed heavily. "I don't know," he said honestly. Slowly his hand went out, and he touched her long, wavy dark hair. His fingers were just a little awkward. "Maybe we'll improve with some practice."

She bit her lower lip. "I…hate being touched," she whispered in a rough whisper.

He winced.

She lowered her eyes to his chest. "Didn't you notice, at the party? I had two men at my feet, but did you see how much distance there was between us? It's always like that. I don't even dance anymore…!"

His hand withdrew from her hair and fell to his side. "God forgive me," he said miserably. "I don't think I can ever forgive myself."

Her eyes came up, shocked. He'd never admitted guilt, or fault before. Something must have happened to change him. But what?

"We'll have to spend some time together before she gets here," he said slowly. "And get to know each other a little better. We might try holding hands. Just to get used to the feel of each other."

Tentative. Like children on a first date. She wondered why she was being so whimsical, and smiled.

He smiled back. For the first time in recent memory, it was without malice or mockery.

"Antonia said that Mrs. Holton was very attractive," she remarked.

"She is," he agreed. "But she's cold, Barrie. Not physically, but emotionally. She likes to possess men.

I don't think she's capable of deep feelings, unless it's for money. She's very aggressive, single-minded. She'd have made a good corporate executive, except that she's lazy."

"Did her husband leave her well-fixed?" she asked curiously.

"No. That's why she's trying to find a man to keep her."

She bristled. "She ought to go back to school and keep herself," she said shortly.

He laughed softly. "That's what you did," he agreed. "You wouldn't even take an allowance from George. Or from me."

She flushed, averting her eyes. "The Rutherfords put me through college. That was more than enough."

"Barrie, I never thought your mother married my father for his money," he said, reading the painful thought in her mind. "She loved him, just as he loved her."

"That wasn't what you said."

His eyes closed. "And you can't forget, can you? I can't blame you. I was so full of hatred and resentment that I lashed out constantly. You were the most easily reachable...and the most vulnerable." His eyes opened again, cold with self-contempt. "You paid for every sin I accused your mother of committing."

"And how you enjoyed making me pay," she replied huskily.

He looked away, as if the pain in her eyes hurt him. "Yes, I did," he confessed bluntly. "For a while. Then we went to the Riviera on holiday with George."

She couldn't think about that. She didn't dare let herself think about it. She moved away from him. "I should unpack."

"Don't go," he protested. "Corlie's making coffee. She'll probably have cake to go with it."

She hesitated. Her big green eyes lifted to his, wary and uncertain.

His face hardened. "I won't hurt you," he said roughly. "I give you my word."

He was old-fashioned that way. If he made a promise, he kept it. But why should he stop sniping at her now, and so suddenly? Her eyes mirrored all her uncertainties, all her doubts.

"What's changed?" she asked miserably.

"*I've* changed," he replied firmly.

"You suddenly woke up one morning and decided that you'd give up an eleven-year vendetta?"

He searched over her face with an enigmatic

expression on his darkly tanned face. "No. I discovered how much I'd lost," he said, his voice taut with some buried feeling. "Have you ever thought that sometimes our whole lives pivot on one decision? On a lost letter or a telephone call that doesn't get made?"

"No, I don't suppose I have, really," she replied.

"We live and learn. And the lessons get more expensive with age."

"You're very reflective, lately," she said, curious. A strand of hair fell over her eyes, and she pushed it back from her face. "I don't think in all the time we've known each other that we've really talked, until the past day or so."

"Yes. I know." He sounded bitter. He turned away from her to lead the way into the spacious living room. It had changed since she'd lived on the Rutherford ranch. This was the very room where Dawson had so carelessly tossed the little silver mouse she'd given him to his date. But it wasn't the same at all. The furniture was different, Victorian and sturdy in its look, but wonderful to sink into.

"This room doesn't look like you at all," she remarked as she perched herself in a delicate-looking wing chair that was surprisingly comfortable.

"It isn't supposed to," he replied. He sat down on the velvet-covered sofa. "I hired a decorator to do it."

"What did you tell her, that you wanted to adopt someone's grandmother and install her here?" she asked.

He lifted an eyebrow. "In case you didn't notice, the house is late Victorian. And I thought you liked Victorian furniture," he added.

She shifted, running her hand along the arm of the chair. "I love it," she confessed in a subdued tone. Questions poised on the tip of her tongue, and she almost asked them, but Corlie came in with a tray of cake and coffee, beaming.

"Just what the doctor ordered," she said smugly, putting the tray on the big coffee table.

"Great huge coffee tables aren't Victorian," Barrie muttered.

"Sure they are. Victorians drank coffee," Corlie argued.

"They drank tea," she replied, "and out of dainty little china cups and saucers."

"They also ate cucumber sandwiches," Corlie returned. "Want a few?"

Barrie made a face. "I'll be quiet about the coffee table if you won't offer me those again."

"It's a deal. Call if you need anything else." Corlie went out, closing the sliding doors behind her.

She helped herself to coffee and cake and so did he. As always he took his coffee black while Barrie put cream and sugar in hers.

"Antonia said that you'd been offered a job heading the math department at your high school next fall," he remarked. "Are you going to take it?"

She looked up over the rim of her coffee cup. "I don't know," she replied. "I love teaching. But that job is mostly administrative. It would take away the time I had with my students, and plenty of them require extra tutoring."

He searched her down-bent face. "You…like children, don't you?"

"Oh, yes." She toyed with her coffee cup, trying not to think about the child they'd made, the one she'd lost so many years ago.

He sat, waiting, hoping that she might finally decide to tell him her secrets. But the moment passed. She went right on eating cake and drinking coffee, and she didn't make another remark. He was hesitant about bringing it up himself. They had a long way to go before she might feel comfortable talking about something so intimate and painful with him.

He changed the subject and conversation reverted to impersonal topics. He went into his study to make some phone calls and she went upstairs to unpack.

She wondered at the change in him, but she was still too raw from the past to let her guard down.

Supper was a cheerful affair, with Rodge and Corlie sitting at the table with Barrie and a taciturn Dawson. They talked. He listened. He seemed preoccupied, and he excused himself to work in the study. He didn't come back, even when Barrie said good-night to Corlie and Rodge and went up to her old room to go to bed.

She lay awake for a long time. Being in the house again brought back memories, so many memories, of Dawson and his antagonism. Then, inevitably, her mind went to the Riviera....

It had been a beautiful summer day. Seagulls had dived and pitched above the white beach where Barrie sat on a big beach blanket and worried about her conservative appearance. Many people were nude. Most of the women were topless. Nobody seemed to pay the least attention, either.

Barrie wanted to sunbathe without white lines, but she was inhibited at twenty-one, and a little intimidated by Dawson in his white trunks. He was exquisite, and she couldn't keep her eyes off him. A thick thatch of curly gold hair, darker than that on his head, covered his broad chest and narrowed down his flat stomach into his trunks. Long, elegantly powerful legs had the same tan as the rest of his body. She imagined that he normally sunbathed without any trunks at all, although she didn't know for sure.

The path of her thoughts embarrassed her and she averted her eyes. But her hands toyed with the ties of her bikini top as she thought daringly how it would be to let it fall, to know that Dawson's gaze was on her bare breasts. She shivered with just the thought of it, and wished she were sophisticated and chic like his usual companions, that she had the nerve just once to do something outrageous and shocking.

She'd glanced at him in what might have seemed a coquettish way as her fingers toyed with the straps and she'd smiled nervously.

Dawson hadn't realized how inhibited she was. He'd formed the idea that Barrie was a born flirt, that she collected men. He'd always seen her shy attempts at affection as deliberate coquetry, because it was the sort of game the sophisticated women he knew played. So when Barrie had darted that curious glance at him, he'd thought she wanted him to coax her into taking off the top. And because she had a lovely young body, and he wanted very much to look at it, he'd played along.

"Go ahead," he'd murmured in a deep, tender voice. "Untie it, Barrie. I want to look at you."

She remembered looking into his eyes and seeing the lazy sensuality in them, the calculating narrowness of them.

"Why the hesitation?" he'd taunted. "You're drawing attention because you're being so damned conservative. None of the other women have any hang-ups about their bodies."

He nodded toward two young women about Barrie's age, dancing along the beach with only bikini bottoms covering their womanliness.

She bit her lip, hesitating, turned just sideways from him, toward the beach.

He'd been beside her, facing her on his knees, his lean hands resting on his muscular thighs. "Barrie?" he'd coaxed softly. And when she looked at him his voice softened and deepened. "Take it off."

He hypnotized her with forbidden longings, with long-buried needs. Her hands fumbled with the single tie at the back of her neck and she loosened it. Her fingers reached around to the other single fastening under her shoulder blades. She looked into his pale green eyes, trembling with new sensations, flushing at the enormity of what she was doing. And she let the top fall away.

She remembered even now the feel of his eyes, the soft intake of his breath as he'd looked at her. She had high, firm, full breasts, pale pink, with darker pink crowns that went rigid under the impact of his level gaze.

She trembled helplessly as he looked his fill. There was a dark flush along his high cheekbones, and he made no pretence of not staring.

Unexpectedly his eyes lifted to hold hers. Whatever he'd seen there must have told him what he wanted to know, because he'd made a sound deep in his throat and stood up. He seemed to vibrate with some violent emotion. Suddenly he'd bent and slipped his arms under her knees and her back and lifted her off the sand. His eyes stared into hers as he slowly, exquisitely, brought her upper body to his so that her breasts flattened gently in the thick hair that covered his broad chest. His skin was as cool from the breeze as hers was hot from the feelings he aroused in her virginal body. She'd stiffened at the shock of the contact.

"No one is looking," he said roughly. "No one gives a damn. Put your arms around me and come closer."

It was shocking, the need she felt. She obeyed him, forgetting her shyness as she ached to feel his body against hers. She remembered burying her hot face in his throat, drinking in the scent of him, feeling his heavy, harsh pulse against her bare breasts as his arms tightened and he walked toward the water with her.

"Wh...why?" She choked.

"Because I'm so damned aroused that I can't hide it," he said half angrily. "The only escape is right into the ocean. Or don't you feel it, too, Barrie? A burning deep in your belly, an emptiness that wants filling, an ache that hurts?"

Her arms contracted and she moaned softly.

"Yes, you feel it," he breathed as he began to wade into the water. His face slid against hers and his mouth suddenly opened as it sought and found her parted lips. She didn't remember the shock of the water. There was nothing in life except that first, burning sweetness of Dawson's hard mouth on her lips, nothing more than the feel of him in her arms, against her bare breasts.

Vaguely she was aware that they were in the warm water, that his arms had released her so that he could pull her into an even more intimate embrace. His long legs tangled with hers, and for the first time, she felt the force of his desire for her. They kissed and kissed, there in the water, oblivious to the whole world, to the line of hotels above the shore, the other swimmers, the noise on the beach.

He moved her, just enough to let his lean hand find and swallow one swollen breast. His tongue eased into her open mouth. His free hand lifted and pulled her, fit her exactly to the hard thrust of him. And she almost lost consciousness at the stabbing ache of pleasure he kindled in her trembling body, there in the water, there in the blue ocean....

She fell asleep with the memories deep in her mind. Unfortunately, those sweet memories merged with some that were much darker. Dawson had finally gained temporary control of himself, and left her alone in the sea to recover from their feverish embraces. But all through the evening meal with George, he'd watched Barrie with eyes that made her feel hunted. The idiotic way she'd smiled at him and encouraged his watchfulness could still make her cringe. She'd thought he was falling in love with her, and she was doing her best to show him that she already felt that way about him. She'd had no idea how he was interpreting her shy flirting.

But it had all become clear after she'd gone to bed that night. The sliding door on her balcony had opened and Dawson had come through it. He'd been wearing a robe and nothing else. Barrie remembered the sweep of his hand as he tore the sheet away from her body, clad only in thin briefs because of the heat and the failing air-conditioning. Her body had reacted at once to his eyes, and even the shock and faint fear hadn't robbed her of the desire that was all too visible to a man of Dawson's experience.

"Want me, Barrie?" he'd whispered as he threw off his robe and joined her on the bed. "Let's see how well you follow up on those teasing little glances you've been giving me all night."

She hadn't had the presence of mind to explain that she hadn't been teasing him. She wanted to tell him that she loved him, that he was her life. But his hands on her body were shocking, like the things he whispered to her in the moonlight, like the feel of his mouth surging over her taut breasts while he made love to her as if he were some demon of the night.

If she'd been the experienced woman he thought her, it would have been a night to remember. But she'd been a virgin, and he'd been completely out of control. She remembered the faint tremor in the hands that had gathered her hips up to the fierce thrust of his body, his cry of pleasure that drowned out her cry of pain. He whispered to her all through it, his body as insistent as his mouth, his hands, until finally he arched up as though he were on some invisible rack, his powerful body cording with ripple after ripple of ecstasy until he convulsed with hoarse, fierce cries and his hands hurt her.

She felt no such pleasure. Her body felt torn and violated. She was almost sick with the pain that had never seemed to stop. When he pulled away from her finally, exhausted and sweaty, she winced and cried out, because that hurt, too.

She wept, curled into a ball, while he got to his feet and put his robe back on. He'd looked down at her sobbing form with eyes she couldn't see, and she didn't like remembering the things he'd said to her then. His voice had been as brutal as his invasion of her, and she'd been far too innocent to realize that he was shocked and upset by her innocence, hitting out to disguise his own stark guilt. It could have been so different if he'd loved her. But in the darkness of her dream, he was a bird of prey, tearing at her flesh, hurting her, hurting her...

She didn't realize that she'd screamed. She heard the door open and close, felt light against her eyelids, and then felt hands shaking her.

"Barrie. Barrie!"

She came awake with a start, and the face above her was Dawson's. He was wearing a robe, as he had been that night. His hair was damp from a shower, and her mind reverted to the night she'd spent in his arms in France.

"Don't...hurt me...anymore!" she whispered, sobbing.

He didn't reply. He couldn't. The terror in those eyes made him sick right through to his soul. "Dear God," he breathed.

Four

BARRIE saw his face contort and as she came back to awareness, she noticed the room around her, the light fixture overhead. "It's...not France." She choked. Her eyes closed. "Oh, thank God, thank God!"

Dawson got up from the bed and moved to the window. He moved the curtain aside and looked out into the darkness. He wasn't looking at anything. He was seeing the past, the horror in Barrie's eyes, the pain that he'd caused.

Barrie sat up. She noticed his lean hand clenching the curtains. It had gone white. He looked beaten, exhausted.

She swallowed hard. Her hands went to her pale cheeks and smoothed over them and then pushed back the tangled dark hair that fell over her breasts. She was wearing a long cotton gown that completely covered her except for her arms and a little of her slender neck. She never slept just in her briefs these days, not even in summer.

"I didn't realize that you still had nightmares about it," he said after a minute. His voice was dull and without expression.

"Not very often," she said. She couldn't tell him that most of them ended with her losing the baby, crying out for Dawson. That hadn't happened tonight, thank God. She couldn't bear for him to know it all.

He turned away from the window and moved back to the side of the bed, but not close. His hands closed in the pockets of his robe.

"It wouldn't be that way a second time," he said stiffly.

Her eyes widened in fear, as if he'd suggested seducing her all over again. The realization infuriated him, but he controlled the surge of anger. "Not... with me." He bit off the words, averting his face. "I didn't mean that."

She drew her knees up and wrapped her arms around them. The sound of the fabric sliding against her skin was abnormally loud. She glanced up at him and the memories began to recede. If she was hurting, so was he. He couldn't fake the sort of pain she saw in his drawn face.

"Haven't you even been curious since then, for God's sake?" he asked. "You're a woman. You must have friends, people you could ask. Surely someone told you that first times are notoriously bad."

She smoothed one hand over the other. Her body slumped with a long sigh. "I can't talk to anyone about it," she said finally. "I only have one best friend. And how could I possibly ask Antonia, when she's known us both for years? She wouldn't need two guesses to figure out why I was asking."

He nodded. "You were a virgin. You needed time to be properly aroused, especially with me, and I lost control much too soon," he added. His eyes searched her face grimly. "That was a first for me. Until you came along, there had never been a woman who could throw me off balance in bed."

Her face lowered. It was an accomplishment of sorts, she supposed.

"I damaged both of us that night," he said gently. "Until I had you, I genuinely thought you were experienced, Barrie, that you were only teasing on the beach when you had to be coaxed into removing your top."

That brought her eyes up to his, shocked. "But I would never have done such a thing!" she protested.

"I had to find that out the hard way," he replied. "Maybe I used it as an excuse, too. I wanted you and I convinced myself that you'd surely had men at your age, that it had all been playacting on your part, all that coy shyness. But it didn't take me long to realize why you'd given in without a struggle. You loved me," he said huskily.

Her eyes closed. She couldn't bear to hear him say it again. He'd taunted her with her feelings after that disastrous night.

She felt the bed depress as he sat down slowly beside her. His hand tipped her head back toward his, making her look at him. "Guilt will drive a man to violence, Barrie," he said, his voice deep and soft in the silence of her room. "Especially when he's done something unforgivable and knows he'll never find forgiveness for it. I taunted you because I couldn't live with what I'd done to you. It doesn't make much sense, now. But at the time, blaming you was the only thing that kept me from putting a gun to my head."

She hadn't said a word. Her big eyes were locked into his as she struggled to understand him.

"I couldn't stop." He took an unsteady breath. "God, Barrie, I tried. I tried. But I couldn't...stop." He leaned forward, his head bent down, defeated. "For months after it happened, I could hear your voice in my nightmares. I knew I was hurting you, but I couldn't draw back."

She didn't understand desire of that sort, pleasure too blind to feel pity. She'd never felt it, although the way he'd kissed her in the ocean had made her hungry for something. "I wanted you, too."

He lifted his head and looked down at her. "You don't understand, do you?" he asked gently. "You've never felt desire that overwhelming. Your only knowledge of real intimacy is forever embedded in pain."

"I didn't know you had nightmares," she said slowly.

"I still have them," he said on a cold laugh. "Just like you."

Her gaze went over his face like searching hands. "Why did you come to my room that night?" she asked softly.

He moved, one long arm going across her body to support him as he leaned closer, so that his face filled her entire line of vision. "Because I wanted you so much that I would have died to have you," he said through his teeth.

The subdued violence in the flat statement surprised her. Perhaps she'd known on some unspoken level how desperately hungry he'd been for her, but he'd never actually said the words before.

"I wanted you so much that I was almost sick with it. I came to you because I couldn't stop myself. And it does no good whatsoever five years after the fact to tell you that I'm sorry."

"*Are* you sorry?" she asked sadly.

He nodded, without blinking an eye. "Sorry. Bitter. Hurt. All the things you were. But there was more to it than just physical pain on your part." He didn't move. He didn't seem to breathe. He took a slow, deliberate breath. "You never told me that I gave you a baby that night. Or that, several weeks later, you lost it. Did you think I wouldn't find out, someday?" he concluded heavily, the pain lying dark and dull in his eyes as he saw the shock register on her face.

Her heart skipped and ran away. "I...how did you find out?" she faltered. "I never even told Antonia!"

"Do you remember the intern who attended to you in the emergency room?"

"Yes. Richard Dean," she recalled. "He'd been a student in your graduating class. But you never saw him, he even said that you didn't mix socially. Besides, he was a doctor, he took an oath never to talk about his patients...!"

"We met at a class reunion a few weeks ago," he confided. "He thought I knew. You're my stepsister, after all, he reminded me. He assumed that you'd told me."

She gnawed her lower lip, staring up at him worriedly.

His lean hand came to touch her mouth, disturbing the grip of her teeth. "Don't," he said softly.

"I forget sometimes," she murmured.

His thumb traced over her mouth gently. He searched her eyes. "He said...that you were utterly devastated," he whispered. "That you cried until he had to sedate you." His face drew up with bitterness. "He said you wanted the baby desperately, Barrie."

She dragged her eyes down to his chest. "It was a long time ago." Her voice sounded stiff.

He let out a heavy breath. "Yes, and you've done your grieving. But I've only just started. I didn't know until Richard told me. It's been a little rough, losing a child I didn't even know I'd helped create."

His face was averted, but she could see the pain on it. It was the first time they'd really shared grief, except when his father had died. But that had only been a few words, because she couldn't stand to be near him so soon after the Riviera.

"Would you have told me?" he asked, staring at the wall.

"I'm not sure. It seemed senseless, after so long a time. You didn't know about the baby. I wasn't sure you'd want to know."

He caught her slender hand in his and linked his fingers with it. "I got drunk and stayed drunk for three days after I got back from my class reunion," he said after a minute. Then he added, expressionlessly, "Richard said that you asked a nurse to call me from the emergency room."

She stared at the big hand holding hers so closely. "Yes, in a moment of madness."

"I didn't know she was a nurse. She mentioned your name and before she could say why she was calling, I hung up on her."

His fingers had tightened painfully. "Yes," she said.

He drew her hand to his lips and kissed it hungrily. His head was bent over her hand, but she saw the faint wetness at the corner of his eye and she gasped, horrified.

As if his pride wouldn't take that sort of blow, letting her see the wetness in his eyes, he let go of her fingers and got up, going back to stand at the darkened window. He didn't speak for a full minute, his hand gripping the curtain tightly. "Richard said it was a boy."

She rested her forehead against her knees. "Please," she whispered gruffly. "I can't talk about it."

He moved from the window, back to the bed. He tore the covers away and scooped her up into his arms, sitting down to hold her tight, tight, across his legs, with his face against her soft throat.

"I've got you," he whispered roughly. "You're safe. Nothing will ever hurt you again. Cry for him. God knows I have!"

The tender gruffness in his deep voice broke the dam behind which her tears had hidden. She gave way to them, for the first time since the miscarriage. She wept for the son she'd lost. She wept for her pain, and for his. She wept for all the lost, lonely years.

A long time later, she felt him dabbing at her eyes with a corner of the sheet. She took it from him and finished the job. And still he held her, gently, without passion. Her cheek felt the regular, hard beat of his heart under the soft fabric of the robe. She opened her hot, stinging eyes and stared across at the dark window, all the fire and pain wept out of her in salty tears.

"It's late," he said finally. "Mrs. Holton arrives first thing in the morning. You need to get some sleep."

She stretched, boneless from exhaustion, and looked up into his quiet, watchful eyes. Involuntarily his own gaze went down to the soft thrust of her breasts under the cotton gown. He remembered the beauty of her body, years after his last glimpse of it.

She watched him staring at her, but she didn't move or flinch.

"Don't you want to run?" he taunted.

She shook her head. Her eyes looked straight up into his. She slid her fingers over the lean, strong hand that was lying across her waist. She tugged at it until it lifted. She smoothed it up her side, over her rib cage, and then gently settled it directly over one soft breast.

His intake of breath was audible, and his body seemed to jump.

"No," he said curtly, jerking his hand down to her waist. "Don't be stupid."

She felt less confident than she had before, but there

was a faint film of sweat over his upper lip. He was more shaken than he looked.

"Don't make me ashamed. It's hard for me, to even think of this, much less...do it," she said. "I only wanted to know if I could let you touch me," she finished with a rueful smile.

The cold hauteur left him. "I can't take the risk, even if you're willing to." He started to move her aside, but she clung.

"What risk?" she asked.

"Don't you know? You don't need to find out the hard way that I can still want you." He laughed coldly. "I'm not sure I want to know, either."

While she was working that one out, he lifted her and placed her gently onto the pillows. He got up and moved back from the bed. "Go to sleep."

"What if you could...want me?" she persisted, levering up on her elbows.

He looked unutterably weary. "Barrie, we both know that you'd scream the minute I touched you with intent," he said. "You couldn't help it. And even if I could feel anything with you, it might be just the way it was before. I might lose my head again, hurt you again."

"I'm not a virgin anymore," she said without thinking.

His face was quiet, expressionless as he looked down at her. "It's a moot point. My body is dead, as far as sex is concerned. For both our sakes, let well enough alone. It's too soon for experimenting."

Before she could speak, he'd gone out the door, closing it behind him with a firm snap. Barrie lay back, turning what he'd said over in her mind.

He knew, finally, about the baby they'd lost. She didn't know if she was sorry or glad, but it had been cathartic to have it all out in the open. He grieved for their child, at least, as she did. But he had nothing to give her, and she still loved him. It was a problem that had no easy resolution, and in the morning a new complication was due to present itself. She wondered how she was going to react to the widow Holton. It would be an interesting introduction, at the very least. Leslie Holton blew in the next morning like a redheaded tornado, driving a brand-new shiny black Jaguar. Peering through the lacy curtains in the living room when she drove up, Barrie couldn't help thinking that the car suited her. Mrs. Holton was sleek and dangerous-looking, a powerhouse no less than the car she drove. She was wearing a black-and-white suit. Its starkness made her pale skin even paler and presented a backdrop for her fiery hair. Wickedly Barrie wondered how much of it came out of a bottle, because the widow was obviously over twenty-one. Way over.

She went out into the hall and met up with Dawson who had just come out of his study. There were dark circles under his eyes. He appeared worn, as if he hadn't slept. He looked across at Barrie, and she realized that he hadn't slept at all.

She moved toward him. Last night had calmed some old terrors, the way they'd talked had changed things in some subtle way. She stopped in front of him and looked up.

"You haven't had any sleep," she said gently.

His face hardened. "Don't push your luck."

Her eyebrows lifted. "Am I?"

"Looking at me like that is chancy."

She smiled. "What will you do?" she chided.

Something equally reckless flared in his pale eyes. "Want to see?"

He moved forward with an economy of motion to scoop her up against his chest. He held her there, searching her eyes at point-blank range.

Her arms tightened around his strong neck and

she looked back at him curiously. He'd wanted the baby, too. That knowledge had changed the way she envisioned him. Even though there was some residual fear of him in her, the memory of the grief she'd seen in his face last night tempered it.

"Doesn't anybody hear the doorbell ringing?" Corlie muttered as she came out of the kitchen and suddenly spotted Dawson holding Barrie off the floor in his arms. "Well, excuse me." She chuckled, sparing them a wicked glance as she went toward the front door.

Barrie started to speak but Dawson shook his head. "Don't disillusion her," he whispered. "Let her hope."

Something in the way he said it made her look at him curiously. His pale eyes fell to her mouth and he hesitated.

"If you wanted to kiss me, you could," she said boldly. "I mean, I wouldn't scream or anything."

"Cheeky brat," he muttered, but he was still looking at her mouth.

"I can always tell when you've been on a trip to the station in Australia," she whispered.

"Can you?" His head bent closer, his mouth threatening her soft lips. His arms contracted a little. Somewhere in the distance, a stringent voice was demanding that Corlie have someone get luggage out of the Jaguar.

"Yes," she whispered at his lips. "You always come back using Aussie slang."

He chuckled softly.

Barrie felt the vibration of his laughter all the way to her toes. It was the old magic, without the fear. She loved him. His arms were warm and strong and safe, and her hands clasped together behind his neck. She lifted herself closer to that hard, beautiful mouth and parted her lips.

"No self-preservation left, Barrie?" he whispered huskily. His own lips parted and moved down slowly. "Baby," he breathed into her mouth. "Baby, baby…!"

The pressure became slow and soft and insistent. It began to deepen and she caught her breath, anticipating the hunger that she could already taste…

"Dawson!"

Their faces jerked apart. Dawson stared at the newcomer just for a moment with eyes that didn't quite focus. "Leslie," he said then. "Welcome to White Ridge." He lowered Barrie gently to her feet and, keeping a possessive arm around her, held his hand out to Leslie.

Mrs. Holton made an indignant sound. "Hello,

Dawson," she said impatiently. "My goodness, isn't that your stepsister?"

"She was," Dawson replied coolly. "Yesterday, she became my fiancée. We're engaged."

Mrs. Holton was clearly surprised. "But isn't that against the law?"

"Barrie and I aren't blood-related in any way," he said. "My father married her mother."

"Oh." Leslie stared at Barrie, who grinned at her. "I'm glad to meet you, Miss Rutherford."

"Bell," Barrie corrected her, extending a hand. She was quivering inside, all raw nerves and excitement. "Barrie Bell."

"I didn't expect this," Mrs. Holton said. She eyed Dawson carefully. "Of course, it's very sudden, isn't it?" She smiled with feline calculation. "In fact, I seem to remember hearing that the two of you didn't even speak. When did that change?"

"Yesterday," Dawson said, unperturbed. He looked down at Barrie. "It was sudden, all right. Like a bolt of lightning." His eyes fell to her soft mouth as he said it, and she caught her breath at the surge of feeling the stare provoked.

Leslie Holton wasn't blind, but she was determined.

"You do, uh, still want to discuss my tract of land near Bighorn?" she asked with a calculating smile.

"Of course," Dawson replied, and he smiled back. "That was the purpose of your visit, wasn't it?"

She shrugged a thin shoulder. "Well, yes, among other things. I do hope you're going to show me around the ranch while I'm here. I'm very interested in livestock."

"Barrie and I will be delighted, won't we, baby?" he added with a glance at Barrie that made her toes curl.

She pressed close to his side, shocked at her surge of hunger to be near him. It was equally shocking to hear his faint breath and feel his arm tighten around her shoulders.

"Certainly," she said. She smiled at Mrs. Holton, but she sounded, and felt, breathless.

"Corlie will show you to your room, and Rodge will bring your bags right up," Dawson said. "I'll be right back." He let go of Barrie with a smile and went to call Rodge on the intercom.

"You teach, don't you?" Mrs. Holton asked Barrie. "You must be on summer vacation."

"Yes, I am. What do you do?" Barrie shot right back.

"Do? My dear, I'm rich," Leslie said with hauteur.

"I don't have to work for a living." Her eyes narrowed with calculation. "And neither will you after you marry Dawson. Is that why you're marrying him?"

"Of course," she murmured wickedly. She glanced at Dawson, who was just coming out of the study again. "Dawson, you do know that I'm only marrying you for your money, don't you?" she asked, raising her voice.

He chuckled. "Sure."

Leslie was confused. She looked from one of them to the other. "What a very odd couple you are."

"You have no idea," Barrie murmured dryly.

"Amen," he added.

"Well, I'll just slip upstairs and rest for a few minutes, if you don't mind," Leslie said. "It's been a long, tiring drive." She paused in front of Dawson and smiled up at him seductively. "I might even soak in the hot tub for a little while. If you'd like to wash my back, you're welcome," she added teasingly.

Dawson didn't reply. He just smiled.

Leslie glowered at him, glanced at Barrie irritably and followed an impatient Corlie up the staircase.

Barrie moved closer to him. "Do we have hot water, or is it still subject to fits of temperament in the spring?"

"We have bucketsful of hot water," he replied. "And a whirlpool bath in every bathroom." He looked down at her. "One of them holds two people."

She had mental images of being naked in it with Dawson, and her face paled. She withdrew from him without making a single move.

He tilted her chin up to his eyes. "I'm sorry. That could have been less crude."

She sighed. "It's early days yet," she said apologetically.

"Very early days." He pushed back her long, soft hair. "You let me kiss you," he added quietly. "Was it all an act, for her benefit?" He jerked his head toward the staircase.

"I don't act that well."

"Neither do I." His gaze fell to her mouth. "If we make haste slowly, we may discover that things fall into place."

"Things?"

He touched the very tip of her nose with his forefinger. "We might get rid of our scars."

She was worried, and looked it. "I don't know if I can—" she began uncertainly.

"That makes two of us," he said interrupting her.

She grimaced. "Sorry."

His chest rose and fell heavily. "One day at a time."

"Okay."

They took Leslie Holton riding that afternoon. She was surprisingly good on a horse, lithe and totally without fear. She seemed right at home on the ranch. If only she hadn't been making eyes at Dawson, Barrie could have enjoyed her company.

But Leslie Holton wanted Dawson, and she was working on ways to get him. The sudden engagement was very strange and she knew for a fact that Dawson had a reputation for avoiding women altogether. She thought Barrie was helping him put on an act, and if it took her every minute of her time here, she was going to unmask them. If Dawson really was cold, Leslie was going to find out why before she left.

Five

UNAWARE of Leslie Holton's plotting, Barrie was trying to concentrate on what Dawson was telling them about the history of the area they were riding through. But her eyes kept straying to the tall, proud way he rode, as if he were part of the horse. He looked good on horseback.

He looked good any way at all.

He caught her staring and smiled gently. Her heart skipped beats. He'd never been this way with her in all the time they'd known each other, and she couldn't believe he was faking it. There was a new tenderness in his eyes. He didn't talk to her in the old, mocking way. If she was different, so was he.

And through it all, there was an attraction that

had its roots in the past. But Barrie was still afraid of intimacy with him. It was one thing to kiss him and hold hands with him. It was quite another to think of him in bed with her, demanding, insistent, totally out of control, hurting her…!

He glanced at her and saw that flash of fear, understood it without a word being spoken.

As Leslie rode ahead, he fell back beside Barrie. "Don't brood on it," he said seriously. "There's no rush. Give it time."

She sighed as she glanced toward him. "Reading my mind?"

"It isn't that difficult," he told her.

She toyed with the reins. "Time won't help," she said miserably. "I'm still afraid."

"My God, what is there to be afraid of?" he asked shortly. "Didn't you hear what I told you? I meant it. I can't, Barrie. I can't!"

She searched his eyes slowly. "You can't with other women," she corrected.

"I can't with you, either," he muttered. "Hell, don't you think I'd know after last night?"

She glanced warily ahead where Leslie was riding. "Last night you were holding back," she said.

"Yes, I was," he admitted. "You'd just had a

nightmare and you were terrified. I didn't want to make it worse. But even this morning," he said heavily, averting his eyes to the horizon. His broad shoulders rose and fell. He couldn't bring himself to admit that even the hungry kiss he'd started to share with Barrie hadn't been able to arouse him.

Barrie noticed his reticence and kept her silence. She glanced around at the budding trees. Spring was her favorite season, although it certainly came later to Wyoming than it did to Arizona, even if May was basically the same in both places. Closer than the budding trees, however, was the irritated way Leslie Holton was glaring back at them.

"We aren't fooling her, you know," she said suddenly, and lifted her eyes to search his. "She thinks we're pretending."

"Aren't we?" he asked with a bitter laugh.

She supposed they were. Only it hadn't felt like pretense that morning on her part.

"That was a bald-faced lie," he murmured after a minute, and the saddle leather creaked as he reined in his horse and turned to look at her. His eyes were level and penetrating. "Suppose we try."

She felt her eyes widen. "Try...?"

"What you suggested last night. Or have you

already forgotten where you put my hand?" he asked outrageously.

"Dawson!"

"You should look shocked. That was how I felt."

"That's right," she agreed, "pretend it was the first time a woman ever offered you any such thing!"

He managed a wistful smile. It had been a very long time since he'd been able to laugh about his body's lack of interest in women. "I can't," he admitted.

"That doesn't surprise me."

He drew up one long leg and wrapped it around the pommel, straining his powerful muscles against the thick fabric of his designer jeans. He leaned against it to study her, pigtailed and wearing similar clothing, jeans and a loose shirt. "You don't wear revealing clothes around me."

She shrugged. "No. Because I don't have to fight you off."

He cocked an eyebrow inquiringly.

She grimaced. "Well, men come on to me all the time, and I don't want any sort of physical relationship. So I flaunt my figure and flirt and talk about how much my family wants to see me get married and have a big family. You'd be amazed at how fast they find excuses to stop seeing me."

He chuckled. "Suppose someday a man calls your bluff?"

"That hasn't ever happened."

"Hasn't it?"

She realized what he meant, and her cheeks burned.

"I don't suppose I even bothered to tell you that I'd never seen a body more perfect," he continued quietly. "Barrie, undressed, you could pose for the Venus de Milo. I'm not sure that you wouldn't make her jealous."

She wasn't sure if it was a compliment or a dig, because their relationship had shifted in the past two days.

"I mean it," he explained, so that there wasn't any doubt. "And if I were still the man I was five years ago, you'd need a dead bolt on your door."

She searched his eyes. "I suppose at one time or another someone's ventured the opinion that your problem is mental and not physical?"

"Sure. I know that already. The thing is," he added with a faint smile, "how to cure it. And you seem to have a similar hang-up."

She shrugged. "From the same source."

"Yes, I know."

She traced around her pommel. "The obvious solution…"

He swung his leg back down and straightened as Leslie, missing them, came back to find them. "I'm not capable," he said shortly.

"I wasn't offering," she muttered. She glared toward Mrs. Holton. "Of course, she would, in a New York minute!"

He cocked an eyebrow. "Maybe I should let her try," he said cynically. "She probably knows tricks even I haven't learned."

"Dawson!"

He glanced at her, and he didn't smile. "Jealous?"

She moved restlessly in the saddle. "I…don't know. Maybe." She searched his face. "I wish I could offer you the same medicine she could. But you'd have to get me stinking drunk," she said on a pained laugh. She averted her eyes. "I'd never forgive you if you did."

"Did what? Get you stinking drunk?"

"No!" she said at once. "Do it…with her," she explained.

His caught breath carried, but before he could reply, Leslie reined in beside them. "Aren't you two coming along?" she drawled. "It's lonely trying to explore a ranch this size on my own."

"Sorry," Dawson said, easing his horse into step beside hers. "We were discussing plans."

"I have a few of my own," Leslie murmured sweetly. "Want to hear them?"

Barrie fell back a little, glaring at them. But Dawson wasn't having that. He stopped and motioned to her to catch up, with eyes that dared her to hesitate. Reluctantly she rode up beside him and kept pace, to Leslie's irritation, all the way home.

She'd thought Dawson would forget what she'd said before Leslie interrupted them. But he didn't. While Leslie was changing clothes before supper, Dawson caught Barrie by the hand and led her into his study that overlooked the cottonwood-lined river below.

He closed the door behind them and, as an afterthought, locked it.

She stood by the desk at the window, watching him warily. "I gather that you wanted to talk to me?" she asked defensively.

"Among other things." He perched himself on the edge of the desk facing her, and searched her wary face. He folded his arms across his broad chest. "You kissed me back this morning," he said. "You weren't doing it in case Leslie was watching, either. You've buried everything you used to feel for me, but it's still there. I want to try to dig it back up again."

She studied her hands in her lap. It was tempting, because, despite everything that had happened, she loved Dawson. But the memories were too fresh even now, the pain too real. She couldn't block out the years of sarcastic remarks, cutting words, that had wounded her so badly.

She didn't know what he was offering, other than an attempt at a physical relationship. He'd said nothing about loving her. She knew he felt guilty about the baby she'd lost, and the knowledge of her miscarriage was very new to him. When he had time to cope with the grief, he might find that all he really felt for her was pity. She wanted much more than that.

She traced a chipped place on one neat fingernail.

"Well?" he asked impatiently.

She lifted her eyes. "I agreed to pretend to be engaged to you," she said quietly. "I don't want to live in Sheridan for the rest of my life, or give up the promotion I've been offered at my school in Tucson." He started to speak, but she held up her hand. "I know all too well how wealthy you are, Dawson, I know that I could have anything I wanted. But I'm used to making my own way in the world. I don't want to become your dependent."

"There are schools in Sheridan," he said shortly.

"Yes. There are good schools in Sheridan, and I'm sure I could get a position teaching in one. But they'd know my connection to you. I could never be sure if I got the job on my merit or yours."

He glared at her. This wasn't at all what he'd expected, especially after the way she'd softened toward him since last night.

"Don't you feel anything for me?" he asked.

She dropped her eyes to the emerald ring on her engagement finger. "I care for you, of course. I always will. But marriage is more than I can give you."

He got off the desk and turned away to the window. "You blame me for the baby, is that it?"

She glanced at his straight back. "I don't blame anyone. It wasn't preventable."

His head lifted a little higher. At his nape, his blond hair had grown slightly over his collar and it had a faint wave in it. Her eyes searched over his strong neck lovingly. She wanted nothing in life more than to live with him and love him. But what he was offering was a hollow relationship. Perhaps once he was over his guilt about the baby, he'd be able to function with a woman again. It was only a temporary problem, she was certain, caused by his unexpected discovery that she'd become pregnant and lost their child. But marriage wasn't the answer to the problem.

"We can have therapy," he said after a minute, grudgingly. "Perhaps they can find a cure for my impotence and your fear."

"I don't think your problem needs any therapy," she said. "It's just knowing about the baby that's caused it…"

He whirled, his eyes flashing. "I didn't know about the baby five years ago!" he said curtly.

She stared at him blankly for a minute, until she understood what he'd just said. Her face began to go pale. "Five years!" she stammered.

He glowered at her. "Didn't you realize what I was telling you?"

"I had no idea," she began. Her breath expelled sharply. "Five years!"

He looked embarrassed. He turned back to the window. He didn't speak.

She couldn't find any words to offer him. It hadn't occurred to her that a man could go for five years without sex. She eased out of her chair and went to the window to look up at him.

"I had no idea," she said again.

His hands were clasped behind him. His eyes were staring blankly at the flat horizon. "I haven't wanted anyone," he said. "When I found out about the baby, I was devastated. And yes, I felt guilty as well. One reason I asked you back here was to share the grief I felt, because I was pretty sure that you felt it, too, and had never really expressed it." He glanced down at her wistfully. "Maybe I hoped I could feel something with you, too. I wanted to be a whole man again, Barrie. But even that failed." His eyes went back to the window. "Stay until Leslie leaves. Help me keep what little pride I have left. Then I'll let you go."

She wasn't sure what to say to him. That he was devastated was obvious. So was she. Five years without a woman. She could hardly imagine the beating his ego had taken. It was impossible to offer comfort. She had her own feelings of inadequacy and broken pride.

"Everything would have been so different if we hadn't gone to France that summer," she said absently.

"Would it?" He turned to look at her. "Sooner or later, it would have happened, wherever we were. I know how my father felt," he added enigmatically.

"I'll stay until the widow leaves. But what about your land? She doesn't seem excited about selling."

"She will be, when I make her an offer. I happen to know that Powell Long is temporarily strapped for ready cash because of an expansion project on his ranch. He won't be able to match what I offer, and she's in a shaky financial situation. She can't afford to wait a long time for a buyer who'll offer more."

She was curious now. "Then if you know she'll sell, why am I here?"

"For the reason I told you in the beginning," he replied. His eyes were old and tired. "I can't let her find out that everything they've said about me is true. I do have a little pride left."

She grimaced. "It won't do any good if I tell you that…"

He touched his forefinger to her mouth. "No. It won't do any good."

She searched his eyes quietly. She felt inadequate. She felt sick all over. Somewhere in the back of her mind, she knew that the only hope he had of regaining a normal appetite was with her. The problem had begun in France. Only she would have the power to end it. But she didn't have the courage to try.

"Don't beat a dead horse," he said heavily, and

managed a smile. "I've learned to live with it. I'll get along. So will you. Go back to Tucson and take that job. You'll do them proud."

"What will you do?" she asked. "There must be a way, someway...!"

"If there was, I'd have found it in five years' time," he said. He turned away from her and started toward the door. "We'd better make an appearance."

"Wait."

He paused with his hand on the lock.

She ran her hands through her hair, drew a finger over her mouth, opened the top button of her blouse and drew part of the shirttail out.

He understood what she was doing. He pulled out his handkerchief and gave it to her. She drew it lightly over the corner of her mouth and handed it back.

Then he unlocked the door, to find Leslie sitting on the bottom step of the staircase. She eyed them suspiciously and when she saw Barrie's attempts at reparation, she made an impatient sound.

"Sorry," Dawson murmured. "We forgot the time."

"Obviously," Leslie said shortly, glaring at Barrie. "I did come here to talk about land."

"So you did. I'm at your disposal," Dawson said. "Would you like to talk over a cup of coffee?"

"No, I'd like to drive into town with you and see some of the sights," she said. She glanced at Barrie. "I suppose she'll have to come, too."

"Not if you'd rather have my undivided attention," Dawson said surprisingly. "You don't mind, do you, honey?" he added.

Barrie was unsettled, but she forced a smile to her tight lips. "Of course not. Go right ahead. I'll help Corlie bake a cake."

"Can you cook?" Leslie asked indifferently. "I never bothered to learn how. I eat out most of the time."

"I hate restaurant food and fast food," Barrie remarked, "so I took a culinary course last summer. I can even do French pastries."

Dawson was watching her. "You never mentioned that."

She shrugged. "You never asked," she said coolly.

"How odd," Leslie interjected. "I thought engaged people knew all about each other. And she *is* your stepsister," she added.

"We've spent some time apart," he explained. "We're still in the learning stages, despite the engagement. We won't be long," he told Barrie.

"Take your time."

He hesitated, and Barrie knew why. She didn't

want to give Leslie any excuse to taunt him. She went forward, sliding her arms around his waist and trying not to notice how he stiffened.

"Remember that you're engaged," she said in a stage whisper, and went on tiptoe to put her lips to his.

They were as cold as ice, like the eyes that never closed, even though he gave the appearance of returning her caress.

"We'll expect something special on the table when we get back," he said, and gently put her away from him.

Barrie felt empty somehow. She knew he wasn't capable of giving her a full response, but she'd hoped for more warmth than he'd shown her. He looked at her as if he hated her. Perhaps he still did.

Her sad eyes made him uncomfortable. He took Leslie's arm with a smile and led her out the door toward the garage behind the house.

"Trouble in your engagement already?" Leslie mused as they drove out of town in Dawson's new silver Mercedes. "I notice that you're suddenly very cool toward your fiancée. Of course, there is a rather large age difference between you, isn't there?"

Dawson only shrugged. "Every engagement has a

few rough spots that need smoothing over," he said carelessly.

"This one was sudden."

"Not on my part," he replied as he slowed to make a turn.

"I begin to understand. Unrequited love?"

He laughed bitterly. "It seemed that way for a few years."

Leslie stared at him curiously, and then all at once she began laughing.

His eyebrows lifted in a silent query.

"I'm sorry." She choked through her laughter. "It's just that there were these rumors going around about you," she confessed. "I don't know why I even believed them."

"Rumors?" he asked, deadpan.

"Oh, they're too silly to repeat. And now they make sense. I suppose you simply gave up dating women you didn't care about."

He hadn't expected that Leslie might be so easy to placate about those rumors. He glanced at her, scowling.

She only smiled, and this time without overt flirting. "It's kind of sweet, really," she mused. "Barrie didn't suspect?"

He averted his eyes. "No."

"She still doesn't suspect, does she?" she asked curiously. "You're engaged, but she acts as if it's difficult for her even to kiss you. And don't think I was fooled by that very obvious lipstick smear on your handkerchief," she added with a grin. "There wasn't a trace of it on your face, or a red mark where you might have wiped it off. She's very nervous with you, and it shows."

He knew that, but he didn't like hearing it. "It's early days yet."

She nodded slowly. "You might consider that she has less experience with men than she pretends," she added helpfully. "She hasn't got that faint edge of sophistication most women of her age have acquired. I don't think she's very worldly at all."

He pulled the car into a parking spot in front of the old county courthouse. "You see a lot for someone who pretends to have a hard edge of her own," he said flatly, pinning her with his pale green eyes.

She leaned back in her comfortable seat. "I was in love with my husband," she said unexpectedly. "Everybody thought I married him for his money, because he was so much older than I was. It wasn't true. I married him because he was the first person in my life who was ever kind to me." Her voice became bitter with memories. "My father had no use for me, because he never believed I was his child. My mother hated me because I had to be taken care of, and she wanted to party. In the end, they both left me to my own devices. I fell in with bad company and got in trouble with the law." Her thin shoulders lifted and fell. "I was sentenced to a year in prison for helping my latest boyfriend steal some cigarettes. Jack Holton was in court at the time representing a client on some misdemeanor and he started talking to me during the recess." She smiled, remembering. "I was a hard case, but he was interested and very persistent. I was married before I knew it." She stared at her skirt, distracted by memories. "When he died, I went a little mad. I don't think I came to my senses until today." She looked up. "Barrie has something in her past, something that's hurt her. Go easy, won't you?"

He was surprised by her perception. But it was beyond him to admit to a relative stranger how Barrie had been hurt, and by whom. "I'll keep it in mind," he replied.

She smiled at him with genuine fondness. "I do like you, you know," she said. "You're a lot like Jack. But now that I know how things stand, you're off the endangered list. Now how much do you want to offer me for that tract of land?"

He chuckled. He hadn't expected it to be this easy, but he wasn't looking a gift horse in the mouth.

When he came back with Leslie, his arm around her shoulder and all smiles, Barrie was immediately on the defensive. She had all sorts of ideas about why they were both smiling and so relaxed with each other. She was furiously jealous and hurt, and she didn't know how to cope with her own reactions.

She was silent at the dinner table, withdrawn and introspective, speaking only when addressed. It was the first glimmer of hope that she'd given a pensive Dawson. If she could still feel jealous about him, there was hope that he hadn't killed all her feelings for him.

So he laid it on with Leslie.

"I think we ought to have a celebration party," he announced. "Friday night. We'll phone out invitations and have a dance. Corlie will love making the arrangements."

"Can she do it, on such short notice?" Leslie asked.

"Of course! Barrie will help, too, won't you?" he added with a smile in his fiancée's direction.

"Certainly," Barrie replied in a lackluster voice.

"I have some wonderful CDs, just perfect for dancing to," Leslie added. "Including some old forties torch songs," she added flirtatiously. "Do you dance, Barrie?" she asked.

"I haven't in quite some time," the other woman replied politely. "But I suppose it's like riding a bicycle, isn't it?"

"It will come back to you," Dawson assured her. His eyes narrowed as he stared at her. "If you've forgotten the steps, I'm sure I can teach you."

She glanced up, flushing a little as she met his calculating stare. "I'm learning all the time," she said shortly.

He lifted an eyebrow and grinned at Leslie. "We'll have a good time," he promised her. "And now, suppose we go over that contract I had my attorney draw up, just to make sure it's in order? Barrie, you won't mind, will you?" he added.

Barrie lifted her chin proudly. "Certainly not," she replied. "After all, it's just business, isn't it?"

"What else would it be?" he drawled.

What else indeed! Barrie thought furiously as she watched him close the study door behind himself and the widow Holton.

She went up to her room and locked the door. She'd

never been so furious in all her life. He'd wanted her to come here and pretend to be engaged to him to keep the widow at bay, and now he was behaving as if it were the widow he was engaged to! Well, he needn't expect her to stay and be a doormat! He could have his party Friday, and she'd be on her way out of town first thing Saturday morning. If he liked the widow, he could have her.

She lay down on the bed and tears filled her eyes. Who was she kidding? She still loved him. It was just like old times. Dawson knew how she felt and he was putting the knife into her heart again. What an idiot she'd been to believe anything he told her. He was probably laughing his head off at how easily he'd tricked her into coming here, so that he could taunt her some more. Apparently she was still being made to pay for his father's second marriage. And she'd hoped that he was learning to care for her. Ha! She might as well cut her losses. She'd tell him tomorrow, she decided. First thing.

Six

BARRIE told Dawson that she'd be leaving after the party. Her statement was met with an icy silence and a glare that would have felled a lesser woman.

"We're engaged," he said flatly.

"Are we?" She took off the emerald ring and laid it on his desk. "Try it on the widow's finger. Maybe it will fit her."

"You don't understand," he said through his teeth. "She's only selling me the tract. There's nothing to be jealous of."

Her eyebrows lifted. "Jealous?" she drawled sarcastically. "Why, Dawson, why should I be jealous? After all, I've got half a football team of men just panting to take me out back in Tucson."

He hadn't had a comeback. The remark threw him completely off balance. By the time he regained it, cursing his own lack of foresight, she'd gone out the door. And until the night of the party, she kept him completely at bay with plastic smiles and polite conversation.

It had been a long Friday evening, and all Barrie wanted was to go back to her room and get away from Dawson. All night she'd watched women, mostly Leslie Holton, fawn over him while he smiled that cynical smile and ate up the attention. He wasn't backing away from Leslie tonight. Odd, that sudden change.

Barrie had been studiously avoiding both of them all night, so much so that Corlie, helping serve canapés and drinks, was scowling ominously at her. But Barrie couldn't help her coldness toward Dawson. She felt as if he'd sold her out all over again.

The surprise came when Leslie Holton announced that she was going to leave and went to her car instead of her room. Barrie watched from the doorway as Leslie reached up and kissed Dawson deliberately. And he didn't pull away, either. It was the last straw. She went back inside with bottled fury. Damn him!

He came back inside just as Barrie was saying goodbye to the last of their few guests. She tried to ease out, but while he said good-night to the departing guest, Dawson's arm came across the doorway and blocked her exit. He seemed to know that she'd withdraw instinctively from his touch, because he smiled without humor when she stepped back.

The visitor left. Dawson closed the door with a snap and turned to her, his narrow green eyes cold and calculating.

"Why?" she asked and tried not to sound afraid.

His eyes ran the length of her, from her loosened wavy dark hair to her trim figure and long, elegant legs in the short black dress.

"Maybe I'm tired of playing games," he said enigmatically.

"With me or Leslie Holton?" she demanded.

"You don't know why I played up to Leslie?" he drawled. "You can't guess?"

Her face colored delicately. "I don't want to know why. I want to go to bed, Dawson," she said, measuring the distance to the door.

He let out a long, weary sigh and moved closer, noticing with resignation her rigid posture and the fear that came into her eyes.

"You run. I run. What the hell difference has it made?" he asked. His hands shot out and caught her shoulders. He pulled her to him, ignoring her struggles, and held her against the lean warmth of his powerful body. "If I ruined your young life, you damn sure ruined mine," he said under his breath, staring at her mouth. "I thought we were getting closer and now we're worlds apart, all over again. Come here."

Two neat whiskies had loosened all his inhibitions. He dragged her to him without caring that he couldn't feel anything physically. He could kiss her, at least…

And he did, with aching need, his mind yielded to the feel and touch and taste of her. He groaned as he drew her even closer, feeling her go rigid against him as his mouth parted her soft lips. But her resistance didn't stop him. He gave in to his hunger without any thought except to show her that he couldn't be aroused by even the most ardent kiss.

But what he expected to happen, didn't. He drew her hips to his and the sudden touch of her long legs against his made him shudder and all at once, his body exploded with hunger, need, anguished desire. His intake of breath was audible, shocking as he felt a full, raging arousal for the first time in almost five years.

He dragged his mouth from hers and looked down

at her with horror and dawning realization. The curse he spat out shocked even Barrie, who'd heard them all at one time or another from very modern grammar school students. His face looked frightening and his hands tightened until they hurt.

She reacted purely with instinct, fighting the pain he was unknowingly inflicting. She struggled away from him, breathing roughly, rubbing the arms he'd held in that steely grip.

He wasn't even aware of having hurt her. He just stood there, glaring at her, shivering with the force of his desire for her. He wanted her with pure obsession and she couldn't bear him to touch her. It was ironic. Tragic. He'd only just discovered that he was still capable with one woman at least, and she had to be the one woman on earth who couldn't bear him to touch her.

He stared at her with narrow, bitter eyes. "God, that was all it needed!" he said in anguish, his face tormented as he met her eyes. "That was damn all!"

He was looking at her as if he hated her, with wild eyes, while she stood gaping at him. He'd said he couldn't feel anything! She didn't realize that she'd said it aloud.

He ran a rough hand through his wavy blond

hair and drew it over his brow as he turned away. "I thought I was dead from the waist down, that I was immune to any woman. I never realized why, even if I suspected it... I might as well be dead!" he said huskily. "My God, I might as well be!"

He threw open the door and went out it as if he'd forgotten Barrie's presence altogether, reaching his car in long, angry strides. He jerked the door open, started it, and took off.

Barrie watched him as if she were a sleepwalker until it suddenly dawned on her that he was acting totally unlike himself. She'd seen him down two neat whiskies, but would that have been enough to make him lose control so completely?

"Dawson," she said to herself, because he was already out of sight.

She stood helplessly in the doorway, trying to decide what to do. He was in no condition to be driving. How could she go to bed now? On the other hand, how could she stay down here? He might be even more violent when he returned. She remembered, oh, too well, what Dawson was like when he was out of control. Corlie and Rodge had gone to bed. She couldn't bear the thought of being alone with him...

But the way he'd driven off had been frightening too. What if he hurt himself?

With a concern that grew by the minute, she rushed to get her wrap and purse and the keys to Dawson's MG that hung by the back door. She'd drive down the road, she thought, just to make sure he hadn't run into a ditch or something. That would make her feel better. And if she didn't see him, she could assume that he was all right and go back to her room. Not that it was going to make her stop worrying. She'd never seen him so shaken, so wild. Dawson never lost control. Well, only that once. But even that hadn't been such a total loss of reason. The alcohol would have made it worse, too.

Her mind made up, she started off in the general direction Dawson had taken. The headlights of the sports car picked up nothing on the side of the road for at least two miles down the deserted highway, and she breathed a sigh of relief. He was probably on his way back to the house even…

Her heart jumped when she saw the flashing lights over the next rise. She knew, somewhere deep inside her, that Dawson was where they were. She stepped on the accelerator and began to pray as a cold sickness grew in the pit of her stomach.

It could have been worse, but not much. The car had overturned. She caught sight of skid marks on the black pavement, and the sheriff's deputy's patrol car on the side of the road. Even as she pulled off the road and stopped, she could hear an ambulance in the distance.

She threw the MG out of gear and left it idling and ran frantically to the median where Dawson's Jaguar lay crushed with its wheels in the air.

"Dawson!" she screamed. Her heart was beating so fast that she shook with it. "Oh, God!"

The sheriff's deputy stopped her headlong flight.

"Let me go." She wept piteously, fighting him. "Please, please…!"

"You can't help him like this," he said firmly. "You recognize the car?"

"It's Dawson," she whispered. "Dawson Rutherford. My stepbrother…is he…dead?"

It seemed forever before he answered. "Not yet," he said. "Calm down."

She looked up at him in the glare of the flashing lights. "Please!" she whispered, reduced to begging as she tugged against his firm hold. "Oh, God, please, please…!"

The officer was basically a kind man, and that look

would have touched a career criminal. With a rough sigh, he let go of her.

Heart pounding savagely, eyes wide with fear, she ran headlong to the car, where Dawson lay in a curious position in the wreckage. Blood was coming from somewhere. When she touched his jacket, she felt it on her hands. She knew not to try to move him. His face was turned away. She touched his hair with trembling hands. It was icy cold, like the skin on his face. Her hands cradled what she could reach of him, as if by touching and holding, she could keep him alive.

"You mustn't...die," she whispered brokenly. "Dawson, please! Oh, God, please, Dawson, you mustn't die!"

There was no movement at all, no answer. He seemed to be pinned. She couldn't tell where in the darkness. Behind her, the ambulance siren came closer. She heard it stop, heard voices. Another vehicle pulled up, too.

Gentle, but firm hands moved her away, back into the care of the deputy. This time she stood silently, unmoving, watching, waiting. She'd thought so many times that she hated Dawson, especially since he'd played up to Leslie, but she'd only been lying to herself. She might have legions of dates, men who wanted her, but there was only one man that she loved. Despite the pain and anguish of the past, her heart was lying in that tangled wreckage. And she knew then, for certain, that if Dawson died, part of her would die with him. She only wished that she'd had time to tell him so.

They had to cut him out of the Jaguar. When they put him on the stretcher, he didn't move. His face was almost white. They covered him with a blanket and carried him to the waiting ambulance. Barrie stared at him, at the ambulance, with dull, dead eyes. Was he gone? He didn't move. Perhaps he was already dead and they didn't want to cover him up in front of her. But her heart was still beating. She was still breathing. Surely if he was dead, she would be, too.

"Come on," the deputy said gently. "I'll drive you to the hospital."

"The…car," she faltered numbly.

"I'll take care of it." With the ease of years of practice, he attended to the car, loaded her into the patrol car and followed the ambulance back to the private hospital in Sheridan.

Barrie drank five cups of coffee before anyone came

to tell her how he was. She didn't think at all. She sat staring out the window into the darkness, praying.

"Miss Rutherford?"

She looked up. "Bell," she corrected dully. "Dawson is my stepbrother." Her eyes pleaded for miracles.

And the doctor had one. He smiled wearily, his green mask dangling from his neck, lying on his stained surgical uniform. Blood, she noticed idly. Dawson's blood.

"He'll make it," he told her abruptly. "He was unconscious when they brought him in, probably due to the concussion he's sustained. But, miraculously, there was no internal damage. He didn't even break any bones, isn't that...Miss Bell!"

She came to lying on a bed in the emergency room. She saw the lights overhead and the whiteness of the ceiling. Dawson was going to live. The doctor had said so. Or had she dreamed it?

She turned her head, and a nurse smiled at her.

"Feeling better?" she asked. "You've had quite a night, I gather. Mr. Rutherford is in a private room, and he's doing fine. He came around a little while ago and asked about you."

Her heart jumped. "He was conscious?"

"Oh, very," she replied dryly. "We assured him

that you were in the waiting room and he didn't say another word. He's going to be all right."

"Thank God," she breathed, closing her eyes again. "Oh, thank God."

"You must be very close," the nurse remarked.

Barrie could have laughed. "We don't have family," she said evasively. "Only each other."

"I see. Well, what a lucky thing that he was wearing his seat belt. He's very handsome," she added, and Barrie looked again, noticing the nurse's pretty blond hair and brown eyes.

"Yes, he is, isn't he?" Barrie replied.

The nurse finished working on her chart. "He's on my ward. Lucky me." She grinned.

Yes. Lucky you, Barrie thought, but she didn't say anything. She got up, with the nurse's help, and went to the restroom to freshen up. She tried not to think on the way. She'd had enough for one night.

After she'd bathed her face and retouched her makeup and combed her hair, she went along to Dawson's room. She peered around the door cautiously, but he was in a private room and alone. He was conscious, as the nurse had said.

His head turned as he heard her step and she

grimaced at the cuts on one side of his handsome face. There was a bruise on his cheek and at his temple. He seemed a little disoriented, and it wasn't surprising, considering the condition the Jaguar had been in. She shuddered, remembering how he'd looked then.

His eyes narrowed. He breathed slowly, watching her approach. "Sorry," he managed to say in a hoarse tone.

She winced and tears overflowed her eyes. "You idiot!" she raged, sobbing. "You crazy idiot, you could have been killed!"

"Barrie," he said softly, holding out a hand.

She ran to him. The walls were well and truly down, as if they'd never existed. She all but fell into the chair beside the bed and lay across him, careless of the IV they were giving him, shivering as she felt his hands on her shoulders, holding her while she wept.

"Here, now," he chided weakly. "I'm all right. Lucky I hit my head and not some more vital part."

She didn't answer. Her body shook with sobs. She clung. She felt his hand in her hair, smoothing it, soothing her.

"Damn," he breathed roughly. "I'm so weak, Barrie."

"Weak is better than dead," she muttered as she

finally lifted her head. Her red, swollen eyes met his. "You're going to have a dandy bruise," she told him, sniffing, dabbing with her fingers at her wet cheeks and eyes.

"No doubt." He moved and winced. "God, what a headache. I don't know if it's the whiskey or the wreck." He frowned. "Why was I driving?" he added, struggling to regain complete control of his faculties after the concussion.

Her heart jumped. "I don't know, exactly," she said evasively. "You…got angry and stormed out to the car."

He whistled softly through pursed lips and smiled half-humorously. "Nice epitaph—dead for unknown reasons."

"Don't," she said, dabbing at her eyes with a tissue from the box by his bed. "It isn't funny."

"Were we arguing again?" he asked.

She shook her head. "Not really."

He frowned. "Then what…?"

The door opened again, and the pretty blonde nurse danced in with a clipboard. "Time for vital signs again," she informed them. "This will only take a minute." She glanced at Barrie. "If you'd like to get a cup of coffee…?"

She didn't have the heart for an argument. "I'll be back soon," she said.

Dawson looked as if he wanted to say something, but the nurse popped her electronic thermometer in his mouth and he grimaced.

Later, Barrie went back to the house and phoned Antonia to tell her what was going on. She'd called Corlie and Rodge the night before, and they were waiting for her when she arrived. She took time to fill them in on Dawson's condition before she phoned her best friend in Bighorn.

"Do you want me to come over and sit with you?" Antonia asked.

"No," Barrie said. "I just needed someone to talk to. He'll be in for another day or so. I didn't want you to worry in case you tried to get in touch with me and wondered where I was. Especially after I'd told you I'd be back in Tucson today."

"Can we do anything?"

Barrie laughed. "No, but thanks. I'll keep you in mind. He's getting plenty of attention right now from a very pretty young nurse. I don't think he'll even miss me when I go."

There was a pause. "You aren't going to leave before they release him?"

"No," Barrie said reluctantly.

"You don't know why he was driving so recklessly?"

"Yes, I think I do," she said miserably. "It was partly my fault. But he'd had too much to drink, too. And he's the one who's always lecturing people about not driving under the influence."

"We can blackmail him for years on this," Antonia replied with a smile in her voice. "Thank God he'll be alive so that we can."

"I'll tell him you said so. If I can get his attention."

She hung up and went into the study, because she felt closer to Dawson there. She hadn't told him the truth about last night. She had a suspicion about why he'd gone out. He'd said it himself. He was only capable with one woman...the one woman he'd scarred too much to ever want sex again. And he couldn't bear the thought of it. How horribly ironic.

It did make sense, somehow. She went to the window to look out. The sky was gray and low with dark clouds. It was going to snow. She needed to get out before the roads became impassable, but she couldn't leave Dawson. What was she going to do? The first thing was to go back to the hospital.

But Corlie refused to let her. "You need food and rest. You've been up all night. Rodge and I will sit with him until you have a little rest."

"You don't have to do that," she began.

"Barrie, you know better than that. He's like our own child, mine and Rodge's. You eat something and we'll stay until you get back to be with him tonight."

"Okay."

Corlie seemed to take it for granted that Barrie was going to stay the night with him. Of course. Everyone still thought they were engaged. She grimaced. Dawson wasn't going to like that one bit. When he was back to himself he was going to hate her all over again. She was his one and only big mistake. He'd been furious at her when he'd stormed out. He seemed to actually hate her because he was aroused by her.

But he was subtly different. When she arrived back at the hospital, he watched her come in with eyes that were alert and searching.

"Feel better?" he asked quietly.

"That's my line," she murmured, smiling at Corlie and Rodge.

Corlie got up and hugged her warmly. "Honey, you're freezing," she chided. "Don't you have something heavier than that windbreaker to wear?"

"It doesn't exactly freeze in Tucson," Barrie reminded her.

"Go to Harper's and buy a coat," Dawson said. "I've got an account there."

"I don't need a coat," she said on a nervous laugh. "And I won't be here long enough to use it. Anyway, it's just a little nip in the air. It's spring."

He didn't reply. His eyes were watchful, curious. "Corlie, you know what size to buy?"

"Yes," Corlie said, grinning.

"Get her one."

"I'll do it first thing tomorrow."

"But…!" Barrie began.

"Hush, child. He's right, you'll freeze in that thing you're wearing. We'll be back early in the morning." She hugged Barrie again.

"Might as well not argue," Rodge said with a grin. "I haven't won an argument with her in thirty-five years. What chance would you have?"

"Not much," Barrie sighed.

They said their goodbyes to Dawson and went out the door, waving.

Barrie edged toward the chair beside the bed, feeling vulnerable now that they were alone. He was much too alert to suit her.

He watched her sit down, his eyes following her. He caught her gaze and held it relentlessly until she flushed and looked away.

"I've remembered," he said.

She bit her lower lip. "Have you?"

"And apparently you've realized why I lost my temper."

The flush got worse. She looked at the floor.

He laughed bitterly. "That's right, Barrie, try to pretend it didn't happen. Run some more." His hand shot out and caught her arm. "Stop that," he said curtly. "Your lip's bleeding."

She hadn't even felt the pain. She pulled out a tissue and held it to her lip. It came away red. "It's a habit," she faltered.

He let go of her arm and sank back against the pillows. He looked older. There were new lines in his face, around his eyes. He looked as if he'd never smiled once in his life.

She clutched the tissue in her hand. "Dawson?"

His gaze came back to hers, questioning.

"Why is it that you weren't...cold...with me?" she asked hesitantly. "I mean, all those other women, like Mrs. Holton...and she's a knockout."

He searched her eyes. "I don't know why, Barrie,"

he replied. "Maybe it's because I hurt you so badly. Maybe it's what hell really is. I want you and you're physically afraid of me. Ironic, isn't it? Do you have any idea, any idea at all, how it makes a man feel to know that he's impotent?"

She shook her head. "Not really."

"All these long years," he said, brushing the unruly hair back from his broad forehead. His eyes closed. "It makes me sick when women touch me, fawn over me. I don't feel anything, Barrie. It seemed to be like that with you. That's why I pulled you against me that way, I wanted to show you what you'd done to me." He laughed with bitter irony. "And I got the lesson, didn't I? It was the most violent, raging arousal I've ever had in my life—with the one woman who shudders at my touch." His eyes closed.

She clenched her teeth as she studied him. She'd loved him all her life, it sometimes seemed. And then in one short night, he'd destroyed her love, her future, her femininity. If his life was hopeless, so was hers.

He glanced at her. "It's been that bad for you, too, hasn't it?" he asked suddenly, with narrowed eyes that seemed to see right through her. "All those damn men parading through your life in a constant, steady stream, in threes and fours. And you've never let one of them touch you, not even in the most innocent way."

She shivered. It was too much. It was too much, having him know that about her. He might as well have stripped her soul naked.

She started to jump up, but he caught her wrist with surprising strength for a man in his condition and jerked her firmly right back down into the chair again.

"No," he said, glaring at her. "No, you don't. You aren't running this time. I said, you've never let anyone touch you, in any way, even to kiss you, since me. Go ahead. Tell me I'm lying."

She swallowed. Her face gave him the answer.

His lips parted. He exhaled softly. "Damn me, Barrie," he said huskily. "Damn me for that."

He let go of her wrist and lay back on the bed. "For the first time in my life, I don't know what to do," he confessed dully.

He sounded defeated. Dawson, of all people. She hated that uncertainty in his deep voice. She hated what they'd done to each other. He was her whole world.

She reached out, very slowly. Her cold fingers just barely touched his bare arm, just at the elbow.

As if he couldn't believe what his senses were telling

him, he turned his head and looked at her pale hand on his arm. His eyes lifted to hers, curious, intent.

She bit her lip again. "I don't want you to die," she said unsteadily.

He looked at her fingers, curled hesitantly around his arm. "Barrie..."

Before he could get the words out, the door opened and the pretty nurse was back again, smiling, cheerful, full of optimism and already possessive about her handsome patient.

"Supper," she announced, putting a tray on the table. "Soup and tea, and I'm going to feed you myself!"

"Like hell you are," Dawson said curtly.

The nurse started. His eyes weren't welcoming at all. They had a very cobralike quality, flashing warnings at her. She laughed with a sudden loss of confidence and pushed the high, wheeled tray over to the bed. "Well, of course, if you feel like feeding yourself, you can." She cleared her throat. "I'll be back to pick it up in a few minutes. Try to eat it all, now."

She smiled again, but with less enthusiasm, and went out the door much more quickly than she'd come in.

Dawson took a pained breath. His head turned toward Barrie. "Help me," he said quietly.

It was intimate, helping him eat. She watched every mouthful disappear past those thin, firm lips, and without wanting to, she remembered the feel of them on her mouth in passion. She'd been innocent and very frightened. He hadn't realized that. His kisses had been adult, passionate, giving no quarter. She knew that he'd never even suspected that she was a total innocent until...

Her flush was revealing. Dawson swallowed the last of the soup and caught her gaze.

"I have my own nightmares," he said unexpectedly. "If I could take it back, I would. Believe that, at least."

She moved restlessly as she put the soup bowl back on the table and helped him sip some of the hot tea. He made a terrible face.

"It's good for you," she said stubbornly.

"It may be good as a hand warmer in a cup on a cold day," he muttered. "If it's good for anything else, I wouldn't know." He lay back down. "If they want to shovel caffeine in me, why can't I have coffee?"

"Ask someone who knows."

He chuckled without humor. His eyes searched hers. "Going to stay with me tonight?"

"It seems to be expected."

His face hardened. "Don't let me put you out. I'm perfectly capable..."

She winced.

He closed his eyes. Beside his thigh, his fist clenched until the knuckles went white.

She pulled her chair closer. Her fingers spread tremulously over his big fist and lingered there. "Dawson, don't," she whispered. "Of course I'll stay. I want to."

He didn't say a word. And still, his hand clenched.

Her fingers pressed down, became caressing.

She knew when his head turned, when his eyes opened. She knew that he was watching her. With a long, helpless sigh, she lifted his hand and put it to her lips. And he shuddered.

She dropped it abruptly, horrified at her own action, and started to get up, red-faced.

But he had her hand now, turned in his, firmly held. He drew it until he could press the palm to his hard mouth. His eyes closed and he made a sound deep in his throat. When he looked at her again, what she saw in his face made her go hot all over.

"Come here," he said huskily.

Her knees became weak. She felt the imprint of his

mouth on her palm as if it were a brand. She never knew whether or not she would have obeyed that heated command, though, because the door opened and the doctor, making rounds, came in smiling. Dawson let go of her hand and the moment was lost.

But not forgotten. Not at all, not through the long night when he slept, because of the pills they gave him, and she lay in the chair and watched him sleep. They seemed to have reached some sort of turning point. Her life lay in that hospital bed now. She had no desire whatsoever to leave him. And it seemed to be the same for him.

When he woke the next morning, a new young nurse came in with soap and a towel and a basin of water. Her eyes were bright and flirting, but when she offered to bathe him, he gave her a look that made her excuse herself and leave.

"You're intimidating the nurses," Barrie remarked with a faint smile. She was tired and half-asleep, but the look he'd given the nurse amused her.

"I don't want them touching me."

"You're not up to bathing yourself," she protested.

His eyes searched hers without amusement, without

taunting. "Then you do it," he said quietly. "Because yours are the only hands I want on my body."

She stared at him helplessly. He wasn't chiding her now. His eyes were warm and quiet and soft on her face.

She got up, a little hesitant. "I've never bathed anyone except myself," she said.

He untied the hospital gown at the neck and, holding her eyes, sloughed it off, leaving the sheet over his lean hips.

She colored a little. She'd never seen him undressed, despite their intimacy.

"It's all right," he said, soothing her. "I'll leave the cover where it is. I can do the rest myself, when you finish."

She didn't stop to ask why he couldn't do it all. Her hands went to the cloth. She wet it, and put soap on it. Then, with gentle motions, she drew it over his face and throat and back, rinsing it and him before she put more soap on the cloth again and hesitated at his arms and chest.

"I'm not in a place, or in a position, to cause you any worry," he said gently.

She managed a smile. She drew the cloth down his arms, to his lean, strong hands, and back up to his collarbone. She rinsed it again before she began to smooth it, slowly over the thick hair on his chest. Even through the cloth, she could feel the warm muscles, the thickness of the hair. She remembered just for an instant the feel and smell and taste of his chest under her lips, when she'd been all but fainting with desire for him.

He felt her hesitate. His hand pressed down on hers. "It's only flesh and bone," he said quietly. "Nothing to be afraid of."

She nodded. Her hand smoothed down to his navel, his flat stomach. He groaned suddenly and caught her fingers, staying them.

His breath came erratically. He laughed abruptly. "I think…you'd better stop there."

Her hand stilled. Involuntarily her eyes slipped past it, and she stared.

"One of the pitfalls of bathing a man," he said, swallowing hard. "Although I won't pretend not to enjoy it. For years, that hasn't happened at all."

Her eyes were curious as they met his.

"You don't understand," he mused.

She smiled faintly. "Not really."

"That doesn't happen with other women," he explained slowly. "Not at all."

"And if it doesn't, you can't—" She stopped.

He nodded. "Exactly."

Evading his intent gaze, she lifted the cloth and rinsed it and then soaped it again. She handed it to him. "Here. You'd better..."

His hand touched hers. He searched her eyes. "Please," he whispered.

She bit her lip. "I can't!"

"Why?" He didn't even blink. "Is it repulsive, to touch me like that, to look at me?"

Her face was a flaming red. "I've never...looked!"

"Don't you want to?" he asked gently. "Honestly?"

She didn't speak. She didn't move, either. His hand went to the sheet and he pulled it away slowly, folding it back on his powerful thighs.

"We made love once," he said quietly. "You were part of me. I'm not embarrassed to let you look. And I'll tell you for a fact, I'd never let another woman see me helpless like this." He took a long, slow breath and felt the tension drain out of him. He was weak and disoriented, and his body relaxed completely. It worried him a little that he couldn't maintain the tension, but when he was well again, perhaps he could find out if he really was capable completely. Unaware of his misgivings, Barrie bit down hard on her lip, and let her eyes slide down. She looked and then couldn't look away. He was…beautifully made. He was like one of the nude statues she'd seen in art books. But he was real.

She tried to use the cloth, but it was just too much too soon. With a smile and a grimace she finally gave in to her shyness and turned away while he finished the chore.

"Don't feel bad," he said gently when he was covered again, and the bath things were put aside. "It's a big step for both of us, I guess. These things take time."

She nodded.

He tugged her down into the chair beside the bed. "Do you realize that we made love and never saw each other undressed?"

"You shouldn't talk about it," she faltered.

"You were innocent and I was a fool," he said. "I rushed at you like a bull in heat, and I never even realized how innocent you were until I hurt you. And I couldn't accept that you were, Barrie," he confessed heavily. "Because if I admitted that, I had to accept what I'd done to you, how I'd scarred you. Maybe my body was more honest than I was. It didn't want another woman after you. It still doesn't. The reaction you get, I can't give to anyone else."

She met his eyes. "I don't…want anyone else, either," she said softly.

"Do you want me?" he asked bluntly. "Are you able to want me?"

She smiled sadly. "I don't know, Dawson."

He took her hand and held it tight. "Maybe that's something that we're both going to have to find out, when I leave here," he said, and it sounded as if he dreaded the outcome as much as she did.

Seven

THEY let Dawson go home three days after he was admitted. The doctor insisted that he be cautious about returning to work, and that if he had any recurring symptoms from the head injury, he was to get in touch. Barrie wasn't happy about them discharging him, but she did have every sympathy with the nursing staff. Dawson in a recovered state was better off without time on his hands. He made everyone uncomfortable.

He'd progressed from the bed to the desk in his study and he'd taken Barrie in there with him to discuss the tract of land Leslie Holton had agreed to sell him.

She stared at the contract on the desk, which had

arrived by special courier that morning. "She wasn't that eager to sell at first. How did you change her mind?" she asked with barely contained irritation.

He leaned back in his chair, his forehead still purplish from its impact with the steering wheel, marred by the thin line of stitches that puckered the tanned flesh.

"How do you think I convinced her?" he taunted.

She didn't say a word. But her face spoke silently.

He smiled cynically. "And that's a false conclusion if I ever saw one," he mused. "I can't do that with anyone except you, Barrie."

She flushed a little. "You don't know that."

"Don't I?" His pale eyes slid down her body which was in a loose knit shirt and jeans, and lingered on the thrust of her high breasts. "Then let's say that I'm not interested in finding out if I can want anyone else."

"You'd been drinking," she reminded him.

"So I had." He stood up. "And you think it was the whiskey?"

She shrugged. "It might have been."

He moved away from the desk, glanced at her thoughtfully for a moment, and then on an impulse, went to close and lock the office door. "Let's see," he murmured deeply, and moved toward her.

She jumped behind a wing chair and gripped it for dear life. Her eyes were wide, wild. "No!"

He paused, searching her white face. "Calm down. I'm not going to force you."

She didn't let go of the chair. Her eyes were steady on him, like a hunted animal's.

He put his hands into his pockets and watched her quietly. "This isn't going to get us anywhere," he remarked.

She cleared her throat. "Good."

"Barrie, it's been five years," he said irritably. After the closeness they'd shared while he was in the hospital, now they seemed to be back on the old footing again. "I've been half a man for so long that it's a revelation to have discovered that I'm still capable of functioning with a woman. I only want to know that it wasn't a fluke, a minute out of time. I want to…make sure."

Her big eyes searched his. "I'm afraid of you like that."

"You weren't just after you had the nightmare," he reminded her. "You weren't the next morning. In fact, you weren't in the hospital when I let you bathe me."

Her hands released the back of the chair. Her short nails had left fine marks in the soft leather. She stared at them. "You weren't…aroused when you pulled back the sheet," she faltered.

"That's what bothers me most, that it didn't last until you tried to bathe me," he said heavily. "Maybe it was just a flash in the pan, the whole thing," he said with black humor. "But either way, I want to know. I *have* to know."

There was something in the way he looked that made Barrie feel guilty. Her own fear seemed a poor thing in comparison with the doubt in his hard face. It was devastating for a man to lose his virility. Could she really blame him for wanting to test it, to know for sure if he'd regained what he'd lost?

Slowly, hesitantly, she stepped away from the chair and let her hands fall to her sides. After all, she'd seen him totally nude, she'd felt his body against hers when it was aroused, and she hadn't succumbed to hysteria. Besides, she loved him. He was here with her, alive and vital. Her mind wouldn't let go of the picture it held—Dawson in the overturned car, his face covered with blood. She looked at him with her heart in her eyes.

His eyes traced her face in its frame of long, wavy dark hair to her soft, parted lips. His hands were still in his pockets, and he didn't move, despite the fact that her expression made him feel violent. She looked as if she cared.

"Are you just going to stand there?" she asked after a minute.

He searched her eyes. "Yes."

She didn't understand for a moment, and then he smiled faintly, and she realized what he wanted. "Oh," she said. "You want me to…kiss you."

He nodded. He still didn't move.

His lack of action made her less insecure. She moved toward him, went close, so that she could feel the heat from his tall, powerful body, so that she could smell the clean scents of soap and cologne that always clung to him. He'd shaved. There was no rasp of beard where she reached up and hesitantly touched his cheek. Involuntarily her fingers slid down to his long, firm lower lip and traced it.

His breath drew in sharply. She felt him tense, but his hands stayed in his pockets.

Curious, she let her fingers become still on his face. There was something in his eyes, something dark and intense. She searched them for a long moment, but she couldn't read the expression.

At least, she didn't understand until she took an involuntary step closer and felt his body against hers.

"No fluke," he said through his teeth. His voice sounded odd. "Now I don't want to frighten you," he continued shortly, "so if you're getting cold feet, this is your last chance to move away."

She wasn't sure if she meant to hesitate, but she did. His hands came out of his pockets and slid to cradle her by the hips. He pulled her, very gently, against him, and then moved her slowly against the raw thrust of his body, shivering.

It wasn't so frightening that way. She was fascinated by what she saw.

"Yes," he said through his teeth. "You recognize vulnerability, don't you?" he asked impatiently, hating the helpless desire he felt even while he thanked God for the ability to feel it. "My legs are shaking. Can you feel them?" He drew her a little closer, to make sure that she could. "I'm swelling. You can feel that, too, can't you?"

It was embarrassing to hear him telling her such intimate things, especially in that angry tone. She flushed, but when she tried to drop her eyes, he caught her chin and made her look at him.

"Stop cringing. I'm not a monster," he said roughly. "I lost control with you at the worst possible time, and I hurt you. I won't hurt you again."

She swallowed. The feel of his body in such close contact made her nervous, but it also excited her to feel him wanting her. She grew dizzy with confused sensations. She shifted, uneasy yet exhilarated at the same time.

He drew in a sharp breath and groaned, and then he laughed. "God, that feels good!" He bit off the words. He actually shivered. His eyes met hers and he moved her against him in the same exotic little motion she'd made without thinking. His teeth ground together and the laughter came again. "I'd forgotten what it felt like to be a man."

His pleasure affected her in the oddest way. She buried her face in his chest, half afraid, half excited. She shivered, too, as his arms enfolded her.

"So you feel it, too, do you?" he asked at her ear. His hands tightened on her hips and he repeated the rough, deft motion and heard her cry out. "Do you like being helpless?" he asked, and his head bent. "Do you like wanting me and feeling powerless to draw away?"

She could hear the resentment, mingled with heated desire, in his deep voice. She opened her mouth to respond and his lips moved over it, opening to fit the shape of it before they settled with a rough, hungry, demanding pressure that made her stiffen with unexpected pleasure.

Pictures of tidal waves flew through his mind as he groaned and forced her body into even more intimacy with his. He wanted her. God, he wanted her. It was a fever that burned so high and bright that he couldn't hide his need. It grew and swelled, the pressure hard against her soft stomach. He could feel her embarrassment as she tried to move her hips away from his, but he wouldn't permit it. He couldn't. He needed her softness against the flare of his masculinity.

He needed her.

His arm forced her closer as his mouth deepened the slow kiss into stark intimacy. She felt the slow, soft penetration of his tongue, the hard caress of his lips, the aching deep groan that shuddered out of his chest.

Her arms were under his and around him. She could feel the heat from the hard muscles under her hands. She could feel his belt digging into her midriff. His powerful legs were trembling as he moved her against him and he groaned again, in anguish.

While he kissed her, his hands went deftly under the knit top to the front catch of her lacy bra, quickly loosening the catch before she could protest. His hands slowly took the weight of her bare breasts, caressing their hard tips, while the kiss went on and on. He felt her body tremble again and heard her soft cry go into his mouth. He couldn't stop. It was just like France, just like that night in her room. Some part of him stood away and saw his own helpless headlong rush into seduction, but he was too far gone to fight it now. He hadn't been a man for years. Now he was in the grip of the most desperate arousal he'd ever felt and he had to satisfy it. He wanted her, needed her, had to have her.

He was practiced, an expert in this most basic of arts. She was, for all her fears, still a novice who'd never known pleasure. He was going to give her that. He was going to make her want the satisfaction his body demanded.

Slowly he began to to slide the fabric of her blouse from her body while his mouth bit at hers in the kind of kisses that were a blatant prelude to intimacy. They threw her off balance so that she made no protest when he removed the top and bra and dropped them onto the carpet. His hands caressed her soft, bare breasts and he drew away a breath so that he could watch them under the tender mastery of his hands.

"They're beautiful," he whispered tenderly, aware at some level of her dazed, wide-eyed stare. His hands caught her waist and he lifted her to his mouth. He traced the hard tips with soft wonder, savoring their taste with lips that cherished her. "You taste of rose petals and perfume," he breathed, nipping her tenderly.

She made a sound that brought his head up. He looked into her eyes, seeing the excitement, the shock of wonder in them. No, she couldn't stop him now. He recognized that blank, set expression on her face. She was in the throes of passion. There was no way she could draw back now, even if she'd wanted to.

Confident, he let her slide down his body and he moved back a step. She didn't try to cover her breasts. After a minute he caught the hem of his own knit shirt and pulled it over his head, tossing it onto the floor with her things.

His chest was sexy, she thought through a haze of pleasure, staring at it, bronzed and muscular with a thick curling mat of hair just a few shades darker than the hair on his head. Without volition, she moved forward and leaned into him, closing her eyes with a shaky sigh as she felt his bare chest against her breasts.

His big hands flattened just under her shoulder blades and drew her closer in erotic little motions that made her shiver.

She felt the heavy, hard beat of his heart under her

ear. She traced the nipple beside her mouth and felt him tauten. Then he groaned and his mouth slid down and found hers. He lifted her clear off the floor and stood holding her, kissing her, in the middle of the sunlit room. For an instant he looked up and glared around the room. There was only the sofa or the desk or the carpet. He groaned.

He had no more time for decisions. Shaking with the terrible need to have her, he couldn't risk having her come back to her senses before...

He laid her down on the carpet in front of the picture window that overlooked the lawn half a story below. Her body, there in the light, had the shimmer of a pearl. He knelt beside her and slowly, tenderly, stripped the clothing from her body, leaving it bare and trembling, all the while tracing her softness with his lips, with his hands, in skilled caresses that made it impossible for her to draw back.

He removed his own clothes then, still a little uncertain that his body was going to cooperate with him despite its tense need. So many years, so much pain, so much hunger. He looked at her and felt his whole body clench as he stood above her, shivering a little in the fullness of his arousal.

She looked at him with faint fear in a single moment

of sanity. It hadn't been this intimate before. In the darkness, she'd had hardly a glimpse of him. Now, standing over her that way, she saw the magnitude of his arousal and flushed.

"I'll be careful," he said quietly.

He eased down beside her, restraining his own desire. He smoothed the hair back from her flushed face and bent to kiss her with aching tenderness, stemming the rush of words that rose to her lips. She wanted to tell him that she was unprotected, to ask him if he was going to take precautions. But his mouth settled hard on her breast and she arched, shivering with hot pleasure, and her last grasp on reason fell away.

The slow, easy movements of his hands and mouth relaxed her. She lay watching him touch her, hearing the deep tenderness of his voice as he whispered to her. The words became indistinguishable as he touched her more intimately. Her body lifted, shivered, opened to him. Her eyes, wide with awe, sought his as the pleasure built to some unexpected plateau and trembled there on the edge of ecstasy as he moved over her at last and his body began, very slowly, to join itself to hers.

She stiffened at first, because it was suddenly difficult, and her eyes flew open, panicked.

He paused, breathing heavily, and bent to kiss her wild eyes closed. He couldn't lose control, he told himself. Not this time. He had to fight his own desperate hunger for her sake. "I won't hurt you," he whispered roughly. His hand caressed over her flat stomach, lightly tracing, soothing. "I won't hurt you, baby. Try to relax for me."

Her eyes opened again, hesitant and uncertain. "You're...so...so...!" she blustered, swallowing. "What if I can't...?"

He groaned, because he was losing control, losing it all over again when he'd sworn he wouldn't, that he could contain the raging desire she kindled. But he couldn't. The feel of her body cost him his restraint.

He moved helplessly against her. "You did before," he said. "God, Barrie, don't tense like that!" he whispered urgently. "Oh, baby, I can't stop...!" His hand suddenly slid between them and he began to touch her expertly, feeling her body respond immediately, uncoiling, lifting helplessly. "Yes!" he groaned. "Yes, yes...!" He shuddered and suddenly his tongue was in her mouth probing, like his body, teasing, penetrating...!

She sobbed. He was doing something to her, something that made a rush of pleasure shoot through her like fiery shafts, that made her body crave what he was doing, what she was feeling…

There was a fullness that grew unexpectedly, that teased and provoked and excited. She was empty and now, now, she felt the impact of the fullness, shooting through her like fireworks, making her body throb in a new rhythm, making her blood flow faster. She could hear herself breathing, she could hear him breathing, she could feel his hips moving, his skin sliding sensuously against hers, above her, as his body moved closer and closer. She couldn't breathe for the hectic beat of her heart. She opened her eyes, her nails biting into his muscular upper arms as she tried to look down, to understand what was happening to her.

"No, don't look," he snapped when she tried to see. He kissed her eyelids, so that they had to close, and his mouth found hers again. His hand was still between them, and she was feeling things so intense that they made her mind spin.

"What are you…doing?" she gasped against his devouring mouth, shivering as the pleasure suddenly gripped her and made her body convulse.

"My God…what do you think I'm doing?" he cried

out, shuddering as his hips pushed down in a pressure that sent the sun shattering behind her eyelids in a burst of pleasure so primitive that she sobbed like a child.

She couldn't tell how he was touching her now, she didn't care. She was moving with him, helplessly. Her taut body felt hot and tight and swollen. She felt it opening to the fullness that was alien and familiar all at once. This, she thought blindly, must be how a man prepared a woman for his body, this…!

His mouth never left her own. She was buffeted in a hard, quick rhythm that increased the fullness and the pressure, and it wasn't enough to fill the emptiness she had inside. Her legs felt the rough brush of his as she heard the anguish that came gruffly from the lips possessing hers. She could hear someone pleading, a sobbing high voice that sounded oddly like her own. She went rigid as the feeling stretched her as tight as a cord and suddenly snapped in the most unbelievable rush of hot pleasure she'd ever known in her entire life.

She felt intimate muscles stretching, stretching, felt her body in rhythmic contractions that threatened to tear her apart. And even as they took her to a level of ecstasy she'd never dreamed existed, the plateau she'd reached fell away to reveal one even higher, more intense…

She cried out, shivering, sobbing, drowning in pleasure. She must have opened her eyes, because his face was above hers, taut and rigid, his eyes so black they might have been coals. His teeth were clenched and he was trying to say something, but he suddenly cried out and his face flooded with color. She watched him in rapt wonder, saw his eyes go black all at once, saw the helpless loss of control, the set rigor of climax that made his face clench. The pressure inside her exploded and she felt his body go rigid, convulsing under her fascinated eyes as his voice cried out hoarsely in an endless moan of pleasure. His chest strained up, away from her, his arms shivering with the convulsive pleasure. He shuddered again and again, and all the while she watched him, watched him…

He felt her eyes, hated them, hated her, even while the world was exploding under him. He thought he was going to faint with the onrush of ecstasy, reaching a level he'd never dared achieve before it left him helpless. Always, he'd been in control. He'd watched women in this anguished rictus, but he'd never allowed a woman to see it happen to him. Until now. He was helpless and Barrie could see. She could see…

what he really felt. Oh, God, no…! He wanted to close his eyes, but he couldn't. She could see everything… *everything*.

The room seemed to vanish in the violence of his rapture. It was a long time before he could open his eyes and see the carpet where his cheek lay against her body. He was shaking. Under him, he felt her labored breathing, felt her cool skin touching his, felt her hands touching his hair, heard her voice whispering shaken endearments, whispering, whispering. Damn her. Damn her!

As she held him, her breasts were wet, like the rest of her body. He was heavy, lying on her. She felt his shoulders and they were cool and damp. She moved her hands and felt his thick gold hair, wet with sweat. When she moved, she felt the pressure of him deep inside her body. She gasped.

When he could breathe completely again, he lifted his head and searched her eyes with barely contained fury at his loss of command, raising himself on both elbows so that she came into focus. He looked odd. He poised above her with a dark scowl.

His jaw tightened. "I saw you watching me," he said. "Did you enjoy it? Did it please you to watch me lose control to the extent that I couldn't even turn my face away?"

The angry words shocked her after the intimacy they'd just shared. She didn't understand the anger that flared in his face. He looked at her with contempt, almost hatred, his lips making a thin line. He took a rough breath and began to lift away, but she hated to lose the intimacy, the oneness he'd shared with her. Her body gripped him in protest at his upward movement, but then she suddenly cried out and her fingernails bit into him.

"Dawson, don't!" she whispered frantically, clutching at him.

He stopped moving at once, afraid that he'd hurt her. He scowled. "What's wrong?" he asked curtly.

Her face was rigid. She could feel the contractions inside her body. "It...hurts when you move," she said, embarrassed. She licked her dry lips. He muttered something that made her color and started to withdraw again, but this time he did it gently, with a slow, steady pressure. It was still uncomfortable, but not painful.

She looked down and blushed as red as a rose as he lifted himself completely away from her.

He rolled away from her and got to his feet, his muscles trembling from the violence of his fulfillment and the fear her cry had aroused. Memories of the night in France came back and he couldn't look at her.

He'd hurt her again. He jerked his clothes back on, hating his helplessness. He was just like his father, he thought furiously, a victim of his own uncontrollable desire. He wondered if Barrie had any idea how it frightened him to be at the mercy of a woman or why.

Barrie didn't understand his coldness, but slowly her pride came to the rescue. She couldn't bear to think of the risk she'd just taken, of the things he'd said to her. She'd welcomed him without a thought for the future, walking like a lamb into the slaughter, just as she had five years ago. Would she never learn? she wondered bitterly.

She drew herself up, wincing at the unfamiliar soreness, embarrassed and hurt as she reached for her things and began to dress, more clumsily than he had. She didn't understand what had made him so angry. He'd wanted her. Had it only been to prove his manhood after all? He'd given her pleasure that she never expected, and at first he'd been tender, almost loving. Now he wouldn't even look at her.

He was breathing a little unsteadily still. She didn't seem to be damaged, at least, thank God. But as his fear for her subsided, his anger at himself only increased. His body ached with the pleasure he'd had from her, but his pride was lacerated. He'd lost himself in her. He'd been helpless, so in thrall to desire that he'd have taken her in the hall, in the car…

He turned away, unable to bear even the sight of her. He was like his father. He was a slave to his desire. And she'd seen him that way, vulnerable, helpless!

She bit her lower lip until she drew blood. "Dawson?"

He couldn't look at her. He stared out the window with his hands tight in his pockets.

She felt cold. Her arms clenched around her body. It was impossible not to understand his attitude, even if she didn't want to. "I see," she said quietly. "You only wanted to know if you…could. And now that you do, I'm an embarrassment, is that it?"

"Yes," he said, lying through his teeth to save his pride.

She hadn't expected him to agree. She stared at him with eyes that had gone dark with shock. The clock had turned back to France, to that night in her hotel room. The only difference was that he hadn't hurt her this time. But she felt just as cheap, just as used, as she had then.

There was really nothing else to say. She looked at

him and knew that the love she'd felt for him since her teens hadn't diminished one bit. The only difference was that now she knew what physical love truly was. She'd gloried in it, drowned in the wonder of his desire for her, given all that he asked and more. But it still wasn't enough for him. Now she knew that it never would be. He hated his hunger for her, that was obvious even to a novice, despite the fact that he'd indulged it to the absolute satiation of his senses. He wanted her, but it was against his will, just as it had been five years ago. Maybe he hated her, too, for being the object of his desire. How ironic that he was impotent with everyone else. How tragic.

She knew that it would do no good to conduct a postmortem. He was uncommunicative, and all her efforts weren't going to dent his reserve. She turned and went to the door, unlocking it with cold hands. Even when she went through it, he never looked her way or said a single word. Nor did she expect him to. He'd frozen over.

She took a bath and changed her clothes. Her shame was so sweeping that she couldn't bear to look at herself in the mirror. There was another fact that she might have to face. He hadn't even tried to protect her, and she'd been so hopelessly naive as to welcome the risk of a child. If she'd had any sense at all, she'd have let him writhe with his insecurities about being a man. If she'd had any sense at all, she'd have run like the wind. Which was, of course, what she was about to do.

It only took her a few minutes to pack. She put everything into her suitcase and garment bag and carried the lot down the staircase by herself. Rodge and Corlie were busy with their respective chores, so they didn't see or hear her go out the front door. Neither did Dawson, who was still cursing himself for his lack of restraint and pride.

He didn't realize she'd gone until he heard the car engine start up. He got to the front door in time to see her turning from the driveway onto the main highway that led to Sheridan.

For a few seconds, he watched in anguish, his first thought to go after her and bring her right back. But what would that accomplish? What could he say? That he'd made a mistake? That giving in to his passion for her had been folly and he hoped they wouldn't both live to regret it?

He closed the front door and rested his forehead against it. He'd wanted to know that he was still a whole man, and now he knew that he was. But only with Barrie. He didn't want any other woman. The desire he felt for Barrie was sweeping and devouring, it made him helpless, it made him vulnerable. If she knew how desperately he wanted her, she could use him, wound him, destroy him.

He couldn't give anyone the sort of power over him that Barrie's mother had held over George Rutherford. He'd actually seen her tease George into a frenzy, into begging for her body. Barrie didn't know. She'd never known that her mother had used George's desire for her to make him do anything she liked. But Dawson knew. A woman with that kind of power over a man would abuse it. She couldn't help herself. And Barrie had years of Dawson's own cruelty to avenge. How could he blame her if she wanted to make him pay for the way he'd treated her?

He didn't dare let Barrie stay. She'd seen him totally at the mercy of his desire, but she didn't, thank God, know how complete her victory was. He could let her leave thinking he'd turned his back on her, and that was for the best. It would save his pride.

From his childhood, he'd known that women liked to find a weakness and exploit it. Hadn't his own mother called him a weakling when he'd begged to be held and loved as a toddler? She'd made him pay for being born. And then George had married Barrie's mother, and he'd seen the destructive pattern of lust used as a bargaining tool, he'd seen again the contempt women had for a man's weaknesses. He'd seen how his father had been victimized by his own desire and love. Well, that wasn't going to happen to him. He wasn't going to be vulnerable!

Barrie thought he'd only wanted to prove his manhood; she'd think he'd used her. Let her. She wouldn't get the chance to gloat over his weakness, as her mother had gloated over his father's. She wouldn't ever know that his possession of her today had been the most wondrous thing that had ever happened to him in his life, that her body had given him a kind of ecstasy that he'd never dreamed he was capable of experiencing. All the barriers had come down, all the reserve, all the holding back.

He'd...given himself to her.

His hands clenched violently. Yes, he could admit that, but only to himself. He'd gone the whole way, dropped all the pretense, in those few seconds of glorious oblivion in her arms. He hated that she'd seen his emotions naked in his eyes while he was helpless, but that couldn't be helped now. It was the first time in his life that he'd ever been able to give himself to pure physical pleasure, and it was probably only due to the enforced abstinence of sex. Yes. Surely that was the only reason he'd had such pleasure from her.

Of course, she'd had pleasure from him, too. It touched something in him to realize how completely he'd satisfied her in spite of her earlier fear. He felt pride that he'd been able to hold back at least that far, that he'd healed the scars he'd given her during their first intimacy.

But wouldn't it be worse for her, now that she knew what kind of pleasure lay past the pain? And wouldn't she be hurt and wounded even more now by his rejection, after she'd given in to him so completely? His only thought had been for his pride, but now he had to consider the new scars she was going to have. Why hadn't he let her go while there was still time? He groaned aloud.

"Dawson?" Corlie called from the kitchen doorway. "Don't you and Barrie want any lunch?"

"Barrie's gone," he said stiffly, straightening, with his back to her.

"Gone? Without saying goodbye?"

"It was...an emergency." He invented an excuse. "A call from a friend in Tucson who needed her to help with some summer school project. She said she'd phone you later."

She hadn't said that at all, but he knew she would phone. She loved Corlie and Rodge. She wouldn't want to hurt their feelings, even if she was furious with Dawson.

"Oh," Corlie said vaguely. "I must not have heard the phone ring." She was curious about his rigid stance and the scowl between his eyes when he glanced at her, but Dawson in a temper wasn't someone she wanted to antagonize. "All right, then. Do you want some salad and sandwiches?"

He shook his head. "Just black coffee. I'll come and get it."

"You've quarreled, haven't you?" she asked gently.

He sighed heavily as he walked toward the kitchen. "Don't ask questions, Corlie."

She didn't, but it took every last ounce of her willpower. Something had gone terribly wrong. She wondered what.

Barrie, meanwhile, was well on her way back to Arizona. She stopped at the first café she came to, certain that she wouldn't have to worry about Dawson following her. The very set of his head had told her that he wouldn't.

She ordered coffee and soup and then sat barely touching it while she relived her stupidity. Would she never learn that Dawson might want her body, but never her heart? This was the second time she'd given in to him. She'd gotten pregnant the very first. Would she, from something so insanely pleasurable? It seemed almost fated that such an experience would produce a child, even if he didn't love her...

Her hand touched her flat stomach and she let herself dream for a space of precious seconds, her eyes closed. Dawson's child, in her body. It would be wonderful to be pregnant again. Somehow she'd carry the child to term. Even if she had to stay in bed forever, she wouldn't lose it...!

She opened her eyes and came back to her senses. No. She removed her hand. She was being fanciful. It wouldn't happen, and even if it did, how would she cope? Dawson didn't want her. She repeated that, refusing to recall his anguish at her loss of their first child, his hunger for a baby. She couldn't let herself dream about Dawson's reaction if he knew she was pregnant. Besides, she thought, lightning rarely struck twice.

She'd simply go back to Tucson and forget Dawson. She'd done it once before. She could do it again!

Eight

BUT it wasn't that easy to forget him. Barrie had started losing her breakfast the day she got back to Tucson, just as she had after that disastrous night in France. She, who never had nausea a day in her life! She'd been home for two weeks now, and it hadn't stopped. It was the absolute end, she thought as she bathed her face at the sink, the absolute end that she could get pregnant so easily with him.

Now that lightning did appear to strike twice, what in the world was she going to do?

She hadn't let any of her lukewarm suitors know she was back in town, so there were no phone calls. She didn't have to worry about a part-time job because, apparently, Dawson had settled the deal with Leslie Holton over her tract of land. He'd have those water rights and he could keep his cattle on the Bighorn land that Barrie owned with him.

Her eyes went to the emerald engagement ring he'd given her such a short time ago. She hadn't meant to take it with her, she'd meant to leave it, but she'd been upset at the time, and she'd forgotten about it. She would have to send it back. Her fingers touched the beautiful ring and she sighed as she thought about what might have been. How wonderful if Dawson had bought her a set of rings years ago, knowing that she loved emeralds, if he'd bought them with love and asked her to marry him and told her that he loved her. Oh, what lovely dreams. But it was reality she had to face now.

She curled up in an armchair, still a little nauseous, and began to make decisions. She could go on teaching, presumably, although it was going to be tricky, under the circumstances. She would be an unwed mother and that wouldn't sit well considering the profession she followed. What if she lost her job? The money she got from her share of George Rutherford's estate, while it helped make her life comfortable, was hardly enough to completely support her. She couldn't risk losing her job. She'd have to move somewhere else, invent a fictitious husband who'd deserted her, died…!

Her stomach churned and she swallowed a rush of nausea. How shocking to be able to tell that she was pregnant so soon after conception, she thought. But it had happened just that way after she'd returned from France. In fact, in some mysterious way, she'd known even while Dawson was taking her. Her eyes closed. Taking her. Taking her. She could feel the harsh thrust of his muscular body, feel all over again the insane pleasure that had spread into her very blood.

She made a sound deep in her throat and opened starkly wounded eyes as the knock on the door coincided with her groan.

She blinked away the memories and got up, swaying a little as she made her way to the door. She didn't want company. She didn't want to talk at all. She leaned her forehead against the cold wood and looked through the peephole. Her heart froze in her chest.

"Go away!" she cried hoarsely, wounded to the heart that Dawson should be standing there.

He looked toward the door, his face pale and set. "I can't."

That was all he said, and not very loudly, but she heard him. Surely he wouldn't know, *couldn't* know.

She smiled at that naive imagining. Of course, he knew, she thought fatally as she sighed and unlocked the door. There was some mysterious mental alchemy that had always allowed them to share their thoughts.

She didn't look up as he entered the apartment, bareheaded, reserved. She closed the door and turned away, to sit back down in the armchair.

He stood over her, his hands in the pockets of his gray suit and looked at her pale, pinched face. Her lack of makeup and the dark circles under her eyes told their own story.

"I know," he said uncomfortably. "God only knows how, but I do."

She looked up, her wounded eyes searching his pale, glittery ones. She shrugged and stared at her clenched hands instead. She was barefoot, wearing a loose dress instead of jeans, because of the nausea. He probably knew that, too.

He let out a long, rough sigh and sat down on the sofa opposite her, leaning toward her with his hands clasped over his knees.

"We have to make some quick decisions," he said after a minute.

"I'll manage," she said tightly.

He turned the diamond horseshoe ring on his

right hand. "You're an educator. Not the most liberal of professions. You won't get that promotion. You may not even be able to keep your job, despite the enlightenment of modern life." He looked up, his pale green eyes lancing into her own. "I want this baby," he said gruffly. "I want it very much. And so do you. That has to be our first concern."

She couldn't believe this was happening, that he was so certain, that she was pregnant. "You can't tell until six weeks. It's only been two," she began, faintly embarrassed.

"We knew while we were making him," he said through his teeth. "Both of us. I didn't take precautions, and I knew without asking that you weren't using anything, either. It wasn't an accident."

She'd known that, at some level. She didn't try to deny it.

"We have to get married," he said.

She laughed bitterly. "Thanks. As proposals go, that's a honey."

His face was tight and uncommunicative. "Think what you like. I've made the arrangements and applied for the license. We'll both need blood tests. It can be done in Sheridan."

She looked up at him, her eyes furious. "I don't want to marry you," she said flatly.

"I don't want to marry you, either," he snapped right back, his face mocking and angry. "But I want that baby you're carrying enough to make any sort of sacrifice, even having to live with a woman like you!"

She jumped to her feet, her eyes flashing, her body shivering with rage, with hatred, with outrage. "If you think I'm going to…!" she shouted at him, when all at once, her face went white and she felt the nausea boiling up into her throat, into her mouth. "Oh, God!" She choked, running toward the bathroom.

She barely made it. There had been a grim satisfaction in seeing the guilt on Dawson's lean, tanned face when he realized what he'd caused. Good, she thought through waves of nausea, she hoped he suffered for it.

She heard footsteps, and then water running. A wet cloth was held against her forehead until the nausea finally passed. She was vaguely aware of him coping with his normal cold efficiency, handling everything, helping her to bathe her face and wash the taste out of her mouth. He lifted her then and carried her into the bedroom, laying her gently on the covers. He propped two pillows behind her and went away long enough to fetch a cold glass of water and help her take a sip. The cool drink settled her stomach, but she glared at him just the same.

He was sitting on the side of the bed. His lean hand went to her damp, tangled hair. He smoothed it gently away from her face and studied her features with faint guilt. He'd tried so hard to stay away, to let go. But the past two weeks had been pure torment. He'd spent them going from ranch to ranch, checking stock and books, and it hadn't helped divert him. He'd missed Barrie as never before. And in some mysterious way, he'd known there was going to be a child. That had brought him here. That, and the feelings he didn't want to have for her.

"I'm sorry," he said tersely. "I didn't mean to upset you."

"Yes, you did," she replied. "You don't want to be here at all. And I'm not marrying any man who has the opinion of me that you do!" she added hotly.

He stared at his hands for a long moment. He didn't speak. The skin of his face was pulled taut by clenched muscles.

She put her hands over her eyes with a shaky sigh. "I feel horrible."

"Were you sick like this…after France?" he asked.

"Yes. It started the very next morning, just like this time. That's how I knew," she said wearily. She didn't open her eyes.

He turned and looked at her, wincing at the fatigue he could see in every line of her face, in the very posture of her body. Without conscious volition, his lean hand went to her belly and pressed lightly there, through the fabric, as if he could feel the child lying there in the soft comfort of her body.

She moved her hands, shocked by the touch of his hand, and saw his high cheekbones ruddy with color as he looked at her stomach.

He felt her gaze and met it with his own. There was no expression at all in his face, but his eyes glittered with feeling.

"Why?" she said heavily, her voice thick with tears. "Oh, why, why…?"

His arms slid under her. He lifted her across his powerful thighs and enveloped her against him, one hand pressing her cheek to his chest in a rough gesture of comfort. She cried, and he held her, rocked her. Outside were the sounds of car horns and pulsing engines and brakes and muffled voices. Inside, closer, there was the sound of her choked sobs and her ragged breathing.

"Don't," he said huskily at her ear. "You'll make yourself sicker."

Her hand clenched against his broad chest. She couldn't remember when she'd been so miserable. He'd made her pregnant and now he was going to marry her, so that their child would have the security of parents. But some part of him hated her, resented her. What sort of life would they have?

As she thought it, the words slipped out, muffled by tears.

His chest rose and fell heavily, his breath audible as it stirred her hair. "We haven't many options," he answered her quietly. His hand smoothed her disheveled hair. "Unless you want to stop this pregnancy before it begins," he added, his voice as cold as winter.

She laughed bitterly. "I can't step on an ant and you think I could..."

His thumb stopped the words. "I know you can't, any more than I can," he said shortly. "I didn't mean it."

"Then why say it?" she demanded.

He tilted her face back and looked into it pensively. "You and I are two of a kind," he said absently. "I strike out and you strike back. You've never been really afraid of me, except in one way." His eyes narrowed as she flushed. "And now you aren't afraid of me that way anymore, either, are you?" he taunted softly. "Now you know what lies beyond the pain."

She pushed at his chest, but he wouldn't let go.

Something glittered in his pale eyes, something fierce and full of contempt and anger. His hand tangled in her thick hair and clenched, pulling so that her face arched up to his.

"That hurts," she protested.

His grip loosened, but only a little. His heart was beating heavily, roughly. She could feel it against her breasts. She could feel something else as well: the involuntary burgeoning of his body and the instant response of her own to it.

He laughed bitterly as he heard her soft gasp. "I was so hot that I couldn't hold back. I couldn't protect you. I couldn't even breathe at the last." His voice grew icy with self-contempt and his hand contracted again, angrily. "I want to make you that helpless in my arms. I want to make you beg me, plead with me, to satisfy you. I want you so maddened with desire that you can't go on living if I don't take you!"

He was saying something to her. Something more

than just words. She looked into his face and saw bitterness and self-contempt. And fear.

Fear!

He didn't realize what he was giving away. His anger had taken control of him. "You think you can break me, don't you?" he demanded, dropping his eyes to her mouth. "You think you can lead me around by the nose, make me do anything because I want you!"

She hadn't said a word. She was still overcome by the enormity of what she was learning about him. She didn't even protest the steely hand in her hair. She lay quietly in his embrace and just listened, fascinated.

"Well, I'm not your toy," he said harshly. "I won't come running when you call or follow you around like a whipped dog begging for favors!"

Odd, she thought, that he didn't really frighten her like this, when he looked ferocious with that scowl between his flashing eyes.

"Can't you talk?" he demanded.

"What would you like me to say?" she asked softly, searching his eyes.

The calm tone eased some of the tension from his body. His hand unclenched and he winced, as if he'd only just realized his loss of control. His jaw tautened and his breathing became deliberate at once.

"You were angry because I watched," she prompted, remembering how unduly enraged he'd been about that.

The color flared along his high cheekbones.

She saw the self-consciousness in his anger. Her hand reached up hesitantly and touched his cheek. He actually flinched.

Her whole body relaxed, forcing him to shift his weight so that he could take hers. She hung in his arms, her eyes quietly clinging to his, and her fingers went from his hard cheek down to the corner of his mouth and then lightly brushed the long lower lip.

"Why didn't you want me to look?" she asked softly.

He didn't speak. His breathing grew rough.

"For heaven's sake, isn't that what sex is all about?" she faltered. "I mean, isn't the whole point of it to let go of inhibitions and restraints with another person?"

"Not for me," he said flatly. "Not ever. I don't lose myself with women."

"No," she agreed, studying him. She could almost see the answer. "No, the whole point of the thing is to make a woman lose all her inhibitions, to humble her so that she…"

"Stop it!"

He put her aside and got to his feet, his breathing

unsteady. He rammed his hands into his pockets and paced to the window, viciously pulling the curtains aside.

She sat up on the bed, propped on her hands, staring at him as all of it jelled in her mind and brought a startling, shattering conclusion.

"That's why you were so vicious to me in France," she said. "You lost control."

He drew in a breath. His fingers went white on the curtain.

"That hasn't ever happened to you, not before, not with any woman," she continued in a hushed tone, knowing it was the truth without a word from him. "And that's why you hate me."

His eyes closed. It was almost a relief to have it said, to have her know it. His broad shoulders slumped as if relieved of some monumental burden.

Barrie had to lie back against the pillows. She felt faint. He wasn't admitting anything, but she knew all the same. She knew so much about him, so many things that she understood on a less conscious level. So why hadn't she realized that it wasn't Barrie he was punishing with his cutting words? It was himself, for losing command of his senses, for wanting her so desperately that he couldn't hold back.

"But, why?" she continued. "Is it so terrible to want someone like that?"

The muscles in his jaw moved convulsively. "I came across them in the hall one day," he said in a rough whisper. "She was teasing him, the way she always teased him, taunting him with her body and then drawing back. She did that to make him give in, to make him do what she wanted."

"She?" she queried, puzzled.

He didn't seem to hear her. "That day, she wanted him to trade cars. She had her heart set on a sports car, and he wasn't ready to give up the luxury sedan he always drove. So she teased him and then told him she wouldn't give in to him if he didn't let her have her way." He let out a cold breath. "He begged her." His eyes closed. "He was crying like a little boy, begging, begging…! And in the end, he couldn't contain it, and he pushed her against the wall and…"

He leaned his forehead against the cold glass, shivering with the memory. "She laughed at him. He was all but raping her, right there in full view of the whole damn household, and she was laughing that he couldn't even make it to the bedroom." He turned, his eyes blazing in a white face. "I got out before they saw me, and then I was sick. I actually threw up. You can't imagine how I hated her."

She was getting a horrible premonition. She'd seen her mother tease George Rutherford, but only with words. And once or twice, she'd heard her mother make some remark about him. But Barrie and her mother had never been close, and she'd spent as little time at home as she could manage, first at boarding school in Virginia and then at college. She made a point of staying out of her mother's way and out of Dawson's. So she'd known very little about her mother's second marriage at all. Until now.

"It was...my mother," she said in a ghostly tone.

"Your mother," he said with contempt. "And my father. She treated him like some pitiful dog. And he let her!"

Her breathing was oddly loud in the sudden stillness of the room. She looked at Dawson and went white. Everything he felt, remembered, hated in all the world was in his eyes.

She understood. Finally it made some terrible sort of sense. She dropped her eyes to her lap. Poor Dawson, to have to witness something like that, to see the father he adored humiliated time and time again. No wonder he drew back from what he felt with Barrie. He didn't want to be helpless, because he didn't trust her not to treat him with the same contempt her mother had had for George Rutherford. He couldn't know that she loved him too much to want to hurt him that way. And of course, he didn't trust her, because he didn't love her. His was nothing more than a helpless physical passion without rhyme or reason, a hated weakness that he couldn't help. He looked at love as a woman's weapon.

"I'm so sorry," she said quietly. "I didn't know."

"How could you not know what she was like? She was your mother!"

"She never wanted me," she confessed stiffly, and it was the first time she'd ever talked about her mother to him, or to anyone else. Her face felt frozen. "She told me once that if abortion had been legal at the time, she'd never have had me in the first place."

He was shocked. His heavy brows drew into a frown as he looked at her, sitting as stiff as a poker in the bed. "Good God."

She shrugged. "My father loved me," she recalled with determined pride.

"He died when you were very young, right?"

"Yes," she said.

He didn't even blink. "You were fifteen when

she married my father." His eyes narrowed. "How many men did she go through before she found him, Barrie?" he asked with sudden insight.

She bit her lip almost through, wincing at the pain.

"Stop biting your lips," he muttered impatiently.

She smoothed her finger over it resignedly. "She had lovers, if that's what you're asking." She glanced at him. "That's why you thought I'd had them," she realized.

He nodded. He moved to the bed and sat down in the chair beside it, fatigue in his face, in his eyes. "She was a bitch."

"Yes," she said, not offended. She searched his face, looking for weaknesses, but he was mending the wall already. "I know you loved your father."

"I tried to," he said shortly. "She came along just when he and I were beginning to understand each other. After that, he had no time for me. Not until he was dying." He looked away. He didn't want to talk about that.

She didn't push. He'd already given away more than he'd meant to, she knew.

After a minute he took a quick breath and his pale eyes searched her thin face. "You've lost weight," he remarked abruptly.

She managed a weak smile. "I started losing meals the day I left the ranch," she confessed, and flushed as she remembered the circumstances.

"I couldn't eat for the rest of the day," he recalled. He stared at the floor. "I shouldn't have let you go like that, without a word."

"What could you have said?" she asked. "I felt used…"

"No!" He was really angry now. "Don't you ever say anything like that to me again. Used! My God!"

"All right, cheap, then!" she countered, sweeping back an annoying strand of hair. "Isn't that how you wanted me to feel?"

"No!"

She glared at him, her lower lip trembling with emotion.

He made a curt gesture with one big hand and his lips flattened. "Damn." He leaned forward, his head bowed, his hands supporting it as he braced his elbows on his splayed thighs.

She picked at the bedspread nervously. "You only wanted to see if you were capable with a woman," she muttered. "You said so."

His hands covered his face and pushed back into his hair. "I had an orgasm," he said roughly.

She recognized the resentment in the words even though she didn't quite understand their content. "What?"

He looked up, glared up, at her. "Don't you know what it is?"

She flushed. "I read books."

"So do I," he replied, "and until France and then that afternoon, that's the only way I knew what it meant."

"You're in your mid-thirties," she said pointedly.

"I'm repressed as hell!" he snapped back. "I never liked losing control, in any way at all with a woman, so I never permitted myself to feel anything...anything like that," he added uncomfortably. His head bent. "I got by on little tastes of pleasure, now and again."

What she was hearing shocked her. He was admitting, in a roundabout way, that he'd never been completely satisfied by a woman until he'd made love to Barrie.

"Oh."

The husky little reply made his head lift. She didn't look like a cat with the cream. She didn't even look smug. She looked...

"You're embarrassed," he said unexpectedly.

She averted her eyes. "That's nothing new, with you," she muttered, and blushed even harder.

Her inhibition made him less irritable, and much less threatened. He watched her with open curiosity.

"Don't stare at me," she grumbled. "I'm not some sort of Victorian exhibit."

"Aren't you?" He leaned forward, with his arms crossed over his splayed thighs. His wavy gold hair fell roguishly onto his wide forehead, tangled from his restless fingers in it. He hadn't remembered how soft her skin was, how radiant it was at close range. It had the sheen of a pink pearl. He'd bought her a string of them once, and balked at giving them to her. They were still in the safe back in Sheridan.

"Did you have one, too?" he asked suddenly.

Nine

SHE didn't know how to answer that. She was intimidated and embarrassed.

He became more relaxed when he saw her expression. She still hadn't smiled, or acted as if his fall from grace in her arms had made her want to gloat.

He leaned back and crossed his legs. "Well, well," he murmured, his eyes narrowing. "What a blush. Are you embarrassed?" he added, emphasizing the word with a mocking smile.

"Yes." She bit her lip. He got up and sat down beside her, his thumb forcing her teeth away from it. His hand spread onto her cheek, gentle and caressing while he studied her pale, pinched face.

"So am I," he confessed unexpectedly. "But maybe

the reason we're embarrassed is because we've never talked about being intimate with each other."

"You've already said quite enough," she muttered stiffly.

He let out an odd, amused sound. "Miniskirts," he mused, "silk hose, four boyfriends at a time, low-cut blouses. And it never occurred to me that it was all an act. You little prude."

Her eyes flashed. "Look who's calling who a prude!!" she raged at him.

His eyebrows went up. "Who, me?"

"Yes, you!" She took a shaky breath. "You gave me hell, shamed me, humiliated me, and all because I opened my eyes at the wrong time! I couldn't really see you anyway," she blurted out, "because what I was feeling was so sweet that—" She stopped in midsentence as she realized what she was admitting.

But if she was embarrassed, he wasn't. His face changed as if by magic, his body became less taut.

He drew in a quiet breath. "Thank you," he said huskily.

She didn't recognize the expression on his handsome, darkly tanned face. "What for?"

His eyes dropped to his hands. "Making the memory bearable."

"I don't understand."

He picked at his thumbnail. "I thought you watched because you wanted to enjoy seeing me helpless."

Tears stung her eyes. She'd always thought of Dawson as invincible, stoic. This man was a stranger, someone who'd known pain and grief and humiliation. She wondered if what he'd let her know about him today was only the tip of the iceberg, if there were other painful memories that went back even farther in his life. Surely it had taken more than her mother's taunts to George Rutherford to make Dawson so bitter about women and his own sexuality.

Hesitantly, she reached out and touched his hand, lightly, her cold fingers unsteady as she waited to see if she was allowed to touch him.

Apparently she was. His hand opened, his fingers curled warmly around hers and then linked slowly with them. He turned his head, searching her eyes.

"Couldn't step on an ant, hmm?" he asked absently, and his eyes softened. "I don't suppose you could. I remember you screaming when you saw a garter snake trapped under the wheelbarrow you were using in the flower beds, and then moving it so the poor thing could escape."

She liked the way it felt to hold hands with him. "I don't like snakes."

"I know."

Her fingers slowly moved against his and she lifted her eyes quickly to make sure that he didn't mind.

His lips twitched with amusement. "You're not very sure of yourself with me after all these years."

She smiled briefly. "I'm never sure how you're going to react," she confessed.

He held her eyes. "Tell me what you felt when we made love in my study."

She flushed. She tried to look away, but he wouldn't let her avoid him.

"We've gone too far together for secrets," he said. "We're going to be married. I hurt you when I pulled back. How?"

She shook her head and dropped her eyes.

"Talk to me!"

She grimaced. "I can't!"

There was a long pause. When she got the courage to look up, he was watching her with an expression she couldn't analyze.

She felt his hand still holding hers. She looked at it, admiring the long, deeply tanned fingers wrapped in her own. Her hand looked very small in that powerful grasp.

"Reassure me, then," he said quietly. "I hurt you. But it wasn't all pain, was it?"

"Oh, no," she said. "There was so much pleasure that I thought I might die of it. I opened my eyes and I saw you, but I felt just barely conscious. Then, you started to draw away and it had been so sweet that I wanted to stay that close to you, so I resisted..." She swallowed. "That's when it started to hurt."

His breath was audible. "You should have told me what you really wanted."

"I couldn't. You looked as if you hated me."

He made a sound deep in his throat. His fingers contracted around hers. "I hated myself," he said roughly. "I've hated myself since we were in France, when I went to your room and all but raped you."

"It wasn't that," she replied. "I wanted you, too. It was just that I didn't know how."

"You were a virgin." He brought her hand to his lips and touched it softly with them. "But I wanted you so desperately that I found excuses to have you."

He was afraid that he'd injured her because he'd lost control. In fact, he was afraid that he might do it again. She felt warm inside, as if he'd shared something very secret with her. And he had. Certainly his loss of control was part of the problem along with bad memories of his stepmother and how she'd humiliated his father.

She touched his wavy hair gently. "After I lost... after the baby," she said. "The doctor told me that I should have had a complete gynecological examination before I was intimate with anyone. I was very...intact."

"I noticed," he muttered. He looked down at her, enjoying the feel of her fingers against his hair. "You said that it hurt when I pulled back, Barrie."

She flushed. "Dawson, I can't talk about this!"

He bent and brushed his mouth softly over her forehead. "Yes, you can," he whispered. "Because I have to know." His cheek rested against hers as he spoke, so that she didn't have to look at him. "In the study, just at the last, when I lost control and pushed down, did it hurt you at all, inside?"

She colored at the memory of how exquisitely he'd lost control. "No."

"Thank God! I hated your mother because of what she did to my father," he said, and his lean hand brushed back her hair. "But that was never your fault. I'm sorry I made you pay for something you didn't do, Barrie," he added bitterly.

"Why didn't you ever talk to me about my mother and George?"

"At first because you were so naive about sex. Then, later, I'd built too many walls between us. It was hard to get past them." He drew her hand to his chest and held it there. "I've lived inside myself for most of my adult life. I keep secrets. I share with no one. I've wanted it that way, or I thought I did." His eyes searched hers. "We'll both have to stop running now," he said abruptly. "You can't run from a baby."

She gaped at him. "Well, I like that!"

"Yes, you do, don't you?" he asked with a gentle smile. "I like it, too. What were you going to do, go away and invent a fictional husband?"

She colored. "Stop reading my mind."

"I wish I could have read it years ago," he returned. "It would have saved us a lot of grief. I still don't know why it never occurred to me that you could become pregnant after that night on the Riviera."

"Maybe I wasn't the only one trying to run," she remarked.

His face closed up. Yes, he had tried to run, tried not to think about a baby at all. Was she rubbing it in? Gloating? Surely she didn't know about his mother, did she? He started to move away, but her hands clung to him, because she knew immediately why he'd withdrawn from her.

"There's a very big difference between teasing and sarcasm," she reminded him bluntly. "Sarcasm is always meant to hurt. Teasing isn't. I'm not going to live with you if you take offense at everything I say to you."

His eyebrows went up. "Aren't you assuming a lot?"

"Not at all. You thought I was making fun of you. I'm not my mother, and you're not your father," she continued firmly. She felt belligerent. "I can't even kill a snake, and you think I could enjoy humiliating you!"

Put that way, he couldn't, either. Barrie didn't have the killer instinct. She was as gentle as her mother had been cruel. He hadn't given that much thought. Now he had to.

He sat back down again, his eyes solemn as they searched over her face. "I don't know you at all," he said after a minute. "We've avoided each other for years. As you reminded me once, we've never really talked until the past few weeks."

"I know that."

He laughed shortly. "I suppose I'm carrying as many emotional scars as you are."

"And you don't look as if you have a single one,"

she replied. Her eyes fixed on him. "Did you give her the silver mouse?"

He knew at once what she was referring to. He shook his head. "I keep it in the drawer by my bed."

That was surprising, and it pleased her. She smiled shyly. "I'm glad."

He didn't return the smile. "I've done a lot of things I regret. Making you look foolish over giving me a birthday present is right at the top of the list. It shamed me, that you cared enough to get something for me, after the way I'd treated you."

"Coals of fire?"

"Something like that. Maybe it embarrassed me, too. I never gave you presents, birthday or Christmas."

"I never expected them."

He touched her disheveled hair absently. "They're in my closet."

She frowned. "What's in your closet?"

"All the presents I bought you and never gave to you."

Her heart skipped. "What sort of presents?"

His shoulder lifted and fell. "The emerald necklace you wanted when you were nineteen. The little painting of the ranch the visiting artist did in oils one summer. The Book of Kells reproduction you couldn't afford the year when the traveling European exhibition came through Sheridan. And a few other things."

She couldn't believe he'd done that for her. "But you never gave them to me!"

"How could I, after the things I'd said and done?" he asked. "Buying them eased the ache a little. Nothing healed it." He picked up her hand and his thumb smoothed over the emerald ring she was wearing on her engagement finger. "I bought you this set when you left France."

That was a statement that left her totally breathless. "Why?"

"Shame. Guilt. I was going to offer you marriage."

"You never did," she whispered in anguish.

"Of course I didn't," he said through his teeth. "When I came by your apartment a week after you'd left France, a man answered the door and told me you were in the shower. He was wearing jeans—nothing else, just jeans, and he was sweating."

She wouldn't have understood that reference once. Now, remembering the dampness of her own body after Dawson's fierce lovemaking, she understood it too well.

"That was Harvey," she said miserably. "He was

my landlord's son at the apartment house where I lived back then. He and his brother were building cabinets in the kitchen. They took a break and while they were doing that, I had a quick shower. I'd been helping them…" She paused. "Harvey never said I'd had a visitor!"

He winced.

"You thought he was my lover," she guessed.

He nodded. "It seemed fairly obvious at the time. I went away eaten up with jealousy, believing that I'd set you off on a path to moral destruction. I was so disheartened that I flew all the way back to France."

She could have cried. If Harvey hadn't been there, if she hadn't been in the shower, if, if, if. Her face told its own story.

"You see what I meant, the morning I came to take you to Sheridan with me?" he asked quietly. "All it takes is a missed message, a lost letter, a phone call that doesn't get answered. And lives are destroyed."

He was still holding her hand, looking at the ring on her finger.

"You knew that I loved emeralds," she said softly.

"Of course I knew." He wasn't admitting how he knew, or why he'd gone to so much trouble to find a wedding set exactly like that one.

Suddenly she remembered. "I saw a ring like this in a magazine, one of those glossy ones," she recalled. "I left it open on the sofa, to show Corlie, because I loved it so much. That was about the time I left for college."

"You had on a pink tank top and cutoffs," he recalled. "You were barefoot, your hair was halfway down your back. I stood in the doorway and watched you sprawled on the carpet with that magazine, and I had to get out of the house."

She searched his eyes. "Why?"

He gave a short laugh. "Can't you guess? Because the same thing happened that always happened when I get close to you. I got aroused."

"But you acted as if you couldn't bear the sight of me!" she blurted.

"Of course I did! I'd have given you the perfect weapon to use against me if I'd let you know how I felt!" he replied without thinking.

He really believed that. She could see it in his pale eyes as they searched her face. He'd spent all those long years protecting himself, avoiding intimacy or even affection because he thought of it as a weakness that any woman would exploit. It was no wonder that they called him the "ice man." In so many ways, he was. She wondered if anything would thaw him out.

Perhaps the baby would be a start. *The baby!* With wonder, her hands went absently to her flat stomach.

The involuntary action brought Dawson out of his unpleasant memories. He followed the motion of her hands and the bitterness left his face.

He reached out and placed one of his big hands over both of hers. "I'll take care of you this time," he said quietly, "even if it means hiring a hospital staff and keeping you in bed for the full nine months."

Her hands slid over his and rested there. "I won't lose this one," she said with certainty.

He made an odd sound and there was a glimmer of real affection in his eyes. "I still can't quite believe it," he said with poignant hesitation.

"Neither can I. Well, so much for that promotion," she murmured dryly. "I'm not living in Tucson alone."

He cocked an eyebrow. "You can teach in Sheridan."

"When he starts school," she agreed.

He searched her eyes. "He?"

"I hate dolls," she murmured shyly. "But I love football and baseball and soccer and wrestling."

He chuckled with genuine amusement. "Chauvinist."

"I am not. I wouldn't mind a daughter, really. I

think Antonia's stepdaughter, Maggie, is precious. I'm sure they're as crazy about her as they are about their new son, Nelson." She shrugged. "Besides, Maggie hates dolls, too. But she loves to read and she knows almost as much about cattle as her dad."

"I like Antonia," he replied.

"You can get used to Powell. Can't you?" she coaxed.

He pursed his lips. "I don't know. Will you make it worth my while?" he murmured with a slow, steady appraisal of her relaxed body.

She couldn't believe she was hearing that. It was the first time in memory that he'd actually teased her. He even looked rakish, with his disheveled wavy gold hair on his forehead and his pale green eyes affectionate. He was so handsome that he took her breath away, but she'd have loved him if he'd been the ugliest man on earth.

"I've shocked you," he mused.

"Continually, ever since you walked in the door," she agreed. She smiled up at him. "But to answer the question, yes, when I feel better, I'll do my best to make it worth your while."

"No more fear?" he asked, and was solemn.

"I don't think so," she replied. "If it's going to be

like last time from now on. And if you won't get furious afterward again."

He took her hand in his and held it tightly. "I'll make sure it's like the last time. As for getting upset…" He grimaced. "It's difficult for me."

"Because you don't trust me yet," she said perceptively. "I know. You'll just have to learn how, I suppose. But I don't think making fun of people is any way to carry on a relationship, if it helps. And I don't think less of you for enjoying what we do together." She blushed. "In bed, I mean."

"We didn't do it in bed. We did it on the carpet." His face hardened. "Like animals…"

She sat up and put her hand over his lips. "Not like animals," she said. "Like two people so hungry for each other that they couldn't wait. There's nothing to be ashamed of in that."

He took a deliberate breath, but his eyes were still full of storms and bitterness.

She traced his long, sensuous mouth with her forefinger. "I'm sorry that my mother made you hate what you feel when we're together, Dawson," she said quietly. "But I'm not like her, you know. I couldn't hurt you. I couldn't even tell you about the baby we lost, because I knew it would devastate you."

He reached for her roughly and enveloped her bruisingly close against him. There was a fine tremor in his arms as he buried his face in the thick hair at her throat.

She smoothed his hair with gentle hands, nestling closer. "But we won't lose this one, my darling," she whispered. "I promise you, we won't."

There was a stillness in him all at once. He didn't lift his head, but his breathing was suddenly audible. "What did you call me?" he whispered gruffly.

She hesitated.

"What?" he persisted.

"I said…my darling," she faltered self-consciously.

He drew back enough to let him see her flushed face. "No!" he said quickly. "Don't be embarrassed! I like it."

"You do?"

He began to smile. "Yes."

She sighed with pure delight as she looked at him.

He studied her flushed face in its frame of disheveled dark, wavy hair. His hands gathered it up and tested its silkiness with pleasure that was visible. "Feeling better?"

She nodded. "I'm a little queasy, but it's natural."

"My doctor can probably give you something for it."

She shook her head. "No. I won't even take an aspirin tablet while I'm carrying him. I won't put him at the slightest risk."

He dropped his eyelids so that she couldn't see the expression in his eyes. "Do you want the baby because of that maternal instinct, or do you want him because he's my child?"

"Are you going to pretend that you don't know?" she mused. "You used to taunt me about how I felt—"

"Yes, I knew." He interrupted curtly and met her eyes. "It hurt, damn it. I was cruel to you and even that didn't make any difference. You can't imagine what torment it was to know that all I had to do was touch you and I could have you, anytime I wanted to. But I had too much honor to do it." His eyes narrowed with pain. "All the same, I hope I haven't killed that feeling in you. I don't know much about love, Barrie. But I want you to love me, if you can."

Tears burned in her eyes as she felt his lips touch her forehead, her eyebrows, her wet eyelids. The tears fell and she couldn't seem to stop them. "I've loved you since the first time I saw you," she whispered unsteadily. "So much, Dawson. So much, so much…!"

He kissed her. His mouth was hungry at first, insistent, almost cruel in its devouring need. But he felt her weakness and his arms loosened their tight grip. His mouth became caressing, tender.

When he lifted his head, he looked dazed. This was his woman. She loved him. She had his child under her heart. She was going to be his wife. He felt as stunned as he looked.

"We can…if you want to," she murmured sheepishly. "I mean, I'm not that sick."

He smoothed back her damp hair. "I wouldn't be much of a man if sex was all I had in mind right now," he replied quietly. "You're carrying my child. I could burst with pride."

It was an odd way to put it, but it touched her. She smiled shyly. "One time and I'm pregnant," she said pensively. "If we don't want twenty kids, I suppose one of us is going to have to do something after the baby comes."

"I'll do something," he said. "I don't want you taking anything that might put you at risk."

"I don't have to take something. I can use something."

"We'll see."

She touched his face, his shoulder, his chest. "I could get drunk on this."

"On what?"

"On being able to touch you whenever I want to," she said absently, unaware of the effect the words had on the man holding her. "I used to dream about it."

"Even after France?" he asked with sudden bitterness.

"Even after France," she confessed. She looked up. "Oh, Dawson, love is the most stubborn emotion on earth."

"It must be," he said.

She leaned forward and kissed his eyelids closed. "When do you want to leave for Sheridan?"

"Now."

"Now? But...!"

"I want to get married," he said firmly. "I want to do it quickly, before you change your mind."

"But, I wouldn't!"

He wasn't sure of that. He'd made so many stupid mistakes already that he couldn't risk another one. "And we won't sleep together again until the ring is on your finger," he added.

"Why, you blackmailer," she said.

He cocked an eyebrow. "I beg your pardon?"

"Withholding your body to make me marry you. Well, I never!"

"Yes, you did," he murmured.

She liked the way his eyes twinkled when he was amused. She smiled. He might not love her, but he liked her, and he wanted her.

"Yes, I did," she agreed. "Okay, if you're in such a hurry to give up your freedom, who am I to stand in your way? I'll pack right now!"

Ten

CORLIE wasn't at all surprised to see Dawson walk in with a radiant Barrie. She hugged them both and went away with a smug expression to make them a pot of coffee.

"Coffee," Barrie began. "I really should have milk…"

Dawson put his finger over her lips and looked sheepish. "Don't. I'll go and tell her we both want milk."

"She'll be even more suspicious of that," she whispered.

He shrugged. "Maybe I'm overreacting. Maybe you are, too," he continued. "We don't even know for sure yet."

She leaned into his body with her eyes closed, feeling secure and at peace for the first time in years. "Yes, we do," she said.

He rocked her in his arms. "Yes, we do," he agreed after a minute. He closed his own eyes and refused to give in to the fear. It would be wonderful to have a child with her. Surely nothing would go wrong, as it had with his mother. And she wasn't going to make him jump through hoops. His eyes opened and he stared past her. He felt troubled and turbulent. Trust came hard to a man with his history. He didn't know how he was going to cope with what lay ahead.

They were married quietly in the local Methodist church with Corlie and Rodge for witnesses. Antonia Long and her husband sent flowers and congratulations, but the baby had a cold and they wouldn't leave him, even for such a momentous occasion as to see Barrie and the "ice man" get married.

Dawson kissed her with a tenderness she'd never expected from him and Barrie felt on top of the world. Since their return to Sheridan, he hadn't touched her except to hold her hand or brush a light kiss across her mouth.

But tonight was their wedding night. She marveled

at her excited anticipation, remembering the pleasure
his body had taught hers to feel. It wasn't fear she was
feeling now when she thought of lying in Dawson's
arms in the darkness. And surely, after the honesty
he'd shown her about his past, they could cope with
his emotional scars. If he wanted to make love with the
lights out, to conceal his vulnerability, she wouldn't
even mind that. She only wanted to lie in his arms
and love him.

But if she expected the wedding band to make an
immediate difference in their relationship, she was in
for a shock. Because that afternoon Dawson, who'd
been restless and prowling ever since the reception,
suddenly packed a bag and announced that he just had
to see a man in California about a seed bull.

"On our wedding day?" Barrie exclaimed, aghast.

He looked more uncomfortable than ever. "It's
urgent. I wouldn't go otherwise. He's threatening to
sell it to someone else."

"You could just buy it," she suggested.

"Not without seeing it first." He closed his bag. "It
won't take long. A few days."

"Days?"

He grimaced at her expression. He tried to speak
and made a curt gesture with one hand instead. "I

won't be away long. Corlie's got the number where I can be reached if you need me."

"I need you already. Don't go."

He paused to tilt her face up to his worried eyes. "I have to." He ground out the words.

She had a feeling that the confinement of marriage was already making him nervous. He'd faced so many things in the past few weeks, including a sudden marriage and a pregnancy. He was trapped and straining at the ropes. And if she didn't let him go now, she might lose him for good. She was wise enough to know that he needed a little time, a little room. Even if it was on their wedding day. She couldn't corner him. She had to let go.

"Okay." She smiled instead of arguing. "If you have to go, you have to go."

He seemed surprised at her lack of protest. His impatience to leave lessened. "You don't mind?"

"Yes, I mind," she said honestly. "But I understand, perhaps better than you realize."

He glared at her. "It's only a business trip. It has nothing to do with our marriage or the baby."

"Of course not."

He didn't like the expression in her eyes. "You think you know everything about me, don't you?"

Her eyebrows raised. "I haven't even scratched the surface, yet."

"I'm glad you realize it."

She reached up and kissed him beside his mouth, very gently, feeling his tall body tense at the unexpected caress. "Do you mind if I kiss you goodbye?" she asked.

He stared at her. "No."

She grinned. "Have a safe trip. Are you taking the Learjet or a commercial flight?"

"Commercial," he said surprisingly. "I don't feel like worrying with maps and vectors today."

"Good. As long as you don't feel compelled to tell the pilot how to fly," she added tongue in cheek, remembering an incident in the past when Dawson had actually gone into the cockpit to instruct the pilot to change his altimeter.

He averted his eyes. "He was a novice commuter pilot and he was so nervous that he had his altimeter set wrong. Good thing I noticed. He'd have crashed."

"I suppose he would have, at that. And he never flew again, either."

"He realized he wasn't cut out for the stress of the job, and he had the guts to admit it." He looked down at her with calmer eyes, searching over her face. "You look better than you did in Tucson," he said. "But don't overdo, okay?"

"Okay."

"And try to eat more."

"I will."

"Don't drive anywhere unless Rodge and Corlie know where you're going."

"Okay."

"And if something goes wrong, call me. Don't try to handle it yourself."

"Anything else?"

He began to look uncomfortable. "Stay away from the horses. You shouldn't go riding until we know for certain."

"You're a case," she murmured with twinkling eyes. "Imagine that, you worrying about me."

He didn't react with humor, as she'd expected. In fact, he looked more solemn than ever. He took a long strand of her hair and tested its soft texture, looking at it instead of her while he spoke. "I've always worried about you."

She sighed, admiring his rare good looks in the tan suit he wore. "I can't believe that you actually belong to me, now," she reminded him, noting his shocked expression.

It should have pleased him to hear the note of possession in her voice. It didn't. Combined with his fears of being vulnerable in her arms, it made him angry. He dropped her hair and moved away. "I'll phone you tonight. Stay out of trouble."

She colored at the snub, because that's what it was. She wasn't through walking on eggshells with him, she realized at once. She'd only just begun.

"Dawson?"

He paused, looking back with obvious reluctance.

She hesitated, frowning. She was going to have trouble approaching him at all from now on. She had to do it right the first time.

"Marriage doesn't just happen," she said, choosing her words carefully. "It takes some cooperation, some compromise. I'll go halfway, but no further."

He looked puzzled. "What do you mean?"

"You're my husband," she said, tingling as she said the word.

"And now you think you own me, because I married you?" he asked in a dangerously soft tone.

Her face felt tight. She just stared at him for a minute before she spoke. "Just remember that I didn't ask you to marry me," she said quietly. "It was *you* who came after *me*. Not the reverse."

His eyebrows rose at the haughty tone. "I came after you to save you from an unwed pregnancy," he informed her with a mocking smile. "Or did you think I had other motives? Do I look like a man who's dying for love of you?" he added with biting sarcasm.

"Of course not," she said in a subdued tone. "I know that you don't love me. I've always known."

He didn't understand the need he felt to cut her, especially now. He'd drained all the joy out of her green eyes, all the pleasure out of her radiant face. She looked tired. If she really was pregnant, as they suspected, upsetting her was the very last thing he should be doing. But she had him now, and he burned for her. He wanted her with a headlong, reckless passion that could place him forever in her power. And that wasn't the only fear he was nursing. He had cold feet and they were getting colder by the minute. He had to get away now, to be alone so that he could get a grip on himself. Dear God, why did she have to look that way? Her very silence made him feel guilty.

Her chin lifted and she managed a smile. "Have a good trip."

His eyes narrowed. "You won't run away while I'm gone?" he asked abruptly, and watched her face color. "Damn it...!"

"Don't you swear at me!" she snapped back. Her lower lip was trembling, her hands clenched at her sides, her eyes glittered with tears of anger and hurt. "And I'm not the one who's running, you are! You can't bear the thought of a wife, can you, especially me!"

Her loud voice brought Corlie into the hall. The housekeeper stopped dead, aghast at the scene before her eyes. There was Dawson with a suitcase, looking as unapproachable as she'd ever seen him, and Barrie crying, shivering.

"You've only just got married," she said hesitantly, looking from one of them to the other.

"Why don't you tell her the truth, Dawson? We didn't get married for love. We got married because we had to!" Barrie sobbed. "I'm pregnant, and it's his fault!"

Dawson's face went white as the words stabbed him like a knife right out of the past. He was oblivious to Corlie's shocked expression as he glared at Barrie. "Don't make it sound like that. You couldn't possibly know for sure yet!" he snapped at her.

"Yes, I could," she said in a ghostly tone. "I used one of those home pregnancy kits, and it says I am!" she growled.

Thinking it was one thing. Hearing it, knowing it, being sure—that was something entirely different. He stood with the suitcase in his hand and he didn't move. She was really pregnant. His eyes went to her stomach, where one of her hands was flattened protectively, and then back up to her hurt, wet face. But he wasn't seeing Barrie. He was seeing his mother, blaming him for her marriage, blaming him, and then at the last, in the casket, with the little casket beside her…

"Well, you're married," Corlie said, trying to find a glimmer of optimism. "And you both love children…"

Barrie wiped her wet eyes. "Yes, we love children." She glared at Dawson. "What are you waiting for? There's a bull standing in a pasture in California just dying for you to rush out there and buy him, isn't there? Why don't you go?"

Corlie glanced at him. "You're going to California to buy a bull on your wedding day?" she asked, as if she couldn't have heard right.

"Yes, I'm going to buy a bull," he said belligerently. He slammed his hat on his head, ignoring his guilt at the way Barrie looked. "I'll be home in a few days."

He stalked to the front door and jerked it open. He knew both women were watching him, and he didn't care. He wasn't going to go rushing to Barrie's bed like a crazed animal begging for favors, and she needn't expect it. She had to learn right from the beginning that he had the upper hand, and that he wasn't going to be some sort of sexual toy for her. She already blamed him for getting her pregnant, for ruining her life. She was going to be like his mother, she was going to torment him. He had to escape while he could.

That he was behaving irrationally didn't even occur to him. Not then, at least.

But by the time he was ensconced in his California hotel suite, the world seemed to snap quite suddenly back into focus.

He looked around him with vague shock. He'd walked out on his wife of two hours, left her alone and pregnant, to go and buy a bull. He couldn't believe what he'd done, what he'd said to her. He must have been out of his mind.

Perhaps he really was, he thought. He'd tortured himself with thoughts of making love to Barrie, but once again he'd have to submit to the madness she created in his body. He'd be helpless, vulnerable, weak. She'd watch him…she'd see not only his surrender to her body, but what he really felt. In the heat of ecstasy he wouldn't be able to hide it from her.

He took a long breath. He'd never faced his own vulnerability with her. In fact, he'd gone to extreme lengths to make sure he didn't have to face it. It had been impossible for him to lower the barriers between them, for fear that she'd want revenge even now for the way he'd treated her. If he let her see the extent of his desire, she'd use it against him. Hadn't his own mother taunted him with his childish weaknesses, ridiculed him, made him look small in front of his father and his friends? Hadn't she pointed out that he was a sissy because he'd cried when his German shepherd had been hit by a car? Hadn't she spent his childhood making fun of him, making him pay, unbeknownst to his father, for a marriage she'd never wanted in the first place? Dawson had been a mistake, she often told him, and she'd had to marry a man she didn't really love because of it...

Funny that he hadn't let himself remember those words until today. Barrie was pregnant and she'd cried that she'd had to marry Dawson because of it. If she hadn't said that, he'd never have gone out the door. Ironic that her own mother had said the same thing about her, he thought, recalling what she'd told him in Tucson. Maybe women didn't really want babies at all except as a means of torturing men and making them feel guilty. He wondered if that thought was quite coherent.

He sprawled on the luxurious sofa in the sitting room, remembering other things, remembering Barrie's soft skin under his, her sweet cries of passion as he drove her into the carpet beneath the heated thrust of his body. He groaned aloud as the memory of the ecstasy she'd given him poured into his mind and made him shiver. Could he live without ever again knowing that pleasure, regardless of the price?

His eyes closed as he lay back. He could always turn out the lights, he thought with dry humor. Then she couldn't look at him. It wouldn't matter if she heard him. He'd hear her, too. She was none too quiet when they made love. His eyes blazed with feeling as he recalled her own shocked pleasure that morning on the carpet. She'd known only pain from him before. He'd taught her that she could expect far more than that.

She'd said she loved him. Good God, how could she love him, when he kept pushing her away? Why couldn't he accept her love, why couldn't he accept his own addiction to her? She was pregnant, and he'd left her in Sheridan on their wedding day out of nothing more than cold fear because he…because he…

He opened his eyes and took a slow, painful breath.

Because he loved her. There. He couldn't admit it to her, but he couldn't hide it from himself. He loved her. He'd loved her since she was fifteen, since she'd given him a silver mouse on his birthday. He'd loved her in France, hated himself for taking advantage of what she felt for him in an attempt to deny that love. But it had grown and grown until it consumed him. He couldn't get rid of it. He couldn't stop. He couldn't give in to it. What was he going to do?

Well, he thought as he managed to get to his feet, there was one thing he could do. He could have a drink, and then he was going to call Barrie and set her straight on a few things!

Barrie was surprised when she heard Dawson's thick voice on the telephone. She hadn't really expected him to call after the furious way he'd left. She'd spent the rest of the day alternately crying and cursing, while Corlie did her best to comfort and reassure her. She'd gone to bed early, sick and disappointed because her new husband couldn't even stand to be in the same house with her. And after the tenderness she'd felt in him in Tucson, too. It had been utter devastation.

Now, here he was on the phone trying to talk to

her, and unless she missed her guess, he was blind, stinking drunk!

"Did you hear me?" he demanded. "I said, from now on, we're only going to make love in the dark!"

"I don't mind," she said, confused.

"I didn't ask if you minded," he muttered. "And you can't look at me while we do it."

"It would never occur to me," she said placatingly.

"And don't say you own me. You don't own me. No woman is going to own me."

"Dawson, I never said that."

"You said I belonged to you. I'm not a dog. Did you hear me?"

"Yes, I heard you." She smiled to herself at his efforts to enunciate properly. The anguish and disappointment of the afternoon had vanished as he poured out his deepest fears without even realizing it. It was a fascinating glimpse at the real man, without the mask.

"I don't belong to you," he continued. He felt hot. He pushed back his hair. He was sweating. Maybe he should turn on the air conditioner. If he could only find it. He bumped into the table and almost upset the lamp. In the tangle, he dropped the phone.

"Dawson?" Barrie called, concerned when she heard the crash.

There were muttered, half-incoherent curses and a scrambling sound as he retrieved the receiver. "I walked into the table. And don't laugh!"

"Oh, I wouldn't dream of it," she assured him.

"I can't find the air conditioner. It must be in this room somewhere. How the hell can they hide something that big?"

She almost lost it then. She had to stifle a burst of laughter. "Look under the window," she instructed.

"What window? Oh, that one. Okay."

There was another pause and some odd sounds, followed by a curse and a thud. "I think I turned on the heat," he said. "It's hot in here."

"You might call housekeeping and ask them to check," she said hesitantly.

"Check what?"

"The air conditioner."

"I already checked it," he muttered. "It's under the window."

She wasn't going to argue. "Did you see the bull?" she asked.

"What bull?" There was a pause. "Listen, there's no bull in here, are you crazy? This is a hotel!"

By now, Barrie was rolling on the floor.

"Are you laughing?" he asked furiously.

"No." She choked. "I have a cough. I'm coughing." She coughed.

There was another pause. "I was going to tell you something," he said, trying to focus. "Oh, I remember. Listen here, Barrie, I can live without sex. I don't even need it."

"Yes, Dawson," she agreed gently.

"But if you want to sleep with me, you can," he continued generously.

"Yes, I would like that, very much," she said.

He cleared his throat. "You would?"

"I love sleeping with you," she said softly.

He cleared his throat again. "Oh," he said after a minute.

The opportunity was too good to miss. He was talking to her as if he'd had truth serum. "Dawson," she began carefully, "why did you go to California?"

"So I wouldn't make love to you," he said drowsily. "I didn't want you to see…how much I wanted to. How much I cared."

Her heart began to swell, to lift, to soar. "I love you," she whispered.

He sucked in a sharp breath. "I know. I love you,

too," he said drowsily. "Love you…so much. So much, Barrie, so much, so much…!" He swallowed. He couldn't quite talk.

Which was just as well, because Barrie was as speechless as he was. She gripped the receiver like a life jacket, staring into space with her heart in her mouth. "But I don't want you to know it," he continued quite clearly. "Because women like having weapons. You can't know how I feel, Barrie," he continued. "You'd torment me with it, just like your mother tormented George because he wanted her so much."

She felt the pain right down to her toes. She'd never known these things about Dawson.

"Listen, I have to go to bed now," he said. He frowned, trying to remember something. "I can't remember why I called you."

"That's all right, darling," she said softly. "It doesn't matter."

"Darling," he repeated slowly. He took a heavy breath. "You don't know how it hurts when you call me 'darling.' I'm buried inside myself. I can't dig my way out. I miss you," he whispered, his voice husky and deep. "You don't know how much. Good night… sweetheart."

The line went dead. Barrie stayed on it, waiting.

After a minute the switchboard came on the line. She heard the operator's voice with a sense of fate. She smiled.

"May I help you?" the operator repeated.

"Yes, you may. Can you tell me how to get to your hotel?"

Corlie muttered all the way to the airport in Sheridan, but she was smiling just the same. She put Barrie on the commuter flight to Salt Lake City, Utah, where she caught the California flight. It was tiring and she was already fatigued, but it seemed somehow the right thing to do, to get to her reluctant husband before he sobered up completely.

She arrived at the hotel very early the next morning and showed the hotel clerk her marriage license. It didn't take much persuasion after that to coax him into letting her have a key to Dawson's room.

Feeling like a conspirator, she let herself in and looked around the suite with a little apprehension. But timidity hadn't brought her this far; courage had.

She opened the door to what must be the bedroom, and there he was, sprawled nude on the covers, as if he'd passed out before he could get under them. Not that he needed to. Bread could have been baked on the floor, judging by the temperature.

Barrie went to the air conditioner and found the switch turned off. She clicked it on high and cool air began to blow in. She stood there for a minute, because she was feeling a little nauseous from the heat. As the cool air filtered up to her face, she began to breathe more easily.

There was a sound and when she turned, Dawson was propped on one elbow, watching her through bloodshot eyes.

Eleven

"GOOD morning," she said, shy now that she was actually facing him after their extraordinary conversation of the previous night.

"Good morning." His eyes searched over her body in jeans and a tank top with a lined jacket over it. Her long hair was a little disheveled, and she looked flushed. He still wasn't certain that she wasn't a mirage. He scowled. "What are you doing here?"

"Turning on the air-conditioning," she said.

He cocked an eyebrow. "Pull the other one."

She lifted her chin and colored a little as her eyes registered his blatant masculinity. He wasn't only nude, he was already aroused, and apparently not the least shy anymore about letting her see. "I'm getting educated."

He smiled mockingly. "We're married. If you don't want to look at me, nobody's making you."

She glared at him. The wall was back up. She'd come all this way on hope, exhilaration that he'd finally admitted his feelings for her, only to find that she'd overstepped her limit again. He wasn't going to admit anything. He was going to go right on keeping her at a distance, refusing to let her see into his heart. The baby wouldn't make any difference. They'd live together like strangers with the child as their only common ground. She could see down the long, lonely years of loving without any visible return of her feelings for him, without hope.

"I came to tell you that I'm going back to Tucson," she said coldly. "That's what you want, isn't it?" she added when he looked shocked. "That's what this trip is all about. You married me because you felt you had to, but now you're sorry and you don't want me around. I make you lose control, and you can't stand that." She straightened. "Well, no more worries on that score. I've got my bags packed and I'll be out of your house by tomorrow!"

He threw his legs off the bed and got up. Nude,

he was more than intimidating. He moved toward her and abruptly lifted her up in his arms, turning to carry her back to bed.

"Put me down!" she snapped at him. "What do you think you're doing?"

"I'll give you three guesses." He tossed her onto the bed and followed her down, catching her flailing hands. He pressed her wrists into the mattress and poised there above her, his eyes pale and steady and totally unreadable.

"I hate you!" she said furiously. Her eyes stung with unshed tears as he blurred in her vision. "I hate you, Dawson!" she sobbed.

"Of course you do." His voice sounded almost tender, she thought, through the turmoil of emotions. But surely it wasn't. His hands slid up to melt into hers, tangling with her fingers as he bent and drew his lips softly, tenderly, over her mouth. His chest eased down, his long legs slid against hers in a silence that magnified her ragged breathing and the sound of his body moving against hers.

He drew her arms around his neck. His hands slid under her, disposing of catches and buttons and zippers. In a melting daze, she felt him undressing her, and all the while, his mouth was making her body sing. He nuzzled her breasts, tasting their hard tips, suckling them, while he removed the layers of fabric until she was as nude as he was. The thick hair on his chest tickled her skin at first, and then made her body tauten with desire.

He never spoke. He kissed her from head to toe, in ways he never had before, his hands touched her with a mastery that would have made her insanely jealous of the women he'd learned it with if she'd been able to think at all. His mouth teased and tempted and finally devoured hers. And all the while, he caressed her as if her pleasure was the most important thing in the world to him. He kindled fires and all but extinguished them over and over again until she was on the edge of madness, sobbing aloud for relief from the tension his expert caresses built in her.

But it was a long, long time later before he finally eased down between her legs and very gently probed the dark, sweet mystery of her body, covering her mouth with his just as he pushed softly and felt her open to absorb him.

She stiffened just a little, but there was no resistance at all to his passage, and he shifted just enough to make her gasp and cling to him before he probed even deeper. All the while, he was tender as he'd never been in the past, slow and quiet and utterly loving. *Loving.* She didn't open her eyes once. She didn't try to look at him. She lay drowning in the pleasure each slow, soft movement of his hips created, sobbing rhythmically under the exquisite throb of pleasure that grew deeper and deeper, like a drum beating in her body, beating, beating…

With maddening precision he built the pleasure to a crescendo that left her whimpering like a wounded thing, clinging fiercely, whispering things to him in her need that would shock her minutes later. But for now, there was no future, no shame. She pleaded helplessly, her whole body rising, shivering in a painful arch, a silent plea for fulfillment. And recognizing the end of her endurance, he moved sharply, suddenly, into complete possession in a slow, deep, endless rhythm that sent her spinning right up into the sun. Her nails bit into his back helplessly as she shuddered, sobbing under his mouth, crying out in anguished delight, tears raining down her cheeks as she endured the most incredible ecstasy she'd ever felt, so deep and throbbing that it was almost pain.

Only then, only when he felt her body convulse in the final spasms of completion did he drive fiercely for his own fulfillment. It was as before, spasms of aching pleasure that built and built and suddenly blazed in his taut body in an explosion of heat and light, making him mindless, shapeless, formless. He was part of her, as she was part of him. There was nothing in the world, only the two of them. Only…this…!

He saw the ceiling without seeing it. He was lying on his back, still trembling from the violence of his satisfaction. He could hear Barrie breathing raggedly. He could feel the dampness of her body where it lay so close and so far from his.

"They say that muscular contractions that violent could break bones without the narcotic of ecstasy to make them bearable," he remarked drowsily when he had his breath back.

She didn't say anything. She was lying on her stomach, half-dead with pleasure and so miserable that she wanted to hide. Sex. Only sex. He hadn't said a word, all the while, and now he was treating her to a scientific explanation of sexual tension.

He rolled over onto his side and looked at her. She averted her face, but he pulled her against him and tilted her chin up.

"Well, do you still want to leave me after *that?*" he asked. "Or would you like to try and convince me that all those outrageous, shocking things you whispered to me were the result of a bad breakfast…Barrie!"

She'd torn out of his arms in a mad dash for the bathroom, and only barely made it in time. She knelt there, her heart breaking in her chest, her eyes red with tears, while she lost her breakfast and everything in between. *The monster!* The monster, taunting her about a response she couldn't help! And where had he learned such skills anyway, the licentious, womanizing…!

While she was thinking it, she was saying it.

Dawson wrapped a towel around his waist and with a resigned sigh, he wet a facecloth and knelt beside her. When the nausea finally passed, he bathed her face and carried her back to bed, tucking her gently under the sheet.

"I want my clothes." She wept. "I can't leave like this!"

"No problem there. Because you aren't leaving." He picked up her clothes, opened the window and threw them out.

She lay in a daze, watching him perform the most irrational act of their long acquaintance. She actually gasped out loud.

He calmly closed the window. Below there was

a loud squeal of brakes. He cocked an eyebrow at her. "That lacy bra probably landed on some poor soul's windshield and shocked him into panic," he mused. "You shouldn't wear things like that in your condition, anyway. It's scandalous."

She held the sheet tucked against her while she struggled with the possibility that Dawson's mind had snapped.

He laughed softly as he stood over her, the towel just barely covering his lean hips. Her expression amused him. "What's the matter?" he asked.

Her hand clenched on the cool cotton fabric. "I didn't bring a change of clothes," she said stiffly. "And now even my underwear—my underwear, for God's sake!—is out there being handled by total strangers! How am I supposed to leave the room, much less the hotel?"

"You aren't," he replied. His eyes slid over her soft, faintly tanned shoulders and he smiled. "God, you're pretty," he said. "You take my breath away without your clothes."

She didn't say anything. She wasn't sure it would help the situation.

He sat down beside her with a rueful smile. "I guess I can't expect you to understand everything at once, can I?" He smoothed back her hair and his eyes were tender on her pale face. "While you're struggling with your situation, I'll have them send up something to settle your stomach. How about some strawberry ice cream and melon?"

Her favorite things. She hadn't realized that he knew. She nodded slowly.

"And some hot tea."

"The caffeine…"

"Cold milk," he amended, smiling.

She nodded again.

He picked up the phone, punched room service and gave the order. Then he went to his suitcase and pulled out one of his nice, clean shirts and laid it on the bed within reach. "I don't wear pajamas," he said. "But that will make you decent when room service comes."

"How about you?" she asked uncomfortably.

He gave her a rueful look. "No guts?" he chided. "Don't want to be seen with a naked man, even if you're married to him?"

She flushed.

"And you were calling me a prude." He got up, tossed the towel onto a chair and pulled on his slacks.

"Better?" he asked when he'd fastened the belt in place around them.

Better. She stared at him with pure pleasure, her eyes drifting over his broad, hair-covered chest down to his narrow waist and lean hips and long, powerful legs. He even had nice feet. She loved looking at him. But that was going to get her in trouble again so she averted her eyes to the bed.

He knew why. He sat back down with a long, heavy sigh and smoothed his big, warm hand over her bare shoulder. It was cool and damp to the touch. Her face was too pale, and a little pinched.

"Go ahead," he invited. "Look at me. It doesn't matter anymore. I suppose I told you all there was to tell last night. I don't remember too much of what I said, but I'm sure I was eloquent," he added bitterly.

She lifted her eyes warily to meet his. She didn't say anything, but her face was sad and resigned and without life.

He grimaced. "Barrie…"

She burrowed her face into the pillow and gripped it. "Leave me alone," she whispered miserably. "You've had what you wanted, and now you hate me all over again. It's always the same, it's always…!"

He had her up in his arms, close, bruisingly close. His face nuzzled against her soft throat through a cushion of thick wavy dark hair. "I love you," he said hoarsely. "I love you more than my own life! Damn it, isn't that enough?"

It was what he'd said last night, but he was sober now. She wanted so badly to believe it! But she didn't trust him. "You don't want to love me," she whimpered, clinging closer.

He sighed heavily, as if he was letting go of some intolerable burden. "Yes, I do," he said after a minute, and he sounded as if he were defeated. "I want you and our baby. I want to hold you in the darkness and make love to you in the light. I want to kiss away the tears and share the good times. But I'm afraid."

"Not you," she whispered, smoothing the hair at his nape. "You're strong. You don't feel fear."

"Only with you," he confessed. "Only *for* you. I never had a weakness until you came along." His arms contracted. "Barrie," he said hesitantly, "if I lose you, I can't live."

Her heart jumped. "But, you aren't going to lose me!" she said. "I'm not going to walk out on you. I didn't really mean it. I thought you wanted me to go."

"No!" he said huskily, lifting his head. He looked worried. Really worried. He traced her soft cheek. "That's not what I meant. I meant that I could lose you when you have the baby."

"Oh, for heaven's sake…!" she exclaimed, stunned.

"Women do still die in childbirth," he muttered uncomfortably. "My mother…did."

She was learning things about him that she would never have dared ask, that she hadn't known at all. She searched his eyes slowly. "Your mother died in childbirth?"

He nodded. "She was pregnant. She didn't want to be, and she tried to have an abortion, but my father found out and made so many threats about cutting off the money she liked to spend that she gave in. She went into labor and something went wrong. They were out of the country, on a trip she'd insisted on taking even that late in her pregnancy. The only medical care available was at a small clinic. It was primitive, there was only an intern there at the time." He sighed heavily. "And she died. He loved her, just as he'd loved your mother. It took him years to get over it. He felt responsible. So would I, if something happened to you."

Her fingers twined around his. It was humbling to realize that he loved her that much. He didn't want to get rid of her at all. He'd gone to the other extreme. He was terrified that he might lose her.

"I'm strong and healthy and I want this baby. I

want to live," she said softly. "I couldn't leave you, Dawson," she added firmly. "Not even to die."

He looked down into her wet eyes and his face was strained, taut. He looked so stoic and immovable that it shocked her when he traced her mouth with a finger that wasn't quite steady.

"You'll learn to trust me one day," she said softly. "You'll learn that I'll never deliberately hurt you, or belittle you, or try to make you feel less of a man because you care about me. And our child will never be mocked or spoken to with sarcasm."

His hand stilled on her face. "And you won't leave me," he added with a bitter laugh.

She smiled. "No," she said gently. "I have no life without you." She took his hand and slid it under the cover to lie on the soft, bare swell of her stomach. "I'm pregnant," she said. "We have a future to think about."

"A future." His hand flattened where she'd placed it. "I guess I'm going to have to stop living on bad memories. It's hard."

"The first step is to look ahead," she told him.

He shrugged. He began to smile. "I suppose so. How far ahead?"

"To the nearest department store," she said with

sudden humor. "I can't spend the day without underwear!"

He pursed his lips and for the first time since she'd arrived, he looked relaxed. "Why not?" he asked. "Are you sore already?"

She stared up at him uncertainly.

"Are you?" he persisted, and his hand moved insinuatingly. "Because I want to make love again."

"It's broad daylight," she said pointedly.

His broad shoulders rose and fell. "It was broad daylight a few minutes ago," he reminded her. His face was solemn. "You kept your eyes closed. Don't do it again. I won't make any more snide remarks about it. I'm sorry I made you ashamed of wanting to watch something so beautiful."

She wasn't sure how to take this apparent change in him. She searched his pale eyes, but there were no more secrets there. He wasn't hiding anything from her.

"I know," he murmured ruefully. "You don't quite trust me, either, do you? But we'll work it out."

"Can we?"

The knock at the door interrupted what he might have replied. Barrie quickly slipped on his shirt and buttoned it while he let the waiter in, signed the bill and handed the man a tip on his way out.

"Take that off," he murmured when he'd locked the door again, nodding toward the shirt.

"I won't," she replied.

"Yes, you will. But we'll let your stomach get settled first," he conceded. He picked up the small dish of homemade strawberry ice cream and sat down on the bed, lifting half a spoonful of it to her lips.

She was surprised, and looked it.

"You fed me when I had the wreck," he reminded her. "Turnabout is fair play."

"I'm not injured," she replied.

"Yes, you are," he said quietly. "Right here." He put the spoon into the hand holding the small crystal goblet and with his free hand he touched her soft breast through the shirt. He felt its immediate response, but he didn't follow up. He lifted the spoon again to her mouth. "Come on," he coaxed. "It's good for you."

She had a sudden picture of Dawson with a toddler, smiling just like that, coaxing food into a stubborn small mouth and she managed a watery smile as she took the ice cream.

"What are you thinking about?" he wondered.

"A little mouth that doesn't want medicine or spinach," she said quietly.

He understood her. His eyes darkened, but not with irritation. He took a long breath and held another spoonful of ice cream to her mouth. Eventually he smiled. "I guess I might as well learn to change diapers and give bottles, too," he mused softly.

"No bottles," she said firmly. "I want to nurse the baby."

His hand stilled halfway to her mouth. He searched her eyes, shocked at the way the statement aroused him.

She could tell from the tautness of his body and the darkness of his eyes, from the faint flush across his cheekbones what he was feeling. She felt her own breath catch in her throat. She could see him in her mind, watching as she nursed the baby...

"You're trembling," he said unsteadily.

She moved restlessly and a self-conscious laugh passed her lips. "I was thinking about you watching me with the baby," she said shyly.

"So was I."

She let her eyes fall to his hard mouth, tracing the firm, sensuous lips. She caught her breath as a wave of hunger swept over her body.

"Good God." He whispered it reverently. He set the goblet aside carefully, because his hands weren't steady. And when he turned back to her, she had the shirt open. She pulled the edges aside, red-faced and taut, and watched him as he looked at her hard-tipped breasts.

Shakily her hands went to his face and she tugged as she lay back on the bed, dragging his mouth to her breast. He suckled her hungrily, fiercely, pressing her back into the mattress with a pressure that was nothing short of headlong passion.

"I'm too hungry. I'll hurt you," he warned off, as he gave in to it.

"No, you won't." She drew him closer, arching under the heat of his mouth. "Oh, Dawson, Dawson, it's the sweetest sensation!"

"You taste of rose petals," he growled. "God, baby, I don't think I can hold it back this time!"

"It's all right," she repeated breathlessly. Her hands helped him get the fabric out of the way. She moved, fixed her body to his, helped him, guided him into sudden, stark intimacy. It should have been uncomfortable, but it wasn't.

He felt the ease of his possession and lifted his head to look into her eyes as he levered above her, softly kissing her. "I'll let you…watch," he whispered, shivering as he felt the tension building in his loins. "I don't mind. I love you. I love you, Barrie. I love you…!"

She watched his face tauten, the flush that spread to his cheekbones as his eyes began to dilate and the movements quickened into fierce, stark passion. He lifted his chest away from hers, his teeth clenched.

"Look…" he managed before he lost control completely.

Barrie went with him every step of the way. She lifted to the harsh, violent demand of his body for the satisfaction hers could give it. She opened herself to him, clung to him, as he cried out in great shuddering waves of ecstasy. Then she, too, cried out as her body exploded into pulsing shards of exquisite color, burning so high from the pleasure that the whole world spun around her.

His voice came from far away and it sounded concerned. "What's wrong?" he asked gently.

"I'm fine." Her eyes opened, wide and green and dazed with satiation. She traced the whorls of damp hair on his body. "I said the most shocking things," she said uncomfortably.

"Wicked, sexy things," he agreed. He smiled. "I loved it."

"Oh."

He bent and brushed his mouth over hers. "There shouldn't be limits on what we can say to each other in bed, what we can do to each other," he explained gently. "I won't ever tease you about it."

"That goes for me, too." She searched his face. "I watched you," she whispered.

He flushed. "I know. I wanted you to."

She smiled self-consciously. "But I couldn't really see much," she added shyly. "Stars were exploding in my head."

"That was mutual. And I couldn't really watch you for the same reason." He chuckled. "I suppose I'm losing my inhibitions, bit by bit."

"Maybe I am, too." She pushed back his damp hair gently. "I like being intimate with you. I like feeling you as close as you can get to me."

He drew her close and rolled onto his back with a long sigh. "Intimacy is new to me," he revealed.

She hit him. "Ha! Where did you learn all those things you did to me this morning? No!" She put her hand over his mouth. "No, don't you tell me, I don't want to know!"

He lifted her onto his chest and searched her angry eyes. "Yes, you do. And I'm going to tell you. I learned them with a succession of carefully chosen, emotionally alienated one-night stands. I learned them without any real participation except for a superficial one. No, don't look away. You're going to hear this." He turned her flushed face back to his. "I have had sex. But until I touched your body, I had never made love. That day on the floor of my study was the first time in my life that I gave myself completely and deliberately to a woman."

She felt hot all over. "You didn't like it."

"I loved it," he said harshly. "I didn't like having you watch it happen to me. I didn't trust you enough." His eyes calmed. "I'm sorry about that, too. We made a baby in the heat of that exquisite loving. I'm sorry I didn't make it a happier memory for you...for both of us."

"I'm not sorry about the baby. Or about watching you," she whispered wickedly. "It was the most exciting, embarrassing thing that ever happened to me."

"I can imagine," he replied quietly. "Because I kept my head long enough to watch you this morning, all through it." His eyes began to glitter. "And now I understand why you had to see my face."

She eased down over his chest and kissed him softly, nibbling his upper lip. "Because you wanted to see the love in my eyes," she whispered.

"Yes. And that's what you saw in mine, above and beyond the desire that was making me helpless, wasn't it?" he asked.

She nodded after a minute. "I didn't recognize it at the time. But, yes it was. It was the love that you didn't want me to see," she realized.

"Yes." He traced her nose with his forefinger, enjoying the lazy intimacy of their sprawled bodies. "I could have saved myself the trouble. You honestly didn't know how I felt until I told you in a drunken rage last night, did you?"

"No, I didn't," she confessed with a chuckle. "And it knocked me so hard that I got on the first plane out here to see if you meant it." She glared at him. "I thought you didn't want me here."

"I was surprised that you came, and delighted at being spared the trouble of flying right out to Sheridan to show you how completely I'd given in to my own feelings toward you."

Her body lay open to his eyes, and he looked at her

with wonder and obvious pleasure. "I couldn't even do this before, did you realize it?" he asked quietly. "It made me feel uncomfortable to see you nude, to look at you openly."

"Then we're making progress."

"Apparently." He traced around her taut nipple and frowned as he saw the blue veins that had become prominent. The nipple was darker, bigger. His hand slid down to her belly and he felt the thickening of her waist. A smile pulled up the corners of his mouth. "My, how you're changing."

She smiled complacently. "I'll be as big as a pumpkin by Christmas."

His hand caressed her. "So you will." He bent and drew his mouth gently over her stomach. "We didn't hurt him, did we?"

"Babies are very tough," she said. She knew he was remembering the one they'd lost. "This one wants to be born," she added. "I feel it."

He lifted his head and searched her eyes. He didn't say anything for a long time. His eyes said all too much.

"You won't lose me," she said deliberately. "I promise you won't."

He took a long breath and let it out. "Okay."

She sat up, pressing close to him. "I'm sleepy."

"So am I. I think a nap might be a good idea. Do you feel better?"

"Oh, yes. I didn't ever feel bad," she murmured with a chuckle. "On the contrary, I felt entirely too good."

He drew her closer. "So did I. I wonder if two people ever achieved such a high at the same time?"

"Should we call the people at the record book and ask…ouch!"

He'd pinched her behind. He chuckled at her outraged expression. "I'll repent. Come here. We'll sleep for a while."

"A while?" she teased as he ensconced them together under the sheet.

His hand cradled her belly. "Life can be sweet after all."

"Hmmm," she murmured drowsily. Her eyes closed. She went to sleep with the sound of Dawson's heart beating softly at her ear.

Twelve

THE phone was ringing off the hook. Barrie opened her eyes, disoriented. The phone was on the bedside table, on the other side of a broad, very hairy chest. She stared at that chest for a moment trying to get her bearings. Then she remembered where she was.

She smiled as she poked him in the ribs and felt him jump, coming awake immediately.

"Phone," she said, shaking him gently.

He reached over and picked it up. "Rutherford," he said shortly. He was quiet for a moment, then he rolled over onto his back and ran a hand through his hair. "What?" he said then. He made a rough sound in his throat. "Hell, no! Good God, man, what sort of person do you think I am?" There was the sound of hurried, apologetic conversation. "You'd damn well better apologize, if you expect me to stay here again or book my people in for another conference. You didn't? Well, that's no excuse. Yes, I should think you are! Very well." He slammed the receiver down and then started laughing.

"What was that all about?" she asked curiously.

He rolled onto his side to prop on his elbow and look down at her. "It seems that the prestige of the hotel was briefly lowered when one of the guests threw a woman's jeans and tank top and very skimpy underwear out of a window. Naturally I had no idea why they should suspect me of... Stop that!" He flicked her cheek with a long forefinger when she started laughing. "You have no idea who did it, either. Remember that. I spend a lot of time here when I travel, and I do want to come back again."

"I still can't believe you threw my clothes out the window!"

He grinned. "It seemed the best way to keep you from leaving." He lifted the sheet and looked at her with eyes as appreciative as any artist's. He shook his head. "God almighty," he breathed. "I've never seen anything so beautiful."

She grinned back. "Lecher."

He drew her against him and held her close with a long, lazy sigh as his legs tangled softly with hers. "Sore?"

"Very."

"So am I," he confessed, chuckling at her expression. "Men aren't made of iron, you know."

"No kidding!"

His arms tightened. "I suppose we'll have beautiful memories for the next few days, at least."

"Several." She touched the faint cleft in his chin gently. "Dawson, I can't go back to Sheridan naked."

"You can't?"

She hit him.

"All right. I'll go shopping." He grinned wickedly. "How about a maternity dress?"

"I don't even show yet," she scoffed.

"Why waste time wearing normal clothes until you do?" he wanted to know. "A man has his pride, Barrie. I'm rather anxious to show off what I've accomplished in such a short time."

Her eyebrows lifted. "*I'm* an accomplishment?!"

"By God, you are," he said huskily. "The most wonderful accomplishment of my life, you and this baby. I must have a guardian angel sitting on my shoulder."

She slid her arms around his neck and reached over to kiss him lazily. "Then so must I, I guess, because you're certainly my most wonderful accomplishment."

He searched her loving eyes with pride and a lingering sense of wonder. "I'm sorry it took me so long to deal with the past," he said. "I wish I'd told you when you were fifteen that I was going to love you obsessively when you were old enough."

Her eyes twinkled. "Did you know so long ago?"

"Part of me must have," he replied, and he was serious as he searched her green eyes. "I was violent about you from the very beginning."

"And I never even suspected why," she agreed. She smoothed her hand over his thick gold hair, tracing the wave that fell onto his broad forehead. "What would have become of us if you hadn't dragged me back to Sheridan to act as chaperone for you and Leslie Holton?"

"I'd have found another excuse to get you home."

"Excuse?"

"I've been managing flirtatious women for a lot longer than five years, honey," he said with a deliberate grin.

"You said you were desperate to get that land!"

"I was desperate to get *you* home," he replied lazily. "There's another tract of land on the north end of the property that's just become available, and I bought it before Powell Long even had time to get a bid in. I didn't need Leslie's tract anymore. Of course, she didn't know that. Neither did you."

"I'm in awe of you," she said, aghast.

He lifted a rakish eyebrow. "That's just right. A woman should always be in awe of her husband."

"And a man in awe of his wife," she returned pertly.

He grinned. "I'm in awe of you, all right."

"Good. I'll do my best to keep you that way."

He stretched drowsily and drew her close. "We can sleep a bit longer. Then we should go home."

"I didn't leave labels in any of my clothes," she pointed out. "The ones you threw out the window, I mean. There's no way they could identify you as the mystery lingerie tosser."

"That's not why I want to go home. It's been just about six weeks, hasn't it? And despite the home pregnancy test, I want proof. I want something I can take up on the roof and wave at people."

She nuzzled her cheek against his chest. "You'll get it," she promised.

And he did. The doctor confirmed not only that Barrie was pregnant, but that she was disgustingly healthy and should be over her morning sickness in no time.

As she and Dawson settled down in Sheridan, she thought back over the long, lonely years they'd been apart and how wonderful it was to have their future settled so comfortably.

Dawson was still sensitive to teasing just at first, but as he and Barrie grew together he became less defensive, more caring, more tender. Over the months of her pregnancy, Dawson was as attentive and supportive as any prospective mother could wish her husband to be. He seemed to have finally dealt with all his fears, even the one of childbirth.

But the most incredible revelation Barrie was ever to see was the look on Dawson's handsome face when he held their twin sons in his arms. As he looked into her worn, delighted face, the expression in his pale green eyes would last her the rest of her life. He looked as if he had the world in that small hospital room. And, as he later told Barrie, he did!

★ ★ ★ ★ ★

Heart of Ice

One

"You didn't!" Katriane wailed at her best friend. "Not at Christmas!"

Ada looked pained and visibly shrank an inch. "Now, Kati…" she began placatingly, using the nickname she'd given the taller girl years ago. "It's a huge apartment. Absolutely huge. And you and I will be going to parties all over town, and there's the charity ball at the Thomsons'… It will be all right, you'll see. You won't even notice that he's here."

"I'll notice," Kati said shortly. Her reddish gold hair blazed in the ceiling light, and her brown eyes glared.

"It's our first Christmas without Mother," Ada tried again. "He's got nobody but me."

"You could go to the ranch for Christmas," Kati suggested, hating the idea even as she said it.

"And leave you here alone? What kind of friend would I be then?"

"The kind who isn't sticking me with her horrible brother during my one holiday a year!" came the hot reply. "I worked myself to the bone, researching that last book. I was taking a rest between contractual obligations...just Christmas. How can I rest with Egan here?"

"He'll be fun to have around," Ada suggested softly.

"We'll kill each other!" Kati groaned. "Ada, why do you hate me? You know Egan and I don't get along. We've never gotten along. For heaven's sake, I can't live under the same roof with your brother until Christmas! Have you forgotten what happened last time?"

Ada cleared her throat. "Look, you planned to set that next big historical in Wyoming, didn't you, on a ranch? Who knows more about ranching in Wyoming than Egan? You could look upon it as an educational experience—research."

Kati just glared.

"Deep down," Ada observed, "you both probably really like each other. It's just that you can't...admit it."

"Deep down," her friend replied, "I hate him. Hate. As in to dislike intensely. As in to obsessively dislike."

"That's splitting an infinitive," Ada pointed out.

"You are an actress, not an educator" came the sharp retort.

Ada sighed, looking small and dark and vulnerable. So unlike her elder brother. "I may wind up being an educator, at this rate," she said. "I am sort of between jobs."

"You'll get another one," Kati said easily. "I've never seen anyone with your talent. You got rave reviews in your last play."

"Well, maybe something will turn up. But, getting back to Egan…"

"Must we?" Kati groaned. She turned, worrying the thick waves of her long hair irritatedly. "Don't do this to me, Ada. Uninvite him."

"I can't. He's already on the way."

"Now?" Kati looked hunted. She threw up her hands. "First my royalty check gets lost in the mail when my car payment is due. Now I wind up with a sidewinder to spend Christmas with…."

"He's my brother," Ada said in a small voice. "He has no one. Not even a girlfriend."

"Egan?" Two eyebrows went straight up. "Egan always has a girlfriend. He's never between women."

"He is right now."

"Did he go broke?" Kati asked with a sweet smile.

"Now, Kati, he's not that bad to look at."

That was true enough. Egan had a body most men would envy. But his face was definitely not handsome. It was craggy and rough and uncompromising. Just like Egan. She could see those glittering silver eyes in her sleep sometimes, haunting her, accusing her—the way they had that last time. She hated Egan because he'd misjudged her so terribly. And because he'd never admitted it. Not then, or since.

She folded her arms over her breasts with a curt sigh. "Well, Mary Savage used to think he was Mr. America," she conceded.

Ada eyed her closely. "He's just a poor, lonely old cattleman. He can't help it if women fall all over him."

"Egan Winthrop, poor? Lonely?" Kati pursed her lips. "The old part sounds about right, though."

"He's thirty-four," Ada reminded her. "Hardly in his dotage."

"Sounds ancient to me," Kati murmured, staring out over the jeweled night skyline of Manhattan.

"We're both twenty-five." Ada laughed. "Nine years isn't so much."

"Fudge." She leaned her head against the cold windowpane. "He hates me, Ada," she said after a minute, and felt the chill all up and down her body. "He'll start a fight as sure as there's a sun in the sky. He always starts something."

"Yes, I know," Ada confessed. She joined the taller woman at the window. "I don't understand why you set him off. He's usually the soul of chivalry with women."

"I've seen him in action," Kati said quietly. "You don't have to tell me about that silky charm. But it's all surface, Ada. Egan lets nobody close enough to wound."

"For someone who's been around him only a few times in recent years, and under the greatest pressure from me, you seem to know him awfully well," Ada mumbled.

"I know his type," she said shortly. "He's a taker, not a giver."

"Neither one of you ever gives an inch," Ada remarked. She studied her friend closely. "But I had to invite him. He's the only family I have."

Kati sighed, feeling oddly guilty. She hugged the

shorter girl impulsively. "I'm sorry. I'm being ratty and I don't mean to. You're my friend. Of course you can invite your awful brother for Christmas. I'll grit my teeth and go dancing with Jack and pretend I love having him here. Okay?"

"That I'll have to see to believe."

Kati crossed her heart. "Honest."

"Well, since that's settled, how about if we go and get a Christmas tree?" Ada suggested brightly.

Kati laughed. "Super," she said and grabbed up her coat to follow Ada out the door. "And if we get one big enough," she mumbled under her breath, "maybe we can hang Egan from one of the limbs."

They trudged through four tree lots before they found just the right tree. It was a six-foot Scotch pine, full and bushy and perfect for their apartment. They stuffed it into the back of Kati's Thunderbird and carried it home, along with boxes of ornaments and new tinsel to add to their three-year supply in the closet.

Ada went out to get a pizza while Kati tied ribbon through the bright balls and hung them lovingly on the tree. She turned on some Christmas music and tried not to think about Egan. It seemed so long ago that they'd had that horrible blowup....

It had been five years since Kati first set eyes on

Egan Winthrop. She and Ada had met at school, where both were majoring in education. Ada had later switched to drama, and Kati had decided to study English while she broke into the fiction market in a small way. Three years ago, after graduation, they'd taken this apartment together.

Egan and Kati had been at odds almost from the first. Kati got her first glimpse of the tall rancher at school, when she and Ada were named to the college honors society in their junior year. Egan and Mrs. Winthrop had both come. Kati had no relatives, and Ada had quickly included her in family plans for an evening out afterward. Egan hadn't liked that. From the first meeting of eyes, it had been war. He disapproved vehemently of Kati's chosen profession, although he was careful not to let Ada or his mother see just how much he disliked Kati. They'd hardly spoken two words until that fateful summer when Kati had flown out to the ranch with Ada for the Fourth of July.

It had been the first year she'd roomed with Ada, almost three years ago. Ada's mother had been diagnosed with cancer, and the family knew that despite the treatments, it would only be a matter of a year or two before she wouldn't be with them. Everyone had gone to the Wyoming ranch for the July Fourth holidays—including Kati, because Ada refused to leave her alone in New York. Kati's parents were middle-aged when she was born, and had died only a little apart just before she finished high school. She had cousins and uncles and aunts, but none of them would miss her during the July vacation. So, dreading Egan's company, she'd put on a happy face and gone.

She couldn't forget Egan's face when he'd seen her getting off the plane with his sister. He hadn't even bothered to disguise his distaste. Egan had a mistaken view of romance writers' morals and assumed that Kati lived the wildlife of her heroines. It wasn't true, but it seemed to suit him to believe that it was. He gave her a chilly reception, his silvery eyes telling her that he wished she'd stayed in New York.

But his cousin Richard's enthusiastic greeting more than made up for Egan's rudeness. She was hugged and hugged and enthused over, and she ate it up. Richard was just her age, a dark-haired, dark-eyed architect with a bright future and a way with women. If he hadn't been such a delightful flirt, the whole incident might have been avoided. But he had been, and it wasn't.

Richard had taken Kati to the Grand Teton National Park for the day, while Mrs. Winthrop soaked up the attention she was getting from her son and daughter. She was a lot like Ada, a happy, well-adjusted person with a loving disposition. And none of Egan's cynicism. Kati had liked her very much. But she and Richard had felt that Mrs. Winthrop needed some time alone with her children. So they'd driven to the park and hiked and enjoyed the beauty of the mountains rising starkly from the valley, and afterward they'd stopped in Jackson for steaks and a salad.

On the way home, Richard's car had had a flat tire. Richard, being the lovable featherbrain he was, had no spare. In that part of the country on a holiday night, there wasn't a lot of traffic. So they walked back to the ranch—which took until four in the morning.

Egan had been waiting up. He said nothing to Richard, who was so tired that he was hardly able to stand. Richard went inside, leaving all the explanations to Kati.

"You live down to your reputation, don't you?" he asked with a smile that chilled even in memory. "My God, you might have had a little consideration for my mother. She worried."

Kati remembered trying to speak, but he cut her off with a rough curse.

"Don't make it worse by lying," he growled. "We

both know what you are…you with your loose morals and your disgusting books. What you do with my cousin is your business, but I don't want my holidays ruined by someone like you. You're not welcome here any longer. Make some excuse to leave tomorrow."

And he walked away, leaving Kati sick and near tears. She hadn't let them show, she was too proud. And she'd managed to get to bed without waking Ada, who shared a room with her. But the next morning, cold-eyed and hating Egan more than ever, she packed her suitcase, gave some excuse about an unexpected deadline and asked Richard to take her to the airport.

They were on the porch when Egan came out the front door, looking irritated and angry and strangely haggard.

"I'd like to speak to you," he told Kati.

She remembered looking at him as if he were some form of bacteria, her back stiff, her eyes full of hatred.

"Go ahead," she told him.

He glared at Richard, who cleared his throat and mumbled something about getting the car.

"Why didn't you tell me what happened?" he asked.

"Why bother, when you already knew?" she asked in glacial tones.

"I didn't know," he ground out.

"How amazing," she replied calmly. "I thought you knew everything. You seem to have made a hobby out of my life—the fictionalized version, of course."

He looked uncomfortable, but he didn't apologize. "Richard had been drinking. It was four in the morning—"

"We had a very long walk," she told him curtly. "About fifteen or twenty miles. Richard wasn't drunk. He was tired." Her dark eyes glittered up at him. "I didn't like you much before, Mr. Winthrop, but I like you even less now. I'll make a point of keeping out of your vicinity. I wouldn't want to contaminate you."

"Miss James…" he began quietly.

"Goodbye." She brushed past him, suitcase in hand, and got into Richard's car. Ada and Mrs. Winthrop had tried to talk her into staying, but she was adamant about having an unexpected deadline and work pressure. And to this day, only she and that animal in Wyoming really knew why she'd left. Even Richard hadn't been privy to the truth.

That episode had brought the antagonism between Egan and Kati out into the open, and their relationship seemed to go from bad to worse. It was impossible for Kati to stay in the same room with Egan these days.

He'd find an excuse, any excuse, to nick her temper. And she'd always retaliate. Like last year…

Egan had been in town for some kind of conference and had stopped by the apartment to see Ada. Kati had been on her way to a department store in downtown Manhattan to autograph copies of her latest book, *Renegade Lover,* a historical set in eighteenth-century South Carolina. Egan had walked in to find her in her autographing clothes—a burgundy velvet dress cut low in front, and a matching burgundy hat crowned by white feathers. She'd looked like the heroine on the front of her book, and he'd immediately pounced.

"My God, Madame Pompadour," he observed, studying her from his superior height.

She bristled, glaring up at him. "Wrong country," she replied. "But I wouldn't expect you to know that."

His eyebrow jerked. "Why not? Just because I'm in oil and cattle doesn't make me an ignoramus."

"I never said a word, Mr. Winthrop, honey," she replied, batting her long eyelashes at him.

The term of endearment, on reflection, must have been what set him off. His lips curled in an unpleasant smile. "You do look the part, all right," he replied. "You could stand on the street corner and make a nice little nest egg…"

She actually slapped him—and didn't even realize she had until she felt her fingers stinging and saw the red mark along his cheek.

"Damn you!" she breathed, shaking with fury.

His nostrils flared; his eyes narrowed and became frankly dangerous. "Lift your hand to me again, ever," he said in that low, cold tone, "and you'll wish you'd never set eyes on me."

"I already do, Egan Almighty Winthrop! I already do."

"Dress like a tramp and people are going to label you one," he rejoined. His eyes cut away from her with distaste. "I wouldn't be seen in public with you."

"Thank God!" she threw after him, almost jumping up and down with indignation. "I wouldn't want people to think I cared so little about who I was seen with!"

At that moment, luckily, Ada had rushed in from her bedroom to play peacemaker. Without another word, Kati had grabbed up her coat and purse and had run from the apartment, tears rolling down her cheeks. It was a miracle that she managed to get herself back together by the time she reached the department store.

That was the last time she'd seen Egan Winthrop.

And she never wanted to see him again. Oh, why had Ada agreed to let him come, knowing the state of hostility that existed between Egan and her? Why!

She put the last ball on the tree, and was reaching for the little golden angel that would sit atop it when she heard the door open.

It must be Ada with the pizza, of course, and she was starved. She reached up, slender in jeans and a pullover yellow velour sweater, laughing as she put the angel in place. As she moved, she knocked into one of the balls, but caught it just in time to keep it from dropping to the carpet.

"Back already?" she called. "I'm starved to death! Do you want to have it in here by the tree?"

There was a pregnant pause, and she felt eyes watching her. Nervous, she turned—to find herself staring at Egan Winthrop. Her hand clenched at the sight of him—so powerful and dark in his gray vested suit—and the fragile ball shattered under the pressure.

"You little idiot," he muttered, moving forward to force open her hand.

She let him, numb, her eyes falling to the sight of his dark hands under her pale one where blood beaded from a small cut.

"I...wasn't expecting...you," she said nervously.

"Obviously. Do you have some antiseptic?"

"In the bathroom."

He marched her into it and fumbled in the medicine cabinet for antiseptic and a bandage.

"Where's Ada?" he asked as he cleaned the small cut, examined it for shards, and applied the stinging antiseptic.

"Out getting pizza," she muttered.

He glanced up. He'd never been so close to her, and those silver eyes at point-blank range were frightening. So was the warmth of his lean, powerful body and the smell of his musky cologne.

His eyes searched hers quietly, and he didn't smile. That wasn't unusual. She'd only seen him smile at Ada or his mother. He was reserved to the point of inhibition most of the time. A hard man. Cold…

Something wild and frightening dilated her eyes as she met that long, lingering look, and her heart jumped. Her lips parted as she tore her gaze down to the small hand that was visibly trembling in his big ones.

"Nervous, Katriane?" he asked.

"Yes, I'm nervous," she bit off, deciding that a lie would only amuse him. If granite could be amused.

"How long did it take Ada to talk you into this visit?" he asked.

She drew in a heavy breath. "All of a half hour," she said gruffly. "And I still think it's a horrible mistake." She looked up at him defiantly. "I don't want to spoil Christmas for her by fighting with you."

His chin lifted as he studied her. "Then you'll just have to be nice to me, won't you?" he baited. "No snide remarks, no deliberate taunts…"

"Look who's talking about snide remarks!" she returned. "You're the one who does all the attacking!"

"You give as good as you get, don't you?" he asked.

Her lower lip jutted. "It's Christmas."

"Yes, I know." He studied her. "I like presents."

"Is anyone going to give you one?" she asked incredulously.

"Ada," he reminded her.

"Poor demented soul, she loves you," she said, eyeing him.

"Women do, from time to time," he returned.

"Ah, the advantages of wealth," she muttered.

"Do you think I have to pay for it?" he asked with a cold smile. "I suppose a woman who sells it expects everyone to…"

Her hand lifted again, but he caught it this time,

holding it so that she had to either stand on her tip-toes or have her shoulder dislocated.

"Let go!" she panted. "You're hurting!"

"Then stop trying to hit me. Peace on earth, re-member?" he reminded her, oddly calm.

"I'd like to leave you in pieces," she mumbled, glar-ing up at him.

His eyes wandered from her wild, waving red-gold hair down past her full breasts to her small waist, flar-ing hips and long legs. "You've gained a little weight, haven't you?" he asked. "As voluptuous as ever. I sup-pose that appeals to some men."

"Ooooh!" she burst out, infuriated, struggling.

He let her go all at once and pulled a cigarette from his pocket, watching her with amusement as he lit it. "What's the matter? Disappointed because you don't appeal to me?"

"God forbid!"

He shook his head. "You'll have to do better than this if you want to keep a truce with me for the next few days. I can't tolerate hysterical women."

She closed her eyes, willing him to disappear. It didn't work. When she opened them, he was still there. She put away the antiseptic and bandages and went back into the living room, walking stiffly, to clean the debris of the shattered ball from the beige carpet.

"Don't cut yourself," he cautioned, dropping lazily into an armchair with the ashtray he'd found.

"On what, the ball or you?" she asked coldly.

He only laughed, softly, menacingly; and she fumbled with pieces of the ball while he watched her in that catlike, unblinking way of his.

"I thought Ada told me you'd stopped smoking," she remarked when she was finished.

"I did. I only do it now when I'm nervous." He took another long draw, his eyes mocking. "You give me the jitters, honey, didn't you know?"

"Me and the cobalt bomb, maybe," she scoffed. She threw away the debris and ran an irritated hand through her hair. "Do you want me to show you to your room, like a good hostess?" she asked.

"You'd show me to the elevator and press the Down button," he said. "I'll wait for my sister and a warmer welcome."

It was Christmas, and he'd lost his mother, and she hated the surge of sympathy she felt. But knowing he'd toss it right back in her face kept her quiet. She went to the window and stared down at the busy street. "Ada, hurry," she wanted to scream.

"I saw your book advertised on television the other day," he remarked.

She turned around, arms folded defensively over her breasts. "Did you? Imagine, you watching television."

He didn't take her up on that. He crushed out his half-finished cigarette. "It sold out at the local bookstore."

"I'm sure you bought all the copies—to keep your good neighbors from being exposed to it," she chided.

His eyebrows arched. "In fact, I did buy one copy. To read."

She went red from head to toe. The thought of Egan Winthrop reading *Harvest of Passion* made her want to pull a blanket over her head. It was a spicy book with sensuous love scenes, and the way he was looking her over made it obvious what he thought of the book and its author.

"I like historical fiction," he remarked. "Despite having to wade through the obligatory sex to get to it."

She flushed even more and turned away, too tongue-tied to answer him.

"How do you manage to stay on your feet with all that exhaustive research you obviously do?"

She whirled, her eyes blazing. "What do you mean by that?" she burst out.

He laughed softly, predatorily. "You know damned good and well what I mean. How many men does it take?"

The door opened just in time to spare his ears. Ada walked in and her face glowed with joy as she saw her brother. She tossed the pizza onto a chair and ran to him, to be swung up in his powerful arms and warmly kissed.

"You get prettier all the time," he said, laughing, and the radiance in his face made Kati feel like mourning. She'd never bring that look to Egan's face.

"And you get handsomer. I'm so glad you could come," Ada said genuinely.

"I'm glad someone is," he murmured, glancing at Kati's flushed, furious face.

Ada looked past him, and her own expression sobered. "Ooops," she murmured.

Kati swallowed her hostility. She wouldn't ruin Christmas for Ada—she wouldn't. She pinned a smile to her lips. "It's all right. He patched me up when I cut my hand. We're friends now. Aren't we?" she asked, grinding her teeth together as she looked at Egan.

"Of course," he agreed. "Bosom pals." He stared at her breasts.

Ada grabbed him by the hand and half dragged him from the room. "Let me show you where to put your suitcase, Egan!" she said hastily.

Kati went to take the pizza into the kitchen and make coffee. And counted to ten, five times.

Two

"How have you been?" Ada asked her brother as the three of them sat around the dining room table munching pizza and drinking coffee.

"All right," he said, staring at the thick brown mug that held his coffee. "You?"

Ada smiled. "Busy. It's helped me not to dwell on Mama."

"She's better off," Egan reminded her quietly.

"I know," Ada said, her eyes misting. She shook her head and grabbed another slice of pizza. "Anybody else for seconds? There are three slices left."

"No more for me," Kati said with a speaking glance at Egan. "I wouldn't want to get more voluptuous than I already am."

"Nonsense," blissfully ignorant Ada said. "You're just right. Come on, have another slice."

"Go ahead," Egan taunted.

"Why don't you?" she dared him.

"And be accused of making a pig of myself?" he asked innocently.

"Who would be so unkind as to call you a pig?" Kati asked sweetly.

"Excuse me," Ada interrupted, "but it's Christmas. Remember? Holly and mistletoe…?"

"Mistletoe?" Egan glanced at Kati. "I'd rather drink poison."

Kati glared back. "Ditto!"

"Let's watch television!" Ada suggested frantically. She dragged Kati into the living room and quickly turned on the set. "I'll clear the table, you keep Egan company."

"You're just afraid of getting caught in the line of fire," Egan accused as his sister rushed out of the room.

But Ada only grinned.

Egan eased down into the armchair he'd vacated earlier and stared at Kati. He'd taken off his coat and vest. Both sleeves of his white silk shirt were rolled up and the neck was opened. He didn't wear an undershirt, and through the thin fabric, bronzed muscles and a thick pelt of hair were visible. That bothered Kati, so she carefully avoided looking at him while the evening news blared into the room.

"How's the writing going?" Egan asked conversationally.

"Just fine, thanks," she replied tersely.

"What are you working on now?"

She swallowed. Ada had finked on her, she just knew it. "Actually, I'm doing another historical."

"On...?"

She cleared her throat. "Wyoming," she mumbled.

"Pardon?" he said.

Her lips made a thin line. "Wyoming," she said louder.

"A historical novel about Wyoming. Well, well. Have you done a lot of research?"

She glanced at him warily. "What do you mean?"

"Historical research," he clarified, watching her. "You'll have to mention cattle-ranching, I imagine?"

"Yes," she said grudgingly.

"Know a lot about it, city lady?" he mocked.

She glared at him. "I have been on a ranch before."

"Sure. Mine." He stared down his nose at her. "I

don't imagine they have many big cattle ranches in Charleston?"

"We have good people," she returned. "With excellent breeding."

His eyebrows arched. "Yes, I know. My grandmother came from Charleston."

She glared at him. "Did she, really?" she asked coldly.

He smiled softly. "She used to say it was where the Cooper and Ashley Rivers meet to form the Atlantic Ocean."

She'd heard that, too, in her childhood in the South Carolina coastal city, and she had to bite her lip to keep from smiling with him.

"She was a redhead too," he continued, waiting for a reaction.

"My hair isn't red," she said, predictably.

"Honey and fox fur," he argued, studying it.

She flushed. That sounded oddly poetic, and she didn't like the tingle that ran through her.

She glanced at her watch. "Excuse me. I'd better put on a dress."

Egan glared. "Going somewhere?"

"Yes." She left him sitting there and went to find

Ada. "Jack's coming for me at seven," she reminded her friend. "I've got to get dressed."

"I'll go keep Egan company. Lucky you, to have a boyfriend in town." She sighed. "Mine's out at sea again."

"Marshal will be back before you know it," she murmured. "Sorry to run out on you."

"You'll have fun." Ada grinned. "And so will I. I like Egan. He's great company, even if he is my brother."

Well, there was no accounting for taste. She couldn't imagine Egan being great company; but then, she wasn't related to him.

She put on a black cocktail dress and wore red accessories with it. Her eyes gave her a critical appraisal. She'd twirled her hair into a French twist and added a rhinestone clip to it, and she liked that elegant touch. She grinned. Jack would love it.

Jack Asher was a reporter for the *New York Times,* a political specialist who was intelligent and fun to be with. She'd known him for several months and enjoyed the occasional date. But things were still platonic between them because she didn't want any serious involvement. She was too independent.

The doorbell rang while she was putting a gloss of

lipstick on her mouth, and she knew Ada would get it. Then she remembered that Egan was here, and rushed to finish her makeup and get back into the living room.

Jack was standing in the hall, talking to Ada while Egan glared at him.

He cleared his throat when Kati joined him, looking painfully relieved to see her.

"Hi, lady," he said with a forced smile. He was blond and blue-eyed and not nearly as tall or muscular as Egan. Sadly enough, in comparison he looked rather pale and dull.

But Kati grinned at him and Ada as if nothing were wrong. "Had to find my purse, but I'm ready when you are. Night, Ada. Egan," she added, glancing his way.

Egan didn't answer her. He was still glaring at Jack with those dangerous narrowed eyes glittering like new silver while he smoked a cigarette. Ada made a frantic gesture, but he ignored her too.

"Night, Ada," Jack said uncomfortably and led Kati out the door.

"Whew!" Jack exclaimed when they reached the elevator. "I felt like an insect on a mounting board for a second there! Is he always like that? So…uncommunicative?"

"Egan?" Kati's eyes flared up. "He's usually much too communicative, if you want to know. We're stuck with him for Christmas. Ada invited him because their mother died earlier this year. She felt sorry for him, being all alone."

"I should think so," Jack said gently. "Well, maybe he talks to her." He frowned. "You don't like him, do you?"

"Not one bit. Not one ounce. Not a fraction." She glared at the elevator.

Jack laughed. "Poor guy!"

"Not Egan. Feel sorry for me. I'm stuck in the same apartment with him for the next week," she moaned.

"You could always move in with me," he offered.

She laughed, knowing the offer was a joke, just as it always had been. They didn't have that kind of relationship. "Sure I could. I can just see your mother's face."

"Mother likes you." He chuckled. "She'd probably be thrilled."

"Only because she could pump me for my latest plots." She grinned. "You know she's one of my biggest fans. Sweet lady."

"She's sweet, all right. Well, where do you want to go? The Rainbow Grill?"

"Let's save it for a special time. How about the Crawdaddy Room at the Roosevelt?"

He chuckled. "You just like to go there because of their pudding," he accused.

"Well, it is terribly good," she reminded him.

"I know, I know. Actually, I like it myself."

She followed him into the elevator and put the confrontation with Egan right out of her mind.

A prime rib, a salad, several hard rolls and a dish of delicious whiskey pudding later, Kati sat drinking her coffee and looking around at the elegant surroundings. She saw a nice little old German waiter she knew from other visits there and smiled at him.

"Friend of yours?" Jack asked her.

"Everybody's my friend." She laughed. "I used to think New York was a cold place until I moved here. New Yorkers just take a little getting to know. And then they're family. I love New York," she sang softly, and laughed again.

"So do I. Of course, I was born here," he added. He looked out the window at the traffic. "I've got tickets for a modern ballet, if you'd like to use them."

"Could we?"

"Sure. Come on."

He led her down a side street where a group of people were just entering what looked like an old warehouse. But inside, it was a theater, complete with live orchestra and lighted stage and some of the most beautiful modern ballet she'd ever watched. The people onstage looked like living art: the women delicate and pink in their tulle and satin, the men vigorous and athletic and vibrant. Kati had been going to the ballet for years, but this was something special.

Afterward, they went to a lounge and drank piña coladas and danced to the hazy music of a combo until the wee hours.

"That was fun," she told Jack when he brought her home. "We'll have to do it again."

"Indeed we will. I'm sorry I didn't think of the ballet weeks ago. I get free tickets."

"Let's do it again even if we have to pay for them," she said, laughing.

"Suits me. I'll call you in a few days. Looks like I may have to fly down to Washington on that latest scandal."

"Call me when you get back, okay?"

"Okay. Night, doll." He winked and was gone. He never tried to kiss her or make advances. With them, it was friendship instead of involvement, and she enjoyed his company very much. Jack had been married and his wife had died. He wanted involvement even less than she did and was glad to be going out with someone who wouldn't try to tie him up in wedding paper.

Dreamily, she unlocked the apartment door and stepped inside. She closed the door and leaned back against it, humming a few bars of the classical piece that had accompanied one of the pieces at the ballet.

"Do you usually stay out this late?" Egan asked from the living room. He was standing by the window with a glass of amber liquid that looked like whiskey in his hand.

She stared at him. "I'm twenty-five," she reminded him. "I stay out as late as I like."

He moved toward her slowly, gracefully, his eyes holding hers. "Do you sleep with him?" he asked.

She caught her breath. "Egan, what I do with anyone is my business."

He threw back the rest of his drink and set the glass on a small table in the hall, moving toward her until she felt like backing away.

"How is he?" he asked lazily. Then he caught her

by the shoulders and held her in front of him, looking down quietly, holding her eyes.

Her lips parted as she met that intimidating stare.
"Egan…"

His nostrils flared. The lean fingers that were holding her tightened. "Is he white all over?" he continued in a faintly mocking tone. "City boy."

"Well, there aren't many cattle to herd up here,"
she said tautly.

"No, but there are too damn many people. You
can't walk two steps without running into someone,"
he complained. "I couldn't survive here. Answer me.
Do you sleep with him?"

"That's non—" she began.

"Tell me anyway. Does he do all those things to
you that you write about in your books?" he asked,
studying her. "Does he 'strip you slowly,' so that you
can 'feel every brush of his fingers…'"

"Egan!" She reached up to press her fingers against
his lips, stopping the words as she flushed deeply.

He hadn't expected the touch of her fingers. He
caught them and held them as if he wasn't sure what
to do with them. His eyes held hers.

"Is that the kind of man you like, Katriane Desiree?" he asked, using the full name that she didn't know he'd ever heard.

She watched him helplessly. "I like…writers," she managed.

"Do you?" He brought her hand to his mouth and kissed its warm palm softly, slowly. His teeth nipped at her slender forefinger.

"Egan," she breathed nervously.

He took the tip of her finger into his mouth and she felt his tongue touching it. "Afraid?" he murmured. "Don't they say that a woman is instinctively afraid of a man she thinks can conquer her?"

She wrenched away from him like an animal at bay. "You'd be lucky!" she whispered. Was that her voice, shaking like that?

He stared at her, sliding his hands into his pockets, and the action stretched the fabric of his trousers tight over the powerful muscles of his legs. "So would you," he returned. "But one of these days I might give you a thrill, honey. God knows, my taste never ran to virgins. And an experienced woman is…exciting."

She felt the blood rush into her face, and she whirled on her heel. If she stayed there one second longer, she'd hit him! Boy, wouldn't the joke be on him if he ever tried to take her to bed! Egan, in bed…

She went straight into the bathroom, oblivious that she might wake Ada, and ran herself a calming cool shower.

Three

KATI didn't sleep. Every time she closed her eyes, she could feel the hard grip of Egan's fingers on her shoulders, the touch of his mouth against her hand. She hated him, she thought miserably; that was why she couldn't sleep.

She dragged into the kitchen just after daylight, with her long gold and beige striped caftan flowing lovingly over the soft curves of her body. Her tousled hair fell in glorious disarray around her shoulders, and her dark eyes were even darker with drowsiness.

With a long yawn, she filled the coffeepot and started it, then she reached for the skillet and bacon and turned on the stove. She was leaning back against the refrigerator with a carton of eggs in one hand and butter in the other when the kitchen door opened and Egan came in, dressed in nothing but a pair of tan slacks.

He stopped at the sight of her and stared. She did some staring of her own. He was just as she'd imagined him without that shirt—sexy as all get-out. Bronzed muscles rippled as he closed the kitchen door; a mat of hair on his chest curled down obviously below his belt buckle. His arms looked much more powerful without a concealing shirt, as did his shoulders. She could hardly drag her eyes away.

"I thought I'd fix myself a cup of coffee," he said quietly.

"I just put some on," she said.

He cocked an eyebrow. "Does that mean I have to wait until you drink your potful before I can make mine?" he asked.

She glared at him. So much for truces. "There's a nice little coffee shop down on the corner," she suggested with a venomous smile.

"I'll tell Ada you're being unkind to me," he threatened. "Remember Ada? My sister? The one whose Christmas you said you didn't want to spoil?"

She drew in a calming breath. "Do excuse me, Mr.

Winthrop," she said formally. "Wouldn't you like to sit down? I'll pour you a cup of coffee."

"Not until you tell me where you plan to pour it," he returned.

"Don't tempt me." She reached up into the cabinet for a second cup and saucer while he pulled out a chair and straddled it.

When she turned back with the filled cups, she found him watching her. It unnerved her when he did that, and she spilled coffee into one of the saucers before she could set them on the table.

"Couldn't you sleep?" he asked pleasantly.

"No," she said. "I'm not used to sleeping late. I'm at my best early in the morning."

A slow, wicked smile touched his hard mouth. "Most of us are," he commented.

It didn't necessarily mean what she thought it did, but she couldn't help the blush. And that increased her embarrassment, because he laughed.

"Will you stop!" she burst out, glaring at him. "Oh, why don't you take your coffee and go back to bed?"

"I'm hungry. Don't I smell bacon?"

"Bacon!" She jumped up and turned it just in time. It was a nice golden brown.

"Going to scramble some eggs, too?" he asked.

"No, I thought I'd let you drink yours raw," she said.

He only laughed, sipping his coffee. "I like raw oysters, but I draw the line at raw eggs. Want me to make the toast?"

"You can cook?"

"Don't get insulting." He stood up and found the bread and butter. "Get me a pan and some cinnamon and sugar."

She stared at him.

"Cinnamon," he said patiently. "It's a spice—"

"I know what it is," she grumbled, finding it. "Here. And I've lined the pan with aluminum foil. It's all yours."

"Ungrateful woman," he muttered as he mixed the cinnamon and sugar in the shaker she'd handed him. He buttered the bread and spread the mixture on top.

"Don't get conceited just because you can make cinnamon toast," she mumbled. "After all, it isn't exactly duckling *a l'orange*."

"I'd like to see you cook that," he remarked.

She cleared her throat. "Well, I could if I had a recipe."

"So could I." He turned on the oven and slid the toast in under the broiler. "Get me a pot holder."

"Who was your personal slave yesterday?" she asked, tossing him a quilted pot holder.

"I liked the old days," he murmured, glancing at her. "When men hunted and women cooked and had kids."

"Drudgery," she scoffed. "Women were little more than free labor...."

"Cosseted and protected and worried over and loved to death," he continued, staring down at her. "Now they're overbearing, pushy, impossible to get along with and wilder than bucks."

"Look who's talking about being wild!" she burst out.

He stared down his nose at her. "I'm a man."

She drew in a breath and let it out, and her eyes involuntarily ran over him.

"No argument?" he asked.

She turned away. "Your toast's burning."

He took it out—nicely browned and smelling sweet and delicate—and put it on a plate while she scrambled eggs.

"I like mine fried, honey," he commented.

"Okay. There's a frying pan, grease is in the cabinet. If you're too good to eat my scrambled eggs, you can mutilate your own any way you like."

He chuckled softly, an odd sound that she'd never heard, and she turned to look up at him.

"Firecracker," he murmured, his eyes narrow and searching. "Are you like that in bed?"

She jerked her eyes away and concentrated on the eggs. "Wouldn't you like to get dressed before we eat?"

It was a mistake. A horrible mistake. Because then he knew what she hadn't admitted since he walked into the room. That, stripped to the waist, he bothered her.

The arrogant beast knew it, all right. He moved lazily until he was standing just behind her...so close that she felt him and smelled him and wanted nothing more out of life than to turn around and slide her hands all over that broad chest.

His hands caught her waist, making her jump, and eased her back against him so that she could feel the warm, hard muscles of his chest and stomach against her back. The caftan was paper-thin, and it was like standing naked in his arms.

She felt his fingers move to her hips, caressingly, and her hand trembled as it stirred the eggs to keep them from burning.

"Egan, don't," she whispered shakily.

His breath was warm and rough in her hair, because the top of her head only came to his chin. The fingers holding her hips contracted, and she felt the tips of them on her flat stomach like a brand.

"Put down that damned spoon and turn around," he said in a tone she didn't recognize.

She was shaking like a leaf, and God only knew what would have happened. But noisy footsteps sounded outside the kitchen door, and an equally noisy yawn followed it. Egan let go of her and moved away just as Ada walked in.

"There you are!" she said brightly, watching her best friend stir eggs. "I'm starved!"

"It'll be on the table in two shakes," Kati promised, hoping her voice didn't sound as shaky as it felt. Damn Egan!

"I'd better get dressed," Egan commented, winking at Ada as he went past her. "I think I bother somebody like this."

Kati made an unforgivable comment under her breath as he left the room.

"At it again, I see," Ada sighed wearily.

"He started it," Kati said through her teeth. "I didn't ask him to walk in here naked."

"What?" Ada blinked.

Kati looked at her friend with a pained expression. "Oh, God, isn't he beautiful?" she whispered with genuine feeling.

Ada chuckled gleefully. "Well, I always thought so, even if he is my brother. But isn't that something of a strange admission for you to make?"

"It slipped out. Just forget it." She dished up the eggs. "I think I'd better put something on too."

"Don't be long," Ada cautioned. "The eggs will congeal."

"I'll hurry."

She ran for her bedroom and closed the door just as Egan opened his. A minute's grace! She got into her jeans, blue T-shirt and shoes, and barely stopped to run a brush through her hair. She hoped it would be a short week. She hadn't expected Egan to have this kind of effect on her. In all the years she'd known him, he'd never even tried to make a pass at her. Now, in less than two days, he'd made more impact on her guarded emotions than any other man had in all her twenty-five years. She was going to have to get a hold on herself. She didn't know what kind of game Egan had in mind, but she wasn't playing.

He was wearing a brown velour pullover when she came back, one that emphasized his dark hair and complexion and the hard muscles she'd already seen.

"We left a little for you," Egan commented as she sat down. He pushed aside his empty plate and poured himself another cup of coffee from the hot plate on the table.

"How kind of you," she said pleasantly. She held up her cup and Egan filled it, studying her far too closely.

"What does your boyfriend do for a living?" he asked unexpectedly.

"Jack isn't my boyfriend," she said. "He's a man I date. And he's a political reporter for the *New York Times.*"

He leaned back in his chair while Ada bit her lower lip and looked apprehensive.

"Is he really?" Egan asked. "He doesn't look like he gets much exercise. A little overweight, wouldn't you say?"

She glared at him. "He works very hard."

He only laughed, and sipped his coffee. "If I took him home with me, I could break him in one day."

"You could break the devil in one day," Kati said, exasperated. "What business is it of yours who I date?"

"Now, that's a good question," he replied. His eyes narrowed, and there was a smile she didn't understand on his chiseled lips. "Maybe I feel sorry for the poor man. He does know what you do for a living, doesn't he? Must be hell on him, having everything he does to you turn up in a book...."

"Egan." Ada groaned, hiding her face in her hands.

"You overbearing, unspeakable, mean-tempered..." Kati began in a low tone. She threw her napkin down onto the table and stood up.

"You sure got up on the wrong side of the bed," Egan commented. "Here I am a guest in your apartment—"

"I'd sooner invite a cobra to breakfast!" she burst out.

"You should have," he murmured, glancing at the plate he'd just emptied. "He might have enjoyed burned eggs and half-raw bacon."

She tried to speak, couldn't, and just stormed out of the room.

She left the apartment before Ada could get out of the kitchen, and wandered around the streets shivering in her thin jacket for an hour before she gave up and went back. It was too cold for pride, anyway. All she'd accomplished was to let Egan see how unreasonably she reacted to his prodding. She'd just have to grit her teeth, for Ada's sake.

Egan was nowhere in sight when she got back, and Ada looked apologetic and worn.

"I don't understand him, I just don't," Ada groaned. "Oh, Kati, I'm sorry. If I'd realized how bad things were between you, I'd never have invited him."

Kati was generous enough not to remind her friend that she'd tried to warn her. She sat down on the sofa with a hard sigh.

"I'll manage. Where is he?" she added darkly.

"Gone to spend the day with some girlfriend of his," Ada said absently. "He said he might not be back until late."

Why that simple statement should make her feel murderous, Kati didn't know. But something gnawed inside her at the thought of Egan with another woman.

"I wonder how much he had to bribe her?" she asked nastily.

"Shame on you," Ada said.

But Kati didn't apologize. And she didn't dwell on her confused emotions, either. She wanted no complications in her life, especially with someone like Egan Winthrop.

She and Ada went shopping later in the day and ate out at a little Italian restaurant just down the street from their apartment. They watched television and eventually went to bed. And Egan didn't come back. Not that night. Not until the next morning.

Kati was sitting on the living room floor with pages littering the area around her. They were galleys of her latest book, which had come that morning by special messenger, and she was going over them. Ada was at auditions for a new play, hoping to be home by lunch if she didn't get held up at the theater during tryouts. That was a laugh. Most of the time, it took hours. Despite the appointments the hopefuls were given, something always went wrong. Ada had never gotten back when she thought she would, and Kati was dreading Egan's arrival. She felt wild when she thought of his not coming in at all, and angry because she didn't understand why. She didn't even *like* the man, for God's sake!

There was a loud knock at the door an hour later, and when she opened it, Egan was standing there looking faintly amused and as immaculate as when he'd left. Still in the same clothes, of course....

She glared at him. "Lose your key?" she asked.

"I thought I'd better not use it, in case you were... entertaining," he said.

She let him in, slammed the door and went back to her comfortable sprawl on the floor.

"Coffee's hot if you want some," she said icily. "I'm busy reading."

"Don't let me interrupt you. I thought I'd have a quick shower and change clothes. I've got a lunch date."

Why, oh, why did she feel like smashing plates? She frowned and concentrated on what she was doing. Minutes later, he was back, dressed in a navy blue pinstripe suit with a white silk shirt and a blue and burgundy tie. He looked regal. Sexy. Unbelievably handsome for such an ugly man. If he was dressing like that in the middle of the day, he must be on his way to the Waldorf, she thought. And God only knew with whom.

"Ada didn't worry, did she?" he asked, checking his watch.

"Oh, no. She's used to people staying out all night," she lied deliberately, lifting her eyes. It shocked her, the flash of reaction in his face before it was quickly erased.

His eyes ran over her: the gray slacks and burgundy silk blouse she was wearing, her feet hose-clad and without shoes. Her hair was loose, and flowed in waves of reddish gold silk down her shoulders; her face was rosy and full of life.

His scrutiny made her nervous, and she dropped her eyes back to the page she was reading.

He moved closer and suddenly bent to pick up a page. His eyebrows rose as he read, and a slow smile touched his mouth.

"You do put your heart into it, don't you?" he murmured.

She reached up and took the page out of his hands, glancing at it. She blushed and tucked it under what she was reading. Why did he have to pick up *that* page? she groaned inwardly.

"Is that what you like with a man?" he continued maddeningly, his hands in his pockets, his eyes intent. "I've never done it in a bathtub, but I suppose—"

"Will you please go away?" she groaned, letting her hair fall over her eyes. "I don't care where you've done it, or with whom, just please go eat your lunch and leave me to my sordid occupation."

"I suppose I'd better. Stockbrokers sure as hell don't have time to waste."

She looked up as he turned to leave. "Stockbroker?" she murmured incredulously.

He glanced down at her from his formidable height with an expression she couldn't decipher. "I'm a businessman," he reminded her. "I do have the odd investment to look after."

"Yes, I know," she said quickly. "I just thought—"

"That because I was out all night, it was with a woman—and that I was meeting her for a leisurely lunch?" he suggested in a menacing tone.

She turned back to her work, trying to ignore him. It wasn't easy when he loomed over her that way.

"The reasons I stayed away might shock you, city girl," he said after a minute.

"I don't doubt it for a minute," she muttered.

"And that wasn't what I meant. It might have something to do with you."

The careless remark brought her eyes up, and he held them relentlessly for so long that she felt currents singing through her body.

"I didn't expect you to start trembling the minute I put my hands on you," he said in a harsh undertone. "Not after all these years. We've been enemies."

"We still are," she said in what she hoped was a convincing tone, while humiliation stuck like bile in her throat.

"Dead right," he said coldly. "And it's going to stay that way. I don't want complications during this holiday."

"Ditto," she said curtly. "And don't go around flattering your ego too much, Egan," she added. "I was half asleep at the time!"

His darkened eyes searched hers in the stillness that followed, and she was aware of him in a way she'd never been aware of a man before. Of his height and strength, of the devastating effect he had on her senses.

"Saving your pride, Kati?" he asked quietly.

She studied her long fingernails. "I like my life as it is," she said. "I'm on the go too much for relationships of any kind. And what you'd have in mind...!" she began.

"Now who's flattering their ego?" he asked shortly, glaring down at her. "My God, I don't mind experience in my women, but I draw the line at promiscuity!"

She scrambled to her feet and was ready to swing when the dark look on his face worked some kind of witchcraft and left her standing helplessly with her fists clenched.

"You slapped me once and got away with it," he said quietly. "If you do it again now, we'll wind up in bed together."

She felt her body tremble at the words. "No," she bit off.

"Yes." His chest rose and fell heavily, and his eyes cut into hers. "Don't you realize that the way we react to each other is like flint and steel? All it would take is a kiss. Just that. And we'd burn each other alive. I've known that from the very beginning."

She hadn't, and the thought of Egan as a lover made her face burn. She had to smother a gasp as she turned away with her arms folded protectively around her slender body.

"Don't worry. You're safe, city girl," he said in a mocking tone. "I'm not that desperate. Just don't push me too far."

She couldn't even face what he was insinuating. Egan was the enemy. He was going to stay that way too, if she had to bite her tongue in two. She stared blankly out the window.

"And it's Ada that's auditioning for acting jobs," he commented sarcastically. "Playing innocent?"

She didn't have to play, but he'd never believe it. He'd just shocked her to her nylon-clad feet, and she was lost for words. It was a little frightening to be threatened with a man's bed, just for provoking him. She hadn't been aware that she *was* provoking him until now. Which automatically led to her asking why she did it, and that was frightening as well.

"Kati," he called softly.

She stiffened. "Will your stockbroker wait?" she asked quietly.

He frowned at her stiff back. "What the hell's the matter with you?"

"You threaten me with sex and then ask me what's wrong?" she burst out, staring at him nervously over one shoulder.

He blinked, as if she'd shocked him. "It wasn't a threat."

She flushed and walked away.

"Will you stop doing your Lady Innocent act and look at me?" he growled.

She walked into her bedroom and slammed the door. On an afterthought, she locked it, too. There was a string of unprintable curses from the vicinity of the living room before the front door slammed violently and the room became quiet.

It wasn't going to be possible to stay in the same apartment with Egan after this, she thought miserably. She'd just have to check into a hotel until he left. Having to put up with his incessant verbal aggression was bad enough; but when he started threatening to make it physical, that was the end. The very end.

The conceited beast—to accuse her of being so vulnerable that she'd jump into his bed at the first opportunity. She groaned as she recalled the touch of his hands on her hips, the wild tremors that had run through her untried body. She gritted her teeth. She'd have to get away from him. Because what if he did that again? The real problem was telling Ada she was leaving without spoiling the poor girl's Christmas.

Four

KATI had half her clothes in her suitcase by the time Ada came home from her tryout. She still hadn't decided what she was going to do, beyond checking into a hotel down the street. She knew for certain that she couldn't take one more night of Egan.

"What are you doing?" Ada asked hesitantly, pausing in the doorway of Kati's room.

"Cleaning out my drawers," came the terse reply.

Ada cleared her throat. "Where are you taking what was in them?"

"To a hotel."

Ada leaned back against the doorjamb wearily. "Egan came home."

"How did you ever guess?" Kati asked pleasantly. She closed the lid of the suitcase.

"You're adults," Ada argued. "Surely you should be able to get along just during Christmas holidays? Peace on earth?"

"There is no peace where your brother is," Kati said vehemently. She tossed back a strand of hair and glared across the room. "I find it no less than miraculous that he can get people to work for him at all!"

The other woman sighed. "Amazingly enough, most of the hands have been with him for years. He has hardly any turnover." She glanced at Kati. "And he gets along wonderfully with women, as a rule. Polite, courteous, attentive—"

"We are talking about the same man?" Kati had to ask. "The big ugly one who's been staying here for two days and one night?"

Ada shook her head, laughing. "Oh, Kati. Kati." She moved out into the hall. "You win. I'll pack, too. We'll let Egan have the apartment and we'll both go to a hotel."

"Now hold on," Kati protested. "It's Christmas, and he's your brother, and the whole point of asking him here—"

"Was not to ruin your Christmas, believe it or not,"

Ada said gently. "You're like a sister to me. How can I let you leave alone?"

Kati bit her lower lip and stared helplessly at the suitcase. She didn't know what to do anymore.

"Maybe if you pretend he's not here?" Ada suggested softly.

Kati looked up. "He won't let me. He keeps making horrible remarks, he says…" Her face flushed, and she couldn't meet the curious look in her friend's eyes. "He has this strange idea about where I get material for my books."

"Suppose I talk to him?"

"That would make it worse." She moved the suitcase aside and sat down heavily. "I'll stay. I can't come between the two of you, not at Christmas."

"You're a doll." Ada grinned.

"I wish I were. Maybe then he'd let me alone," came the muttered reply.

"Just treat him like someone you've never met before," Ada suggested.

"That's an idea."

"Anything's worth trying once."

"Yes. Where do you keep the arsenic?"

"Shame on you! It's Christmas!"

"All right, I'm easy," Kati agreed. "Where's the holly stake?"

Ada threw up her hands and left the room.

It was late that evening when Egan came in, looking disheveled and out of sorts. He glared at Kati as if every ill in the world could be laid at her feet.

"We, uh, saved you some supper, Egan," Ada said.

"I'm not hungry," he returned gruffly, but his eyes still didn't leave Kati.

"I'll bring you some coffee," Kati said pleasantly and with a polite smile.

Egan stared after her blankly. "Concussion?" he asked Ada.

Ada laughed, going to help her friend in the kitchen.

"It's working," she whispered as they filled a tray. "He thinks you're sick."

"When hasn't he?" Kati muttered. She sliced some pound cake, added some dessert plates, forks and napkins to their coffee service, and carried the loaded tray into the living room.

Egan was sprawled in the big armchair that he'd appropriated since his arrival. He glared up from its depths as Kati put the tray down on the coffee table.

"I said I wasn't hungry," he repeated.

"Oh, the cake isn't for you," Kati said sweetly. "It's for Ada and me."

That seemed to make him worse. He sat up and took the cup of black coffee Kati poured him, sipping it. He seemed to brighten all at once. "Too weak," he said, staring at her.

She ignored the challenge. "Is it?" She tasted hers. "Yes," she lied, "it certainly is. I'll make some more."

"Don't bother," he returned curtly, leaning back with the cup and saucer held on the palm of one large, lean hand. "It'll do."

She nibbled at her cake and idly watched television. The program they had chosen was a romantic comedy about detectives.

"Isn't he dashing?" Ada sighed as the leading man came into view.

"Oh, rather," Kati said theatrically. "So handsome." She glanced at Egan with a lifted eyebrow.

Egan glanced back at her with hard eyes. But he didn't say a word.

"Did you settle that business with our stockbroker?" Ada asked when the commercial came on.

"Yes," Egan replied curtly. He finished his coffee and stood up. "I think I'll get some sleep. It's been a trying day. Good night." He walked out without a word to Kati.

"It's barely nine," Ada murmured, scowling after him. "Egan never goes to bed this early."

"Maybe it's his conscience bothering him," Kati suggested. "About the abominable way he's been treating me?"

"Dream on, my best friend" came the sighing reply.

The phone rang and Ada dragged herself over to answer it, brightening when she heard the caller. "It's Marshal!" she whispered to Kati.

Kati grinned. Ada's boyfriend had been away for several weeks, and the joy of homecoming was in her eyes. She moved the phone into the hall while Kati finished watching television.

"He wants us to double up tomorrow night at the Rainbow Grill. Want to ask Jack?" Ada asked.

"I'd love to, but Jack's still out of town. How about Friday night?"

"Fine! I'll make sure it's okay with Marshal."

"You'll make sure what's okay?" Egan asked, stopping in the doorway with his tie in his hand and his shirt unbuttoned over his broad chest.

"A date, Friday night," Ada volunteered. "Want to come along? I've got a super girlfriend—"

"I can get my own women," he said with a tilt of his mouth. "Friday? I'll ask Jennie. What time?"

Kati's heart sank, and it showed in her eyes. Egan happened to look her way; he smiled with pure malice.

"What's the matter, honey, will I cramp your style if I come along?" he asked her.

Kati remembered almost too late the role she'd chosen to play. Polite hostess. No personalities. No hostilities. Christmas. Good cheer.

She gritted her teeth. "You're welcome, of course," she said with a frozen smile.

Egan's heavy eyebrows lifted. "My God, get a doctor," he told Ada.

Kati smiled even brighter. "Now, I think I'll say good-night, too. I have this headache…"

"But it's only nine," Ada wailed. "Don't both of you go to bed and leave me alone."

"Don't you want peace and quiet?" Egan asked his sister.

Ada glanced from one to the other of them and sighed. "Well, I think I'll come, too. I need my beauty sleep, I guess."

"Some of us might benefit from it," Kati muttered, glaring up at Egan.

He chuckled softly. "Think I'm ugly?"

She flushed. Her eyes involuntarily ran over the craggy contours, the broken nose, the hard, cruel mouth. For some odd reason, she couldn't quite look away. His eyes caught and held hers, and they stood staring at each other in a silence that blazed with new tensions.

"Excuse me," Ada murmured, trying to hide a grin as she edged past Kati's frozen form and into her own bedroom. "Good night!"

Egan's chest was rising and falling roughly as he stared down at Kati. "Do you?" he asked in an odd tone.

She swallowed. Her throat felt as if it were full of cactus. Her lips parted, and Egan watched them hungrily. She realized all at once that he hadn't just been making threats earlier in the day. He wanted her!

"I...I'm tired," she managed, starting to move.

One long, hard arm came out, barring her path. "I wasn't threatening you this afternoon," he said tautly. "I was telling you how it would be. You can't be blind enough not to see how we are with each other, Kati," he added half under his breath.

She moved gingerly away from that long arm. "I... have a boyfriend...whom I like very much," she said shakily.

He eased forward, just enough to let her feel the warm strength of his body, the heat of his breath against her reddish gold hair. "Liking isn't enough."

Her eyes came up to meet his. "Isn't it?"

His fingertips touched her throat like a breath, feeling its silky texture, stroking it sensuously. "You smell of roses," he said in a husky whisper.

Her fingers caught his, trembling coldly against their warm strength as she tried to lift them away from her throat.

He caught her hand and moved it to his chest—easing it under the fabric and against thick hair and warm muscle—and her breath jerked in her throat. He felt as solid as a wall, and the wiry pelt of hair tickled her fingers as he flattened them against him. His expensive cologne filled her nostrils, drowning her in its masculine scent.

"Forgotten what to do, Kati?" he murmured roughly. "Shall I refresh your memory?"

She lifted her eyes dazedly to his, and they were wide and curious as they met his glittering gaze.

His head bent so that his hard face filled the world. "'She tore his shirt out of the way,'" he quoted huskily, "'and ran her fingers, trembling, over his hard, male…'!"

"No!" Recognizing the passage, she flushed hotly. Immediately, she dragged her hand away and shrank from him as if he'd burned her.

He laughed, but there was an odd sound to it, and his eyes blazed as she reached behind her for the door-knob to her room.

"Doesn't your reporter friend like having you do that to him?" he asked huskily. "Or does he prefer what comes later?"

She whirled on a sob, pushing open the door. She started to slam it, but he caught it with a powerful hand and she couldn't budge it.

"I hate you," she breathed shakily, frantic that Ada might hear them.

"So you keep telling me," he replied. "You're the one with no scruples, honey, so stop flying at me when I throw them back at you."

"I'm not what you think I am," she cried.

"No kidding?" he murmured insolently, letting his eyes punctuate the insult.

"You go to hell, you ugly cowboy!" she said furiously.

He studied her flushed face and black eyes amusedly. "Ada used to talk about her sweet-tempered, easygoing friend. Before I ever met you, I imagined a retiring little violet. You were a shock, honey."

"What do you think you were?" she returned.

He laughed softly. "No woman's ever pulled the wool over my eyes. It didn't take reading your books to tell me what kind of woman you were. All I had to do was watch you in action."

"The car broke down," she reminded him. "Richard and I had to walk for miles...!"

"Aren't you tired of lying about it? I told you," he added, letting his eyes narrow sensuously, "experienced women turn me on."

"Then why don't you go out and find the friend you spent the night with?" she retorted hotly.

His eyebrows went up and he grinned. "Did that bother you?"

She brought her heel down hard on his instep, without warning; and while he was off balance, she slammed the door and locked it.

"Kati!" he growled furiously.

"Go ahead, break it down!" she dared him. "I'll be screaming out the window until the police come!"

There was a muffled curse; a door opening; Ada's voice, almost hysterical; and Egan's, angry but conciliatory. Minutes later, two doors slammed almost simultaneously. With an angry sigh, Kati started stripping off her clothes and heading toward the shower. She was furious enough not to mind that the water was ice-cold.

Five

EGAN was gone, blessedly, when Kati woke up late the next morning. Jack called to say he was back in town and asked Kati out for dinner. Grateful for the respite, she was waiting for him on pins and needles at six that afternoon.

Ada had been sympathetic about her brother's strange behavior, adding that he had a sore foot and it served him right. It was the first time Kati ever heard Ada say anything against Egan.

"Do you think I'm scandalous?" Kati asked unexpectedly when she and Jack were relaxing over coffee after a satisfying steak.

He stared at her. "You?"

"Because I write what I write," she added. "It's important."

"No, I don't think you're scandalous," he said honestly and smiled. "I think you're extremely talented, and your books are a joy to read."

"You don't think I lead a wild life?"

He only laughed. "No, I don't. What's wrong? Are you getting unpleasant letters again?"

"Oh, no. It's..." She sighed and propped her chin on her hand. "It's Egan."

"Please, don't spoil a perfect evening," he said with a restless movement. "He has a glare that could stop a clock."

"Tell me about it," she muttered. "He's giving me fits about what I write."

"Doesn't he realize the difference between fiction and fact?"

"Not if he doesn't want to," she said with a short laugh. "Egan makes up his rules as he goes along. He's a law unto himself out West."

"I got that idea, all right." He studied her sad face and reached out impulsively to pat her hand. "He'll leave after Christmas," he said bracingly.

"Roll on, New Year," she murmured, and sighed as she sipped her coffee.

They went dancing after dinner, and for a while Kati forgot all her troubles. She drew interested glances in the black dress she was wearing. It had a peasant bodice with a full, swirling skirt, and left her creamy shoulders bare. With her hair in a high coiffure, and a minimum of makeup, she wore the designer gown with a flair.

She felt on top of the world, until she went into the apartment and found Egan waiting in the hall.

"Where's lover boy?" he asked, glaring past her at the closed door. "Doesn't he come in for a nightcap?"

He was wearing a dress shirt rolled up to the elbows and half unbuttoned in front, with his black slacks. Obviously, he hadn't spent the evening at home, either, and his proprietary air irritated Kati even more. She was still fuming from last night.

"He doesn't wear a nightcap," she said with sweet venom, "and I don't lend mine."

His chin lifted at an arrogant angle and he looked at her long and hard, his dark eyes narrowing on her bare shoulders.

Self-conscious with him, she hunched her shoulders so that the elastic top came back into place, demurely covering everything south of her collarbone.

"Shy of me?" he asked quietly, moving forward.

She felt like running. Where was Ada, for heaven's sake? She couldn't get past him to her room to save her life, and she knew it.

"Where's Ada?" she asked quickly.

"In her room, talking to Marshal," he said. "Why? You're a big girl, now; you don't need protecting, do you?"

Oh, yes, she did, but obviously she couldn't count on her best friend tonight.

She felt the impact of his rough, warm hands—with a sense of fatalism. Her body jerked under the sensation as he deliberately began to slide the fabric away from her shoulders and down.

"Isn't this how you had it?" he breathed, bending. His chest rose and fell roughly, and she drowned in the warmth of his body.

"Egan…" she began.

"Don't talk. Stand still." His mouth smoothed over her shoulder, leaving a fiery wake. His fingers held her upper arms, digging in as his teeth nipped slowly, tenderly at the silken flesh.

"Don't," she moaned, eyes closed, throat arching as if it invited him—begged him—to do what he pleased.

"You want it," he whispered huskily. "So do I.

Desperately…!" She felt his tongue and the edge of his teeth as he moved over the warm expanse of her shoulders and her collarbone in a silence blazing with promise.

His breath sounded oddly jerky as he drew her body against him. "You taste like the sweetest kind of candy," he said under his breath, and his fingers were hurting, but she was too shaken to care. "Baby," he whispered, his mouth growing urgent now as it found her throat, the underside of her chin. His hands moved up to catch in her hair, careless of its neat bun, as he bent her head back and lifted it toward his hard, parted lips. "Baby, you make me ache…!"

His mouth was poised just above hers, and at that moment she'd have given him that and anything else he wanted. But before he could lower his head, the sound of a door being opened shattered the hot silence.

"Oh, damn," Egan ground out. His fingers bruised her, and his eyes were blazing as he pushed her away and turned as if he were blinded by his own passion—a frustrated passion like of which was making her tremble.

"Marshal's sick of the sea, but they won't let him come home," Ada sighed, oblivious to the wild undercurrents around her. "Why couldn't I find myself a man instead of a sailor? Hi, Kati. Have a good time?"

"Sure," Kati said, smiling through a haze of unsatisfied longing. She glanced toward Egan and saw his eyes, and she flushed wildly. Her eyes went to his mouth and back up; and he muttered something terrible under his breath and slammed into his room without even the pretense of courtesy.

"What's the matter with him?" Ada asked softly.

"Beats me," her friend replied blandly. "Gosh, I'm tired. We went dancing and my feet are killing me!"

"Well, I hope you don't wear them out before Friday night," Ada laughed. "Sleep well."

"I'll do my best," came the muttered reply, and she went into her room and almost collapsed. He hadn't even kissed her, and she was trembling like a leaf. Heaven only knew what would happen if he ever really made a heavy pass. She couldn't bear to think about it! She went to bed and lay awake half the night brooding, only to wake with a splitting headache the next morning.

Egan brooded all day. He moved restlessly around the apartment, like a man aching for the outdoors. Even Kati felt vaguely sorry for him.

"You'll wear ruts in the carpet," she murmured

after lunch, while Ada was taking her turn at the dishes.

He turned with his hands rammed deep in his pockets and stared at her. "If I do, I'll buy you a new one."

"That wasn't what I meant," she said, trying hard to hold on to her temper. She searched his hard face, but she couldn't quite meet his eyes. "You hate being indoors, don't you?"

"With a passion," he agreed shortly. "I couldn't live like this."

"New York is full of things to see," she suggested. "There's Central Park, and the Statue of Liberty, the Empire State Building—"

"I've already seen them once," he said. "And I've walked the streets. What I want, I'm not going to find out there."

She lifted her eyes and had them trapped.

He moved closer so quickly that she hardly saw him coming before he was towering over her. "I want you," he said, his voice like warm velvet in the sudden silence of the room. "I'm through pretending."

"Well, I don't…I don't want you," she said in a breathless little voice. "I have a boyfriend—"

"No competition whatsoever," he returned. "What

are you afraid of? I'm not brutal in bed. I wouldn't hurt you."

She flushed deeply, and just stopped herself from slapping him. "I liked it better when you hated me," she said angrily, glaring up at him.

His eyes searched hers. "Was it ever that?"

Her lips parted, but before she could find an answer, Ada was through with the dishes and Kati stuck to her like glue until it was time to leave for dinner that evening.

Jack grinned as he saw Kati in her burgundy velvet dress. "What a dish," he murmured. "And I like your hair down like that."

"Thank you. You aren't bad yourself. Jack, you know Marshal," she said, indicating the tall, dark young man beside Ada.

"Sure." Jack extended his hand. "Good to see you again."

"Same here," Marshal replied. He hugged Ada close. "I still love the sea, but sometimes I get a little hungry for the shore."

"I can imagine. Uh, wasn't your brother supposed to join us?" Jack asked Ada with evident reluctance.

"He's meeting us at the Rainbow Grill," Ada said. "And I made reservations in advance."

"Good girl," Jack said. He took Kati's arm. "Well, let's get it over with," he murmured under his breath.

"It will be all right," she promised as Ada and Marshal fell back. "We can have the waiter pour wine over his head if he starts anything."

"You don't think he would?" Jack asked, horrified.

She patted his arm. He wasn't the type for public scenes, although Kati wouldn't have minded dousing Egan any old where at all. "No, I don't," she promised. "Don't worry. Everything will be fine."

She was to remember those words vividly a little later, when Egan joined them at their table overlooking the colorful lights of the city sixty-five floors down. He had on his arm a windblown little blonde who looked and dressed like a woman who loved money, and her first glance at the other women was like a declaration of war.

"So this is Ada," the blonde gushed, heading straight for Kati.

"Wrong woman," Kati said shortly. "That's Ada."

The blonde shrugged, gave a careless smile and turned to greet a highly amused Ada. "So you're Ada. How nice to meet you at last. I've just heard so much about you from Egan. We've known each other for a long time, you know. He calls me every time he gets to New York. I'm a model."

As if that didn't stick out a mile, Kati thought as the blonde sat down near her and almost choked her with expensive perfume.

"Isn't this the most gorgeous place?" the blonde enthused. "I love the atmosphere. And isn't the combo great?"

Kati couldn't say. She hadn't been able to hear them play, or hear their sultry-voiced vocalist sing, for the newcomer. And just as she was wondering how she'd eat because of the perfume, Egan slid into the seat beside her and ruined her appetite completely.

"Jennie Winn, this is Katriane James and her date," Egan volunteered.

Kati glared at him. "Jack Asher," she supplied.

"Nice to meet you, I'm sure," Jennie murmured. "What do you do, Mr. Asher?" she asked Jack and batted her impossibly long eyelashes at him.

He perked up immediately, the turncoat. "I'm a political columnist, for the *Times*," he said.

Jennie beamed. "Are you, really? Oh, I just adore intelligent men."

Kati had to muffle a giggle with her napkin. Really, she was behaving impossibly, but that blonde couldn't be for real!

"Something amuses you, Miss James?" Egan asked with ice in his tone.

She got herself under control. "I got strangled, Mr. Winthrop," she managed.

"On what? The air?"

"Now, Egan, honey," Jennie crooned, glaring past him at Kati. "You just relax, and later I'll take you back to my place and soothe you."

Kati bit almost through her lip to keep from howling. She didn't dare look at Egan—it would have been the very end.

"Jennie, look at the menu," Egan said curtly.

"Whatever you say, sugar."

"I want the beef Wellington," Ada said. "How about you, Kati?"

"Do they serve goose here?" Egan asked under his breath.

"If they do," Kati replied with a venomous smile, "yours is probably sizzling on the grill right now, sugar."

He glared at her and she glared back at him. Sensing disaster, Jack quickly intervened.

"Kati, didn't you want to try that duckling in orange sauce?"

She tore her eyes away from Egan's and smiled across the table. "Yes, I did."

By then the waiter was back, elegant in his white jacket, to take their order. By and large, Kati loved New York waiters. They had a certain flair and grace of manner that set them apart, and they were unfailingly polite and kind.

"I want prime rib," Jennie said nonchalantly. "Rare, honey."

"A woman after my own heart," Egan murmured. "I'll have the same."

Kati wanted to mutter something about barbarism, but she kept her mouth shut with an effort. And when the food came, she was far too involved in savoring every morsel to waste time on Egan Winthrop.

But the coffee and dessert came, eventually, and while Kati toyed with her superb English trifle, Egan leaned back and eyed Jack.

"I read your column on the Washington scandal," he told the younger man.

"Did you?" Jack asked with a polite smile.

"Interesting, about the deficit in the agency's budget," he continued. "Apparently your man was allocating funds on paper that never reached the recipients. The audacity of politicians constantly amazes me, and so does the apathy of the public."

Jack perked up. "Yes. What I can't understand is how he expected to get away with it," he said, forgetting his dessert as he went into the subject.

Egan matched him, thought for thought, and the ensuing conversation fascinated Kati. She listened raptly, along with everyone else at the table except Jennie—who looked frankly bored to death.

"You know a hell of a lot about politics for a rancher, Mr. Winthrop," Jack said finally, on a laugh.

"I took my degree in political science" came the cool reply. "Ranching pretty much chose me, rather than the other way around. When my father died, there was Ada and my mother to look after, and no one else to assume control of the property. There was a lot of it." He shrugged. "The challenge is still there," he added with a smile. "Cattle are a lot like politics, Mr. Asher. Unpredictable, hard to manage and sometimes just plain damned frustrating."

Jack laughed. "I imagine so."

"Oh, can't we stop talking about such boring things?" Jennie asked in a long-suffering tone. "I want to go to the theater, and we've got tickets to that hit musical on Broadway. We'll be late if you talk all night."

Egan gave her a look that would have stopped traffic.

Jennie flushed and cleared her throat. "I mean, whenever you're ready, sugar," she said placatingly.

Kati lifted her chin with faint animosity. She'd have told him where to go, instead of pleading with him like that. He knew it, too. Because he glanced at her and caught the belligerent gleam in her eye, and something wild and heady flashed between them when he smiled at her.

Her lips trembled, and she grabbed her coffee cup like a shield.

"See you later," Egan told them, picking up the tabs. "My treat. I enjoyed the discussion," he told Jack.

Before anyone could thank him, he and Jennie were gone and Jack was shaking his head.

"And I thought he hated me. My God, what a mind. He's wasted out West."

Ada beamed. "He was offered an ambassadorship, did you know?" she asked. "He knows everybody in Washington, right to the top. But he turned it down because of mother and me. Since then, he's given everything to the ranch."

"Not quite everything," Marshal murmured. "His girl was a knockout."

"I'd have liked to knock her out," Kati muttered, flushing at Ada's shocked look. "Well, she must have bathed in perfume; I could hardly breathe," she said defensively.

But Ada only grinned, and Kati hated that knowing look. So she was jealous! She caught her breath. She was jealous? Of Egan? She picked up the untouched wineglass and helped herself.

Egan wasn't home when they finally got back to the apartment, and Kati could just picture him with that sizzling blonde. It made her ache in the oddest way. She took a shower and got ready for bed and then paced and paced around her room.

"Is something bothering you?" Ada asked minutes later, coming in to check on her. It wasn't like Kati to pace. "You're getting to be as bad as Egan about wearing ruts in the carpets."

Kati lifted her shoulders helplessly, grabbing at the ribbon strap that kept sliding off. The green gown was far too big, but she liked its roominess. "I'm just restless."

Ada studied her friend quietly. "He's a man," she said softly.

Kati blushed all the way down her throat and turned away.

"I'm sorry, I shouldn't have said that," Ada said hesitantly. "But, you see, I can't help noticing the way you look at him. And the way he looks back. Normal people don't fight like the two of you do. Anything that explosive has to...well, there has to be something pretty powerful to cause it, don't you see?"

"I hate him," Kati said through her teeth. "That's powerful, all right."

"But you want him."

Kati's eyes closed. "Tomorrow is Christmas," she said. "The day after, he'll go back to Wyoming and I'll go back to my sordid books, and we'll both be better off. There's no future with your brother for any woman, Ada, and you know it." She turned around, her face stiff with control. "He's not the happily-ever-after kind."

Ada looked worried. "He says that, but no man really wants to get married, does he? It kind of takes the right woman."

Kati laughed huskily. "A woman like Jennie. She suits him just fine, doesn't she?" she asked venomously.

Ada shook her head. "She numbs the hurt, that's all. He's a lonely man."

"He got hurt once and never wants to be again, is that how it goes?" Kati asked.

"I don't think Egan can be hurt, Kati," came the soft reply. "He doesn't let anyone close enough. I know less than nothing about his private life. But I think he's more involved with you right now than he's ever been before."

"He's never touched me," she bit off.

"Yes, I know. I didn't mean physically," Ada said. "I mean emotionally. Don't you realize that's why he hits at you so hard?"

"He hits at me because he wants me," she told the other woman bluntly. "He said so. He thinks I'm easy."

Ada looked horrified. "Well, did you tell him the truth?"

"Of course not! I don't owe your horrible brother any explanations— Let him just keep his disgusting image of me!"

Ada frowned slightly. "Kati, he isn't a man to let go of something he sets his mind on. I think you'd better tell him."

"Why bother? He'll be gone day after tomorrow," she repeated.

"Kati—"

"Go to bed and stop worrying about me," Kati said

gently, and hugged her concerned friend. "Egan and I will go on being enemies, because I won't give in and he'll give up. He makes a nice enemy."

"You wouldn't think so if he'd ever really been yours," Ada replied.

"Anyway, we both need our sleep. It will all work out, somehow. Sleep well."

Ada gave up. She smiled as she went out. "You, too."

But Kati didn't. Not until the wee hours of the morning. And Egan still hadn't come home. He was with that blonde, kissing her with that wide, cruel mouth that had tormented hers so sweetly....

Something woke her. She didn't know what. But she felt the light on her eyelids and the coolness of air on her skin, and her dark, drowsy eyes opened slowly.

He was standing beside the bed, wearing nothing but a pair of slacks, with his broad chest sensuously bare and a cup of black coffee in one hand. And he was looking at her in a way that brought her instantly alert and wary; his glittering silver eyes were on fire.

She frowned slightly as she realized that he wasn't looking at her face. Her eyes shifted, and she noticed to her embarrassment that the loose gown had shifted in the night, leaving one perfect breast pink and bare.

Her hand went to jerk the bodice back up.

"No, Kati," he said in a husky undertone, and his eyes went back up to hers. "No. Let it happen."

He moved close, setting the coffee on the table. He dropped smoothly down beside her, and she hated the sudden weakness and hunger of her body as she stared up at him. Her hair was spread out on the pillow like a ragged halo of red and gold, her cheeks rosy with sleep, her eyes sultry. And he looked just as disheveled, just as attractive to her, with his hair tousled, his muscular arms and chest bare and tanned.

His hands went under her head, both of them, and he eased down so that his chest rested on her partially bare one.

She gasped at the unfamiliar sensation of skin on skin, and her eyes dilated under the piercing scrutiny of his.

"I'm going to kiss you until you can't stand up," he said roughly, bending. "My God, I want your mouth…!"

He took it, with a hard, hungry pressure that frightened her. Her slender hands lifted quickly to his shoulders and started to push—until they discovered the rough silkiness of his skin, the power in his bunched muscles. She ran her hands slowly down his arms, feeling the tension of the hard muscles, and back up again, to the hard bone of his shoulders.

Meanwhile, his mouth was slowing, gentling. He lifted it so that it was poised just over hers, and he looked at her for a long moment.

"You don't like it hard, do you?" he asked in a gruff undertone. "I do. Hard and hot and deep. But I'll make the effort, at least."

He bent again, coaxing her lips. It was an education in sensual blackmail. She lay tense under the crush of his torso, feeling each brief, soft contact like a brand. Her lips parted because she couldn't stop them, her breath was coming in short gasps and her heartbeat was shaking her. She hadn't known that women felt like this, despite the novels that bore her name. All her research had come from books, from films and television and bits and pieces of gossip. But what Egan was teaching her bore no resemblance to any of that. He was making her catch fire, and she was moving and reacting in ways that embarrassed her.

"That's more like it, baby," he breathed. "Much, much more like it. Now," he whispered, letting his hands slide down the long, bare line of her back, "now, if you want my mouth, come up and get it."

Blind, aching, she arched up and caught his hard

mouth with hers, kissing him with enough enthusi-asm to make up for her lack of experience at this kind of impassioned caress.

She felt his tongue go into her mouth, and she moaned sharply at the intimacy.

He lifted his dark head as if the sound had shocked him, and looked down at her rigid, anguished features. His free hand tugged slowly at the other strap of her gown and his eyes followed its movement.

"Do you want me, Kati?" he asked quietly. "Shall I get up and lock the door?"

Her mind cleared instantly with the words as she stared up into his blazing eyes. He was asking her a straightforward question, and the answer would have been an unqualified *yes*. But he was offering a quick, temporary merging of bodies that would shame her when her sanity returned. And what in heaven's name would Ada think?

As if he sensed the indecision, his hand stilled on her arm. "Second thoughts?" he asked softly.

"I…can't," she whispered, searching his narrow eyes.

"I understand," he murmured, glancing toward the door with a wry smile. "We're not likely to be alone much longer."

He thought it was because of Ada, and it didn't really matter, did it? Whatever the reason, the result was going to be the same.

He looked back down at her and shifted so that the thick hair on his chest rubbed against her soft bareness; he smiled at her reaction.

"Like it?" he murmured arrogantly, and his hand came up to tease the softness under her arm, making her gasp.

"You have to stop that," she told him in a halting tone.

"Do I?" He bent and brushed his mouth lightly over hers while his fingers toyed with the silken skin and edged slowly, relentlessly, toward the hardening nub that would tell him graphically how he was affecting her.

"Egan?" she whispered in a voice that sounded nothing like her own. Her fingers lifted, catching in his hair, and her body was no longer part of her. It was his, all his, and every inch of it was telling him so.

His nose rubbed against hers as his mouth brushed and lifted; and his fingers made nonsense of principles and morals and self-respect.

"Kati?" he whispered, sensuously. He nipped at her

lower lip. "Kati, take my hand and put it where you want it."

It was the most wildly erotic thing she'd ever heard or dreamed or thought. Helplessly, she reached out for his hand and carried it to the aching peak, and pressed it there.

"Oh, God," she ground out, trembling, her face pressing into his hot throat, her body shuddering with the force of her own hunger.

"Silk," he whispered, his own voice rough and unsteady. "You're silk. So soft, so whisper-soft." His mouth found hers and he kissed her so tenderly that tears welled in her eyes, while his hand cupped and his thumb caressed, and it was the sweetest ache in the world that he caused her.

And then, all at once, the bodice was back in place, the sheet was over her and she was lying, shaking, in the bed as he propped up pillows and set her against them like a big doll.

"Ada," he ground out, handing her the cup with hands that trembled.

Her own trembled, and between them they just got it steady as Ada opened the door without knocking and came in yawning.

"Morning," she murmured, grinning at them. "I've

got breakfast. Bring your coffee with you. Thanks for taking it to her, Egan."

"My pleasure," he murmured, and went out without a backward glance.

"Bad mood again?" Ada grimaced. "I thought it might mellow him up if I sent him in with your coffee. I guess I goofed again. Well, hurry up and dress, I've got something special!" Ada added and went out the door laughing.

Kati sat there with tears suddenly rolling down her cheeks, so shaken and frustrated that she wanted to scream the roof down. She should have listened to Ada, she told herself. Ada had known what she didn't—that Egan was relentless when he wanted something. And what he wanted now was Kati.

Six

ADA had made fresh croissants—so light and flaky they could almost fly—and she had real butter to go on them. But Kati didn't taste anything she ate. She felt as if she were in the throes of some terrible fever, and every time she glanced at Egan, it got worse.

He was wearing a shirt and his boots now, with his dark slacks, and he was still beautiful. Kati could hardly drag her eyes away.

"You must have been late last night," Ada remarked to her brother. "I didn't hear you come in."

"I let myself be talked into going to a party after the show," he muttered. "Damned bunch of freaks. It was like a drugstore in there."

"You left," Ada said with certainty.

"I left. And took Jennie with me. And she screamed bloody murder all the way back to her apartment." He laughed shortly. "Which got her nowhere at all. She knew how I felt about that from the beginning, I never made any secret of it."

"Things are different in the city, Egan," Ada said sadly. "Very different."

His head lifted. "Geography doesn't change what's right and what isn't," he said shortly.

"I know that," Ada agreed. "I don't like it any more than you do, but I don't feel I have the right to dictate to the rest of the world. Kati and I just keep to ourselves."

He glanced at Kati then, his eyes sweeping over her pale jersey blouse and slacks possessively. "Are you an old-fashioned girl in that respect, at least?" he asked, but he didn't sound so sarcastic as usual. "Do you drink and pop pills and smoke pot?"

"I drink cola," she replied. "And I do take aspirin when my head hurts." She watched him with wide eyes. "But I don't think I've ever tried to smoke a pot. What kind of pot did you have in mind?"

He burst out laughing. It changed his entire face, erased some of the hard, leathery lines. He looked faintly attractive, despite that cragginess. "My, my, aren't we sharp this morning?"

She lowered her eyes before he could read the embarrassment in them. "Eating improves my mind."

"I know something better," he remarked just as she lifted the coffee cup to her mouth.

"Don't move!" Ada gasped as hot coffee went all over the table and into Kati's lap. "I'll get a towel!"

She disappeared, and Egan mopped at her legs with a napkin.

"That was damned poor timing on my part," he muttered. "I didn't mean to make you hurt yourself."

She looked up into his silver eyes, astonished. "That's a first," she breathed.

He looked back, his gaze intent. The napkin rested on her thigh. "Did I tell you how lovely you are?" he asked under his breath. "Or what it did to me to touch you like that?"

She felt her lips part helplessly. "Egan, about...what happened—"

"I want it again," he breathed, bending so that his mouth threatened hers. "I want you against me so close that I can feel your heart beating."

"You don't understand," she whispered weakly.

"You want me," he returned huskily. "That's all I need to understand."

It was true, but it wasn't that uncomplicated. And before she could tell him how complicated it really was, Ada was back and the moment was lost. And she was trembling again.

She walked around like a zombie, going through the motions of helping Ada in the kitchen. They invited Marshal and Jack over for dinner the next day, since neither of them was going to try to go home for Christmas. And getting everything ready was a job.

Egan watched television and paced. Finally he got his jacket and hat and went out, and Kati almost collapsed with relief. She ached every time she looked at him, until it was torment to be within seeing distance.

He came in just as the annual Christmas Eve specials were beginning on the public broadcasting station, and he tossed his hat onto the hall table and shed his jacket.

"Culture," he murmured, watching the opera company perform.

"Go ahead, Mr. Winthrop, make some snide remark," Kati dared, feeling young and full of life because her heart leaped up just at the sight of him.

He smiled at her, with no malice at all on his dark face. "I like opera."

"You?"

"Well, there was a report awhile back on music and milk production," he told her, dropping easily into his armchair, "and it seems that cows produce more milk when they're listening to classical music."

Kati smiled. "It must cost a lot."

"What?"

"Having the orchestra come all the way out to the ranch."

"You little torment," he accused and reached out to tug a lock of her long hair playfully.

Ada, watching all this, just stared at them.

"Something wrong?" Egan asked her.

Ada shrugged. "Not a thing in this world, big brother."

He grinned at her. "Where's your boyfriend?"

"Begging for liberty on his knees," she told Egan. She laughed. "If he gets it he'll be here any minute."

"I'd bet on him." He glanced at Kati. "How about yours?" he asked tautly.

"Jack's making calls to his family," she said. "He won't be over until tomorrow."

He didn't say anything, but he settled down in the

chair to watch the programs with an oddly satisfied smile.

Marshal came a few minutes later, and Egan even joined in when they sang Christmas carols during the next program. They drank eggnog and ate cake, and Kati thought she'd never been so happy in her life.

Ada led Marshal under the mistletoe on his way out at midnight and kissed him lovingly, winking at Kati as the two of them moved out into the hallway.

"I'm going to walk Marshal to the elevator," she called back. "Don't wait up."

"Don't fall down the elevator shaft!" Kati called after her.

The door closed on a giggle. Which left Kati alone with Egan and trembling with new and frightening emotions.

He stood up, holding out his hand. She put hers into it unhesitatingly and let him lead her to the mistletoe. His lean, strong hands caught her waist and brought her gently against the length of his hard body.

"I've waited all day for this," he whispered, bending.

She stiffened, but his hands smoothed down over her hips and back and he nudged his face against hers gently.

"I know how you like it, baby," he breathed. "I won't hurt you this time, all right?"

She was beyond answering him. Her body throbbed. Throbbed! It was the most incredible physical reaction she'd ever had in her life, and she couldn't control it.

His mouth opened and hers opened to meet it, inviting the new intimacy, and she drowned in the magic of the long, sweet kiss. She breathed him in, the tangy fragrance of cologne and, closer, the minty hotness of his mouth.

"I want you," he whispered, his voice shaking.

She drew back a little, trying to catch her breath and regain her sanity. It was impossible, but she couldn't even speak. They were simply torturing each other with this kind of thing. But how could she explain it to him?

He rested his forehead on hers and his eyes closed on ragged breaths. Against her hips, his body was making an embarrassing statement about his feelings, and she withdrew just enough to satisfy her modesty.

"Still playing games, Kati? You don't have to put on any acts for me. That virginal withdrawal—"

"Egan, you have to listen to me," she managed, looking up.

"I've got an apartment two streets over," he said on

a harsh breath. "One even Ada doesn't know about. We could be there in fifteen minutes, and she'd never have to know."

Her breath caught in her throat. His eyes were blazing with it, and she knew her own legs were trembling. For one wild second she looked up at him and knew how it would be between them. She could almost feel the length of him without clothes: the silken slide of skin on skin, the aching pleasure of being touched by those lean, expert hands...

"Come with me, Kati," he said unsteadily. "We're just torturing each other. I've got to have you."

"I can't," she ground out. She lowered her chin so that her tormented eyes were on a level with his chest, and her trembling fingers pressed against his warm shirt.

His fingers tautened on her waist, moved to her hips and jerked them into his. "I ache," he whispered. "You know what I'm feeling."

Her eyes closed. She wasn't stupid; she could imagine that it was ten times worse for him than it was for her. But she couldn't undo all the years of conditioning. Flings weren't for her. She had too much conscience.

"I'm sorry," she whispered. "I'm so sorry, Egan, but I can't."

He drew in an angry breath, and she stiffened because she knew he was going to go right through the ceiling. She couldn't even blame him; she should never have let him touch her.

But oddly enough, he didn't say a word. He loosened his grip on her hips, allowing her to move away, and drew her gently into his arms. He held her, his head bending over her, his heartbeat shaking both of them, until his breathing was normal again.

Her hands felt the warm strength of his back even through his shirt, and she loved the protected feeling she got from being close like this. Her eyes closed and, just for a moment, she allowed herself the luxury of giving in completely, of pretending that he loved her.

"I could make you," he whispered at her ear. "I could take the choice away."

"Yes, I know," she agreed softly. Her cheek nuzzled against his chest.

"This kind of passion is a gift," he said quietly. "I could give you pleasure in ways you've never had it with another man. Not because I'm any damned prize in bed, but because we react to each other like dynamite going up."

"I can't," she replied softly. "I want to, but I can't."

His hand smoothed her long hair gently. "Because of him?"

She drew in a steadying breath. She was going to have to tell him, and it wasn't going to be easy.

The door opened, thank God, and Ada walked in, stopping dead when she saw the two of them wrapped in each other's arms.

"Wrestling match?" she guessed. "Who's winning?"

"Mistletoe," Egan murmured, nodding upward. "Damned potent stuff. She's got me on my knees."

"That'll be the day," Ada grinned.

Kati pulled away, and he let her go with obvious reluctance. "And I didn't poison you, either," she murmured, trying to keep it light.

"Didn't you?" he returned, but there was a difference in him now, a strangeness.

"No fighting," Ada said. "It's Christmas day."

"So it is," Egan said. "Where's my present?"

"Not until morning," Ada returned.

"Damn." He looked down at Kati. "I like presents. What did you get me?"

"Not until morning," she echoed Ada.

He lifted an eyebrow. "I hate waiting," he murmured, and only Kati knew what he meant.

"All good things come to him who waits, though," Ada interrupted; and then wondered why Kati blushed and Egan laughed.

The girls went in to bed, but Kati didn't sleep. She wanted Egan. And there was more to it than that. She was beginning to feel something she'd never expected. She thought ahead to the next day, when he'd leave for Wyoming, and the world went black. She couldn't imagine a day going by without the sight of him. Just the sight of him.

She sat straight up in bed and stared at the wall. She hadn't known that it could happen so quickly. Of course, it could be just physical attraction. She did want him very much, and it was the first time she'd wanted any man. She knew nothing about him really, except bits and pieces. So how, she asked herself, could she be in love with him?

"Love," she whispered out loud. She licked her dry lips and put it into words. "I...love...Egan." The sound of it made tingles all the way to her toes, and when she closed her eyes she could feel his mouth on hers; she could taste the minty warmth of his lips. Shivers went all over her like silvery caresses, and she caught her breath.

You have to forget all that, she told herself. Because what Egan wanted was the limited use of her body, to sate his own hunger. And once he'd had it, he'd be off to new conquests. Like Jennie. Her eyes clouded with bridled fury. Jennie! She'd like to rip the girl's hair out.

She lay back down and closed her eyes. Well, that was his kind of woman, anyway. All she had to do was grit her teeth and bear it until he left. Then she could pull her stupid self together and forget him. Her eyes opened. It was over an hour before she could close them in sleep.

Seven

THE thought of the condominium bothered Kati. She couldn't help remembering that Egan had said Ada didn't know about it, which meant he kept it for only one reason. If he was willing to take Kati there, he must have taken other women too. In the cold light of morning, she was glad she'd had the sense to resist him. Egan only wanted her. Someday, with a little luck, there would be a man who'd love her.

But if she was inclined to be cool and collected, Egan wasn't. He watched her covetously when she joined them for breakfast. His silver eyes roamed over the pretty red vest and skirt she was wearing with a long-sleeved white blouse, and he smiled appreciatively.

"Very Christmassy," he murmured.

She smiled as coolly as possible. "Thank you."

She allowed him to seat her, expecting Ada to plop down beside her as usual. But instead, Egan slid into Ada's usual place, so close that his thigh touched hers when he moved.

"I can help," Kati volunteered quickly.

"No," Ada said as she dished up everything and carried it to the table. "Just sit. We'll both have enough to do later."

So she sat, nervously, hating the close contact because she could feel Egan as well as smell the warm, manly fragrance of his body. He was dressed up, too, in a navy pinstripe suit that made him look suave and sophisticated. And all the time she picked at her bacon and eggs, he watched her. It was as if he were launching a campaign, with her as the objective. And it was getting off to a rousing start.

Ada noticed the tension and smiled. Kati flushed at that smile, because she knew her friend's mind so well.

It didn't help that Ada finished early and announced that she just had to have a shower before she dressed.

"Afraid to be alone with me?" Egan teased gently when the door closed behind his sister.

"Oh, yes," she admitted, looking up with fascinated eyes.

His own eyes seemed unusually kind and soft, and he smiled. "Why?" he asked. "Because of last night?"

She lowered her eyes to his smooth chin, his chiseled mouth. She remembered the feel of it with startling clarity.

"Don't hide." He tilted her face back up to his and studied it quietly. "I can wait. At least, until you've had time to break it off with Asher."

So that was what he thought! That was why he'd been so patient last night. He assumed that she was sleeping with Jack and had to end the affair before...

She caught her breath. "But I can't—"

"Yes, you can," he said. "Just tell him how it is. He doesn't seem to be so unreasonable to me. In fact—" he laughed shortly "—he hardly touches you in public. A man who's committed to a woman usually shows a little more warmth."

"I don't like that kind of thing, around people," she murmured.

"Neither do I, for God's sake," he bit off. "But when people get involved, it happens sometimes. A look, a way of touching, a hand that can't let go of another hand—there are signs. You and Asher don't show them."

"He's…very reserved," she returned.

"So are you. Even alone with me." He leaned closer and brushed his mouth over hers like a breath. "Ada won't be gone that long. And then we'll be surrounded by people. And I won't be able to do this to you…."

His hand contracted behind her head, catching her hair, tangling in its fiery depths to press her mouth to his. As if passion were riding him hard, he bit at her closed lips and shocked them into parting. And then she was his. Totally his, as he explored the soft warmth of her mouth expertly, possessively.

When he stopped, her hands were clenched in his thick hair, and she moaned when he lifted his mouth.

"No more, baby," he whispered huskily. "We don't have the luxury of privacy, and I had a hard enough time sleeping last night as it was. A man can only stand so much."

Her eyes opened slowly and she looked up at him drowning in the silver of his eyes. "I didn't mean to tease," she whispered. "It wasn't like that."

"I know that," he replied quietly. "You were with me every step of the way, from the first second I touched you. Circumstances have been the problem.

I need to be alone with you. Completely alone." He drew in a slow breath. "Come back to Wyoming with me, Kati."

Her eyes dilated. "What?"

"You said you had to research that damned book. All right. I'll help you. Fly out with me in the morning, and I'll show you everything you need to know about ranch management."

She studied his hard face. She knew exactly what he was saying: "during the day." His eyes were telling her that he had different plans for the night, and she already knew exactly what *they* were.

"Still afraid?" he asked thoughtfully, watching the expressions change on her young face. "Let's get it out in the open. Why? Do I strike you as a brutal man? Do you think I'd be kinky in bed or something?"

Her face burned and she looked down. "I've never thought about it."

"Liar. You've thought about it every second since yesterday morning, just like I have." He bent his head and kissed her quickly, roughly. "It was just the way I told you it would be. We touched each other and exploded. I wanted you, and it made me rough at first. But it won't be that way anymore. I promise you, Kati. I'll be as tender a lover as you could want."

"You...you never seemed gentle," she said involuntarily. "And you've been so harsh with me...."

He brushed a lock of hair back from her cheek and frowned as he looked down at her. "It's the way you write, damn it," he said. "So...openly."

"Egan, I don't make love with strange men in bathtubs," she said. It was one of the ironies of her life that she could write torrid romances at all. But the writing never embarrassed her. It was as if the characters did what they wanted to, taking over as the words went onto paper. The situations arose from the characterizations, not out of her own personal experience.

He shrugged. "That may be. But no man likes to think he's being used for research."

Her eyes opened wide. Her eyebrows went straight up. "You don't imagine that I...that I'd even consider—" She felt herself puffing up with indignation. "Oh, you monster!"

She jerked up from the table, glaring down at him as she fought tears of pure fury. "What do you think I am, damn you, an exhibitionist? What I write comes out of nowhere! The characters create themselves on paper, and their own motivations produce the love scenes! I do not write from personal experiences with a multitude of lovers!"

"Now, Kati," he began, rising slowly.

"But you just go on thinking whatever you please, Egan," she continued. "You just go right ahead. I don't care. I don't need you at all!"

And she turned, tears in her eyes, and ran from the room, colliding with Ada.

"Hey, what's the matter?" Ada asked gently.

"Ask Dracula!" came the broken reply, and she threw a last accusing glare at Egan before she went into her room and slammed the door.

It was a bad start for the day. And it didn't help that when she got herself together and came back out, Egan had vanished. She'd overreacted, and she was ashamed. But his opinion of her had hurt in unexpected ways and brought home how he considered her widely experienced.

Wouldn't he be shocked, she thought miserably, to know how innocent she was?

In fact, the love scenes in her books were mild compared to those in other genres. They were sensuous, but hardly explicit. That was why she was able to write them. She didn't have to go into a lot of explanations that she'd have to dig out of anatomy books anyway—because she didn't know the first thing about fulfillment, except what she'd learned secondhand.

"Will he be back?" Kati asked miserably when Ada told her that Egan had walked out.

Ada lifted her shoulders helplessly. "I don't know. Things were going so well this morning. What happened?"

"He accused me of doing my own research for the love scenes," she muttered. "In bathtubs with strange men." She hid her face in her hands. "You can't imagine how it hurt to have him think so little of me!"

"Then why not tell him the truth, my dumb friend?" Ada asked. "He doesn't read minds, you know."

"Because..." She clenched her fists and hit the air impotently. "Because," her voice lowered, "the only thing about me that attracts him at all is my 'experience.'"

Ada gaped at her. "You're in love with him," she said half under her breath.

Kati smiled sadly. "Doesn't it show? Hasn't it always shown? Ada, I'd walk over a gas fire just to look at him."

"And I thought you hated him."

"I did. Because he hated me, and I knew it would never be more than that." She smoothed her hair.

"And now it's worse, because he's like a bulldozer and I'm terrified of him."

"I warned you," Ada reminded her. "He's utterly relentless."

"He wants me to go home with him," she said.

Ada's face brightened. "He does?"

"Don't be silly, I can't go! If I do, he's bound to find out what an absolute idiot I am, and then where will I be? He'll throw me out on my ear!"

"And then again, he might not."

"I'm no gambler, Ada. Losing matters too much. I'd rather stay here and pull the pieces together. Maybe it's just a physical infatuation and I'll outgrow it," she added hopefully.

"If you'd walk through fire just to look at him, darling," Ada said gently, "it's got to be more than physical. And you know it."

"But what can I do?" Kati wailed. "Ada, I'm not the kind to have affairs. I'm too inhibited."

"Not when you write, you aren't!"

"That's different. When I write, I'm a storyteller, telling a story. In real life, I get too emotionally involved, and then I can't let go. And Egan hates even the idea of involvement."

"He looked pretty involved to me this morning.

He could hardly take his eyes off you long enough to eat," Ada remarked.

"You know why, too."

"Men are attracted first, then their emotions get involved. Look at Marshal and me! He liked my legs, so he called me. And now here we are almost engaged!"

"And here it is Christmas and I've ruined it again," Kati moaned.

"No, you haven't. Egan will be back when he cools down. He's mad at himself, I'll bet, not at you." She smiled. "He didn't mean to hurt you."

Tears welled up in her eyes and she turned away. "I never meant to hurt him, either."

"Then cheer up. It will all work out, honest it will."

"So you keep saying. I'll try to listen this time."

They had everything ready just as Marshal and Jack arrived, and the four of them stood around and talked until noon.

"Should we wait for Egan?" Marshal asked.

"Well," Ada said, biting her lower lip, "I don't know when he'll be back."

Even as she said the words, the front door opened and Egan walked in. He tossed his Stetson onto the hall table.

"Waiting for me? I got held up at Jennie's," he

added, glancing toward Kati with pure malice in his eyes.

So much for Ada's helpful optimism, Kati thought as she took off her apron. She didn't even look at him again, and her entire attitude was so cool and controlled that she felt she deserved an Oscar for her performance all the way through the holiday meal. The turkey was perfectly browned, the ham beautifully glazed. Egan, at the head of the table, carved, and Ada passed the plates down. He said grace, and everyone was far too busy to talk for the first few minutes.

Kati was just bursting with fury about Jennie. She could imagine what Egan had been doing and why he'd been held up. She was rigid with the effort not to get up and fling the turkey carcass the length of the table at him.

"The cherry pie is delicious," Jack offered as he finished his last mouthful and followed it with the rich black coffee Ada had made.

"Thank you," Kati said with a smile.

"Kati does all the desserts," Ada told Marshal. "I'm no hand at pastry."

Egan hadn't touched any of the pies or fruitcake. He barely seemed to eat anything, like Kati. Her eyes found his across the room, and it was like lightning striking. She felt the longing she'd been fighting down all day coming to life again. It was incredible that she could look at him and go to pieces like this.

"Well, I hate to eat and run," Jack said, "but I promised my cousin I'd stop by and see him and his family this afternoon. There are so few of us left these days."

"Yes, I know what you mean," Ada said quietly, and her face showed the loneliness Kati knew she must feel this first Christmas without her mother.

"I'm sure you do. I'm sorry, I didn't mean to bring up such a sad subject," Jack apologized.

Ada smiled. "Don't be silly. Happy Christmas, Jack. I'm glad you could come."

"Me, too," Kati said, avoiding Egan's eyes as she got up to walk Jack to the door.

"I enjoyed it," Jack said. "Merry Christmas!"

Kati saw him out into the corridor. "I'll see you later, then."

Jack stared down at her quietly. "Do you realize how that big cattleman feels about you?" he asked unexpectedly.

Her face paled. "What?"

"He watched you as if he'd bleed to death look-ing. And the one time I smiled at you, I thought he was going to come over that table to get me." He laughed self-consciously. "If you get a minute, how about telling him that we haven't got anything serious going? I'd like to keep my insurance premiums where they are."

She laughed too, because they were friends who could ask such things of each other. "I'll do my best. Want to spend New Year's with us?"

"As far as I know, I don't have a thing planned. But," he added with a wink, "you might. So let's leave it alone for now, and I'll call you. All right?"

"All right. Merry Christmas," she added.

"You, too." He bent and kissed her lightly on the cheek. He was just lifting his head when Egan appeared in the doorway with eyes that glittered dangerously.

"You're taking a long time just to say goodbye," he muttered.

"Discussing the weather," Jack said quickly. "Damned cold outside! In here, too. Bye, Kati!" And he took off for the elevator with a grin.

Egan caught Kati's hand in his, holding it warmly, closely, and pulled her just inside the door. They were out of view of the living room, and when he closed the outside door, they might have been alone in the world.

"I can't stand it," he ground out, gripping her arms as if he were afraid she'd fly out of his reach. "You're driving me out of my mind, damn it!"

"You started it," she bit off, keeping her voice down.

"I didn't mean it, though," he returned in a harsh undertone. His hands loosened their grip, became caressing, burning her even through the blouse's long sleeves. "Kati, I'm so used to hitting at you…but this morning I didn't mean to."

Her lower lip trembled as she looked up at him. "You went to her," she said shakily.

Every trace of expression left his face, and only his eyes showed any emotion at all. They glittered at her like silver in sunlight. "I didn't touch her," he said huskily. "How could I? All I want in the world is you!"

Her lips parted, and before she could speak, he bent and caressed them slowly, sensuously, with his own. His breath was suddenly ragged, uneven, and the hands that were on her arms moved up to cup her face and hold it where he wanted it.

"Are you going to fight me every inch of the way?" he asked in a strained tone.

"I'm not," she protested dazedly.

"Then kiss me," he murmured.

She didn't understand what he meant until the pressure of his mouth forced hers open and she felt his tongue in a slow, even penetration that made her blood surge.

She gasped, and he deepened the kiss even more. She felt his body tremble, and he groaned softly—deep in his throat—like a man trying to control the impossible. He whispered her name under his breath and his arms went around her like chains. He crushed her into the taut muscles of his body until she hurt, and she didn't care. She wanted to be closer than this, even closer, with nothing in the way…!

"Kati?" Ada called from the living room.

In a fever of hunger, Kati watched Egan lift his head and take a slow, steadying breath.

"We're talking, all right?" he asked in what sounded like an almost normal tone.

"Oh, excuse me!" Ada called back. "Never mind!"

Egan's eyes burned down into Kati's. "Are you all right?" he whispered, watching the tears shimmer in her eyes.

"Yes. I…just…just feel kind of shaky," she stammered.

He took her hands to his hard chest and held them

over the vest. "So do I," he said. "From the neck down. My God, you stir me up!"

Her eyes searched his slowly, curiously. "You're a passionate man," she whispered. "I imagine most women make you feel that way."

He shook his head very slowly. "I'm not promiscuous, Kati. I'm selective. It takes a very special woman."

She felt unreasonably flattered, but then, she wasn't thinking straight. How could she, this close to him, wanting him with a fever that was burning her alive?

"I'm scandalous, remember?" she said. "I seduce men to help me with my research—"

He stopped the words with a touch to her lips. "I'm not a virgin. How can I sit in judgment on you?"

"If you'd listen to me," she said softly, "I'd tell you."

"I don't want to hear it," he said curtly. "The past is over. We'll go from here. Are you coming home with me?"

And there was the question she'd wanted and dreaded, staring her in the face. She looked at him and knew she wasn't going to be strong and sensible. She could feel herself falling apart already.

"You won't…expect too much?" she asked hesitantly.

"Listen," he said, brushing his fingers over her

warm cheek, "as far as I'm concerned, you're coming to learn about ranching for a book. You don't have to pay for your keep, Kati. In any way," he emphasized. "I'll let you come to me. I won't ask more than you want to give."

She lowered her eyes to his vest and wondered again, for the hundredth time, what it would be like with him—and knew that it was suicide to think about it.

"Come home with me," he said, tilting her face up to his. "The snow's sitting like a blanket on the Tetons, and the river's running through it like a silver thread. I'll show you where the buffalo used to graze and the mountain men camped."

He made it sound wildly romantic, and his eyes promised much more than a guided tour. It was crazy! She was crazy!

"I'll go home with you, Egan," she whispered.

His breath caught and he studied her eyes for a long moment before he bent to kiss her softly, slowly on her swollen lips. "There's a bear rug in front of the fireplace in my den," he breathed at her lips. "I've wondered…for years…how it would feel on bare skin, Kati."

A tiny, wild sound escaped from her throat, and

he lifted her in his arms to kiss her roughly, possessively, until the whole world compressed into Egan's mouth and arms.

"Er-ahmmmm!" came a loud noise from the doorway.

Egan drew away with shaky reluctance and let Kati slide back to her feet just as Ada peeked around the corner.

"Marshal and I wondered if you'd like to go walking and look at the city," Ada asked, trying not to look as pleased as she felt.

"I'd like that," Egan said, smiling down into Kati's rapt face. "Would you?"

"Yes," she said dreamily.

"I hope you don't mind living alone for a couple of weeks, Ada," Egan added as he grabbed his hat and topcoat. "Because I'm taking Kati to Wyoming."

"You are?" Ada burst out, her face delighted.

"To help her with the book," he added, glaring at his sister. "Research, period."

"Oh, of course," Ada said, getting a firm grip on herself. "What else?"

Kati didn't dare look up. It would have blown her cool cover to pieces. Then Egan caught her small hand in his big one as they went to the elevator, and every thought in her head exploded in pleasure. Her fingers clung, locking into his. She walked beside him feeling as if she owned the world, oblivious to the beauty of New York City in holiday dress. Her present was right beside her.

It was almost dark when they came back to the apartment, after looking in store windows and eyeing the decorations around Madison and Fifth Avenues. Then they exchanged presents, and Kati was overwhelmed when she opened Egan's gift. It was a silver bracelet—pure silver with inlaid turquoise, and surely not a trinket. She looked up, pleasure beaming from her dark eyes, to thank him.

"Do you like it?" he said on a smile. "I like mine, too."

She'd given him a new spinning reel, something Ada said he'd appreciate. Although, at the time, pleasing Egan hadn't been on Kati's list of priorities, now she was glad she'd bought it. She saw the real appreciation in his eyes.

All too soon it was bedtime, and Ada was seeing Marshal out in a protracted good night.

"You'll have to get up early," Egan told Kati as they said their own good-night at the door of her room. "I want to be out of here by eight."

She smiled. "I'll pack tonight. I have to bring my computer."

"One of those portable ones with a built-in telephone modem?" he asked knowledgeably.

She nodded. "It's my lifeline. I can't manage without it. It even has a printer built in."

"I carry one with me when I travel," he said. "We inventory our herds on computers these days, and use them to print out the production records for sales. I even sell off cattle by videotape. Ranching has moved into the twentieth century."

"I'll feel right at home," she said, laughing.

"I hope so," he said, his face softening as he looked down at her. "No strings, baby. I won't back you into any corners."

She nodded. "Sleep well."

"Without you?" he murmured wistfully. "No chance."

He bent and kissed her lightly. "Night."

And he was gone.

She walked into her room and closed the door, feeling impossibly happy and terrified all at the same time. What was going to happen when, inevitably, Egan discovered that her reason for going wasn't his reason for inviting her? Because things were bound to come to a head. And either way, he'd discover for himself that she wasn't the worldly woman he thought her. What would he do? She shuddered. He'd probably be furious enough to put her on the first plane to New York.

She reached for the doorknob. She almost went to tell him that she'd changed her mind. But the prospect of even a few days alone with him—to glory in his company—was like the prospect of heaven. And she was too besotted to give it up. Just a day, she promised herself. Just one day, and she'd confess everything and let him do his worst. But she had to have that precious time with him. It would last her all her life. It would be all she'd ever have of him.

Eight

HER first sight of the Tetons as she and Egan flew over Jackson Hole made Kati catch her breath.

Seated beside Egan in the ranch's small jet, she stared down at the velvety white tops of the jagged peaks with wonder.

"Oh, it's beautiful," she whispered. "The most beautiful thing I've ever seen!"

"You've never been here in the winter, have you?" he asked, smiling. "I'd forgotten. Honey, if you think this is something, wait until I get you on the Snake."

"Snake?" Her ears perked up and she looked at him apprehensively.

"River," he added. "From the ranch house, we

overlook the Snake, and the Tetons look like they're sitting over us."

"I knew it was spectacular in the spring and summer," she sighed, staring back out the window. "But this is magic."

He watched her with quiet, smiling eyes. "I was born here, but it still sets me on my heels when I come home. A lot of battles have been fought over this land. By Shoshone and Arapaho and the white man, by ranchers and sheepmen and rustlers."

She glanced at him. "Are there still rustlers out West?"

"Of course, but now they work with trucks. We have a pretty good security system, though, so we don't lose many. Feeding the cattle during the winters is our biggest problem," he said. "We're pretty fanatical about haying out here, to get enough winter feed. A cow won't paw her way through the snow to get food, Kati. She'll stand there and starve first."

"I didn't know that," she said, fascinated.

"You've got a lot to learn, city lady," he said with a soft laugh. "But I'll teach you."

That, she thought, was what she feared. But she only smiled and watched the familiar lines of the big two-story white frame house come into view as they headed for the landing strip beyond it.

"How old is the house, Egan?" Kati asked after Egan had told the pilot to take the jet to the Jackson airport where it was based.

"Oh, I guess around eighty or ninety years," he said. He led her to a waiting pickup truck. "My grand-father built it."

"And called it White Lodge?" she asked, remembering that the ranch also was called by that name.

"No. That was my grandmother's idea. She was Shoshone," he added with a smile.

She studied him quietly. "And your grandfather? Was he dark?"

He nodded. "The sun burns us brown. Despite all the damned paperwork, I still spend a lot of time on horseback."

"Hi, Boss!" Ramey yelled out the window of the pickup truck.

"Hi, Ramey!" Egan called back. He opened the door and put Kati inside, jerking a thumb at Ramey to get him out from behind the wheel.

"I ain't such a bad driver," Ramey grumbled.

"I don't care what kind of driver you are," Egan

reminded him as he got in next to Kati and shut the door. "Nobody drives me except me."

"On account of Larry ran him into a tree," Ramey explained as he shut his own door just before Egan started down the snowy ranch road. The young boy grinned at Egan's thunderous look. "Broke Larry's nose."

"Hitting the tree?" Kati asked innocently.

"Hitting the boss's fist afterward" Ramey chuckled.

Kati glanced at Egan. "And I thought you were the sweetest-tempered man I'd ever met," she said dryly.

Ramey's eyebrows arched. He started to speak, but Egan looked at him and that was all it took.

"Don't reckon you got a Chinook tucked in your bag somewheres?" Ramey asked instead, his blue eyes twinkling.

"A what?" Kati asked blankly.

"Chinook," Egan said. "It's a warm wind we get here in the winter. Melts the snow and gives us some relief." He looked over her head at Ramey. "How's the feed holding out?"

"Just fine. We'll make it, Gig says. Gig is our foreman," Ramey reminded her. "Kind of came with the ranch, if you know what I mean. Nobody knows how old he is, and nobody's keen to ask him."

"The answer might scare us," Egan chuckled. "Damn, this stuff is deep!"

He was running in the ruts Ramey had made coming to the landing strip, but it was still slow, hard going, and powdery snow was beginning to blow again.

"It'd be faster if we walked," Ramey suggested.

"Or rode." He shot a quick glance at Kati, letting his eyes run over her beige dress and high heels and short man-made fur coat. "God, wouldn't you look right at home on horseback in that? I almost made you change before we left Ada's."

She started to object to the wording and then let it go. Why start trouble?

"No comeback?" Egan chided. "No remarks about my tyrannical personality?"

"Why, Mr. Winthrop, I'm the very soul of tact," she said haughtily.

"Especially when you're telling me to go to hell," was the lightning comeback.

She flushed, noticing Ramey's puzzled look.

"We, uh, sometimes have our, uh, little differences," she tried to explain.

"Yes, ma'am, I recall," Ramey murmured, and

she remembered that he'd been nearby when she had walked furiously off the ranch that summer.

She cleared her throat. "Well, you do have the Tetons at your back door, don't you?" she asked Egan, who seemed to be enjoying her discomfort.

He followed her gaze to the high peaks rising behind the house. "Indeed we do. And the river within sight of the front door," he added, indicating the winding silver ribbon of the Snake that cut through the valley far below the house.

"Elk and moose and antelope graze out there during the winter," he told her. "And buffalo used to, in frontier days."

"I've never seen a moose," she said.

"Maybe this time," he told her.

She watched as Egan's elderly housekeeper waddled onto the front porch, shading her eyes against the blinding white of the snow. Egan left the truck idling for Ramey and lifted Kati off the seat and into his hard arms. The sheepskin coat he wore made him seem twice as broad across the chest and shoulders.

"You're hardly equipped for walking in the snow," he murmured, indicating her high heels. "I hope you packed some sensible things."

"Hiking boots, jeans and sweaters," she said smartly.

"Good girl. Hold on."

She clung as he strode easily through the high blanket of snow and up onto the steps, his boots echoing even through the snow against the hardwood. Dessie Teal was watching with a grin, her broad face all smiles under her brown eyes and salt-and-pepper hair.

"I never would have believed it," she muttered as Egan set Kati back on her feet. "And I don't see a bruise on either one of you."

"We don't fight all the time," Egan said coolly.

"Well, neither do them Arabs, Egan," Dessie returned, "but I was just remarking how nice it was that you and Miss James seemed to be in a state of temporary truce, that's all."

"She came to research a book about Wyoming in the old days," Egan told the old woman gruffly, his eyes daring her to make anything else of it.

Dessie shrugged. "Whatever you want to call it. A book about frontier days, huh?" she asked, leading Kati into the house. "Well, you just go talk to Gig, he'll tell you more than any book will. His daddy fought in the Johnson County range war."

Kati asked what that had been about and was treated to fifteen minutes of Wyoming history, including references to the range wars between cattlemen and sheepmen, and the ferocity of Wyoming winters.

"My brother froze to death working cattle one winter," Dessie added later, when Kati had changed into jeans, boots and a sweater and was drinking coffee with the housekeeper in the kitchen. "He fell and broke his leg and couldn't get up again. He was solid ice when one of the men found him." She shivered delicately. "This ain't the place for tenderfeet, I'll tell you." She paused in the act of putting a big roast into the oven. "How come you and Egan ain't fighting?"

"He's trying to get me into bed," Kati returned bluntly and grinned wickedly at the housekeeper's blush.

"I deserved that," Dessie muttered and burst into laughter. "I sure did. Ask a foolish question… Well, I might as well make it worse. Is he going to?"

Kati shook her head slowly. "Not my kind of life," she said. "I'm too old-fashioned."

"Good for you," Dessie said vehemently. "Honest to God, I don't know what's got into girls these days. Why, we used to go two or three dates before we'd hold hands with a boy. Nowadays, it's into bed on the first one. And they wonder why nobody's happy.

You gorge yourself on candy and you don't want it no more. At least, that's how I see it."

"You and I should join a missionary society," Kati told her. "We don't belong in the modern world."

Dessie grinned at her. "Well, speaking for myself, I ain't in it. Can't get much more primitive than this, I reckon, despite all the modern gadgets Egan bought me for the kitchen."

"I understand what you mean." She leaned back in the chair and sipped her coffee. "Did Egan really not want to be a rancher?" she asked.

Dessie measured that question before she answered it. "I don't think he knew exactly what he did want. Politics used to fascinate him. But then, so did business. And that's mostly what ranching is these days—it's business. He has Gig to look after the practical side of it while he buys and sells cattle and concentrates on herd improvement and diversification." She grinned sheepishly. "What big words!"

"Is he happy?" Kati asked, because it mattered.

"No," Dessie said quietly. "He's got nobody except Miss Ada."

Kati studied her coffee cup, amazed at how deeply that hurt her. "He's...not handsome, but he has a way with him. And he attracts women," she added, remembering Jennie.

"Not the right kind of women" came the tart reply. "Not ever one he could bring to this ranch. Until now."

Kati blushed to the roots of her hair.

"Now what are you doing?" Egan growled from the doorway, taking in Kati's red face and Dessie's shocked expression at his sudden appearance. "Talking about me behind my back, I guess?"

"Well, who else is there to talk about?" Dessie threw up her hands. "I never see anybody except you. Well, there's Ramey, of course, but he don't do nothing interesting enough to gossip about, does he?"

Egan shook his head on a tired sigh. "I guess not. Damn. You and your logical arguments." He took off his hat and coat. "What's for dinner? I'm half-starved."

"You're always half-starved. There's some sliced turkey in the refrigerator, left over from my solitary Christmas dinner I had all by myself, alone, yesterday."

Egan glanced at the old woman. "Did you have a good time?" he asked.

"I told you I ate by myself!" Dessie growled.

"Well, I guess that means you didn't have any company," Egan said pleasantly.

"Wait," the housekeeper said, "until tonight. And see what I feed you for supper."

"Let me die of starvation, then," he said. "I'll call up Ada and tell her you won't feed me, and see what you do then!"

Dessie threw down her apron. "Hard case," she accused, her lower lips thrusting out. "Just hit me in my weakest spot, why don't you?"

Egan grinned, winking at Kati, who was seeing a side of him she hadn't dreamed existed. She liked this big, laughing man who seemed so at home in the wilderness.

He even looked different from the man in the pinstripe suit in Ada's apartment. He was wearing denim now, from head to foot, and a pair of disreputable brown boots that had seen better days—along with a hat that was surely obsolete. The only relatively new piece of apparel he had was the sheepskin coat he'd just taken off. But he seemed bigger and tougher and in every way more appealing than the sophisticated executive.

"You look different," Kati remarked absently, watching him.

He cocked an eyebrow as he carried turkey and mayonnaise to the table. "I do?"

"His looks ain't improved," Dessie argued.

"Just mind your own business, thank you," he drawled in her direction and watched her go back to her roast. "And don't burn that thing up like you did the last one!"

"I didn't burn nothing up," she shot back. "That stupid dog of yours got in here and reared up on my stove and changed the heat setting!"

"Durango doesn't get in the house," he told her. "And he isn't smart enough to work a stove, despite being the best cattle dog I own."

"Well, I wouldn't turn my back on him," she muttered. She put the roast in the oven and closed the door. "Excuse me. I got to go to the cellar and get apples. I thought you might like an apple pie. Not that you deserve one," she added, glaring back as she went out the door.

He only laughed. "Get the bread, honey, and I'll make you one too," he told Kati.

"Where is it?"

"In the bread box."

She got up and went to the cabinet to get it, but before she could turn around, he was behind her, the length of his body threatening and warm.

"Fell right into the trap, didn't you?" he breathed,

turning her so that her back was against the wall. With his hands on the wall beside her, he eased down so that his body pressed wholly on hers, in a contact that made the blood surge into her face.

"God, it's wild like this, isn't it?" he said unsteadily. "I can feel you burning like a brand under every inch of me."

She opened her lips to speak, and he bent and took them. His mouth was cold from the outdoors, but hers warmed it, so that seconds later it was blazing with heat. A moan growled out of his throat into her hungry, wanting mouth.

She felt his tongue, and her eyes opened suddenly, finding his closed, his brows drawn, as he savored the pleasure. But as if he felt her looking at him, the thick lashes moved up and his darkening silver eyes looked straight into hers.

On a caught breath he lifted his lips just fractionally over hers. "Now, that's exciting," he whispered. "I've never watched a woman while I kissed her."

But obviously he was going to, because his eyes stayed open when he bent again, and so did hers. The hunger and need in his kiss inflamed her, and her hands found their way to the top button on his shirt.

She'd never wanted to touch a man's bare skin. She

couldn't remember a time in her life when the thought had appealed. But it did now. She could feel the crush of his hips and thighs over hers, and explosive sensations were curling her toes.

Her fingers toyed with his top button while she tried to decide how risky it would be. He was hungry enough without being tempted further, and she wasn't sure she could handle him.

He lifted his head and watched her fingers. "Are you always this unsure of yourself with a man?" he asked under his breath. "Or is it just me? Touch me if you want to, Kati. I won't lose my head and bend you back over the kitchen table."

The wording made it sound cheap, made her sound cheap. The color went out of her face and she eased away from him.

He swore quietly, watching her get the bread and some saucers and start making sandwiches in a strained silence.

"What do you want from me?" he ground out.

She drew in a steadying breath. "I'd settle for a little respect. Not much. Just what you'd give any stranger who came into your house." Tears welled in her eyes as she spread mayonnaise. "I'm not a tramp, Egan Winthrop."

He watched a solitary tear land with a splatter on the clean tabletop, and his hands caught her waist convulsively, jerking her back against him.

"Don't…cry," he bit off, his fingers hurting.

"Don't touch me!" she threw back, twisting away from him.

He held on to the edge of the table, glaring as she wiped the tears away and finished making the sandwiches. She pushed his at him and went to put the knife in the sink.

He poured coffee into her cup and his, put the pot away and sat down. She followed suit, but she ate in silence, not even looking at him. Fool, she told herself. You stupid fool, you had to come with him!

Dessie came back to a grinding silence. She stared at them, apples in her apron, and grimaced. "I leave you alone five minutes and you start a war."

Egan finished his coffee and got up, not rising to the bait. "I've got work to do."

He grabbed his coat and hat and stamped out the door. Kati brushed away more tears. Dessie just shook her head and started peeling apples. After a minute, she got another bowl and knife and pushed them at Kati.

"Might as well peel," she told her. "It'll give your hands something to do while your mind works."

"Mine doesn't work," Kati replied coldly. "If it did, I'd still be in New York."

"Not many people get under his skin like that," Dessie commented with a slow grin. "Good to know he's still human."

"Well, I'd need proof," Kati glowered.

"I think you'll get it," came the laughing reply. "Now, peel, if you want an apple pie."

Kati gave in. And it *was* rather soothing, peeling apples. She had a feeling she was going to make a lot of pies before she got her research done.

Nine

AFTER that little episode, Egan became remote. He was the perfect host, polite and courteous, but about as warm as one of the rocks on his land.

Kati decided that if he could play it cool, so could she. So she was equally polite. And distant. Oddly enough, there were no more violent arguments like the ones they had in the past. Once in a while, she'd notice Egan watching her over the supper table before he disappeared into his study to work, or during a rare minute in the morning before he went to his office down the road. But he kept to himself, and the affectionate, hungry man who'd brought her to the ranch seemed to have vanished into his former, cold counterpart.

But she did accomplish one of her goals. She learned enough about ranching to do a nonfiction work on it.

The logistics of supplies fascinated her. Egan's cows and second-year heifers were bred to drop calves in February and March. So during January, the ranch manager and his men were very much involved in pre-calving planning. That meant buying ear tags, identifying first-calf heifers, checking breeding dates to estimate calving dates and arranging for adequate facilities.

Because of the increased herd, more calving pens had to be added, but those were erected during the fall. The cowboys were closely watching the cows now to make sure there were no problems. One of the older hands told her that he always hated being a cowboy during this time of the year and at roundup in the spring, when the cattle had to be branded, vetted, and moved about fifty miles away to summer pasture.

Listening to the men tell about their adventures took up the better part of her days. She was careful not to interfere with their work, having been cautioned by the boss about that. But she was around during breaks and sometimes after dinner, with her pad and pen in hand, asking questions.

It would have been all right if Ramey hadn't asked

her to go to a dance with him. Egan happened to overhear the question, and before Kati could even get her mouth open to say "No, thanks," Egan was on top of them.

"If you're through irritating the men," he told her cuttingly, "they need their rest."

She rose, embarrassed to tears but too proud to show it. "Excuse me, I didn't realize—"

"But, boss," Ramey groaned, "she wasn't bothering us!"

There was a loud tumult as the other cowboys in the bunkhouse agreed with pathetic eagerness.

"All the same, good night," Egan said in his coldest tone. He held the door open; Kati, seeing defeat, shrugged, calling a smiling good-night to the men and walked knee-deep in the melting snow back to the truck she'd commandeered for the drive down.

"This way," Egan said curtly, taking her arm. He led her to his pickup truck and put her inside.

"I was just asking questions," she muttered. "You told me not to interfere with their work."

"I didn't say you could sleep with them," he growled.

"You pig!" she burst out. Her eyes blazed; her lips

trembled with fury. "How dare you accuse me of such a thing!"

"Ramey asked you out—did you think I didn't hear him?" he asked. He fumbled for a cigarette, surprising her, because she'd seen him smoke only once or twice in the past few days.

"I was going to refuse," she replied. "He's a nice boy, but—"

"But not experienced enough for a woman like you, right?" he asked, smiling insolently.

Her breath stopped. "What exactly do you mean, 'a woman like me'?" she asked deliberately.

"What do you think I mean?"

She clutched the pen and pad in her hand and stared straight ahead.

"No comeback?"

"I won't need one. I'm going home."

"Like hell you are."

"What do you plan to do, Mr. Winthrop, tie me up in a line cabin?"

"Who taught you about line cabins?"

"Gig," she said uncomfortably, remembering the long, amusing talk she'd had with the sly old foreman.

"Gig never talks to anybody, not even me."

"Well, he talks to me," she shot back. "But I guess you'll accuse me of trying to get him into bed too!"

"You'd hate it," he said, lifting the cigarette to his mouth. "He only bathes once a month."

She tried to keep her temper blazing, but she lost and hid the muffled laugh in her hands.

He glanced at her, his eyes sparkling. "If I stop making objectionable remarks to you," he said after a minute, "do you suppose we might try to get along for the duration?"

"I don't think that's possible," she said, glancing at him. "You won't even give me the benefit of a doubt."

"I've read your books," he reminded her.

"How in God's name do you think Edgar Rice Burroughs wrote *Tarzan of the Apes?*" she exploded. "Do you believe that he swung from trees in darkest Africa? When he wrote the first book, he'd never even seen Africa!"

He pulled up at the front door and cut off the engine. "Are you trying to tell me that a woman could write a sexy book without having had sex?" He laughed. "No dice, baby. I'm not stupid."

"That depends on your definitions," she returned hotly. "About me, yes, sir, you are stupid."

"Only when you kiss me in that slow, hot way,"

he murmured, smiling wickedly, "and try to take off my shirt."

She slammed the pen against the pad impotently and glared at him.

"All right," he said after a minute and crushed out the cigarette. "I'll apologize for the crude remark I made in the kitchen. Will that pacify you?"

"I want to make something crystal clear," she returned, gripping the pad tightly. "As far as I'm concerned, I'm here to research a book."

His eyes darkened and he studied her closely. "Put it in words, not innuendos."

"I don't want to be mauled around," she replied.

"Tell Ramey. He was the one who wanted to take you off into the woods," he said on a laugh.

"So did you!" she accused.

He shook his head. "No. I wanted to take you into my bed. There's a difference."

"Geographical," she countered.

He sighed and reached out to smooth a long, unruly strand of her hair. "I want you. I haven't made any secret of it. You want me, too. It's just going to take more time than I thought."

"I won't sleep with you," she told him.

"You will," he replied softly, searching her eyes. "Eventually."

"Is that a threat?" she asked, finding her fighting feet.

"No, ma'am," he said, grinning.

She glared at him uncertainly. "I don't understand you."

"You've got a whole lot of company," he told her. He dropped her hair. "Better get some rest. And don't go back to the bunkhouse at night. Keeps the boys awake."

"I have to find out some things about calving," she protested.

"Do you? What do you want to know?" he asked with a wicked smile.

"Oh, stuff your hat...!" she began.

"Now, now, you mustn't shock me," he told her as he got out of the truck. "I'm just an unsophisticated country boy, you know."

"Like hell," she muttered under her breath.

He opened her door and lifted her into his arms. She started to struggle, but he held her implacably and shook his head.

"Don't fight," he said. "We've spent days avoiding each other. I just want to hold you."

She felt a rush of feeling that should have made her run screaming the other way. But instead, she put her arms—pad and pen and all—around his neck and let him carry her. By the time he got to the steps, her face was buried in his warm throat and her heartbeat was shaking her.

"We haven't made love since we were in New York," he whispered as he carried her into his study and deliberately locked the door behind him.

She felt her lips go dry as she looked up at him. He was taking off his hat and coat, and the way he was staring at her made her feel threatened.

"No more games, Katriane," he said softly. He took away the pad and pen, and, bending, took off her warm coat and dropped it beside his on the chair. He lifted her off the floor. "I won't hurt you. But I've gone hungry too long."

There would never be a better time to tell him the truth. But just as she started to, he bent and pressed his open mouth against the peak of her breast. She cried out, shocked speechless at the intimacy of it even through two layers of cloth.

He didn't say a word. She felt him lower her, felt the soft pile of a rug under her back. And then his body was spreading over hers like a heavy blanket, making fires that blazed up and burned in exquisite torment.

His mouth moved up to hers, taking it with a power and masculine possessiveness that she'd never felt before. She wasn't even aware of what his hands were doing until he lifted her and she felt the slight chill of the room and the heat of the blazing fire in the hearth on her bare flesh.

"Egan," she protested shakily as he laid her back down.

"God, you're something!" he breathed, looking down with wild, glittering eyes on what he'd uncovered. His hands went to the buttons on his shirt and unfastened them slowly, methodically. He pulled the shirt free of his jeans and stripped it off, revealing bronzed skin that shimmered smoothly in the light of the fire.

Her eyes fastened on him hungrily, loving every rugged line of him, wanting the feel of his hard muscles against her own trembling softness.

There was only the crackle of the fire as they looked at each other, only its reddish glow in the room. She knew what he was going to do, but she was powerless to stop him. She loved him. Oh, God, she loved him!

He came down slowly, easing his chest over hers by

levering himself over her on his arms. His eyes held hers every second as he brushed his chest against her taut breasts and watched the wild, sweet surge of her body upward to make the contact even closer.

"Don't hold anything back with me," he said under his breath. "And I'll please you until you scream with it."

His mouth eased down as his chest did, and she reached up to catch his head in her hands, tangle her fingers in his hair while he kissed the breath from her swollen mouth.

She experienced her own power when she felt the tremor in his long body; and without thinking about consequences, she tugged his head up and shifted to bring his lips down to the bareness of her body.

"Kati!" he burst out as if she'd surprised him, and he dug his hands in under her back. His mouth opened, and she felt his tongue, his teeth at flesh that had never even known a man's eyes.

Her body rippled in his arms, on waves of sweetness, and she moaned as his mouth learned every smooth inch of her above the waist. He rolled suddenly onto his back, bringing her with him, and she felt his hands going under the waistband of her jeans onto the softness of her lower spine.

"Look at me," he said in a husky tone.

She lifted her head just as his clean, strong hands contracted, and he smiled at the hunger he could read in her eyes.

He nipped her earlobe with his teeth and whispered things that excited and shocked, all at once, embarrassing things that she'd only read until that moment.

"Egan," she protested weakly.

"Just relax," he whispered, bringing her hips back against his in a slow, sweet rotation. "Let me show you how much I want you."

He ground her hips into the powerful, taut muscles of his own. She cried out as he freed one hand to bring her shaking mouth down onto his, thrusting his tongue up into it in a rhythm that said more than words.

"My room," he whispered. "Right now."

He rolled her over and handed her the blouse and sweater he had taken off her minutes before. "You'd better put those on," he said in a taut undertone. "In case Dessie's still up."

She clutched the cool things to her, staring at him like someone coming out of a trance.

"Well?" he ground out. "My God, you felt what you've done to me. I need you, damn it!"

She swallowed, trying to find the right words. "I need you too, Egan," she said shakily. "But there's something you'd…you'd better know first."

"What? That you aren't on the Pill?" he demanded. "It's all right, I'll take care of it. I won't let you get pregnant."

She blushed and lowered her eyes to the jerky rise and fall of his chest. Her fingers tightened on the shirt and sweater. "I'm a virgin."

"My God, that's a good one." He laughed coldly. "Try again."

"I don't have to," she said, trying to hold on to her pride and her self-respect, both of which were slipping. "I've told you the truth."

"Sure, I'm a virgin, too," he told her. "Now can we go to bed?"

"Go right ahead," she said with venom in her tone. "But without me! Didn't you hear what I said, damn you, I'm a virgin!"

"At twenty-five?" he asked in a biting tone. "Writing the kind of books you write?"

"I've told you until I'm blue in the face that I don't research those love scenes—most of which are foreplay with a hint of fulfillment!" She flushed, avoiding his eyes. "And some of that is obligatory—I can't get historical fiction published without it. And as for men…" she added, lifting her face to glare at him, "…most of them have felt as you do, that a woman's place in the modern world is to be available for sex and then disappear before anyone gets emotional. I can't live like that, so I don't indulge."

"Never?" he burst out.

"Never!" she returned. "Egan, didn't Ada ever tell you about my parents?"

His breathing was steadier now, but he still looked frustrated and full of venom. "That they were old?"

She took another steadying breath of her own. "My father was a Presbyterian minister," she whispered. "And my mother had been a missionary. Now do you understand?"

He looked as if he'd been slapped. His eyes went over her, right down to the fingers that trembled on her discarded top. "Why didn't you tell me?" he ground out. "My God, the things I said to you…!"

He got to his feet and grabbed up his shirt, shouldering angrily into it. "Get out of here," he said coldly.

She managed to get to her feet gracefully, pausing as she tried to decide between running for it and dressing first.

"Put on your blouse, for heaven's sake!" he snapped,

and turned away again to light a cigarette with jerky motions.

She put on the blouse and pulled the sweater on over it without ever fastening a button. She couldn't even look at him as she walked toward the door. Her fingers fumbled with the lock, and when she pulled the door open, he still hadn't turned or said a word. She closed it quietly behind her with trembling fingers and went upstairs as quickly as she could. When she was safely in her room, with her own door locked, she burst into tears.

Ten

IT WAS the most agonizing night Kati remembered spending. Egan had bruised her emotions in ways she hadn't dreamed possible. Rejecting her was enough of a blow. But couldn't he have done it gently? She cringed, thinking of the way he'd been, the things he'd said until she confessed. Ada had warned her. Why hadn't she listened?

Worst of all was the fact that she'd been more than ready to give in to anything he wanted of her. She'd wanted him to know the truth because he was so hungry that she was afraid of being hurt the first time. But her revelation had backfired. Instead of comforting her, he ordered her out of the room and turned his back.

Well, at least she knew how he really felt now, she told herself miserably. She knew that he'd only wanted her, and there was no feeling on his part except desire. She couldn't remember ever hurting so much. She loved him. What she'd felt in his hard, expert embrace was something she'd never get over. But he'd turned away as if such devastating interludes were just run-of-the-mill. To him, they probably were. With good-time girls like Jennie.

She got up well before daylight. She packed quickly and dressed in her boots and jeans and a burgundy sweater. She decided to go downstairs and have breakfast, and make sure Egan had left the house before she called a cab. It was eight o'clock, and he was usually long gone by then. She didn't know how she could face him if he was still there, not after last night. It made her color, just remembering the things they'd done together.

Her footsteps slowed as she reached the kitchen. She pushed the door open partway and found Dessie puttering around the stove. With a sigh of relief, she pushed it open the rest of the way and came face-to-face with Egan, who was just behind it picking up his hat from the counter.

She actually jumped aside. He looked down at her

with an expression she couldn't read. His eyes were dark silver, cold, angry.

"I want to talk to you for a minute," he said curtly.

He didn't give her a chance to protest. He propelled her through the door and down the hall to the living room. He shut the door behind them and stared hard at her.

"Before you start," she said in a painfully subdued tone, "I realize it was all my fault, and I'm sorry."

He pulled a cigarette from his pocket and lit it, his fingers steady. "We won't talk about last night," he said. "Stay the week out, finish your research. If you run off this morning, you'll just upset Dessie and Ada."

"What do you mean, if I run off?" she countered defensively.

"Aren't your bags packed already?" he asked, lifting his head at an arrogant angle.

Damn his perception, she thought furiously, turning her eyes to the curtained windows. "Yes," she snapped.

"Then unpack them. You came here, obviously, for a different reason than I brought you," he said with the old, familiar mockery. "Since your work is obviously so important, by all means indulge yourself. Just stay out of the bunkhouse after dark. We've got a couple of new men that I don't know well."

"The only people I really need to talk to are Gig and Ramey," she told him with what dignity she could muster. "Would you mind if I asked them up to the house?"

"Don't be ridiculous," he shot back through a cloud of smoke. "I don't play the master around here. The men are always welcome."

"I didn't mean it that way," she said. She wrapped her arms around her. "Please don't hate me, Egan."

He stood, breathing slowly, deliberately, while his eyes accused. "You knew why I invited you here, Kati," he said after a minute, and his manner was colder than the snow outside. "I didn't make any secret of wanting you. I assumed you felt the same way."

Her eyes lowered to his shirtfront. "I thought I could go through with it," she confessed. "But, last night—" She swallowed. "I was afraid that if I didn't tell you the truth, you'd hurt me."

He made an odd noise deep in his throat and turned away, smoking his cigarette quietly while the clock on the mantel ticked with unnatural loudness.

"I told you once that I like my women experienced. I meant it. I have no taste whatsoever for virgins." He took another harsh draw from the cigarette and moved restlessly around the room, oblivious to her slight flinch. "You're safe for the duration, Miss James," he said finally, glaring at her. "I wouldn't touch you now to save this ranch."

She would have died before she'd let him see how much that hurt. Her face lifted with what pride she had left. "I won't get in your way," she promised quietly.

"Well, that's comforting," he said sarcastically, and with a smile she didn't like.

Her arms tightened where she had them folded over her breasts. "If that's all, I'd like to have some coffee."

"Help yourself."

She left him, her heart around her ankles. It had been better when she hated him, when she didn't have the memory of his hungry ardor to haunt her. But he'd closed all the doors just now, and there wouldn't be any openings again. He'd as much as said so. Virgins didn't interest him.

She laughed miserably to herself. At least he hadn't guessed that she was in love with him. He hadn't understood that she couldn't have given herself without loving, and that was a blessing. She'd finish her research and get out of there. And once she did, she never wanted to see Egan again. It would be too painful.

For the rest of the day, she went through the motions of living without really feeling much of anything. Dessie noticed, but was kind enough not to say anything.

Finally, faced with imminent insanity or work, Kati chose work. She got out the portable computer and began to write, putting all her frustrations and irritations down on paper in a letter to Egan telling him just what she thought of him. She read it over and then erased every word from the screen without ever having fed it to her printer. She felt much better. Then she began work on the book.

Somehow, writing took all the venom out of her. She created without knowing how she did it, watching the characters unfold on paper, feeling the life force in them even as she put the words down. When she looked at the clock, she realized that she'd been working for hours. She put the information on tape and then ran it off on the printer for hard copy. After a shower, she went downstairs to see if she could help Dessie with supper.

"No need," Dessie told her with a grin. "We're

having beef stew and homemade rolls and a salad. Suit you?"

"Oh, yes! I love beef stew!" she enthused.

"You'll like this—it's our own beef. Want to sit down while I dish it up?"

Kati eased into a chair, noticing that only two places were set. "Just us two?" she asked as casually as she could.

"Boss is helping at the calving sheds. Had a handful of first-time heifers calving tonight, and they've already had to pull one. Gets expensive if you lose too many calves," she explained.

"Is the snow still melting?"

"No, worse luck," Dessie grumbled as she put the food on the table. "Weatherman says it's going to come again tonight. I've seen it so that the snow was over the door."

Kati's heart lodged in her throat. "That high?"

"This is Wyoming" came the laughing reply. "Everything's bigger out West, didn't you know? Now, don't you worry. The boys would dig us out if we got snowed in. And we could get another Chinook."

"I remember a painting by Russell," Kati murmured. "A drawing of a cow freezing in the snow, surrounded by wolves, with the legend Waiting for a Chinook. I didn't understand it until now."

"See? You're learning." She nibbled at her stew, watching the younger woman curiously. "Uh, you wouldn't care to tell me a little about this new book? I've read all your others."

Kati's face brightened. "You have?"

"Sure. Well, I know you, sort of." She shifted in the chair. "Gave the girls at the bookstore a charge when I told them that." She glanced up. "I like the books, though, or I wouldn't spend good money on them."

"Just for that," Kati said, "I'll tell you the whole plot."

And Dessie sat, rapt, sighing and smiling, while the entire book was outlined.

"What does the hero look like this time?" Dessie asked finally. "Is he blond like your others?"

"No, this one is dark and has silver eyes."

"Like Egan?"

Kati's face flamed red. "His eyes are...gray," she protested.

"Not when he's mad, they ain't. They're silver, and they gleam." She reached over and patted the young woman's hand. "Listen, I don't tell Egan nothing. I won't spill the beans, so don't start clamming up.

These eyes of mine may be old, but they don't miss a lot. Besides," she added, sipping coffee, "this morning he ate sausage."

"What does that mean?"

"Egan eats bacon or ham. He hates sausage. I cook it for me." She grinned. "He wouldn't have noticed if I'd fed him raw eggs. In a nasty temper, he was."

And Kati knew why, but she wasn't rising to the bait. "Maybe his tastes have changed."

"Oh, I know that," Dessie said casually. "Yes, I do. Have some more stew."

The snow came all night, but Egan didn't appear. It was late the next morning before Kati got a glimpse of him. He came in cursing, stripping off his jacket as he strode toward his study.

"Damned bull," he muttered. "I should have had his horns cut off... Dessie!" he yelled.

She came running, her apron flapping, while Kati stood frozen on the staircase.

"What?" Dessie asked.

"That big Hereford bull of mine got Al," he grumbled. "Get some bandages and disinfectant and I'll drive you down to the bunkhouse to bandage him until I can get the doctor here. I've sent Ramey to fetch him." He jerked up the phone. "Kati!" he called.

She walked in as he was punching buttons. "What can I do?" she asked hesitantly.

"You can stay with Al's wife and keep her quiet," he told her. He held up his hand and spoke into the phone. "Brad, have the boys tracked that wolf yet? Well, call Harry Two Toes and get him to meet me at the house in twenty minutes. Tell him I'll pay him a thousand dollars for that damned wolf. Right." He hung up the receiver. "Al's wife, Barbara, is pregnant with their first child," he continued, his eyes dark and steady on hers. "I won't let her see him. She gets hysterical at the sight of blood, and she's miscarried twice already. Will you stay with her?"

"Of course," she said without hesitation. "How old is she?"

"Twenty. Just a baby herself. Al was trying to check a sore on that damned bull, and he turned wrong. It's my fault, I should have had him dehorned," he said shortly as he rose from the desk. "Got Al in the stomach. That's a bad place to get gored."

"If he works for you, he must be tough," she said quietly. "He'll be all right, Egan."

His eyes searched hers for a long moment. He turned away. "Get a coat, honey."

She thrilled to the endearment, although she knew

that he was worried and probably hadn't realized he was saying it. She ran up the stairs to get her overcoat and knitted hat, and hurried back. Dessie was already wearing a thick corduroy coat of her own, a floppy old hat and high-top boots.

"Let's go," Egan murmured, herding them out into the snow where the truck was parked.

It was slow going. The road was half obscured by the thick, heavy flakes that fell relentlessly. It seemed to take forever to get to the bunkhouse. Egan had Kati wait in the truck while he got Dessie inside and checked to see how Al was. He was back minutes later.

"He's stopped bleeding, at least on the outside," he said heavily as he pulled the truck back onto the ruts. "But he's lost color and he's hurting pretty bad. He'll need to go to the hospital, I'm damned sure of that. I told the boys to get him into one of the pick-ups and put a camper over it and take him into town. I had Ken call Ramey on the radio and have him go on to the hospital instead of to the doctor's and alert the emergency room."

"It's starting out to be a rough day, isn't it?" she asked, thinking of the poor man's wife as well, who still had to be told about the accident.

"Worse." He lit another cigarette. "We had two cows brought down by a wolf and savaged."

"One wolf?" she asked.

"He's old and wily," he told her shortly. "I've lost cows and calves to him for several months now, and I'm at the end of my patience. I'm going to get an Arapaho tracker I know to help me find him."

"You must be losing a lot of money if the wolf is bringing down that many cattle."

"That's not why. I hate killing even a mangy wolf, with the environment in the mess it's in. But you've never seen a cow or a horse that's been attacked by a wolf." His jaws set. "They don't quite kill the animals, you see."

She did, graphically, and her face paled. "Oh."

"We'll trap him and free him in the high country." He turned the truck into the driveway of a small house not far below the bunkhouse.

"Will wolves attack people?" she asked uneasily.

"Not you," he said, half amused. "You won't be walking this ranch alone."

"That's not what I meant." She glanced at him silently.

"Worried about me?" he asked mockingly.

She turned away. "Maybe I was worrying about the wolf," she grumbled.

He got out and helped her over the high bank of snow. She noticed that he didn't offer to carry her this time, and she was glad. It was torture to be close to him, with all the memories between them.

"Try to make her rest as much as you can," Egan said before he knocked on the door. "I'll have Ramey call here just as soon as the doctor's examined Al."

"All right. I'll take care of her."

The door opened, and a pretty young girl with dark hair and eyes opened it. "Egan!" she said enthusiastically. "What brings you here?"

His eyes went from her swollen belly back to her face and he grimaced. He pulled off his hat. "Barbara, my new Hereford bull gored Al," he said softly. "He's all right, but I've had the boys drive him in to see the doctor."

The girl's face went pale, and Kati stepped forward quickly, as Egan did, to help her back inside and onto a chair.

"I'm Kati," she told the girl as she led her to the chair and eased her bulky figure down into it. "I'm going to stay with you. He'll be all right, Barbara. Egan said so."

Egan looked down at her with a faint smile in his eyes. "I'll be out on the ranch with my tracker," he told Kati. "But if Al isn't home by dark, you'll stay in the house with us, Barbara."

"Yes, Egan," Barbara nodded numbly.

Kati left her long enough to walk out onto the front porch with Egan.

"Keep her as quiet as you can," he said. "If you need help, get Dessie."

"I will," she promised. She looked up at him, quietly searching the craggy lines of his face, loving him so deeply that she'd have followed him barefoot through the snow.

He glanced down at her, and the darkness grew in his eyes as they held hers.

"The wolf," she said uneasily. "You won't take chances?"

He moved close, framing her worried face in his hands, and stared down into her eyes for a long moment. "I never take chances, as a rule," he said. "Of course, I blotted my book with you."

"I don't understand."

"What would you call trying to seduce a virgin on a bearskin rug?" he asked dryly.

She flushed and he laughed.

"I lost my head that night," he told her. "I could have broken your young neck when you told me the truth."

"Yes, I know, and your temper hasn't improved since," she said miserably. "I shouldn't have said anything, I guess."

"I'd have blown my brains out afterward if you hadn't," he said. "Kati, I wasn't in any condition for initiation ceremonies. You had me so worked up, I didn't know my name. That's why it took me so long to get over it."

"Oh," she murmured, studying him. He didn't look so formidable now. He looked…odd.

"I can't get too close to you, baby, don't you know? I don't want you any less right now than I did the first time I kissed you," he breathed, bending to her mouth. "But I could seduce you now without even trying. And that wouldn't be a good thing."

"It wouldn't?" she whispered, watching his mouth brush and probe gently at hers in the cold air.

"Don't they say," he whispered back, "that good girls almost always get pregnant that first time?"

"Egan…!" she moaned as his mouth found hers.

He lifted her against him and kissed her roughly, his mouth cool and hard and sure as it moved over hers. His gloved hand caught at her nape and brought her face closer; and she heard a deep, rumbling sound echoing out of his chest.

"We've got to stop this," he ground out as his mouth slid across her cheek, and he wrapped her up tightly in his arms. "It's just a matter of time before I go off the deep end if we don't. I could eat you!"

"Yes, I know," she whispered achingly. "I feel the same way."

He rocked her slowly in his arms while the wind whistled around the house and snow blew past them. "I have to go, Kati."

Her arms tightened. "Be careful. Please be careful."

He was breathing heavily, and his eyes when he lifted his head were silvery and wild. "I used to be," he said enigmatically. He let her go and tugged at a lock of her hair with rough affection. "See you, city girl."

She nodded with a weak smile. "So long, cowboy."

She turned and went back into the house before he could see the worried tears in her eyes.

"Would you like some coffee?" she asked Barbara with perfect poise. "If you'll show me where you keep everything, I'll even make it."

Barbara dabbed at her eyes and smiled. "Of course. Thank you for staying with me."

"I'm glad to do what I can for you," Kati replied. "Come on. Your man will be all right. You have to believe that."

"I'm trying to," the young girl replied. She glanced at Kati as they went into the kitchen. "Is Egan your man?"

Kati flushed. "No," she managed. "No, he's my best friend's brother. He's helping me with some research on a book I'm writing."

"You write books?"

"Yes. Those big historical things," Kati offered.

"It must be lots of fun." She got down cups. "I wanted to be a singer, but I married Al instead. We've been together two years now." She stared out the window at the thickening snow. "I love him so much. And we've been so excited about this baby."

"What do you want?" Kati asked, seeing an opening. "A boy or a girl?"

"Oh, a boy," Barbara said. "I've been knitting blue booties and hats. He'll be all right, won't he?"

"Egan said he would, didn't he?" Kati hedged.

Barbara smiled wanly. "I guess so. Egan's never lied."

Kati nodded, but her own mind was on that killer wolf and Egan out hunting it. An animal that would savage cattle three or four times its size would think nothing of attacking a man. She closed her eyes to the possibility. She couldn't bear thinking about it.

Two hours went by before the phone rang, and Kati answered it herself.

"Barbara?" came Ramey's voice.

"No, Ramey, it's Kati. How is Al?" she asked quickly.

"Madder than a skinned snake." Ramey chuckled. "He wants Egan to give him that bull for steaks."

"He's all right!" Kati told Barbara, laughing; and Barbara sat down heavily with a tired sigh.

"The boss might do it, too," Ramey laughed, "despite how much he paid for him. They're going to keep Al overnight, but he wants Barbara with him. Pack her a bag, will you? They're going to put a bed in the room for her."

"I sure will. Are you coming after her?"

"Guess I'll have to. Boss is still out with Harry."

That was a worrying thought. "Will it take them long to find the wolf, do you think?" she asked hesitantly.

"Anybody's guess, Miss James. See you."

"'Bye."

She hung up the phone with numb fingers. "Al

wants you to spend the night with him at the hospital. They've even fixed you a bed," she said cheerfully. "He's going to be fine, but Ramey said they want to keep him overnight."

"Oh, thank God, thank God!" Barbara whispered. She took a minute to pull herself together before she became practical. "I'll pack my bag right now. Oh, my poor Al!"

Kati helped her get ready, knowing how she might feel in the same circumstances. And Egan was out tracking that wolf right now. What if something happened to him? How would she manage?

Ramey came and dropped Kati by the house on the way to depositing Barbara at the hospital. Kati waved them off and rushed to find Dessie.

"Is Egan back?" she asked the housekeeper.

Dessie shook her head. "It may take all night. Or longer," she told the obviously worried younger woman. "Kati, he's a rancher. This isn't the first time he's had to go tracking a predator. I doubt if it will be the last. It's something you get used to. Back in the old days," she added with a faint smile, "it was rustlers they chased. And they shot back."

"In other words, the wolf is the lesser of a lot of evils." Kati sighed. "Well…" She stuck her hands in the pockets of her jeans. "I guess I'll go work on my book."

"You do that. I'll straighten up the kitchen. Will you be all right by yourself? You won't get scared if I go on to bed?"

"Of course not." She was used to Dessie's early hours by now. "I'll just curl up in a chair and watch TV while I jot down a few notes. Today has been an education."

"I don't doubt it. Sleep well. Barbara doing okay, was she?"

"Yes. Just worried, and that's natural. But she handled it well."

"She's a cowboy's wife," Dessie replied. "Of course she did."

Kati nodded. She was beginning to understand what that meant. She wandered into the living room and watched television until bedtime. Still, Egan hadn't come back.

She paced and watched the clock and listened for the sound of a vehicle. But it didn't come. She thought about going up to bed, but knew she wouldn't sleep. So she curled up on the sofa to watch a late-night talk show. Somewhere in the middle of a starlet's enthusiasm for designer clothes, she fell asleep.

The dreams were delicious. Someone was holding her, very close; she could feel his breath at her ear, whispering words she couldn't quite hear. She smiled and snuggled close, clinging to a hard neck.

"Did you hear me?"

The sound of Egan's voice brought her awake. Her eyes opened heavily, and she blinked as she saw him above her.

"What time is it?" she asked sleepily.

"Six o'clock in the morning," he said, studying her. He was standing and she was locked close in his arms. She looked around and realized that they were in her bedroom. He'd carried her all the way from the living room and she hadn't known....

"I meant to go to bed," she protested.

"Yes, I imagine you did."

Her eyes searched his drawn face: the growth of beard on his cheeks and chin; the weariness that lay on him like a net. "Did you get the wolf?" she asked softly.

"Yes, honey, we got him." He bent to lay her on the bed and looked straight into her eyes. "Were you waiting up for me, Katriane?"

"No, I was watching television," she protested quickly.

He sat down beside her on the bed, still in his sheepskin coat and the wide-brimmed old hat he wore. He put his fingers over her mouth; they were cold from the outdoors, and he smelled of the wind and fir trees.

"I said," he repeated softly, "were you waiting up for me?"

"Well, you said the stupid creature would attack people, didn't you?"

"I didn't think you'd mind too much if he took a plug out of me," he murmured, studying her sleepy face.

"Isn't that the other way around?" she muttered. "You're the one with all the grudges, not me."

"I wanted you, damn it!" he burst out, glaring at her, and all the controlled anger was spilling out of him. "Wanted you, you naive little idiot! You write about it with a gift, but do you understand what it's like? Men hurt like hell when they get as hot as you got me that night!"

She dropped her eyes to his chest. "I wasn't going to say no," she managed curtly.

"But you knew I would," he returned. "You knew I'd never take you to bed once I had learned the truth. It's not my way."

"I wasn't thinking," she muttered.

"Neither was I. I brought you home thinking I could have you. You knew it. Then, just when I'm involved to the back teeth and aching like a boy of fourteen, you turn it off. Just like that."

She couldn't bear the accusation in his deep voice, the anger. Her eyes closed and her fingers clenched by her side.

"And the worst part," he continued, with barely leashed fury in his tone, "is that I think you did it deliberately, despite that lame excuse you gave about not wanting me to hurt you. I think you set me up, Kati, to get even."

That hurt more than all the other accusations put together. It made tears burn her eyes. "What an opinion you have of me," she whispered shakily, trying to force a smile to her lips. "First you think I'm a tramp, and then you try to seduce me, and now you think I'm a cheat besides."

"Don't try to throw it back on my head!" he growled.

"Why not?" She sat up, glaring. "Why not? You were the one who kept putting on the pressure, weren't you? And every time I tried to explain, you shut me up!"

"You knew why I invited you," he shot back. "For God's sake, what did you come out here expecting, a proposal of marriage!"

That was so close to the truth that it took all her control not to let him see it. "Of course not," she replied instead, as coolly as she could. "I expected to be allowed to research my book. And you told me," she added levelly, "that there were no strings attached. Didn't you?"

He sighed angrily but he didn't deny it. His eyes searched over her flushed, angry face, her narrowed eyes. "I guess I did."

Her breasts rose and fell softly, and she looked down at her hands. "As soon as the snow melts a little, I'll leave. I'll need some more data on Wyoming history and a few other related subjects, but I can get that in Cheyenne."

"Writing is all that matters to you, isn't it?" he asked coldly.

She met his eyes. "Egan, what else do I have?"

His heavy brows drew together. "You're young."

"I'll see my twenty-sixth summer this year," she replied. "And all I have to show for my life is a few volumes of historical fiction in the 'J' section of the library. No family. No children. No nothing."

"I'm almost thirty-five and in the same predicament, and I don't give a damn," he told her.

She studied his hard face. "I'm not even surprised. You don't need anyone."

"I do need the occasional woman," he replied.

"I'm sorry, but I don't do occasionals," she told him. "I'm the forever-after type, and if you'd really read any of my books, you'd have known it before you ruined everything."

"I ruined everything?" He glared at her thunderously. "You couldn't get your clothes off fast enough!"

"Oh!" Shamed to the bones, she felt the tears come, and she hated her own weakness. She tried to get up, but he caught her, his hands steely on her upper arms.

"I didn't mean to say that," he ground out. "Damn you, Kati, you bring out everything mean and ornery in my soul!"

"Then it's a good thing I'm leaving before you just rot away, isn't it?" she said, weeping.

He drew in a deep, slow breath. "Oh, baby," he breathed, drawing her close against him under the unbuttoned sheepskin coat. "Baby, I don't want to hurt you."

His voice was oddly tender, although she barely

heard the words through her sobs. She'd hardly cried in her life until Egan came along.

His arms enclosed her warmly and she felt his cold, rough cheek against hers as he held her. "You've had a hard time of it, haven't you? I wouldn't have asked you to stay with Barbara, but I needed Dessie more to get Al patched."

"I didn't mind, truly I didn't. She was so brave."

"She's had to be. Living out here isn't easy on a woman. It's still hard country, and winters can be terrifying. Spring comes and there's flooding. Summer may bring a drought. A man can lose everything overnight out here." He stroked her hair absently. "It was even harder on Barbara. She was a California girl."

"She loves him, Egan."

He laughed shortly, the sound echoing heavily in the dark room. "And love is enough?"

"You make it sound sordid," she murmured at his ear, stirring slightly.

"Well, women set great store by it, I suppose," he said quietly. "I never did. What passed for love in my life was bought and paid for."

She flinched at the cynicism and drew back to look at him. This close, she could see every line in that craggy face. It held her eyes like a magnet, from the kindling silver eyes to the square chin that badly needed a razor.

"Haven't you ever loved anyone?" she asked gently.

"My mother. Ada."

"A lover," she persisted, searching his eyes.

"No, Katriane," he told her somberly. "The few times I tried, I found out pretty quick that it was the money they wanted, not me. What was it you called me that last time we got into it—a big, ugly cowboy?"

"I meant it, too," she said, not backing down. "But what I was talking about had nothing to do with looks. No, Egan, you aren't at all handsome. But you're all man, so what difference does it make?"

He stared at her, and she flushed, averting her eyes. She hadn't meant to let that slip out.

His fingers toyed with her hair and worked their way under her chin to lift it. He was closer than she'd expected—so close that all she could see was his nose and mouth.

"It's been…a long time since anyone waited up for me. Or worried over me," he said huskily. His breath came heavily. "Kati, you'd better not let me have your mouth."

But she wanted it. Ached for it. And her eyes told

him so. He caught his breath at the blatant hunger in them.

"I'll hurt you," he ground out.

"I don't even care…!" She reached up, opening her arms and her heart, and dragged his open, burning mouth down onto hers.

He was rough. Not only in the crushing hold he had on her slender body, but the bristly pressure of his face and the ardent hunger of his mouth. His fingers tangled in her long hair and twirled it around and around, arching her neck.

His lips lifted, poised over hers, and he was breathing as raggedly as she was. "Open your mouth a little more," he said shakily. "Let me show you how I like to be kissed."

Her eyes opened so that she could look into his, and his hands clasped the back of her head as he ground his mouth into hers again, feeling it open and tremble and want his.

"Kati," he breathed as he half lifted her against him, while the kiss became something out of her experience. "God, Kati, it's so sweet…!"

She clung to him, giving back the ardent pressure until he groaned and his rough cheek slid against hers and he held her, breathing in shudders at her ear.

"Stop letting me do that," he ground out, tightening his arms. "It only makes things worse!"

"Yes," she whispered shakily. Her face nuzzled against his, her eyes closed, her body aching for something it had never had.

She began to realize what was happening to him, and it was her fault. She sat perfectly still in his arms and let him hold her until his breathing was steady, until the slight tremor went out of his arms.

"I'm sorry," she whispered.

"Yes, I know, but it doesn't help," he murmured.

"Well, don't put all the blame on me!" she sobbed, trying to push him away.

"I'm not trying to. Stop fighting me."

"Stop making horrible remarks."

He laughed. Laughed! He rubbed his face against hers affectionately; it felt like a pincushion. He lifted his head, and his eyes were blazing with laughter and something much harder to identify. He looked down at her, searching her eyes, her face, and looking so utterly smug that she wanted to hit him.

"You are something else," he said, and she remembered the words from the night he'd made love to her by the fire. She blushed scarlet, and he lifted an eyebrow. "Remembering, are you?" His eyes went down to her blouse and stayed there. "I'll never forget."

Her eyes closed because she couldn't bear the heat of his gaze. "Neither will I. I never meant—"

"Don't," he whispered, bringing her close again. "We made magic that night. I had this opinion of you, you see. For a long time. Kati, I wasn't telling the truth when I said I'd read your books, I'd only read a passage or two. Just enough to support my negative assessment of your character." He lifted his head and looked down at her. "Night before last, I read one. Really read it. There are some pretty noticeable gaps in those love scenes." He searched her eyes. "But some pretty powerful emotions in them, all the same. They were beautiful."

Her eyes burned with tears. "Thank you."

He touched her cheek softly. "I'd like very much to make love with you that way, Kati," he whispered. "I'd like to lie with you on a deserted beach in the moonlight and watch your body move, the way that pirate did in your last book…."

"Don't," she pleaded, burying her face in his shirt. She didn't feel at all like the very cool author who spoke to writers' clubs with such poise. She felt… young.

"So shy with me," he whispered, lifting her across his lap. "And I was the first, wasn't I? The first man to look at you, to touch you, to be intimate with you. My God, I ache just thinking about it, when it never mattered a damn before how many men I'd followed with a woman." His hands smoothed over her back gently while his face nuzzled hers. "I'm like a boy with you, Kati. When we share those deep, hot kisses, I shake all over."

Her fingers made patterns on his shirt, and she loved the bigness and warmth of his body so close to hers. But he was admitting to nothing except desire. And she wanted much, much more.

"We'd better go and eat, I suppose," he murmured. "And I need a shave and a bath." He lifted his head and studied her pink cheek where his had scraped it, and he smiled slowly. "If we made love and I hadn't shaved, you'd look like that all over," he commented.

It brought to mind pictures that made her ache, and she couldn't get away from him quickly enough.

"There's just one thing," he added, watching her with a lazy smile. "If I ever turn up in one of those damned books, you're in trouble."

"I don't write about real people," she defended, and prayed that he'd never see the first few chapters of her new book before she had time to turn the hero back into a blond.

"You'd better not," he said; and although his voice was pleasant, there was a hard glint in his eyes. "What we do together when we make love is private. For the two of us alone."

She frowned. "You can't believe I'd do that!"

He searched her eyes slowly. "I'm not a writer. Explain it to me."

"It would take hours," she told him.

"I'm not leaving for the rest of the day," he told her. "Let me get my bath and shave. I'll meet you downstairs. You can ask me anything else you need to know about the ranch while we're at it."

The prospect of spending a day alone with him was heady and sweet. "All right," she said.

He winked and went out the door, already a different man. For the rest of the day, they talked as never before. He told her about the early days of the ranch and how his grandfather came by it. He told her about his own plans for it; his dreams; the career he once thought he wanted in politics. In return, she explained to him how she felt her characters come alive on paper and take over the actual writing of the book, right down to the love scenes. She explained how she researched the historical facts and how she'd learned to grit her teeth and smile when people asked where she had learned so much about intimacy when she was unmarried and apparently living alone.

"You see, it's just that you can't write fiction without a little romance." She sighed. "And these days, the more sensuous the better. I won't go the whole hog and write explicit scenes, but the sexiest books are the biggest sellers. I must be pretty accurate, though, because my reader mail is mostly kind."

He shook his head, sitting quietly by the crackling fireplace, watching her. "A virgin. Writing what you write. My God."

"Well, most fiction about scientists isn't written by scientists. Most fiction about lawyers isn't written by lawyers. It's just a matter of research, like anything else," she added.

"You do it very—"

The telephone interrupted him. Expecting news about Al, he sprang to his feet to answer.

"Hello?" His face changed. "Yes, how are you, Jennie?"

Kati felt her body go rigid. That woman! So they did have something going, even after he'd left New York.

"Yes, I know." He toyed with a pen-set on the desk. "Umm-hmm. Yes, we did, didn't we?" He smiled. "Here? No, I don't think that's a good idea, honey. We're snowed in. That's right, about five feet of it. No, we've closed the landing strip. You'd have to fly in to Jackson. Maybe. Tell you what, let's put it off until spring. Yes, I know you don't, but that's how it is, Jennie. No strings, remember? I told you at the very beginning how it was going to be. That's right. Sure. Next time I'm in town. So long." He hung up and turned, watching the expressions cross Kati's face.

"She wanted to stop over for a week or two on her way to California for a screen test," he volunteered. "I said no. Anything else you'd like to know?"

"She…was very pretty," Kati muttered.

"Surely she was. And experienced," he added deliberately. "But she wanted ties and I didn't."

"Freedom is your big problem, isn't it?" she asked on a laugh. "Well, don't look at me as if I had a rope in one hand—I don't want strings any more than you do," she lied, and looked away just in time to miss the expression that froze his face.

"I thought all you women wanted marriage," he said in an odd voice.

"Not now I don't," she returned as casually as she could. "I'm too involved in work."

"Going to remain a virgin for life, I gather?" he asked cuttingly. "Give up a home and children so you can keep writing those damned books?"

She looked up with a deliberate smile, in spite of the glittering anger in his eyes. "I like writing those damned books."

He turned away. "So I noticed. Don't let me hold you up, you probably have a lot of work to get through if you're leaving by the end of the week."

And he walked out of the room, leaving her speechless. Well, what had he expected her to say, she wondered achingly—that she loved him? That she'd lie on the floor and let him walk on her if she could stay with him?

Fat chance! If he could brush Jennie off so easily, when he'd obviously had an affair with her, what chance did she have? Probably he was just biding his time until he could get her into his bed. He knew she'd surrender, she thought miserably, he knew very well that she couldn't resist him. And once she'd given in, he'd be letting her down easily, just the way he'd done Jennie. And he'd be in pursuit of some new woman. With a tiny moan, she went upstairs and opened the case that held her computer. What a miserable end for a wonderful day!

Eleven

IT WASN'T hard to avoid Egan after that. He wasn't home. He worked from dawn until late at night and appeared only briefly to eat. He treated Kati with grudging courtesy, but he didn't come near her.

She packed Friday morning to go back to New York. The snow was melting again, and the skies were sunny and clear. Perhaps, she told herself, it was an omen.

"I sure am going to miss you," Dessie said gruffly as she had breakfast with Kati and Egan. "Been nice, having another woman around the place."

"I'll miss you, too," Kati said genuinely as she finished her eggs and drank her coffee. "I've learned a lot while I was here."

"I reckon Gig's talked more in the past week than he has since I've known him," Egan said mockingly. He leaned back precariously in his cane-bottom chair to study her as he smoked a cigarette. He seemed to smoke all the time these days. "Have you satisfied your curiosity about ranch life, Miss Author?" he added.

"Yes," she said, refusing to let him irritate her. "And about the cattle business. Thank you for letting me come."

"My pleasure. Anytime." He swallowed the rest of his coffee and got to his feet. "Ramey's going to drive you to the airport."

"Ramey?" Dessie burst out. "But, Egan, you never let Ramey— "

"Just never mind, if you please," he told the old woman, a bite in his voice. He glanced at Kati hard, and his eyes accused.

"I'll clear this stuff away," Dessie murmured quickly and retreated into the kitchen with two empty platters.

"Have a safe trip home," he told Kati quietly. "And give Ada my love."

"I'll do that," she said stiffly.

He started to pass by her, paused, and suddenly jerked her out of the chair by her arms, hurting her as he dragged her against his chest.

"Damn you," he breathed furiously, with silver eyes that glittered dangerously. "Do you think your career is going to keep you warm at night? Will it give you what I did on that bearskin rug by the fireplace?" he demanded.

Her body melted against his and she wished she had the strength to hit him, but she was drowning in his eyes and the feel of his taut, powerful body.

"What are you offering me?" she asked. "A night in your bed?"

His hands tightened on her arms and he looked hunted. "I don't want you to leave," he said gruffly. "We'll work it out somehow."

"How?" she persisted. "Egan, I'm not like Jennie. I can't take an open affair."

"What do you want, then?" he asked under his breath, watching her. "Marriage?"

She searched his angry eyes defeatedly. "You'd hate me for that," she said with quiet perception.

"I don't know," he replied. "We might get used to each other, make a go of it."

She reached up, touching his face softly with her fingertips. "You'd better stick to girls like Jennie," she said softly. "I couldn't settle for what you'd be able to give me. I couldn't live on crumbs."

"I'm a rich man," he said curtly. "You could have anything you wanted, within reason. And in bed, I'd be everything you'd ever need."

"I know that," she agreed. Her fingers traced his hard mouth, feeling its automatic response with wonder. "But it's still not enough."

"Why not, for God's sake?" he growled, catching her wandering fingers roughly in his own.

"Because I'm in love with you, Egan," she said proudly, watching the reaction flare in his eyes, harden his face. "You can't match that with money or sex. I'd wither away and die of neglect and pity. No, I'd rather be totally alone than on my knees at your heart."

His lips parted and he couldn't seem to find the right words. He touched her hair hesitantly. "You love me?" he whispered huskily, frowning as if he found the words incomprehensible.

"Occupational hazard," she whispered, trying not to cry. "I'll get over it. Goodbye, Egan."

His fingers tightened in her hair. "No, not yet," he said uncertainly. "Not just yet. You don't have to go right now—"

"Yes, I do," she said, on the verge of tears. "I'm running out of pride—" Her voice broke, and she tried to get away, but his arms tightened like a vice and he held her despite her struggles.

"Don't," he whispered, shaken. "Don't fight me. My God, Kati, don't run."

"Egan," she moaned.

"Egan!" Dessie called sharply from the kitchen. "It's the hospital on the phone! Something about Al— Can you come?"

He cursed under his breath, looking down at the tears on Kati's cheeks with eyes that frightened her. "Don't move," he said shortly. "Not one step. You hear me?"

She nodded, but the minute he was out of sight, she grabbed up her bag and made a run for the front door. She couldn't face him again, not after the fool she'd made of herself. If she couldn't have his love, she didn't want his pity. She couldn't bear it!

As luck would have it, Ramey was just getting out of the pickup truck. She dived in on the passenger side.

"Ramey, can you get me to the airport in Jackson in a hurry?" she asked quickly. "There's an emergency— I have to leave!"

"Emergency?" Ramey jumped back in and started the truck. "Why sure, Miss James. Don't you worry, I'll get you there!"

He turned the truck, and Kati reached down and very unobtrusively cut off the two-way radio.

"That noise is just awful," she murmured, "and I have such a headache. Can't we leave it off just until we get to town?" she asked with a pitiful smile.

He hesitated, then he grinned. "Sure. I don't reckon we'll need it."

"Good!" And then she began to talk furiously to keep his mind occupied. It didn't hurt her, either, to stop thinking about Egan and the look on his face when she'd confessed. She didn't know if she'd be able to hear his name again without going mad.

It seemed to take forever, and despite the four-wheel drive and snow tires, they almost bogged down a few times. But Ramey got her to the airport. It wasn't until she was getting out that she realized she'd left her computer at the ranch.

"I'll tell the Boss," Ramey assured her. "He'll get it to you."

That wasn't a comforting thought; the Boss would be out for blood. But she smiled anyway. "Thanks." She'd just do those chapters over on her stationary computer at the apartment, she assured herself; she could remember most of them.

"Have a good trip!" Ramey called and was off with a wave of his hand.

There was a seat on an outgoing plane to Cheyenne. She'd hole up there for a few days, letting only Ada know where she was. She wasn't strong enough to resist Egan, so she wasn't going to try.

She kept watching the door, although she couldn't help wondering why. Egan wouldn't come after her. Besides, she thought, he'd never make it through the snow anyway.

She checked her bag, went aboard with only her purse, and sat down heavily in her seat. It was over. She was leaving. Now all she had to do was get her mind off Egan and find some way of not thinking about him for the rest of her life. Facing Ada was going to be hard. Living with her would be sheer torture. She knew she'd die every time Ada mentioned her brother.

The plane was running now, and she knew it wouldn't be long until takeoff. She was just starting to fasten her seat belt when she heard a commotion in the back of the plane.

A sheepskin coat came suddenly into view, with a hard, furious face above it.

While she was getting over the shock, Egan reached

down, unfastened her seat belt and scooped her up in his hard arms, purse and all.

"You can't do this!" she burst out, oblivious to the amused eyes of the other passengers.

"Like hell I can't," he replied curtly and carried her off the plane.

"Oh, Egan, let me go!" she wailed as he walked back toward the terminal, burying her embarrassed face in his warm collar.

"I can't," he whispered huskily, and his arms tightened around her.

Tears rolled down her cheeks. He wanted her, that was all, but she didn't have the strength to walk away again, even if he'd let her. So she lay in his arms, crying softly, and let him carry her all the way to his pickup truck.

He put her in and got in beside her, picking up the radio mike as he started the truck. He gave his call letters and told somebody he was on his way back with Kati and signed off.

"My bag," she began.

"I hope it has a nice trip," he said curtly, glaring at her as he pulled out into the road. "I told you to stay put."

"I couldn't," she muttered miserably, staring into her lap. "I was too embarrassed."

"Bestselling author," he scoffed, glaring toward her. "The sensual mistress of the ages. And you can't tell a man you love him without blushing all over?"

"I've never done it before!" she burst out, glaring back at him.

His silver eyes gleamed. "You're doing a lot of firsts with me, aren't you, city girl? And the biggest and best is still to come."

"I won't sleep with you, Egan," she said angrily.

"Won't you?" He lit a cigarette and smoked it with a smile so arrogant she wanted to hit him.

"I want to go home!"

"You are home, honey," he replied. "Because that's what White Lodge is going to be from now on."

"Do be reasonable," she pleaded, turning toward him. "You're asking me to give up everything I believe in!"

"That's where you're wrong, Kati. I'm not asking."

"I'll scream," she threatened.

He gave her a wicked smile. "Yes, you probably will," he murmured softly.

"Oh, damn," she wailed.

"Now just calm down, honey," he told her. "When

we get back to the ranch, I'll explain it all to you. Right now, you'd better let me keep my mind on the road. I don't want to spend the rest of the day sitting in a ditch."

She sighed. "How's Al?" she asked dully, remembering the phone call.

"On his way home. He called to get one of the boys to drive him. Now hush."

She folded her arms across her chest, feeling miserable and cold and helpless. He was taking the choice away from her, and she didn't know what to do. Didn't he realize what he was forcing on her? She wouldn't be able to go on living afterward, because the memory of him would burn into her like a brand and she'd never be free again. How could he be so cruel?

It seemed to take much less time getting back to White Lodge than it had leaving it. Egan pulled up at the steps and cut off the engine.

"I won't go in," she muttered.

"I figured you were going to be unpleasant about it," he said on a sigh. He got out, lifted her from the cab of the truck and carried her into the house.

"Dessie, take the phone off the hook," he told the amused housekeeper. "I've got a lot of explaining to do, and I don't want to be interrupted."

"Just keep in mind I'll be out here with my frying pan," Dessie told him, winking at Kati. "And keeping the coffee hot."

He laughed under his breath, carrying Kati into his study. He slammed the door behind him and put her down so that he could lock it.

She retreated to the fireplace, where a fire was crackling merrily, and glanced down at the bearskin rug. She quickly moved away, and Egan watched her as he took off his hat and coat, his eyes sparkling with amusement.

"It wasn't that bad, was it?" he asked, nodding toward the rug. "I thought you enjoyed what I did to you on that."

"Don't you have work to do?" she asked, moving behind his desk.

"Afraid of me, Kati?" he asked softly, moving toward her.

He looked devastating. All lean grace and muscle. His dark hair was mussed, and his eyes were sensual.

"Egan, let me go to New York," she said unsteadily, backing up until the wall stopped her.

He moved toward her relentlessly, until she was trapped between the hard wall and his taut body. He put his hands deliberately beside her head, the way he had in the kitchen that morning, and she trembled with the hunger to feel that hard body crushing down on hers.

"Now we talk," he said softly, watching the emotions play on her face. "You told me you loved me. How? Is it just a physical thing, or is it more?"

Her lips parted on a rush of breath and her body ached for him. He poised there, taunting her; and, involuntarily, she moved against the wall.

"Tell me," he whispered, "and I'll do what you want me to do."

She swallowed, so weak with love that she couldn't even protest that arrogance. "I love you in every way there is," she told him. "Every single way."

"I've got a nasty temper," he reminded her quietly. "I like my own way. And I've lived alone for a long time. It won't be easy. There are going to be times when you'll wish I hadn't carried you off that plane."

Her body felt like jelly as she looked up at him. "I love you," she whispered. "I love you!"

He eased down over her, letting her feel the full, devastating effect the words had on him, and he smiled at the mingled hunger and embarrassment in her face.

"I'll want a son," he murmured, watching the effect of that soft statement. "Maybe three or four of them."

She smiled slowly, wonderingly. "I'd like that, too," she said, trembling as she realized what he was saying.

"No big wedding, though," he added under his breath as his body began to move slowly, sensuously, against hers. "Just the minister and some of the boys and Ada."

"Yes," she whispered, lifting her mouth, pleading for his.

"And if a word of what I'm about to do to you gets into print," he threatened with his mouth poised just above hers, "I'll chase you to Jackson with the truck."

"Yes, darling," she whispered back, standing on tip-toe to reach his open mouth with hers. "Egan, what are you going to do to me?"

"Come here and I'll tell you," he murmured on a soft laugh.

She felt his fingers taking away the sweater and opening the blouse, but she was too busy unbuttoning his shirt to care. Seconds later, hard, hair-roughened muscle pressed against soft, bare breasts; and she moaned, lifting her arms around his neck as she moved hungrily under him.

"Not here," he groaned. He lifted her and carried her to the rug, easing her down onto it.

"You can't imagine," she managed shakily as he

lifted himself over her trembling body, "how many books I've read this scene in."

"You can't imagine," he countered, "how different this is going to be from reading." His hands slid under her, lifting her to the hard pressure of his hips, and he watched her with glittering silver eyes as she cried out. "You see?" he whispered unsteadily. "Kati, I'm drowning in you. Drowning in the feel of you, the taste of you."

He bent, and she gave him her mouth totally, moving instinctively under the weight of his taut body, loving the heaviness and hunger that was crushing her in pleasure.

"Like this," he whispered, guiding, and she felt him in a new and shocking way, and her eyes flew open incredulously.

His face, above hers, was hard with desire, his eyes glittering with triumph as he saw her pleasure in her eyes. "Now," he breathed, and his hands went under her thighs. "Now, just do what I tell you."

She felt his mouth on hers through a fog of incredible hunger, and somewhere in the middle of it, she began to cry. It was the sweetest maelstrom in the world. She felt the rough silk of his skin under her hands, and she touched him in ways she'd never dreamed of touching a man. Her legs tangled with his while he taught her sensations that shocked and burned and stung with pleasure.

"Please, Egan," she whispered into his ear, gasping as he lifted her hips closer. "Please, please!"

"I want you just as much," he whispered back. "But we're not going all the way."

"Egan!" she groaned.

"Trust me, Kati," he whispered. "Give me your mouth, and lie still."

She did, and somewhere in the back of her mind she felt as if she were dying as his body stilled on hers and his mouth began to lose its obsession with hers. He stroked her and whispered to her, and she cried helplessly as the urgency began to recede, to calm into a pleasant exhaustion.

"You and I," he whispered, "are going to burn up when we make love for the first time. I've never felt in my life what I feel when you put your hands on me."

She smoothed his dark hair with fingers that still trembled, and nuzzled against the hair over his hard chest. "Will it be enough?"

His lips brushed over her closed eyelids. "Look at me, little virgin," he whispered. "I want to watch your eyes when I say it."

Her heavy eyelids lifted and she saw his eyes burn like sunlight.

"I love you, Kati," he whispered softly. "I loved you the night you came walking home with my cousin, and I was so eaten up with jealousy that I ate you alive. I've loved you every day since and fought it with everything in me."

Her lips parted but she couldn't speak. Oh, God, it was like having every dream of love she'd ever dreamed come true all at once!

"I thought you were having a fling," he said tightly. "Until the night we lay here together and you told me the truth. And I wanted to go through the floor, because I'd misread the whole situation, and I'd said things to you that still make me uneasy." He brushed the hair away from her cheeks and let his gaze drift down to her soft bareness. His jaw clenched and he dragged his eyes back up to hers, while his fingers stroked over skin no man had touched before. "Then you said you didn't want ties, and I realized that I did. I wanted my ring on your finger, for all time. But you were leaving. And I couldn't find the right words." He sighed heavily. "I was trying to, when you told me you loved me."

"I thought I'd embarrassed you," she said softly.

"You'd given me the moon, Kati," he replied, watching her. "The moon, the sun, the stars—I was speechless, just savoring the feel of it, the sound. And then Al called, and you got away. I'd have gone down on my knees to you…!"

"Egan," she breathed, drawing him close with possessive arms, clinging passionately to him. "Egan, it tore me apart to go! But I was afraid you'd pity me."

"I pitied myself for being so damned stupid—for ever letting you out of my sight. It will be the last time, too. As soon as I get a license, we're getting married. Tomorrow, if possible."

"But, I don't have a dress!"

"Get married in blue jeans, for all I care," he told her. "I just want to give you my name. My heart. My life."

Her eyes closed on a wave of pleasure. Tears welled up in them, at the magnificence of loving and being loved in return. She shuddered.

"Cold?" he whispered, concerned. "I'd forgotten how little we have on."

She did blush then, as he handed her her blouse and bra and watched her struggle to rearrange her jeans.

"Don't stare," she pleaded.

"I can't help it. You're so lovely," he said with a

grin. He propped himself on an elbow, devastating without his shirt. "I guess we'll have to have at least one daughter to look like you." He caught her hand when she finished buttoning buttons and clasped it warmly to his hard, furry chest. "Can you live here with me and not miss the excitement of the city?"

"My darling," she said softly, "I carry my excitement around in my imagination, and I can work on the roof if I have to. There's a post office in Jackson. I have you to keep me warm and love me. What else do I need?"

He smiled slowly. "A good supply of sexy nightgowns," he murmured.

"Now, in that last book I wrote," she whispered, easing down beside him, "the heroine had this very modest white gown…"

"Which the hero ripped off on page fifty-six," he chuckled softly. "Yes, I know, but I like that scene in the bathtub. So, suppose tomorrow night you and I try it out?"

"I thought you were afraid of my research turning up in books," she laughed.

"Not since I've been reading them," he replied. "Anyway, they're giving me some good ideas."

She lifted her arms around his neck and pulled him

down. "Suppose we just work on this bearskin-rug scene a little more?" she whispered at his lips. "I don't think I've got it the way I want it just yet."

"After we're married," he whispered back, his voice husky with emotion as he stared into her eyes, "we'll lie here together and go all the way. I'll let you feel this rug under you while I lie over you and—"

"Egan," she groaned, trembling, hiding her face.

He laughed softly as he pressed her back into it. "I can see that having a virgin for a wife is going to be educational," he mused.

"It's sort of the other way around right now, though," she reminded him. "You're the one doing the teaching."

"So I am." He rubbed his nose against hers. "And I'll tell you a secret, city girl. It's a hell of a lot more fun than fighting."

She smiled. Indeed it was, she thought as his lips nuzzled against hers. She caressed his back lovingly, and she wondered if Ada was going to be surprised when they called her. Somehow, she didn't think so. She reached up and pulled Egan's head down to hers. Outside, the snow began to fall softly, again.

★ ★ ★ ★ ★